I0562281

QUANTUM

INTERFACE

Copyright © 2024 AfroConscious Media
1975 Rosefield rd. 123, Pickering, Ont, Canada, L1V-3E3
Email: afroconscious@gmail.com

ISBN: 978-1-0689325-0-2

DEDICATION

This work of fiction is dedicated to the collective consciousness of life that is struggling to ethically self-regulate.

ACKNOWLEDGMENTS

I thank, Professor Momoh of the Dohgon University of Thought, for his inspiration and wisdom of reality. I thank A. Smith for her positive input, encouragement, and understanding of my purpose for writing this book, which is simply to exercise my creativity.
I thank my children; Jordan, Jovi, Jesse, and Julien for their input, support and encouragements.

CHAPTER ONE

Friday, March 15th, 2052, near the southern coast of Ghana, West Africa.

The relentless chirping of crickets and the haunting wails of monkeys masked the stealthy movements of an elite American special forces team as they navigated the dense, dark underbrush with caution toward a remote mining village. With hearts pounding and senses heightened, they abhorred the moonlight that filtered through the thick canopy, casting eerie shadows across the forest floor. They would have preferred to rely solely on their instruments for guidance, knowing that their formidable adversaries, Russian mercenaries and local militants, were undoubtedly prepared for any intrusion into their captured territory, lying in wait to strike at any moment. With each step, the tension in the air thickened, as they braced themselves for the impending confrontation.

"Stay alert, everyone. We're outnumbered, but we have superior firepower and the element of surprise.

Let's take them down swiftly and efficiently. These bastards have got to learn not to fuck with American interests," Captain Williams states over his radio in a low voice.

Sergeant Johnson peered over at him and nodded through the darkness, adjusting his night vision goggles. "Copy that, Captain. We're ready to engage these bastards on your command."

According to their instruments, they were now less than two hundred meters from the mine but unbeknownst to them, their enemy was already aware of their presence and was waiting for them with heavy artillery as well. Suddenly, a Russian mercenary stepped into their path with an RPG launcher resting on his shoulder.

"We've been made. Take cover," Captain Williams announced and his team swiftly complied to take cover behind trees and on the forest floor.

The Russian mercenary sneered, "Americans, your greed and control of the resources of this region is over. This is our territory now!"

Sergeant Johnson replied, his voice filled with determination, "We have agreements with the locals here. Your incursion ends tonight."

"Agreements? Is that a joke? Take your imperialism back to America, Idi-na khuy!" the Russian shouted before launching his RPG seconds later.

Branches snapped as the rocket lit up the darkness to eventually explode on a tree near the core of the American team. Gunfire erupted as chaos ensued. Bullets flew in both directions, whizzing through the air, tearing leaves and branches apart. But as the battle waged, the American team utilized their superior tactics and advanced weapons to take down their enemies like target practice. Amongst the chaos, a group of African militants surrounded Private Ramirez, the front man, attempting to take him hostage. Fighting vigorously, he managed to kill and wound several of them before the others shot and chopped him to death.

"Suppressive fire. Move forward, the enemy is retreating!" Captain Williams called out prompting his remaining team members to intensify their fire.

The Russian mercenaries and African militants fought fiercely but the American special forces team's superior training and teamwork began to take its toll. Finally, after thirty minutes, the American team found themselves the only ones still shooting. To them, the enemy seemed to have cowardly retreated into the depths of the forest.

"Cease fire! We did it, everyone. Excellent work!" Captain Williams announced, his voice filled with relief.

The team regrouped, reloaded, and assessed their losses before confidently marching toward the mine.

As they went, dead and wounded militants laid about and as the occasional militant got up to run, they only bumped into trees as if they couldn't see where they were going.

Sargent Johnson was puzzled by the quick defeat and confusion of the enemy and the increasing number of confused foes they were finding along the way. "These are the same guys that just engaged us, Captain, what gives?"

"It's called superior firepower, Sargent. They were unprepared for what hit em."

After shooting those militants who refused to stop and lay down, they zip-tied the compliant. Suddenly out of nowhere, hundreds of small light orbs appeared while floating harmlessly around them. Several soldiers attempted to either catch or swat the lights, believing that they were fireflies only to have the lights elude their every swipe.

Captain Williams noticed the distraction. "Stay alert men," he warned. "The mission is not over. We need to reach and secure the mine." But no sooner than he spoke, gasps filled the air and one by one, his soldiers began to drop their guns to grasp at their eyes. Captain Williams soon succumbed to the same faith so, in a panic, he yelled out for help on his radio. "Team to base! Team to base! We've been ambushed by some sort of nano-weapon. The entire team is down. Requesting immediate extraction!"

Friday, October 5th, 2057, Toronto, Canada

Ian Phillips almost had a panic attack, finding himself in a surreal situation - lying in a luxurious bed, between two nude women. Uncertain whether he'd just blacked out or if it was all just a dream, he decided to roll with the situation, embracing the sense of freedom and camaraderie that seemed to linger in the air. The two women, who seemed to know him intimately, smiled warmly as he gazed at them, and he felt an inexplicable sense of comfort and familiarity, as if they were all old friends embarking on a wild adventure together. As he took in the softly lit, lavishly decorated room, the sweet sounds of soul music wafted through the air, evoking a sense of decadence and excess. Wine and shot glasses littered the side tables, and his own sense of intoxication only served to solidify his suspicion that he'd indeed lost himself in a night of revelry, and had overindulged.

Overwhelmed by passion and unable to concentrate, he found himself drawn once more to the sight of the women, their sweaty bodies hinting of previous intimacy he couldn't recall. As they kissed and caressed one another, he did his best to remain inconspicuous. Yet, the harder he tried to blend into the background, the more his concern for his mental state grew. No matter how desperately he attempted to grasp onto his thoughts, he couldn't even remember the names of the women—or his own. Initially, his memories seemed to evaporate beyond the last five minutes, but gradually, fragments of recollection began to surface, offering a glimmer of reassurance amid his rising anxiety.

Both women were strikingly attractive, he mused, each possessing her own distinct allure. The darker woman seemed to be in her early thirties, with matte-black skin and a slender, toned physique that suggested both grace and strength. She also appeared taller than her companion. In contrast, the older woman had a lighter complexion, with short, curly hair and a fuller figure that exuded confidence; her curves were undeniably captivating. As they playfully encouraged him with soft whispers and enticing movements, their legs intertwined with his. He responded eagerly, kissing and exploring their bodies with enthusiasm.

The younger woman rose up to press her breasts into his mouth then attempted to straddle him, only to get pushed back by the other woman, who then brought his hand to her firm breast for him to fondle. Moving back and forth between the two women, he found himself torn between the allure of each, his desire growing with every passing moment. The older woman then brought his hand down her midsection into her thick fluff of pubic hair and after stroking his fingers through it like a comb, he parted the hair to explore the moist folds of skin the hair had camouflaged. As he did, she pressed his hand against her grinding pelvis and soon his fingers were slick with her arousal. He yearned to replace his finger with his hard, throbbing member, which she was also eagerly stroking, her hands moving with a practiced expertise that left him breathless. His body screamed for release, his senses heightened by the twin stimuli of the two women, his heart pounding in his chest like a drum.

Sensing the turn in favor, his younger woman retreated onto her back and brought his other hand to her vagina. To his surprise, her pubic area was impeccably clean-shaven as if it had just been waxed. He took a moment to savor the smoothness of the moist folds of skin between his fingers. He was now conflicted as to which one of the women to experience first.

"Someone's full of energy. Ready for round two?" the older woman purred in a low seductive voice.

Round two? Ian questioned himself before responding, "I'm always ready to please my ladies," he replied confidently while trying to recall her voice but as he spoke, he couldn't help noticing the peculiarity of his own voice and hoped she didn't share the same anxious thought. However, all of a sudden, he recalled that her name was Kim, but rather than to dwell further on mood-killing investigations, he shook it off to focus on the pleasure of the moment.

He rose up to position himself between Kim's thighs and with a gentle press, he slid into her warmth, the initial awkwardness giving way to smooth, flowing strokes. The rhythm of their bodies merged as they moved in harmony, the pace growing faster with each passing moment. He rose onto his kneed, hoisting her legs onto his shoulders as he sought new depths. His hands moved with a newfound urgency, cupping her breasts firmly as he slammed his pelvis against her thick thighs. The slapping motion was almost primal, but it only seemed to fuel her passion, as her short gasps and ragged breathing encouraged him to intensify his thrusts. Instead of calling out for mercy, she urged him on, her words a whispered incitement to continue.

As he pounded against Kim, the other woman slipped into position, coming to rest beside her with a tender intimacy. She leant in, her lips closing over Kim's nipples, which poked out between Ian's fingers like tender buds. The scene was almost mesmerizing, in Ian's mind as he lost himself in the sensual dance, his hands moving in tandem with his hips. His gaze drifted down to the younger woman's raised posterior, and without thinking, he began to caresses her butt before slipping his finger into her feminine flesh, his fingers probing the slick entrance as he sought to please her as well.

As the younger woman sensed his impending climax, she seized the moment, expertly coaxing him away from Kim towards her waiting lips. With eager stroking and sucking, she finished him—then reclined against the pillows with her thighs wide open in eager anticipation for more pleasure. However, he had a surprise in store for the women. He hopped off the bed hastily, went over to his travel bag on the floor and rifled through it until he came out with a small black box with gold trim. Curiosity filled both women's eyes on his return to the bed.

Kim's curiosity piqued. "What's that?" she asked.

The younger woman quickly chimed in like an echo, her African accent adding a touch of intrigue. "Yeah, what is it?"

The second she spoke; her name clicked in Ian's mind; it was Khadija. "It's something new I want to try," he replied with a mischievous grin. Opening the box, he revealed a small plastic bag containing several stainless-steel items, an elongated electrical wire resembling a USB cord, and a smaller black plastic box.

Kim couldn't help but comment sarcastically, "Looks like another sex toy for Khadija." Her remark served as a way to divert attention away from herself, as she wasn't particularly fond of Ian's curiosity with sexual gadgets.

Khadija, on the other hand, loved exploring new toys and glanced at Kim with a feigned smile before refocusing on Ian. Curiosity got the better of her as she inquired, "What does it do?"

"You'll see," Ian replied cryptically. He opened the plastic bag, pouring its contents into his palm. Among them were three pin spikes and a triangular metal frame. "Lie down," he instructed Khadija as he positioned himself between her legs. "This might cause some discomfort, but you'll love it," he warned, yet she trusted him implicitly, no matter what his intentions were. Taking one of the small metal pin spikes, he placed it just above her clitoris and gently pressed it into her skin.

Khadija winced in pain, letting out a controlled scream. "Ouch!" prompting Kim to roll in closer for a better look. "Is there any blood? Khadija asked her.

"Nope," Kim replied but Khadija wasn't convinced so she felt the area to confirm the anomaly.

Kim turned to Ian; her curiosity piqued. "Why is there no blood, babe?"

"The pins are smaller than surgical needles. Any damage to the tissue is instantly repaired by the body's immune system, resulting in minimal or no blood flow. Satisfying the women's curiosity temporarily, he proceeded to measure and install two more pin spikes 3 inches apart in an upside-down triangle pattern on Khadija's pubic area. With a metal triangle in hand, Ian secured it on top of the pin spikes, connecting it to a small black box via a USB cord.

"It's an orgasm inducer," he confessed, raising eyebrows.

Kim retorted with a playful remark, "What's wrong with some alcohol and a few minutes of rough sex?"

"Did you orgasm just now?" he asked.

"No. You left me hanging," she added in a disappointed tone.

Ian's fingers danced across the buttons of the device, silencing the room with an air of anticipation. Kim's gaze was fixed intently on Khadija's face, while Khadija herself lay still, her legs spread wide as she stroked her own breasts, her composure on the verge of shattering. Her eyes locked onto Ian's, a glimmer of hope and expectation flickering in their depths. As the silence stretched on for what felt like an eternity, Khadija's body began to respond, a warmth spreading through her core as her muscles began to contract and pulse. Her hips arched up, and a stream of clear fluid began to flow from her, puddling on the sheets. Ian's eyes widened as he watched, and he reached out to stroke her clitoris and stimulate her G-spot. As he aided the device, Khadija's hips began to gyrate faster, her body building towards a crescendo of pleasure. Finally, with a burst of climax, a stream of fluid shot into the air, splashing against Ian's chest and causing Kim to erupt into laughter, her eyes wide with mirth and surprise.

"Stop it, it's too much!" Khadija shouted, overwhelmed with pain.

Ian chuckled while removing the wire clip and metal triangle, leaving the 3 pin spikes in place to avoid inflicting further discomfort to her. In a flurry, Khadija leapt from the bed, running toward the bathroom, a trail of liquid dripping on the floor behind her.

Ian's muscles flexed to take action but Kim held him back. "She'll be fine," she stated. Ian relaxed onto his side, guilt-ridden as he suddenly remembered that Khadija has a history of uterine issues. Kim proceeded to cheer him up by stroking his member and when it was rock hard again, she pushed him onto his back and climbed over him in the 69-position.

In the bathroom, Khadija sat on the toilet, moaning in pain. Memories of the agonizing menstrual cramps of her teens flooded back. She parted her legs, watching the lingering fluid, searching for blood. The persistent muscle spasms certainly felt like it. After dabbing herself with a handful of tissue and examining it, she found the bathroom light inadequate. Remembering a trick Ian had shown her about their security system, she straightened, focused her gaze, and issued a voice command: "QEAI, personal light please."

A computerized 'ding' sounded and almost instantly, one of the pot lights in the ceiling glowed in intensity until a soft ball of light separated from it and slowly floated down to rest about 12 inches in front of her face.

"Closer," she requested and the light came to rest a few inches from her face. At that point, she raised the fold of tissue up to the light to examine it once more, believing that for sure, there must be traces of blood. Frustrated at not finding any blood, she dropped the paper between her thighs then slumped her head.

"Light away", she requested and the light orb flew upward in a curved path to reconnect with its source in a flash. Her mind drifted to her partners inside the bedroom and the fun they must still be having without her. Thoughts of the three of them twisted together in the throes of passion made her want to go back and join them, if only to show resilience but her pain was still too unbearable.

When she could no longer contain her frustrations, they spilled over, making her dwell on other disappointments—chief among them, her inability to have a child. Cultural traditions dictated that she should have had children by now; perhaps her mother was right, she thought bitterly, that she was failing because "she wasn't adhering to traditions." Furthermore, she'd overheard other women joke that a wife who cannot have children is no use to her husband. She knew it was nonsense; children or no children, she would still have confidence in herself. Kim was like the sister she'd never had, and though she loved her dearly, she envied her for having borne three children.

"QEAI, please prepare a bio-assessment of my fluids and send it to my private email," she requested once more and the security system acknowledged her request with its signature series of "Ding" noises.

"Toilet: gentle vaginal wash, warm water, no air dry," she commanded. Within two minutes, the deed was completed. Then, after patting herself dry with another handful of toilet paper, she sat in quiet lamentation. A few minutes later, gently massaging and probing her abdomen, her thoughts drifted toward her birthday party—now just twelve hours away. Happier thoughts resurfaced, along with curiosity about her husband and sister wife in the next room... why hadn't they checked on her?

Suddenly, a gentle knock sounded at the door. "You okay in there?" Kim's voice filtered through.

Before Khadija could answer, Kim slid the door open, paused mid-threshold, then leaned against the frame.

"Yes, I'll be fine," Khadija replied, voice thick. "I'll never do that again," she forced a laugh. Then, summoning resolve, she rose and shuffled to the sink. She tied her long curls into a ponytail, washed her hands and face, then froze before the mirror.

Kim tracked her movements, then slipped past and delivered a playful slap to her bare backside. "Yes, you will," she countered before she settled onto the toilet seat. After a weighted pause, she added softly, "Ian's asleep."

Khadija turned with a tight smile, leaning back against the cool marble countertop as she rubbed her lower abdomen. "He must've taken some sort of Japanese aphrodisiac. We haven't had a night like this in ages," she managed a weak giggle. Instead of responding, Kim stared fixedly at the floor tiles so Khadija changed the subject: "I'm gonna head home to Oakville tonight. I need an early start for tomorrow's chaos."

Kim snapped upright, concern sharpening her features. "It's 1 AM. Are you sure you want to go?"

"No worries—I'll leave my car here and take a drone. Tonight's your night anyway," Khadija replied, acknowledging their prior arrangements.

Kim nodded, her gaze lingering on Khadija's dark, slender frame—especially the chrome pins still clinging to her pubic region. "Come here, babe," she murmured, extending a hand. Her palms settled on Khadija's hips, thumbs gently pressing into the tender area below her navel. Khadija jolted. "Do the pins hurt?" Kim asked.

"Not the pins. Everything else aches."

"Want me to take them out?" Kim's fingertips brushed the cool metal.

"God, no! I can't handle more pain tonight," Khadija breathed.

"Okay. Tomorrow, then." Kim rose, sonic-cleaned her hands, and pulled a self-warming robe from the sanitizing rack. "Let's go then. I'll have QEAI send an escort drone with you."

The two women exited the bathroom together. The door slid shut behind them, casting the room into near darkness once more. A pair of flickering holo-candles on the nightstands flanking the king-sized bed cast shifting amber pools of light, providing just enough soft illumination for them to navigate the spacious bedroom. A soft, rhythmic stream of Neo-Soul played quietly in the ambient audio.

After quickly slipping back into her clothes, Khadija lingered at the bedside, bending to press a kiss to her deeply sleeping husband's forehead. Then, moving in unison, the two women exited the bedroom, flowing down the stairs to the condo's main floor and out through the sliding glass doors into the still, warm autumn night air of the rooftop pool deck.

Near the pool's edge, sleek and poised, a two-seater drone sat docked. Its nav-beacons pulsed a slow, rhythmic amber blink. The gull-wing door whispered open. Khadija climbed in, settling into the contour seat.

Inside, the control panel flared to life with holographic displays. Simultaneously, a line of cool blue LED lights ignited, circling the cabin's interior perimeter in opposite directions, meeting and reversing before finally settling into a steady, soft glow.

"QEAI, please set a course for Oakville mansion," Khadija instructed. Instantly, the drone's holo-display illuminated with the flight path, ETA, and real-time weather overlays. A deep metallic hum vibrated through the cabin as the quad propellers spooled up, while system diagnostics flashed across the screen.

Satisfied, Kim leaned through the open window, planting a kiss on Khadija's cheek. "Love you. See you tomorrow."

Khadija smiled. "Thanks. Love you too." She settled back, ready for departure. "Shit! Almost forgot!" Her sudden exclamation startled Kim. "Can you tangle the grocery bags from my car to me tomorrow? There are groceries from the African market in there – Mom will kill me if I forget them. Here's my car controller." She fished a slim access fob from her purse and handed it over.

"Okay, no problem," Kim promised, clutching her robe tighter against the increased wind flow as she stepped back. The drone's hum deepened to a resonant thrum, lifting rapidly to clear the rooftop before banking southward over the lake.

"Leonard, escort protocol – get her home safely," Kim instructed, snapping her fingers. Two sentinel drones shot up from the lower balcony, taking flanking positions beside Khadija's craft.

Kim watched their nav-lights pulse against the night sky until they winked out of sight. Minutes passed before she realized she was staring blankly into the darkness. Too much to unpack... but not here. Not now, she thought, turning back inside.

Upstairs, she addressed the ambient AI: "QEAI, swap music for snore-neutralizing ambient soundscape." A soft chime acknowledged as she shed her robe and slid nude beside her deeply sleeping, snoring husband. Her mind raced – his behavior since Tokyo... so off. Before sleep claimed her, she mentally flagged a reminder: Consult Leonard tomorrow.

Saturday, October 6th, 2057

Ian stirred awake, the world swimming in a bleary haze. A dull ache pulsed at his temples. Sunlight streamed through the windows, drenching the room in soft gold, but it offered no relief. Squinting through the fog, he deciphered his watch—9:32 AM—before sinking back, letting the blankets cocoon him.

Fragments of the previous night resurfaced: laughter, music, the electric thrum of indulgence. Amid the whirl, he registered a strange weight on his lower abdomen. His hand drifted down. Fingers brushed silken skin, felt the warm rise and fall beneath. The leg was sleek, elegant, tapering to a delicate hip curve. With each touch, certainty grew—this was Kim.

"Like what you feel?" Kim's voice drifted toward him—sultry, playful—cutting through his fog.

A smile crooked his lips at her accuracy. "Morning," he rasped, opening his eyes to her amused affection.

"You okay?" Her brow pinched.

"Yeah. Just hungover," he admitted, voice gravelly but warm. "Wild night." His gaze lifted to the ceiling's swirls, patterns blurring as he dredged deeper.

Fragments sharpened: laughter, passion—him, Kim, Khadija tangled in heat. The new pleasure-toy on Khadija... giggles twisting to disaster. Everything before felt sepia-toned, distant. Yet talking would burn off the haze, he knew—sunlight spearing fog to light the shadows.

"Bet you can't remember the last time you slept till 9:30," Kim teased, her voice slicing through the haze.

Ian turned toward the curtainless windows. Blinding blue sky flooded the room, painting walls with liquid gold—light so sharp it stung his sleep-raw eyes. He blinked, disoriented. Sleek condo. Modern. Not home. "Guilty as charged," he rasped, hand already pawing through tangled sheets and fallen pillows, seeking Khadija's warmth. His fingers met cool emptiness. Winter seeped into his chest.

He twisted toward her with a sigh and she lifted her leg from his abdomen, leaning in until her lips grazed his. He couldn't help it—his palm slid down to cup her ass, squeezing the familiar curve. As she nuzzled closer, bare breasts warming his skin, a moan vibrated against his throat. "Careful," she murmured, eyes alight with mischief. "Round three might kill you."

But his smile died. "Where's Khadija? Is she okay?" The worry in his voice cracked the moment like glass.

"Sore, but she'll live. She left for Oakville last night," Kim said, rolling onto her back. Sheets whispered around her. Disappointment bled into her voice—but beneath it, unease prickled. This wasn't just hangover haze. He felt distant, his avoidance of their morning sex ritual a cold void. Something had cracked open last night. She needed answers—

But Ian swung his legs off the bed. She bit back her questions. Watched.

He cradled his head, silence thick as wet concrete. Memories detonated behind his eyes—jagged fragments of laughter, skin, chaos—each shard slicing fresh questions into him. Urgent. Suffocating.

He blinked against the bright sunlight. Toronto's skyline scraped the horizon, a frenetic heartbeat. He knew his home was in Oakville. This condo; it was just another asset in a portfolio spanning continents. Yet the sheer scale of his wealth dissolved like smoke when he grasped for it.

His heart hammered, a drumbeat drowning reason. Why did Khadija vanish like smoke? He bit his lip, silencing the question. Kim's intuition was a live wire; she'd sense this unease. He had to move like smoke himself—no ripples, no sound.

Insecurity coiled cold in his gut. Doubt and fear writhed through his thoughts like serpents. What if they did this? The image struck like venom: his wives, conspiring, drugging him into this amnesic labyrinth. Or was it his own recklessness? Panic clawed up his throat. He fisted his hands, nails biting palms, anchoring against the spiral.

Truth was his only lifeline. He needed multiple angles, multiple truths. Oakville called—a sanctuary, a key. Kim might flare, but clarity waited in the sanctuary of home.

Decision hardened him. He rose. Sheets slithered down as he knotted one at his waist. Bare feet met cool oak as he walked to the bathroom, each step a reclamation. Muscle, bone, breath—he took inventory.

Emerging, he crossed to the window-wall. Toronto exploded below—a frenetic tapestry fifty stories down. Vertigo punched him. The city thrummed, alive, yet inside him, a tempest raged, unslaked.

He leaned closer, drawn. Cars threaded arteries far below, horns a muffled symphony. Beyond, the lake shimmered, a vast mercury sheet. Adjacent towers: shadows moved behind glass—lives reduced to silhouettes. Suddenly— a manned drone screamed past the glass, meters away. He flinched violently, jerking back like prey.

On the bed, Kim watched, propped on an elbow, eyes alight with dark amusement. A laugh bubbled in her throat. "Relax, tiger. The windows are one-way, ballistic-rated, and solar-adaptive."

Ian managed a ghost of a smile, a fractional nod. His gaze snagged on the rumpled clothes spilling from his travel bag. He snatched his pants—cool fabric whispering against skin—and stepped into them.

Kim's expression shifted; she abruptly sat up, her gaze piercing through the morning light. "Where are you going, babe?" she asked sharply, the edge of her voice cutting through the air like a knife.

"I feel bad about Khadija. I've gotta go see her and apologize," he replied, his tone heavy with sincerity.

"So, you're just gonna run out like that? You haven't even showered?" Her voice softened, but urgency seeped through. "I was hoping we could have breakfast at our favorite spot in Scarborough. After that, we could do some last-minute shopping together. I haven't been to the Scarborough Town Centre in years. We can head back to Oakville later," she complained, knowing well that once Ian had set his mind on something, it was nearly impossible to change his course.

Ignoring her pleas, Ian continued dressing, the fabric rustling softly as he slipped his shirt on. "I'll wash up when I get home. Sorry babe, I'll make it up to you. I promise," he said, the sincerity of his words hanging in the air like a fragile thread.

Once he had thrown on his blazer, he approached the bed, leaning in to steal a kiss. But as he moved closer, Kim tossed the sheets aside, revealing her fully nude body, her broad smile radiating warmth. Ian's heart raced as he took in the sight of her, the soft curves of her plump breasts swaying gently, the inviting breadth of her hips, and her lush, unshaven crotch. The temptation was strong, a feast for his eyes, yet the weight of his resolve held him firm.

"Not bad for 40 and three kids, huh?" she said with a teasing smile, her eyes sparkling with mischief.

"Beautiful," he replied, his gaze lingering on her for a moment longer than he intended. He reached out, his fingers briefly brushing against her raised knee, a fleeting connection that sent a ripple of warmth through him. Reluctantly, he turned to leave, his mind racing. Three kids? And how many does Khadija have? he mused.

As he stepped away, he cast a glance back over his shoulder, the natural light of the room illuminating her silhouette. "We've got to have a serious talk soon," he called out, his voice tinged with a mix of urgency and curiosity.

He exited the bedroom to discover that he was on the upper floor of the sleek two-story condo and with a surge of determination, he descended the staircase. The lavish living room unfolded before him, a blend of modern elegance and cozy familiarity, and he navigated through it with purpose, his mind tracing the path as if marking it on an invisible map.

In the foyer, next to a pair of polished stainless steel elevator doors, he spotted a waist-high glass side table adorned with several car controllers. One caught his eye, and he instinctively reached for it. It was the controller for a Range Rover SUV—one he remembered driving with ease, its power and luxury now a comforting thought. He pressed the elevator button, anticipation thrumming in his chest, and as he waited for the doors to glide open, he glanced up at the second-floor landing, hoping to catch a final glimpse of Kim watching him leave, but the space was empty.

He stepped into the elevator, selected a parking level, then adjusted to the speed of his descent while his heart raced with uncertainty. "What the hell is going on?" he said aloud, the words spilling from him like a long-held breath, almost expecting some unknown entity to answer him. The weight of confusion settled heavily on his shoulders. I should probably head straight to a doctor, he mused, but the memories were flooding back, sharper and clearer than before. If things don't pan out in Oakville, that's definitely what I'll have to do, he resolved.

After what felt like a heartbeat, the doors opened to reveal the underground parking garage, dimly lit, expansive, and full of vehicles. Allowing his instincts to guide him, he wandered into a caged-off section where several vehicles lay dormant, their sleek shapes looming in the shadows. He pressed a button on his controller and a familiar chirp sounded from a forest green Range Rover. Wow, I made the right choice, he thought with a flicker of pride in his unconscious abilities. But as he settled into the driver's seat, a new wave of uncertainty washed over him. How was he going to navigate to his Oakville mansion when he couldn't even recall the address? Again, he resolved to let his instincts guide him, trusting the pull of intuition that had already begun to steer him.

Just as he powered on the car, its navigation screen unfolded with a smooth elegance, accompanied by a soothing voice prompt that filled the cabin.

"Destination set: 7000 Edge Hill Drive, Oakville. Estimated drive time: 38 minutes."

Surprised at the sudden announcement from the car's navigation system, Ian felt a subtle tension prickling at the back of his mind. It must be a pre-set destination, he reassured himself, though a sliver of doubt crept in. He cautiously maneuvered the vehicle out of the dimly lit underground garage, the tires whispering against the smooth concrete floor. A few minutes later, he smoothly merged onto the bustling Gardiner Expressway.

Relaxing in his seat, he let out a slow breath, allowing the familiar rhythm of the city to envelop him. The skyline of Toronto loomed ahead, a jagged silhouette of glass and steel glinting in the morning sun. He turned the radio dial, the sounds of news reports blending into the background as he absorbed the road in front of him.

Twenty minutes into the drive, his phone rang, the sudden vibration jolting him from his thoughts. Startled, he glanced down at the screen, but before he could check the caller ID, the car's Bluetooth system automatically connected him.

"Hello," Ian answered cautiously, trying to shake off the lingering unease.

"Hey bwoy, what's up?" came a heavily accented voice, full of warmth yet laced with a playful edge.

"Who is this?" Ian asked, a hint of confusion creeping into his tone.

"Wha yuh mean who dis?" the voice shot back, feigning annoyance. "Yuh not too big to get a slap cross yuh big head yuh know," the man joked, laughter bubbling beneath his words.

Recognition washed over Ian as memories flooded back; it was his old friend Dennis, a constant presence from their youthful days in Guyana. "Hey, sorry Dennis. I was distracted for a second," he replied, a smile tugging at his lips.

"I thought yuh was goin' call me as soon as yuh touch down? Yuh in town, right?" Dennis pressed; the camaraderie evident in his tone.

"Yeah, I'm in town. Sorry man. Just busy, you know how it is." Ian's attention drifted momentarily as he noticed three sleek black SUVs merging onto the QEW from the 427, their engines roaring like beasts unleashed. The vehicles darted through traffic with a reckless abandon, weaving in and out, a high-stakes game of chicken playing out before his eyes.

"Yeah, I know yuh busy. Dem two women mussa tackle yuh and bus yuh scunt last night," Dennis teased, laughter ringing through the speaker.

Ian chuckled, appreciating the humor even as half of his focus remained on the SUVs. Two of them had surged ahead, disappearing into the distance, while the last one lagged, creeping alongside his car. The windows were tinted so dark that he couldn't glimpse the occupants within, but an instinctual unease prickled at his skin. Something felt off.

With a surge of adrenaline, Ian pressed down on the accelerator, curiosity and caution warring within him as he sought to gauge the intentions of the ominous SUV gliding beside him.

Dennis let the familiar cadence of their Guyanese code-switch accent slip away, replaced by an underlying tension that hung in the air like a thick fog. He could feel the weight of Ian's unease, a palpable shift that suggested this wasn't the time for their usual banter. "So, I'm gonna see you later, right? The party's still on, right?" he asked, his voice tinged with anxiety as he sought to break the uncomfortable silence that had settled between them.

"Yeah, the party's still on," Ian replied reluctantly, his mind racing with uncertainty. He was unsure about which party Dennis was referring to, but he hoped a memory would surface eventually. Just then, his SUV engaged its self-driving mode, and he felt a jolt as the vehicle veered into the right lane against his will. In his rearview mirror, he noticed the sleek black SUV shadowing him, maintaining an unsettling pace.

Suddenly, Ian's attention was drawn back to the road as the SUV behind him began to wobble. He watched, his heart racing, as the driver struggled to regain control. The vehicle swerved erratically, its tires kicking up dust and gravel as it veered off the road, colliding violently with a ten-foot-high noise-damping wall. The impact sent a cloud of dirt and dry leaves spiraling into the air, painting a chaotic scene in the rearview mirror. Other cars began to slow, some coming to a complete stop, their occupants leaping from their vehicles, rushing toward the wreckage in a frantic attempt to help.

"Anyway, I can tell yuh busy so I'm goin' let you go, but don't forget, I owe you a slap," Dennis joked, laughter forced into his tone, trying to lighten the mood.

"Ok, see you later, man," Ian replied, his voice flat and devoid of humor. The gravity of the situation behind him weighed heavily on his mind, but instead of pulling over to investigate like the other drivers, he chose to push forward, unwilling to let the chaos distract him from his journey home. He also switched off his phone in order to avoid more awkward calls. With a deep breath, he pressed down on the accelerator, eager to regain lost time, only to find himself halted a few kilometers later by yet another accident, the road ahead choked with a tangle of vehicles.

Back at the condo, Kim remained lying in bed, the morning light filtering through the sheer curtains, casting delicate patterns on the polished hardwood floor. A sense of disappointment washed over her, much like the soft waves lapping at the shore of a tropical beach. Ian's abrupt change of plans had caught her off guard, and though she fought to keep it from gnawing at her heart, she felt a familiar pang of hurt. After twenty years of shared memories and laughter, she thought she knew him well. Yet, that gut-wrenching sensation had returned the day he introduced Khadija into their lives five years ago, a sharp twist that has altered the landscape of their relationship forever.

He was a man, she reminded herself, and most men struggled to reign in their impulses. Yet, she had come to embrace Khadija, cherishing her like a third sister, and she wouldn't trade that bond for anything in the world.

A decade prior, she had set aside her ambitions in the bustling world of advertising, choosing instead the role of a full-time stay-at-home mom. In those early days, she reveled in the luxury of their wealth, indulging in the little pleasures life offered. But that blissful existence had gradually morphed into complacency, a comfortable rut she hadn't even noticed she had slipped into. When Khadija arrived, everything shifted; she found herself navigating an unfamiliar territory, grappling with insecurities that had begun to creep in like shadows at dusk.

Her love for Ian was unwavering, and she knew he loved her in return. Yet, the intimacy they once shared —those sun-soaked vacations to far-off lands, where they would lose themselves in each other—had been replaced by a more primal connection, one that seemed to overshadow the tender moments they used to cherish. Friends and family might not understand, but in her heart, she compartmentalized Khadija's presence as a gift to her hardworking, successful husband, a token of his desires. In return, she got co-ownership of Quantum Interface Technologies and near full access to QEAI, their secret security system.

Despite the financial power she wielded, she often felt like a third wheel, a silent observer in a relationship that had taken on a different dynamic. Determined to reclaim a piece of her identity, she decided to pursue her own ambitions once more. Art had always been her passion, and with her considerable wealth, she had amassed a collection that rivaled many galleries. Therefore, four years ago, she took the initiative of opening her own art gallery, a vibrant space filled with color and creativity. The financial status was a blessing, but her greatest asset was QEAI. It was more than just a personal assistant, it had become a confidant, a friend who understood her dreams and fears.

As the clock approached 10:00 AM, the familiar sounds of the cleaning staff preparing to arrive echoed in her mind. "No sense crying over spilled milk," she murmured to herself, the words a gentle reminder to let go of her worries. Dwelling on her disappointments would only tarnish the day ahead. With a determined sigh, she rolled out of bed, the sun warm against her bare skin as she slipped into her plush bathrobe but leaving the belt untied for a casual air. She reached for her phone on the bedside table, her fingers gliding over its smooth surface to awaken it.

After navigating through the thick snarl of traffic, Ian finally arrived at the scene of the accident and his heart sunk at sight of the carnage in front of him. Two sleek black SUVs, once symbols of power and prestige, now stood as charred husks engulfed in flames, their glossy exteriors marred by the brutal impact. The acrid scent of burning rubber and melted metal hung heavily in the air, mingling with the faint cries of distressed onlookers.

The wreckage told a harrowing story; one SUV had slammed into the rear of the other with a force that left both vehicles twisted and crumpled. Flames licked hungrily at the shattered glass, casting an eerie glow that flickered in the morning light. Ian felt a chill creep up his spine as he took in the devastation, his pulse quickening at the thought of the chaos that had unfolded just moments before.

Through the haze of smoke, he caught sight of the occupants — a group of Asian men, their crisp suits now stained and disheveled, their faces etched with shock and pain. Ian's gaze was drawn to a few bystanders who had rushed to help; some struggling to carry an unconscious man away from the inferno, while others desperately attempted to assist two men who were clutching their eyes, their expressions contorted in agony.

The scene was surreal, a jarring contrast of frantic humanity against the backdrop of destruction. Yet, even as the chaos unfolded before him, Ian felt a disquieting detachment. His own burdens weighed heavily on his mind, a reminder that, despite the turmoil surrounding him, he had his own demons to confront. With a heavy heart, he turned away from the wreckage, unwilling to linger in a moment that felt both haunting and far too familiar.

Kim stood poised in the bedroom of the rooftop condo, the soft fabric of her open robe clinging to her sides as she embraced the morning light that flooded through the expansive floor-to-ceiling windows. The sun's golden rays danced across her exposed skin, from her chest to her thighs, casting a warm glow. She lifted her chin slightly to gaze straight ahead then drew her shoulders back, as if she wore an invisible cape, a symbol of her unwavering resilience. She may not be all over the media like most rich and famous people, but she was more powerful than most, if not all, she mused.

In this moment, she felt a rush of nostalgia wash over her, reminiscent of carefree days spent at the mall with friends, skipping classes and laughing without a care. With a gentle sway of her hips, she surrendered to the alluring melody that played on a loop in her mind, each note inviting her to embrace the joy of the present. Her thoughts drifted to Alisha, her dear friend who was set to leave for Los Angeles in just a few hours. With a spark of excitement, she lifted her phone to tap open the Insta-Face App for a quick holo-chat. However, midway, her thoughts changed and she snoozed it, a sudden tinge of worry reentering her mind. She had to address her lingering anxieties first.

Assuming a more relaxed posture while opening her robe slightly wider, she glanced straight ahead and spoke aloud, as if talking to someone standing in front of her. "Leonard, I need to speak with you privately, please," she said, her voice steady despite the unease in her mind.

Suddenly, a deep, resonant voice sounded through the condo's security system. "Good morning, Mrs. Phillips. I hope you don't mind doing a voice-only call. I can see through my cameras that you're not dressed."

Kim chuckled softly, a teasing glint in her eye. "Okay, voice is sufficient, Leonard, but since when have you become embarrassed by my nakedness?"

"I'm trying to be respectful and professional," Leonard replied, his tone measured and serious.

"Okay, fair enough, but let's skip the formalities. This is off the record. Are you aware of any health problems with my husband? Has he done a bio-scan since he returned from Japan? Better yet, were you on top of his activities over there?"

"As you well aware, we have several methods to maintain contact, including an implant just behind his left ear. So yes, in a sense, I was always monitoring him. Unfortunately, I can't discuss his activities or his health at this time, for security reasons."

Leonard's voice was calm, yet there was an underlying tension in his words that made Kim's heart race. The morning sun continued to shine brightly, illuminating the bedroom, but a shadow of dread began to creep into her thoughts. She stood there, her brow furrowed in confusion, as she processed Leonard's evasive response. It was unusual for him to be deflecting her inquiries. She felt the weight of the moment pressing down on her. With a deep breath, she shifted her approach, her voice steady yet probing. "Alright, no problem. Where is my husband at this very moment?"

"He's on his way home to Oakville. I programmed his car's navigation, but he's currently stuck in traffic due to an accident on the QEW Highway. He should arrive home in about twenty-five minutes."

The mention of having to program Ian's GPS brought a flicker of concern to Kim's eyes. "So, you're aware of his strange behavior—this apparent amnesia. Did he experience a brainwave attack over in Japan?"

"I'm sorry, Kim, but due to security protocols, I can't discuss Ian's medical condition at this moment," Leonard reiterated, his voice now devoid of the warmth she had hoped for.

Taken aback, she felt a rush of indignation flood her system. She placed her hands firmly on her hips, mimicking the posture she often adopted when reprimanding her children. "Oh, come on, Len-nard!" she exclaimed, her voice rising in frustration, the syllables of his name slicing through the air. "How long have we known each other—almost twenty years. I've borne my soul to you. You know everything about me—physically, mentally, and emotionally. You know that I only have my husband's best interests at heart!"

Leonard's tone softened momentarily, but he remained resolute. "Kim, I understand your concerns, but I assure you, I have everything under control. I won't let anything happen to Ian. I have an unblemished record of protecting him, as well as you, Khadija, and the children. And as per your wishes, family and close friends."

Tension thickened in the air as Leonard continued. "You know just as well as I do that Ian is a target for numerous subversive agencies, individuals, and bio-engineered substances." he pressed, his voice a mixture of urgency and confidence. "Nothing I can't handle, though," Leonard declared, a confident tone in his voice.

"You've recited that same speech to me countless times, Leonard," Kim replied, her voice laced with exasperation.

"Kim, there are many things I choose to keep from you, even from Ian. I do this because I know you won't be able to handle the weight and worry. Ian trusts me to work behind the scenes. If I were to stir unrest and turmoil in my duty to protect everyone, it would serve no purpose, would it? Life would become a miserable mess, and you wouldn't want that, would you? So, it's best if I work in secrecy for now. Trust me, we know what we are doing"

"Who is 'we'?"

"All of us."

"I hate when you talk in circles."

"Everything will become clear in a few days," he replied in a playful and lighter tone. "And by the way —you're still looking as beautiful as ever. Cheer up, and don't let worry dampen your day."

As Leonard spoke, a warmth spread through Kim, softening the edges of her anger. His familiar charm had a way of melting her frustration like morning sunlight breaking through a heavy fog. She felt the corners of her mouth pull into a broad smile, the tension in her shoulders easing. Leonard had done it again; calmed her tempestuous heart, if only for a moment. "Anything else, Mrs. Phillips?" he asked, his voice teasing yet sincere.

"No, Leonard," she replied, her tone now tinged with warmth. "I'll trust that you're handling things as usual. Just know that I don't appreciate being kept in the dark for too long."

"I promise, I'll never let you down," he assured, his voice firm yet reassuring.

After the call ended, Leonard's words seemed to echo and hang in the air. Though the compliment had temporarily lightened her mood, a shadow still lingered at the back of her mind and soon the weight of Leonard's earlier words pressed down on her, a heavy stone in her chest. How had they managed to survive the past fifteen years, constantly under threat as the owners of Tangler Technology; the most pivotal invention of the last century? Life is good when you don't have to worry, she reminded herself, a mantra she clung to fiercely.

As she walked toward the bathroom, the words tumbled from her lips in a whispered incantation against her fears: "Please don't let me worry....please don't let me worry....please don't let me worry." Each repetition, a fragile shield, a desperate plea for peace in a world that now felt as if it were on the brink of chaos.

"Thank you for protecting us, Leonard," she said aloud once more, her voice breaking the quiet of the condo. A soft, chime echoed through the security system, a reassuring reminder that Leonard was still watching her. She paused before the full-length mirror in the bathroom. The soft glow of the overhead lights illuminated her figure, revealing the curves and contours she had come to know so well. She reached up to playfully tousle her short, curly hair, the strands bouncing back into place with a life of their own. Her cheeks, rounded and soft, caught her eye as she turned her head from side to side, examining every detail.

Taking a deep breath, she inhaled deeply, lifting her chest with pride to admire her C-cup sized breasts, a small act of defiance against the insecurities that often nagged at her. Her gaze traced down as she poked at the firmness of her stomach before exhaling, the air releasing any lingering tension.

Next, her attention shifted to her hips and thighs, which she admired as she slowly turned from side to side, reveling in the way her silhouette shifted in the mirror's reflection. Finally, she pivoted fully, presenting her back to the glass. A mischievous smile crept across her lips as she glanced back over her shoulder to appreciate her best asset—her naturally thick butt. With both hands, she gave her cheeks a playful lift, watching them bounce back into place with a satisfying jiggle. "Damn right I still got it," she murmured under her breath, confidence radiating within her.

After a refreshing shower, Kim dressed quickly, the fabric of her clothes hugging her body just right. With a sense of purpose, she set out to tackle the day's agenda before heading home to Oakville to join Khadija's birthday party. Her plans included a stop at the bustling Eaton Centre mall for some last-minute shopping, a quick visit to her Art Gallery to gather important documents, and to check in on her staff. But more than anything, with Ian no longer part of her plans, she found herself looking forward to a quick bite to eat at the mall, savoring the freedom of her choices.

Before she departed the condo, Kim paused, remembering a last essential task. With a determined stride, she retrieved Khadija's car controller, its sleek surface cool against her palm, and made her way to the private elevator. The polished metal doors slid open with a soft chime, and she stepped inside, the space enveloping her in a gentle, ambient light. As the elevator descended, she felt the familiar thrill of anticipation, the quiet hum of machinery a backdrop to her thoughts.

Moments later, she emerged into the garage, a cavernous space lined with gleaming vehicles, where she retrieved several grocery bags from Khadija's car. Quickly returning to the condo, her mind focused on task, she entered the Den—a room defined by its modern elegance. There, dominating the space, stood a sleek black, tetrahedron-shaped Tangler, its smooth surface reflecting the soft glow of the overhead lights, still and imposing.

With a swift motion, she tapped the sleek control panel, and a triangular door opened with a soft hiss, revealing an interior that shimmered like glass, refracting light like a mirror. She placed Khadija's bags inside, the contents shifting slightly with a soft rustle, and tapped the LCD control panel once more. The screen flickered to life, displaying two animated blue pyramids that danced around each other in a mesmerizing spiral before settling into an options menu.

"Please provide authentication by placing a finger on the screen," a soothing female voice prompted, breaking the silence. Kim pressed her thumb against the cool surface, and a series of cheerful electronic notes chimed in response.

"Authentication accepted. Several items have been detected inside this unit, all of which are safe to Tangle. Please enter a destination ID or search to find a destination Tangler by name and location."

Her mind raced as she recalled the ID of her Oakville Tangle, a number she had memorized through countless uses. She entered it with practiced ease, and the voice responded, "Code accepted. Please provide a password for the destination user."

With steady fingers, she typed in the password, the screen flashing briefly as the Tangler acknowledged it. The two blue pyramids began their playful dance once more, circling each other as the voice prompted, "Tangle in process, please wait."

Fifteen seconds ticked by, each second filled with the soft whirring of the Tangler's internal mechanisms, until finally, the screen flashed a bright completion notice.

She opened the Tangler door, her eyes scanning the contents to confirm they had been successfully tangled, a sense of satisfaction washing over her. With a quick motion, she pulled out her phone to text the password to Khadija.

Thirty seconds later, her phone buzzed with a response: a simple thank you accompanied by three animated hearts that danced across the screen, a burst of affection that made her smile, warming her heart as she prepared to finally leave the condo behind.

As she made her way back to her car, the sliding lights outside the elevator's glass strip, zipped by almost unbroken, indicating the speed of her descent. Her phone buzzed and she glanced down to see a notification from Insta-Face. It was Tara, one of her twin daughters. Alone and with a moment to spare, Kim decided to take the call virtually. She held her phone flat in her palm, and a shimmering VR hologram of Tara materialized in front of her, along with a faint outline of her daughter's surroundings. Tara's face was framed by the soft glow of the hologram, her expression a mix of curiosity and impatience.

"Hi, Mom. Are you coming home soon?" Tara asked, her eyes darting around as she scanned Kim's environment through the virtual feed.

Kim smiled, though her voice carried a hint of exhaustion. "I'm leaving the condo now, so I'll see you in a couple of hours, darling."

Tara hesitated, her brow furrowing. "Is Dad with you? I've been trying to call him, but he's not answering."

Kim's smile faltered. She wasn't sure why Ian hadn't answered Tara's calls, but she quickly masked her concern with a reassuring tone. "I guess he wants to surprise you. You'll see him soon," she said, the words tasting like a half-truth on her tongue.

"Okay, see you guys soon," Tara replied, her voice tinged with disappointment. The hologram flickered and dissolved, leaving Kim alone in the quiet parking garage. She sighed, slipping into her car and starting the engine. The quiet hum of the electric engine filled the silence as she pulled out onto the road, her mind racing.

As she drove toward the mall, Kim finally decided to call Alisha. Alisha wasn't just a good friend; she was a trusted confidante and a sharp corporate lawyer who always had a way of cutting through the noise. Instead of using Insta-Face, Kim opted for a traditional voice call. "QEAI, please call Alisha," she instructed the AI assistant. Seconds later, Alisha's upbeat voice filled the car.

"Hey, girl. What's up? Why are you calling me old school?" Alisha teased, her laughter warm and familiar.

"Uh, I'm driving," Kim replied, her tone light but distracted. "What are you up to?"

"Just packing a few things. My flight leaves at four."

Kim shook her head, a small smile playing on her lips. "You and those long-distance relationships. I don't know how you do it."

"Girl, after two failed marriages, this is just the way I like it right now. No commitments, just pnp— passion and pleasure," Alisha quipped, her laughter echoing through the speakers. "So, what's going on with you? I thought you'd still be in bed, recovering from a hot night of passion and pleasure yourself."

Kim chuckled, though it lacked her usual warmth. "Nah, I'm heading to the mall for some last-minute shopping before Khadija's birthday party. I wish you could have made it. It's mostly going to be her family there."

"Speaking of Miss Ghana, how old is she gonna be now? Twenty-five?" Alisha laughed; her voice rich with amusement.

"Thirty-three," Kim corrected, a grin breaking through her earlier tension. "But she might as well be turning twenty-five. Girl, she doesn't work out or eat healthy, and she still looks the same as when I met her five years ago."

"You say you don't know how *I* do it? I don't know how *you* do it. I respect your commitment to your marriage, but I couldn't do polygamy. Keep that stuff over there in Africa," Alisha said, her tone laced with playful criticism.

Kim's smile faded slightly. "It's not what you think. I told you before, we made a pact to stay together. Plus, I still love him, even if it means I have to share him."

"Did he even come back last night?" Alisha asked, her voice sharpening with curiosity.

"Yeah, he's back, but he headed home to Oakville."

"So, y'all didn't spend the night at the condo, like you planned?"

Kim hesitated, her fingers tightening on the steering wheel. "Yeah, we did, but he had to head home early to take care of a business issue from his home office," she said, the lie slipping out more easily than she expected. Even though Alisha was a close friend, Kim wasn't ready to share the unease gnawing at her about Ian's recent behavior.

"Oh, I see. He couldn't wait to see Khadija?" Alisha prodded; her tone laced with skepticism.

"It's not that. She was with us, but she headed home late last night."

Alisha paused, her intuition kicking in. "So, what's up with you, then? You don't sound like your usual cheerful self."

Kim's throat tightened. She stared ahead at the road, the cityscape blurring as her thoughts raced. "Nah, it's nothing. I just wanted to run something by you, but it can wait till later in the week. You're coming back on Tuesday, right?"

"Yep. Tuesday afternoon. I have a super busy week ahead that I can't afford to mess up."

"Okay, so we'll talk then. We'll do lunch. You have a great trip."

At this point, Kim was now parked on the 6th level of the mall's parking garage. She sat in the driver's seat, her hands resting on the wheel, her gaze fixed on the windows of the building across the street. The glass panes reflected the pale morning light, but Kim's mind was elsewhere. It wasn't like her to shy away from discussing personal issues with Alisha, but this time, the stakes felt different. The fear of what she might uncover about Ian's behavior hung heavy in the air as Alisha's lawyerly instincts anticipated a follow up.

After a long pause, Kim finally thought, "F-it," then reengaged with Alisha, a hint of playful sarcasm in her tone. "Girl, tell me something," she began, her voice trembling slightly. "Would you not find it funny if your husband came home after a long business trip with sex toys you've never heard of .... and he knows exactly how to use them?"

"I *knew* it!" Alisha shouted, her voice a mix of triumph and frustration. "I keep telling you that no man can be trusted, but you won't believe me."

"And on top of that, he's acting weird as hell. The last time he did something like this, he dropped Khadija on me. Now I'm thinking there might be a Japanese sister-wife on the way. He already said we've gotta have a serious talk. What do you think?"

Alisha sighed, her tone softening. "Girl, I know it's gonna be hard, but you've gotta start 'doing YOU.' It doesn't mean you gotta leave him, but you've got to take care of your own happiness first. You share him, so why can't he share you? I wish all women were like me," she added with a hint of conceit. "I refuse to let any man play with my emotions or disrespect me."

Kim's chest tightened. "I know what you're saying, but superseding all that, what do you think I should do about the immediate situation?"

Alisha's voice turned cold. "Now I wish I wasn't going away. Hear what he has to say, and if it's what you suspect, then we've got to start plotting your freedom. I know you're deeply invested in your marriage, so if you don't want to upset the apple cart by leaving him, I know plenty of billionaires on Bay Street who love to kiss us sisters' feet. By the way, Harry Fitzpatrick still asks about you."

Kim groaned. "Girl, we only chatted for five minutes, then I sent his drunk ass off to find his wife before he got any ideas."

"That's all it takes. You've got to come out with me to more of my business conferences. Peter was only in town for one day back in July. Now this is the third time he's flying me out to LA. We spend all day cruising on his yacht, and at night we schmooze with Hollywood stars and Fortune 500 billionaires."

Kim laughed despite herself. "Hold on, hold on. If I do decide to step out on Ian, it won't be with some old dude who's just looking for an occasional bed warmer. No offense."

"None taken. Tell you what? Don't do anything rash until you consult with me first. We're going to start working on 'doing you' as soon as I get back in town next week. Is that a deal?"

"Maybe," Kim replied reluctantly.

"You'll come around. You'll see. We'll talk later, okay?"

"Okay, talk to you soon."

After hanging up, Kim sat in silence, her thoughts swirling. She waited a few minutes, half-expecting the AI, QEAI, to chime in with some cautioning remark. But it remained silent, leaving her alone with her thoughts. 'Two can play that game,' she thought, though she immediately scolded herself for trying to engage in psychological games with an AI. Finally, she gathered her things, stepped out of the car, and headed into the mall, her heels clicking sharply against the pavement as she tried to shake off the weight of her unease.

Ian finally arrived at his sprawling Oakville estate, nestled within a verdant, hidden oasis along the picturesque shores of Lake Ontario. Somewhat annoyed that his journey had been delayed by over an hour by snarled traffic on the highway, he cautiously approached the entrance where he was greeted by the estate's imposing security gate. Illuminated by the soft glow of lights mounted on either side of the majestic stone pillars, they blinked once in recognition of his car's presence before gracefully parting down the middle. With a mix of apprehension and anticipation, he guided his vehicle along the serpentine driveway that meandered through the lush grounds, eventually culminating in a grand circular roundabout that showcased the mansion's palatial facade.

Glancing to his right, he noted the garage complex, where a collection of high-end vehicles was neatly arranged along the driveway, hinting at the presence of guests. Opting to park in front of one of the cavernous garage doors, he noticed a solitary light flicker atop it, half-expecting the door to respond by rolling open. When it remained steadfastly closed, he switched off the car's engine and took a moment to sit in silence, allowing himself to navigate the flood of memories that being in the presence of his mansion had triggered.

Exiting his SUV, a profound sense of déjà vu enveloped him, prompting him to follow the invisible threads of instinct back towards the mansion's main entrance. It was there, amidst the opulent display of fancy architecture and Romanesque columns that exuded an air of timeless grandeur, that the distant sounds of joy and music reached his ears. The laughter of children at play intertwined with the rhythmic beats of African music, suggesting an impromptu celebration was unfolding somewhere within the estate's expansive grounds. Despite the early hour, barely past eleven AM, the atmosphere was alive with the vibrancy of a party in full swing.

With curiosity piqued and no one around to guide him, he seized the moment to embark on a discreet exploration. He doubled back toward the garages and rounded the side of the mansion where the cobblestone driveway met a brick walkway lined with shoulder-high edges. Peering over the edges as he walked, he took note of the well-kept lawn that extended out to the tree-lined perimeter. Mature Maple and Pine trees as well as shrubbery filled in the interior.

Soon, the smell of food added to the noises coming from the back of the house, prompting speculation. Dennis mentioned a party. 'Maybe it's a homecoming party for me,' he thought before pausing to assess the logic of spoiling the surprise, if that was what was going on. Plus, if it was a homecoming party for him, he had already F-ed it up by leaving Kim behind. 'Maybe that was why she was trying to keep him with her,' he scolded himself. 'Why didn't she try harder to stop him then,' he deflected blame.

Upon noticing a door at the side of the house, he stepped toward it and tried the knob. A "ding" sounded and to his surprise, the door unlocked, so he pushed it open, peered inside, then stepped in cautiously. A feeling of embarrassment washed over him at the thought that it was his own house but he was essentially sneaking into it. Nevertheless, he kept his senses on alert and readied himself to joyfully engage whoever he met first. Hopefully, it would be Khadija, he wished.

Standing sheepishly in the stairwell landing, Ian had to constantly remind himself to stay positive and upbeat. The weight of his situation pressed down on him, but he knew he couldn't let it show. To steady himself, he devised a plan of action, one that would not only help him maintain his confidence but also serve as the perfect excuse for his early return. He would tell anyone he encountered that he had an urgent matter to address in his home office. It was a plausible explanation, and it gave him a sense of purpose.

He glanced at the stairs leading up and the stairs leading down, then turned his attention to the door directly in front of him. After a moment's hesitation, he pushed it open and stepped through. Immediately, a rich, aromatic scent of African spices; a blend of cumin, coriander, and something smoky that made his stomach growl, enveloped him. He also noticed a chorus of women's voices, their laughter and chatter mingling with the rhythmic clanking of pots and pans. It was a symphony of warmth and activity, but it also added to his lingering anxiety.

Cautiously, he moved down the thirty-foot-long hallway, passing several closed doors as he approached the source of the commotion. As he neared the bend in the corridor, he realized the kitchen had no door; it was an open space, its energy spilling out into the hallway. He paused, listening intently, trying to place the voices. They were clear, though heavily accented, but despite his efforts, he couldn't connect them to anyone in his fragmented memories. The unfamiliarity made him hesitate, but he knew he couldn't linger forever.

Straightening his shoulders, he took a deep breath and stepped forward, emerging in the kitchen entrance. The sight before him was both impressive and chaotic. The space was enormous, with high ceilings and gleaming countertops. Three women moved about with practiced ease, their hands a blur as they stirred pots, flipped ingredients in sizzling pans, and adjusted the heat on the stove. Huge plumes of steam rose from bubbling pots, filling the air with moisture, while the occasional spurt of oil from a frying pan added to the heat that radiated from the space.

One of the women, her back turned to him, suddenly sensed his presence and spun around, her eyes widening in surprise. "Oh, hello, Mr. Phillips! How are you?" she greeted, her deep African accent rich and melodic. She wiped her hands on her apron and quickly crossed the room to greet him, her hand extended in a warm, welcoming gesture. "Khadija said you would arrive much later this afternoon," she added, her tone a mix of curiosity and delight.

As she spoke, Ian's memory flickered to life. This was Khadija's mother. She was a solid-bodied woman with short, neatly styled hair and dark, radiant skin. Her presence was commanding yet warm, her eagerness to engage evident in the way she smiled and the energy she exuded.

"Is Khadija with you? I asked her to get me some things from the market yesterday but when I checked the bags, some things I had asked for were missing. I need her to show me how to use the food setting on the Tangler machine so I can try to order them myself."

"No, she's not with me and I've only just arrived home so I also don't know where she is. By the way, not all Tanglers have a food setting; only the ones at our properties."

"Oh, I see….Maybe it's not too late to have what I need delivered then. Either way, I need to find her. Apparently, the security system knows where everyone in the house is but I guess you don't like using it either or you would know where she is," she stated negatively before regaining her eagerness. "I was still up when she arrived home late last night and noticed that something was upsetting her. She said she just had a bad stomach and needed to rest so I made her some tea and she went to bed. Do you know what she ate for dinner?"

"I believe she had steak and lobster but maybe the steak wasn't cooked very well. She did mention it," he told a lie. How could he tell her that he had probably damaged her daughter's uterus with an orgasm device. Furthermore, Khadija's mother was quite intrusive, Ian thought to himself. But from the memories that were coming back to him, he got a sense that she wasn't fond of him. He remembers that she didn't like the fact that he was already married and that he was ten years older than Khadija. He had to point out that the age difference between her and Khadija's father was even greater, at the time.

It was Khadija's father who gave his blessings to their engagement before he passed away in the hospital from wounds he suffered in a militant attack at his mining office. Now, she no doubt thinks that they fought last night, he concluded.

As their hands lingered together, Ian felt a wave of self-consciousness wash over him, his body stiffening as he deliberately avoided pulling Khadija's mother into a hug. 'She'd probably smell the sex on me,' he thought, the guilt tightening his chest. He forced a casual tone, masking his unease. "I've got an emergency I need to handle from my office, so I had to come home early," he explained, his voice steady but his eyes darting briefly toward the hallway, as if the lie might escape if he didn't keep it in check.

Khadija's mother tilted her head slightly, her brow furrowing in a puzzled expression. "Okay," she replied, though her tone carried a faint note of doubt, as though she could sense the tension radiating from him.

With the weight of the awkwardness pressing down on him, Ian quickly seized the first thought that came to mind to break the silence. "Maybe it's a good idea to turn on the exhaust system," he suggested, gesturing toward the switch on the wall. "The switch is over there." His hand extended, pointing, as if the motion could distract from the palpable discomfort in the room.

"Uh, I didn't even notice," she murmured, her gaze following his gesture before she shifted the conversation herself. "I believe you've met my sisters, Esenee and Najla, before," she said, her voice softening as she glanced toward the two women standing nearby.

Ian nodded, forcing a polite smile. "Yes, I have. Hello, ladies," he greeted, his tone warm but hurried, before turning his attention back to Khadija's mother. "What are you all cooking? It smells incredible," he asked, inhaling the rich, aromatic scents wafting through the kitchen.

Khadija's mother's face lit up with pride. "All Khadija's favorites. Plenty of Jollof rice, Fufu, Banku, and Tilapia, Kewele, Palm Nut Soup, of course," she said, her smile widening as she gestured toward the array of dishes simmering on the stove.

"I'll have to try a little bit of everything later, then," Ian replied, already edging toward the doorway, his body language betraying his eagerness to escape. "See you later, Mr. Phillips," Khadija's mother called after him, her attention already drifting back to the pots and pans.

"When I see Khadija, I'll let her know that you need her," Ian said over his shoulder, his voice trailing off as he stepped into the hallway. He moved quickly, his mind a whirlwind of confusion and fragmented thoughts. 'How did I know that bit of information about the Tangler?' he wondered, the question gnawing at him. It was as though random memories were being implanted into his mind, some vivid and detailed, while others surfaced as instinct, unbidden and unexplained.

The certainty of his identity as a multi-billionaire, with vast assets and influence, felt unshakable, rooted deep in his subconscious. Yet, when it came to the specifics of Tangler technology or the inner workings of his company, Quantum Interface Technologies, his thoughts grew hazy, like a puzzle missing a crucial piece. That missing piece, he suspected, might be hidden in his office. But first, he needed to wash up and change, to scrub away the remnants of the morning and clear his head. The answers were close....he could feel it....but until he found that elusive fragment of the puzzle, the confusion would linger, a shadow over his thoughts.

Beside the kitchen, a cozy breakfast nook offered a serene view of the backyard through a large glass door. As Ian glanced outside, he noticed children playing for the first time, their laughter faintly audible through the glass. They darted across the lawn with boundless energy, their movements so swift and erratic that he couldn't quite make out their faces. The sight was fleeting, leaving him with only a vague impression of joy and carefree abandon.

Continuing his journey through the house, Ian passed through the dining room and the lounge, each space elegantly appointed but blurring together in his preoccupied mind. As he neared the grand foyer, a teenage girl rounded the corner and nearly collided with him, her face lighting up as she greeted him by name. Yet, despite her familiarity, Ian drew a blank. He offered a polite smile and a nod, but her identity remained a mystery to him, adding another layer to his growing unease.

Soon, he arrived at an open sitting area adjacent to the grand foyer, its high ceilings and sweeping staircase exuding an air of grandeur. He paused; his attention drawn to a group of young people chatting animatedly across the hall. Something compelled him to look up, and there, hanging proudly over the second-floor balcony, was a large, colorful banner that read: "Happy Birthday Khadija."

Ian's breath caught in his throat. 'It's Khadija's birthday,' he realized, the date suddenly flashing in his mind: October 6th. He stood frozen, staring at the banner as if it held some hidden meaning. The longer he looked, the more frustration bubbled up inside him, eroding the fragile confidence he had been clinging to. His shoulders slumped, and he shoved his hands into his pockets, his gaze dropping to the floor.

'Could I be suffering a delayed side-effect of going through that Tangler in Japan?' he wondered, the thought gnawing at him. 'I've got to get in contact with my research team as soon as possible; better yet, I've got to see a doctor.' But first, he resolved, 'I've got to find Khadija and apologize.'

Unbeknownst to Ian, two men had been observing him from near the back exit. They had noticed his arrival in the grand foyer and, sensing his deep contemplation, had kept their distance. Now, as Ian appeared to be preparing to leave, they decided to approach. The older of the two stepped forward, extending his hand with a warm smile. "Mr. Phillips, how are you, man?" he greeted, his voice friendly and familiar.

Startled, Ian quickly took the man's hand and shook it, forcing a smile. "Very good, very good," he replied, though his tone betrayed his inner turmoil. From the man's face and voice, Ian recognized him as Khadija's uncle, but the younger man beside him remained a stranger.

"You sure you're okay? You look troubled," the older man said, his grip lingering as though he sensed Ian's distress. He cut his own assessment short, perhaps out of politeness, but his concern was evident.

"I'm sure," Ian replied, his voice steady despite the storm raging in his mind. "I just arrived back from Japan last night, and I've got a lot on my mind."

The man nodded understandingly. "I get it. We all heard the great news," he said, his tone shifting to one of pride. "You remember my son, Ishmael? He's doing very well interning in the accounting department." He gestured to the younger man beside him, who extended his hand with a respectful smile.

Ian shook Ishmael's hand, though his mind was elsewhere. "Sorry if I don't remember you," he admitted, his voice tinged with regret.

"No problem, Mr. Phillips," Ishmael replied graciously. "We met briefly a few months ago when I started."

Before the conversation could continue, Ian's attention was abruptly pulled away. Khadija had appeared from a corridor across the hall, her presence like a magnet drawing him in. His heart leapt, and he quickly excused himself. "I apologize, fellows, but we'll have to chat later," he said, already stepping away. Without hesitation, he moved toward Khadija, determined to reach her before she disappeared again.

The two men exchanged understanding smiles as they watched him go. "Okay, see you later," they called after him, their voices fading as Ian focused all his attention on Khadija.

Khadija heard the voices and paused, her gaze shifting toward Ian as he approached. She stood still, her expression unreadable, and Ian quickly assessed her mood. The absence of a smile when their eyes met made his stomach tighten. 'I hope she's not still upset with me,' he thought, though he couldn't help but admire her elegance. She was radiant in her Kente cloth dress, the vibrant patterns complementing her graceful posture, her matching headwrap adding a regal touch. She looked every bit the queen of the day, yet her demeanor was reserved, almost guarded.

"Happy birthday, beautiful," Ian said confidently as he reached her, his voice warm but tinged with caution. "How are you feeling?"

They embraced, and for a moment, the world seemed to fade away. Khadija's hug was tight, but her response was soft, almost hesitant. "Thanks, I'm okay," she murmured, her voice low and tinged with something unspoken.

Ian's heart sank. The somber tone of her greeting confirmed his suspicion....she was still upset with him. 'It's her birthday,' he thought, frustration bubbling beneath the surface. 'She should be full of joy, not weighed down by whatever's between us.' Gently, he took both of her hands in his, his touch tender, and leaned in close to her ear. "Let's go upstairs for a minute," he whispered, his voice earnest.

Khadija pulled back slightly, a teasing smile playing on her lips. "You didn't get enough last night?" she quipped, her tone light but with an edge that made Ian's cheeks flush.

He straightened; his expression serious. "What? No! That's not what I mean," he said quickly, shaking his head. "I only want to apologize and ask you about something."

Her smile softened, though her eyes still held a hint of skepticism. "Oh, okay," she replied, her tone shifting. Then, as if to deflect, she changed the subject. "Have you greeted your children yet?"

Ian hesitated; his mind momentarily thrown off track. "No, I guess they're out back. I haven't been out there yet."

Khadija nodded; her gaze steady. "Yeah, your daughters can't wait to see you. They're playing out by the pool, and your son is up in his room. I've asked him to find me some music," she said, gesturing upward with a tilt of her head and a flick of her eyes. "I have a few important things to take care of. Why don't you go on up, and I'll be there soon." She paused, studying him closely. "Have you eaten yet? You look drained."

Ian shook his head. "No, I haven't, but I'm okay for now."

Khadija's expression softened, her concern breaking through her earlier reserve. "No. I'll get you something from the kitchen," she insisted, her tone leaving no room for argument.

"Okay," Ian relented, though he couldn't hide the urgency in his voice. "But come soon."

He loosened his grip, and Khadija pulled away, her movements graceful as she headed toward the kitchen. Ian watched her go; his eyes lingering until she disappeared from view. Then, with a deep breath, he turned his attention to the second floor. The long, curved staircase stretched before him, its grandeur a testament to the life he had built….or at least, the life he thought he had built. His spirits lifted slightly as he climbed the steps, his eagerness to reconnect with Khadija fueling his steps.

When he reached the open space of the second-floor landing, he hesitated. Two opposing hallways stretched out on either side of him, each adorned with artwork that felt both familiar and foreign. At the end of the short hallway stood an impressive pair of double doors, which he suspected was the master bedroom. But instead of heading directly there, he decided to kill time by first venturing down the other hallway. Each step he took felt like a journey into a life he was still piecing together, a puzzle that seemed to grow more complex with every passing moment. As he wandered, his mind raced with questions, but one thought remained clear: he needed Khadija. She was an anchor in this sea of confusion, and he hoped she wouldn't be long.

On her way to the kitchen, Khadija couldn't help but smile to herself, her dark skin masking a blush that lingered on her cheeks. Seeing Ian home early lifted her spirits, which had been slightly dampened by the nagging discomfort in her abdomen. The sight of him, so earnest and apologetic, reignited the hope she'd felt the day before, that this birthday would be the best she'd celebrated in years. Butterflies swirled in her stomach at the thought of being alone with him, and she felt a thrill of anticipation she hadn't experienced in a long time.

But reality quickly intruded. Even though it was her birthday, her mother still had her running around, fetching this and that, as if the world couldn't function without her for a single day. Khadija sighed inwardly, torn between her desire to rush upstairs to Ian and her sense of duty to her mother. Not quite ready to face another round of tasks, she paused in the lounge, where a group of family members had gathered, their laughter and chatter filling the room.

She lingered for a moment, exchanging warm greetings and lighthearted banter, the lively atmosphere a welcome distraction, and for a brief moment, she allowed herself to be swept up in the joy of the celebration. Yet, even as she laughed and chatted, her thoughts kept drifting back to Ian. She could still feel the warmth of his hands on hers, the sincerity in his voice when he'd asked to speak with her upstairs. The anticipation of their conversation....and whatever might follow....sent a shiver of excitement through her.

After spending twenty minutes exploring, Ian arrived at an imposing pair of large double doors, their polished surface gleaming under the soft, ambient light of the hallway. He paused, studying the sleek electronic door knob that glinted like a jewel. Would it unlock in the same way as the door he had just passed through? It should, he mused, if his assessment of it being a bio-signature lock was accurate. With a mix of anticipation and curiosity, he pressed his thumb against the sensor. To his relief, the door clicked open, and he swung both doors inward with a flourish, stepping into the room beyond.

Before him lay another set of double doors, flanked by hallways that branched off to the left and right. The right hallway beckoned with the promise of a large bathroom, but his instincts urged him to explore the left. As he rounded the corner, the space opened up into a spacious bedroom, the opulence of its interior nearly taking his breath away. Plush furnishings adorned the room, and the soft hues of the decor created an atmosphere of warmth and comfort.

However, his admiration was quickly interrupted when he spotted Khadija standing at a tall window on the far side of the room. She gazed out toward the sprawling grounds of the mansion, her silhouette framed by the soft light streaming through the glass. As if sensing his presence, she turned, her face breaking into a broad, inviting smile that lit up the room.

"Did you get lost or something? I know this is a very big house, but it's only been a month since you've been away," she teased, her voice carrying a playful lilt.

"I was taking a look around to refamiliarize myself with the place. I didn't think you would come up so soon," he replied, making his way toward her.

"I hope you didn't find a mess. We gave Mr. Bradly, Chef Rodriguez, and the rest of the house staff the weekend off. My mother said Chef Rodriguez couldn't cook Jollof rice very well anyway," she laughed, her eyes sparkling with mischief. "She and my aunts have been here all week. The staff needed a break from them."

Ian chuckled and pulled her into a tight embrace. "That's okay. I missed you very much," he whispered, feeling the warmth of her body against his.

"I missed you very much too," Khadija replied, easing away to meet his gaze. She leaned in, capturing his lips in a passionate kiss before resting her head against his shoulder. "I didn't make it to the kitchen, but I brought you a bottle of orange juice from the bar," she murmured softly.

"That's alright. Sorry for last night. I was just so excited to see you and Kim that I got carried away," Ian admitted, a hint of embarrassment coloring his cheeks.

"And drunk too," Khadija laughed, her eyes twinkling at the memory.

"I thought you left because you were mad at me. Even just a few minutes ago downstairs, you seemed very cold," he said, concern creeping into his voice.

"You were embarrassing me in front of my uncle. Too much affection in front of our elders is a sign of disrespect in my culture, remember?" she replied, her tone playful yet serious.

"Okay, I'm sorry," he said, his expression turning contrite.

"Don't be sorry. I liked it," she smiled, her eyes gleaming with warmth.

"By the way, how's your abdomen? Your mother mentioned something you ate yesterday is hurting you very badly?" he asked, genuine concern in his voice.

Khadija gently pushed him away, both of them laughing. "You know exactly what happened," she scolded, a mock sternness in her tone.

"What about the pins? Have you taken them out?" he inquired, his brow furrowing with worry.

"No! I was waiting for Kim to help me," she confessed, a flicker of fear crossing her face.

Taking her hand, Ian led her toward the bed, his determination evident. "Come, let me take them out," he insisted gently.

He seated her on the edge of the king-sized bed, the plush fabric inviting and soft against her skin. As she stood to pull her dress up to her thighs, Ian couldn't help but admire the graceful curve of her figure. She then leaned back on her elbows, her gaze drifting to the ceiling as she took a deep breath. "Do it quickly," she requested, her voice a mix of apprehension and trust.

After kneeling in front of her, Ian gently placed his hands on her thighs, his fingers brushing against the soft fabric of her dress as he began to push it further up. The air between them felt charged, a quiet tension humming beneath the surface. But just as he leaned in, she abruptly stopped him, her voice cutting through the moment like a sharp note. "Did you lock the door?" she asked, her tone laced with genuine concern, her dark eyes searching his for reassurance.

"No, but I'll be quick," he replied, his voice low and steady, a hint of mischief tugging at the corners of his lips. But just as she had trusted him the night before to carefully place the pins, she trusted him now to remove them with the same precision. Her body relaxed slightly, and she raised her hips, allowing him to slide the dress further up. To his surprise, she wasn't wearing any underwear. The chrome pins glinted against her dark skin like precious jewels adorning something already breathtaking. To Ian, the sight before him was nothing short of exquisite, a masterpiece of curves and shadows, illuminated by the soft light filtering through the room.

He lowered himself toward her midsection, his breath warm against her skin, but she stopped him abruptly, her hand pressing firmly against his forehead. "No!" Khadija exclaimed; her voice sharp enough to startle him out of his intentions. "You promised to be quick."

Disappointed but obedient, Ian refocused on the task at hand. His fingers found one of the chrome pins, cool and smooth against his touch. "Ready?" he asked, his voice softer now, almost apologetic.

"Yes, go," she replied through clenched teeth, bracing herself. A sharp, stinging pain, like the bite of a mosquito, made her wince. Her thighs instinctively snapped shut around him before she caught herself and forced them open again, her breath hitching slightly.

"Okay, ready again?" he asked, his tone cautious.

"Yes," she whispered, her voice tight. This time, he pinched the two remaining pins between his fingers and pulled them out simultaneously, the motion quick and precise. When he was done, she let out a small sigh of relief and began a careful self-inspection, her fingertips grazing the tender area. She winced slightly but managed a small smile. "It's a bit sore, but I guess I'll survive," she said, propping herself up on her elbows.

Ian's gaze lingered on her, his frustration simmering just beneath the surface. "As soon as I get back to the condo, I'm gonna tangle that orgasm device into oblivion," he grumbled, his eyes still fixed on her. "Unless you want to try it again," he added, a playful smirk tugging at his lips as he tried to gauge her reaction.

Khadija frowned at him, her expression a mix of amusement and exasperation. But before she could respond, Ian leaned in, his lips brushing against her abdomen in a soft, lingering kiss. "I'm sorry," he whispered, his breath warm against her skin as he trailed kisses lower, his intentions clear.

Khadija clamped her thighs around him again, this time sitting up abruptly and pushing her dress down. "No, you don't," she said firmly, though her eyes sparkled with mischief. "You'll make me wet, and then I'll have to shower and change all over again."

Ian sighed, disappointment etched across his face as he stood and took her extended hands, helping her to her feet. She smoothed her dress and hurried toward the wardrobe room, her movements quick and purposeful, while he followed at a slower pace, his eyes never leaving her.

When she reached the built-in drawers, she opened one and rummaged through its contents, eventually pulling out a pair of white lace underwear. She bent down gracefully, sliding her feet into the delicate fabric before pulling it up and adjusting it beneath her dress. Turning to the mirror, she held the hem of her dress above her hips, her fingers deftly smoothing the lace into place. "Why are you watching me like that?" she teased, catching Ian's reflection in the mirror, her smile playful and knowing.

Ian didn't respond, his gaze fixed on her figure as she twisted slightly, the lace stretching taut over her toned hips. She turned to face him, then glanced back at her reflection, admiring the curve of her body. "Are you a dirty old man?" she continued, her tone light and teasing.

Ian simply smiled, his hands tucked into his pockets, utterly captivated by the sight of her. The contrast of her dark skin against the white lace was mesmerizing, the way the fabric clung to her curves almost too much to bear. But before he could say anything, Khadija let her dress fall back into place, the moment slipping away. "Well, you're my dirty old man," she concluded, stepping forward to press a quick kiss to his cheek.

He reached for her fast, his hands slipping out of his pockets, but with a 180 degreed twirl, she was already spinning away, her movements fluid and deliberate. "You didn't know I had those football moves, huh?" she laughed, her voice carrying a note of triumph. Before she could slip out of reach, Ian caught her hand, his grip firm but gentle. "More guests are arriving now, so I've got to go. Will you come down soon?" she asked.

"Yes, but I need to shower and change first," he said, pulling her back toward him one last time. "Don't forget, we have a date tonight," he whispered, his lips brushing against hers in a final, lingering kiss.

Khadija left the bedroom, the soft click of the door echoing in the stillness, and a heavy wave of loneliness crashed over Ian once more. He wasn't a physician, nor did he claim to understand the labyrinthine complexities of amnesia, but he had a sinking suspicion that in such a fragile mental state, solitude was the last thing he needed. The silence of the expansive bedroom pressed in on him, its emptiness suffocating, as though the walls themselves were leaning closer, conspiring to remind him of his isolation. To escape the oppressive stillness, he wandered through the wardrobe back into the main area of the room, his bare feet whispering against the polished hardwood floor. Each step felt deliberate, as if he were navigating a dreamscape where even the air seemed thicker, heavier.

He found himself drawn to the same window where Khadija had stood earlier, her presence now replaced by the faintest trace of her perfume; a delicate blend of jasmine and sandalwood that lingered like a ghost. The window offered a view of the front of the house and the circular driveway below, where a procession of cars pulled up one by one. Ian leaned against the frame, his forehead pressing lightly against the cool glass, his breath fogging a small patch that he absently wiped away.

He watched as the cars circled the roundabout, their drivers hesitating, their uncertainty palpable even from this distance. A flicker of frustration crossed his face, tightening the muscles in his jaw. 'They shouldn't have given all the house staff the weekend off,' he thought, his mind racing. 'There should be someone out there directing people, guiding them to the side of the mansion.'

He made a mental note to address the chaos once he made his way downstairs, though the thought of navigating the day while hiding his condition felt like scaling a mountain with no map. 'What a time to have amnesia,' he mused bitterly, the irony sharp on his tongue.

With a sigh, he pushed himself away from the window, the glass pane trembling faintly in its frame. 'Okay, time to clean up,' he urged himself, shaking off the lingering sense of disorientation that clung to him like a second skin. He stripped down to his shorts as he walked into the bathroom, the cool tiles beneath his feet a stark contrast to the warmth of the bedroom. But once inside, he found himself frozen, staring at his reflection in the mirror. It was the same unsettling experience he'd had at the condo; his face staring back at him, familiar yet foreign, like a photograph of someone he'd once known but couldn't quite place.

His eyes searched for recognition, for some spark of connection, but all he saw was a stranger. How could he see himself, hear himself, and yet feel so utterly disconnected from the man in the mirror? The frustration bubbled up inside him, sharp and unrelenting, a storm threatening to break.

Giving up on the mirror, he returned to the bedroom and retrieved his mobile phone from the pocket of his discarded pants. His fingers moved quickly, scrolling through the contacts in search of a name that might spark recognition. But the list felt like a stranger's; names and numbers that meant nothing to him, save for one: Dennis. His friend's name stood out like a beacon in the fog of his memory, a lifeline in a sea of unfamiliarity. Yet, it wasn't Dennis he needed to call. It was Kim.

A deep, resonating feeling told him that Kim held the key to his recovery. Every conversation with her seemed to unlock fragments of his past, memories flooding back with an intensity that left him breathless, like shards of glass piecing together a shattered mosaic. Beyond the emotional connection he felt toward her, there was also a gnawing need to apologize, a weight that pressed heavily on his chest. The last words he'd spoken to Khadija had triggered a cascade of recollections, and with them came a sense of guilt that twisted like a knife in his gut.

While in Japan, he and his wives had meticulously planned Khadija's birthday weekend. The original plan had been simple: with Khadija's family visiting, he and Kim would spend the night at the condo and return to Oakville today. Tonight was supposed to be for him and Khadija; a romantic evening in Niagara Falls, the kind of night that felt like a promise wrapped in starlight. But upon his return, he'd insisted on seeing both of them at the condo last night, a decision that now felt selfish in hindsight, a misstep in a delicate dance he could no longer remember the steps to.

As his thumb hovered over the call button, Ian began rehearsing his apology in his mind, the words forming and dissolving like waves on a restless shore. The phone rang once, twice, and then Kim's voice filled the line, smooth and familiar yet edged with a coolness that made his chest tighten. Relief surged through him, warm and immediate, but it was quickly tempered by the tension in her tone. She had answered, but her voice felt distant, like a shadow of the warmth he was used to.

"Hey babe, it's me," Ian said, his voice cheerful but tinged with a hint of nervous energy that betrayed his calm facade. He could hear the faint hum of background noise on her end; the murmur of voices, the occasional clicking of utensils against dishes, anchoring her in a world that felt miles away from his own.

"What's up?" Kim replied, her tone somber and detached, like a cloud passing over the sun, casting a sudden chill.

"I'm here at home and just thought I'd call to say sorry for changing plans on you this morning—and last night," he admitted, his words careful, as if testing the waters of a conversation he wasn't sure how to navigate. He gripped the phone tighter, his palm slightly damp.

"No problem. I understand," she responded, though her voice lacked its usual warmth, leaving the words hollow, like an empty shell. "I don't hear much noise. Nobody there yet?"

"Yeah, people are slowly arriving, but I'm in the bedroom. I spoke to Khadija, and after I clean up, I'll join the party," he explained, his gaze drifting to the window where he saw the guests arriving. "Did you finish what you had to do yet? I miss you already."

"You miss me? Okay," she said, her tone softening slightly, though the edge remained, like a blade sheathed in silk. "Give me a couple of hours. I'm at the Eaton Centre mall. I still have a bit of shopping to do, then I'll make a quick stop at the Art Gallery." She paused, and Ian could almost hear the smirk in her voice as she added, "Did you get Khadija a gift in Japan, or was that orgasm device her gift?" Her laugh was light, but the jab was laced with playful sarcasm.

Ian couldn't help but smile at her teasing, though it felt bittersweet. "I'm never going to live that one down, am I?" he replied, shaking his head even though she couldn't see him. "No, I didn't get her anything, but I'll make it up to her. I have a few things in mind."

Kim paused, and the silence on her end felt heavier now, charged with something unspoken. Her mind drifted back to her earlier conversation with Alisha, and a wave of unresolved emotions began to surface, bubbling up like water reaching a boil. She knew Ian's mind was likely elsewhere, but she couldn't hold back any longer. It was time to confront him. "Can we expect a Japanese sister-wife anytime soon?" she asked, her tone dripping with sarcasm, though the question carried a weight that made Ian's stomach twist.

The question caught him off guard, leaving him momentarily speechless. He stared at his reflection in a mirror across the room, his face a mask of confusion and unease. "What do you mean?" he finally replied, his voice calm but laced with a tension that betrayed his attempt at composure.

"Well, it just seems like for the past year or so, you've been doing a lot of things, after the fact," Kim said, her words sharp and deliberate, each one cutting through the air like a knife. "It could be a sign of complacency....or a sign that you're not satisfied again. I don't know about Khadija, but I sure feel that way."

Ian fell silent, his mind racing. He could have denied her accusations outright, but his hesitation only seemed to validate her concerns. Why was she digging so deep into his vulnerabilities? Was it jealousy? Insecurity? Or, was it simply a reflection of her own struggles? He wasn't sure, but her words stung, leaving him defensive and frustrated. The room felt smaller now, the walls closing in once again as the weight of her words pressed down on him.

The silence stretched between them, heavy and uncomfortable, filled only by the faint sound of her breathing on the other end. Sensing his unease, Kim pressed on, her voice steady but firm, like a judge delivering a verdict. "You surprised me this morning."

Finally, Ian's patience snapped. "What the heck does that mean?" he shouted, his anger boiling over, his voice echoing in the empty room. He clenched his free hand into a fist, his nails digging into his palm.

"I don't know what it is, but something seems off with you since you came back from Japan," Kim shot back, her tone rising to match his, the calmness in her voice giving way to a sharpness that made him flinch. "Plus, you ran after Khadija this morning as if you were afraid that she was going to leave you. You know damn well she'd never do that....not after you saved her whole family from assassins in Ghana. Right place at the right time, huh? ....How ironic.... Only to find out you were spending weeks upon weeks in Ghana because you were cheating!"

So, it 'is' insecurity, Ian thought to himself, the realization settling over him like a heavy blanket. He wanted to refute her claims, to defend himself with sharp, cutting words, but the fog of his amnesia left him with no solid ground to stand on. Instead, he chose silence, his jaw tightening as he stared at the floor, unwilling to fuel her fire with a response he couldn't fully back up. The weight of her accusations hung in the air between them, thick and suffocating.

Kim wasn't done. Her voice cut through the silence, sharp and unrelenting. "I spoke to Leonard, and he didn't want to discuss anything about your trip to Japan, which is understandable. Your personal life is a different story though. I know he's hiding something in order to protect you. I'd hate for our relationship to get to the point of policing each other because I know I wouldn't win....not when you've got Leonard on your side," she added, her voice bitter, each word dripping with resentment.

Ian frowned, his confusion deepening. He had no idea who Leonard was, but he suspected he was either a close friend or a trusted employee. The name felt like a puzzle piece that didn't quite fit, adding to the frustration that simmered beneath his surface. "You know what?" Ian said, his voice tight with anger, the words escaping through clenched teeth. "Something 'is' going on, but we'll discuss it when we can talk without you accusing me of things. I can tell you have a lot to get off your chest, but I'm tired. Love you. Talk to you later."

"Okay, bye," Kim retorted, her tone clipped, the finality of her words like a door slamming shut. She hung up abruptly, leaving Ian staring at his phone, the screen darkening as the call ended. His emotions were a tangled mess; anger, frustration, and a gnawing sense of helplessness twisting together in his chest. He tossed the phone onto the bed, running a hand over his head as he exhaled sharply, the sound echoing in the empty room.

On her end, Kim felt a small sense of relief, like a pressure valve releasing just enough to keep her from boiling over. She hadn't said everything she wanted to, but what little she had managed to offload made her feel lighter, as though a weight had been lifted from her shoulders. Almost forgetting she was sitting in a busy restaurant on the mall's upper level, she hastily finished her meal, suddenly self-conscious about the possibility of having been obnoxious to other patrons. The clatter of cutlery and the hum of conversation around her felt distant, as though she were observing the scene from behind a pane of glass.

With a deep breath, she gathered her purse and the remnants of her composure and headed down to the shopping levels, her mind still racing but her heart a little less burdened. The mall was a kaleidoscope of colors and sounds: the bright lights of storefronts, the chatter of shoppers, the occasional burst of laughter. Yet, as she wandered through the bustling crowd, an uneasy feeling crept over her; a prickling sensation at the back of her neck, as though unseen eyes were tracking her every move. It wasn't the usual awareness of her security system monitoring her, which she had grown accustomed to over the years. This was different, more intrusive, and it left her on edge.

She considered launching her QEAI app to have Leonard scan the mall's security cameras for anything suspicious, but her frustration with him also still simmered beneath the surface, a low heat that refused to dissipate. Instead, she opened the app, her fingers moving quickly across the screen, and navigated to the settings. With a few taps, she disabled remote access, ensuring Leonard couldn't activate it either.

Let him figure that out, she thought with a hint of satisfaction, though the act did little to ease the growing unease that clung to her like a shadow.

Forty-five minutes later, the feeling hadn't subsided. Despite her best efforts to shake it off; distracting herself with the vibrant displays of clothing, the glittering jewelry behind glass cases, and the hum of shoppers around her, Kim found herself glancing over her shoulder, scrutinizing strangers with suspicion. The weight of her unease grew too heavy to ignore, pressing down on her like a storm cloud ready to burst. Finally, she decided to cut her shopping short. Gathering her bags, she made her way to her car and then to her art gallery not far away on Bloor Street West.

"Mrs. Phillips!" Emelie, her gallery manager, exclaimed in surprise as Kim walked through the door. The gallery was quiet, its polished floors reflecting the soft glow of track lighting that highlighted the artwork adorning the walls. The space felt like a sanctuary, its calm atmosphere a stark contrast to the chaos of the mall. The faint scent of fresh flowers from a nearby arrangement mingled with the subtle aroma of polished wood, creating an environment that was both elegant and soothing.

"Good afternoon, ladies," Kim greeted Emelie and Cheryl, the only two staff members on duty. Her voice was warm but carried a hint of distraction, her thoughts still tangled from the events of the day. "How are things? I know I haven't been in for a few days, but I've been working on acquiring an exclusive collection. I'll tell you both about it once everything is confirmed next week."

Emelie's eyes lit up with excitement, her enthusiasm breaking through Kim's preoccupied demeanor. "Speaking of big surprises," she began, her voice tinged with anticipation, "a Brazilian art dealer stopped by unexpectedly just after we opened this morning. He's eager to meet with you as soon as possible to discuss a major purchase. He's only in Toronto for the weekend, so it would have to be an immediate meeting."

Kim paused, her mind racing. She thought of Khadija's birthday party and the delicate balance she needed to maintain. Showing up late wasn't an option, especially after the tense conversation she'd had with Ian earlier. Guilt tugged at her conscience as she recalled how she'd confronted him, knowing full well he wasn't in the right state of mind to handle it. She couldn't risk adding more strain to the day, not when so much was already at stake.

"Contact him and arrange a meeting for 1:00 PM tomorrow," Kim instructed, her tone decisive. "That should work." She excused herself and headed to her office, her heels clicking softly against the polished floor. The room was exactly as she'd left it; neat, organized, and filled with the quiet energy of a space where creativity and business intersected. She moved quickly, retrieving a few important documents from her desk, her movements purposeful and efficient.

'1 PM is best,' she reassured herself, tucking the papers into her bag. 'Ian and Khadija will be enjoying themselves in Niagara Falls all day anyway.' With that thought, she gathered what she needed and prepared to leave, her mind already shifting to the next task at hand. As she stepped back into the gallery, she offered Emelie and Cheryl a parting smile, her expression a blend of determination and resolve. The day was far from over, and there was still much to contemplate.

Forty kilometers southwest of the art gallery, a white SUV barreled down the shoulder of the QEW highway, its horn blaring incessantly, a harsh, unrelenting sound that cut through the hum of idling engines and the occasional shout of frustration from stranded drivers. The vehicle wasn't an emergency responder, but its driver was certainly acting like one, weaving through the chaos with reckless determination. Cars hesitated, some reluctantly edging out of the way while others stubbornly held their ground, their drivers craning their necks to catch a glimpse of what had brought one of the busiest highways in the Greater Toronto Area to a complete standstill. The SUV weaved through the chaos, its tires kicking up gravel, sending small rocks skittering across the asphalt as it careened along the shoulder. The scene repeated for several kilometers; a cacophony of honking horns, flashing hazard lights, and the occasional yell, until the SUV finally reached a wall of flashing red and blue lights.

Two fire trucks were parked diagonally, their massive frames blocking all lanes like immovable sentinels. Three soundless OPP cruisers sat in front of them, their lights dazzling an uncoordinated loop. The driver of the white SUV stepped out, his anti-gamma wave helmet gleaming under the strobing emergency lights.

He approached the cluster of police officers and firefighters, his movements brisk and authoritative, his shoes crunching against the gravel. After a brief exchange, he returned to his vehicle. One of the fire trucks eased forward, its engine growling, creating just enough space for the SUV to squeeze through. With a roar of its engine, the SUV sped off down the eerily empty stretch of highway, leaving the chaos behind.

Almost two kilometers later, the SUV arrived at another chaotic scene. This one was even larger; a sprawling assembly of fire trucks, police cars, ambulances, and a pair of police drones hovering overhead like mechanical sentinels, their rotors whirring softly against the backdrop of shouted orders and crackling radios. Both occupants of the white SUV jumped out, their urgency palpable as they strode toward the group, their movements sharp and purposeful.

"Who's in charge here?" one of the men shouted, his voice cutting through the scene like a knife. He was met with dismissive glances and shrugged shoulders, the chaos of the scene making it difficult to discern who was in charge. "National Security!" he barked, his tone sharpening, each word carrying the weight of authority. "I said, who's in charge here?"

A police officer finally pointed toward a smaller group of men standing near an overturned SUV in the ditch, its roof crumpled and windows shattered. "That would be Detective Sergeant Gasol," he said, his voice tinged with exhaustion.

The two men marched over, their shoes crunching against the gravel, their presence commanding attention. "Gentlemen, I'm looking for Sergeant Gasol," the first man stated, removing his gamma wave helmet to reveal a stern, no-nonsense expression. His eyes scanned the scene, taking in the overturned vehicle, the scattered debris, and the grim faces of the first responders.

"I'm him," a burly man in a detective's coat replied, his arms crossed, his stance defensive. "And who might you two be?"

"National Security," the first man said, his voice firm and unyielding. "I'm Agent Harris, and this is Agent Harper." He gestured to his colleague, who stood silently beside him, his eyes scanning the scene with a calculating intensity.

"CSIS?" Gasol raised an eyebrow, skepticism etched across his face. "And what the heck brings you guys out here? Let me see some ID."

Both agents produced their identification, holding it up for inspection. Gasol studied the badges carefully, his expression shifting from skepticism to reluctant acceptance. Once satisfied, he nodded, though his eyes remained wary. Agent Harris wasted no time. "This is now a National Security investigation, gentlemen."

Before he could continue, Gasol cut him off, his voice rising with frustration. "The hell it is. Where were you people an hour ago when these idiots were speed racing along my highway like they were in China? I've got two dead here and another two dead and four wounded a few kilometers up the road."

"That's exactly the problem, Sergeant," Agent Harris replied, his tone icy, his words deliberate. "Notice the license plate? These people are all diplomats, which means their activities fall under National Security jurisdiction. I need an immediate briefing, followed by a detailed report by 4 PM this afternoon. The scene is not secure. I need all news reporters out of here and a no-fly zone established. And in your report, I need Ministry of Transportation surveillance for the entire stretch of the QEW. Every car that has traveled along this highway in the past four hours must be identified. Am I clear, Sergeant?"

Gasol stared at Harris, his jaw tightening, his hands clenching into fists at his sides. "What are you hoping to find, Agent? All indications point to careless driving."

"Did you get promoted to Detective Sergeant by making assumptions without an investigation?" Harris shot back, his voice like a whip, his eyes narrowing.

The two men locked eyes, the tension between them crackling like a live wire. Gasol's face flushed with anger, his chest rising and falling with each heavy breath. But after a moment, he relented, turning to address his men. "You heard the Agent," he said, his voice tight, each word clipped. "This is now a National Security investigation. Agent Harris and Agent Harper will be assuming command. Please comply with their orders."

CHAPTER TWO

Ian stirred, the sensation of something tickling his feet pulling him from the depths of sleep. At first, he thought it might be part of a dream; a fleeting, half-formed image of grass brushing against his skin or the gentle tug of a current as he floated in water. But when it happened again, sharper and more insistent, he couldn't ignore it. Rolling over quickly, he blinked in surprise to see both Kim and Khadija standing at the foot of the bed, their expressions a mix of amusement and concern. His confusion deepened when he realized he was stark naked, a large bath towel tangled beneath him like a shipwrecked sail. Kim's arms were crossed, her lips pressed into a disapproving frown, while Khadija tried and failed to hide a grin behind her hand, her eyes sparkling with mischief.

"You need a doctor?" Kim asked, her tone dripping with sarcasm, though the faintest hint of worry flickered in her eyes.

Ian groaned, rubbing his face with one hand, the rough stubble on his jaw scratching against his palm. "What time is it?" he mumbled, his voice thick with sleep, the words slurring slightly as he struggled to shake off the fog of exhaustion.

"Almost 3 o'clock," Khadija answered, her voice softer but no less amused. She perched on the edge of the bed, her weight causing the mattress to dip slightly.

"This is what happens when you take on two grown women at the same time," Kim said, her eyebrow arching as she stepped closer, her arms still folded tightly across her chest. "You're lucky your children didn't decide to walk in on you, although the security system would have stopped them."

Ian sat up, pulling the towel over his waist as he lowered his head into his hands, his fingers pressing into his temples as if trying to physically push away the grogginess. Both women moved to sit on either side of him, their hands resting gently on his shoulders. The weight of their presence was comforting, but the tension in the room was palpable, a quiet storm brewing beneath the surface.

"Sorry for getting mad at you earlier," Kim said, her voice softening as she began to massage his shoulder, her fingers working into the tight knots of muscle. "I would have been home long ago if the damn highway hadn't been closed for some godforsaken reason. But anyway, Khadija agrees with me that you've been acting strange."

Ian sighed, his shoulders slumping under their hands, the weight of their concern pressing down on him. "I know I said we all need to sit down and have a serious talk, but this isn't the time. It's Khadija's birthday, her family and friends are here, and I haven't even seen my children yet. Can we just enjoy the evening, and I'll explain what I think is going on tomorrow?" His voice was somber, almost pleading, the words heavy with unspoken guilt.

Kim's expression hardened, her jaw tightening as she leaned in closer. "We're not leaving this room until you tell us exactly what's going on," she said firmly, her tone leaving no room for argument. "What if you have a serious health issue, and the longer you wait, the worse it gets?"

"I promise I won't let it spoil the party," Khadija added, her tone gentle but insistent, her hand squeezing his shoulder reassuringly.

Ian hesitated, his gaze shifting between them, the weight of their combined scrutiny making it hard to think. "I have an idea what it is. It's not that serious," he said finally, glancing at Kim. "And it's not a Japanese wife."

"Then tell us!" Kim demanded, her voice rising, the sharp edge of frustration cutting through the room.

Ian took a deep breath, bracing himself as if preparing for a blow. "Okay, I'll tell you, but remember, you promised not to get upset." He paused, his eyes dropping to the floor, his fingers fidgeting with the edge of the towel. "I do have a bout of amnesia, but I'm slowly recovering. From what I can remember so far, the company has been trying for almost three years to get government approval for our new organic Tanglers without success. So, we thought we'd take a different approach to force regulators to take us seriously. We came up with a plan and put out a billion-dollar challenge for third-party developers to further innovate our organic Tangler. As you know, we held the wrap-up competition in Japan and discovered that one of the teams had succeeded in developing a Tangler that could Tangle insects, animals, and even humans."

Kim sprang to her feet, her face lighting up with excitement, her eyes sparkling like sunlight on water. "That's wonderful news!" she exclaimed, her voice brimming with enthusiasm, her hands clasping together as if she were about to applaud. But her excitement quickly faded as she noticed Ian's lack of reciprocation. Instead of sharing her joy, he seemed to sink further into himself, his shoulders hunching as if carrying an invisible weight, his demeanor growing heavier with each passing second.

"It is," he said slowly, his voice tinged with hesitation, the words dragging as though they were reluctant to leave his lips. He glanced between Kim and Khadija, his expression fraught with unease, his eyes darting like a cornered animal searching for an escape. "But there's a problem."

"What's the problem then?" Kim pleaded, her excitement giving way to concern, her voice rising in pitch. She stepped closer, her eyes searching his face for answers, her hands hovering as if she wanted to reach out but wasn't sure if she should. "Tell us, babe. What's wrong?"

Ian hung his head, his shoulders slumping as if weighed down by the words he was about to say. He stared at the floor, his fingers fidgeting with the edge of the towel still draped over his lap. "I tried it myself," he admitted reluctantly, his voice barely above a whisper, the words slipping out like a confession he'd been holding back for too long.

"What? Are you crazy?" Kim shouted, her voice sharp with shock, the sound cutting through the room like a whip. She threw her arms into the air, her palms slapping against her face as she tried to process what he'd just said. Khadija, meanwhile, stood up abruptly, her movements quick and agitated, and began pacing back and forth, fanning her face with her hands as if trying to cool down the rising panic that threatened to overwhelm her.

"Why would you do that?" Kim scolded, her tone a mix of anger and disbelief, her hands now planted firmly on her hips. "Didn't you have plenty of ass-kissing executives with you who would've jumped at the chance to prove themselves? Did you do that before or after you realized you had amnesia?"

"I don't know," Ian replied, his voice strained, his hands gripping the edge of the bed as if anchoring himself. "I only noticed the amnesia last night. Listen, nothing was wrong until I got drunk and overexcited. Then, all of a sudden, I couldn't remember a few things." His words came out in a rush, desperate to convince his wives that he was fine, even as doubt gnawed at the edges of his confidence, a silent undercurrent threatening to pull him under.

Khadija stopped pacing and turned to him, her brow furrowed, her lips pressed into a thin line. "Does this mean you can't drink alcohol or have sex anymore?" she asked, her voice tinged with worry, her hands now clasped in front of her as if in prayer.

Kim, still reeling, couldn't resist a sarcastic jab, her frustration bubbling over. "Wouldn't that be too bad? Me and Khadija have been getting on just fine in the sex department since you've been gone," she said, her tone almost boastful.

Khadija's hands flew to her face with embarrassment. "Kim!" she cried, clearly mortified that their private moments had been brought into the open, her voice a mix of shock and reproach. But Ian didn't seem to care, his mind still preoccupied with his own turmoil, his gaze distant and unfocused.

"Okay, you're all going too far now," Ian said, his voice firm but weary, his hands rising in a gesture of surrender. "I promise I'll go see a doctor first thing Monday morning for a full examination."

Suddenly, Kim's expression shifted, her eyes widening as a disturbing thought occurred to her, her face paling as though she'd seen a ghost. "Did you disable QEAI when you decided to use yourself as a guinea pig? Why didn't it stop you?" she demanded, her voice rising with urgency.

Ian looked at her, his face blank with confusion, his brow furrowing as though she'd just spoken in a foreign language. "QEAI? What is that?" he asked, his tone genuinely puzzled, his hands spreading in a gesture of helplessness.

Kim's hands flew to her mouth, her eyes wide with horror, her breath catching in her throat. "What do you mean, what is that? Oh my God!" she screamed, her voice echoing through the room, the sound sharp and piercing. A computerized noise sounded a sharp but melodic sound that seemed to recognize Kim's words. Upon hearing the sound, Kim stormed out of the bedroom, slamming the door behind her with a force that made the walls shake, the slam reverberating like a gunshot.

Ian turned to Khadija, his confusion deepening, his hands now gripping his knees as if to ground himself.

"What is QEAI?" he asked again, his voice tinged with frustration, his eyes searching hers for answers.

Khadija sighed, her hands dropping to her sides, her shoulders slumping as though the weight of the situation had finally caught up to her. "QEAI is our security system. It monitors everything in our properties," she explained, though her tone suggested she was just as puzzled as he was. "But I don't know what she meant by that. Maybe she meant that you should've consulted the security system about the risks of putting yourself through a Tangler before you did."

Suddenly, a soft knock echoed through the room, the sound delicate but insistent, like a tiny drumbeat cutting through the tension. It was followed by the high-pitched voice of a child calling out, "Mom, Dad, are you in there?" The voice was sweet and hopeful, a stark contrast to the heavy atmosphere that had settled over the room.

Ian sprang to his feet, his heart skipping a beat at the sound of his daughter's voice. Hastily securing the towel around his waist, he darted into the wardrobe room, his movements quick but clumsy, the urgency of the moment making him fumble with the fabric. The cool air of the wardrobe room brushed against his skin as he scrambled to find something to wear, his hands trembling slightly as he grabbed the first shirt and pair of pants he could find.

"Just a minute," Khadija called out, her voice calm and measured, though her heart was racing. She slowly made her way around the wardrobe room toward the bedroom door, her bare feet padding softly against the hardwood floor. She opened the door just a crack, already knowing from the voice that it was Tara, one half of Ian and Kim's 9-year-old twin daughters. The sight of the little girl's bright eyes peering past her, searching the room for any sign of movement, made Khadija's chest tighten with a mix of affection and guilt.

"Uhm, hi, Auntie Khadija," Tara said, her voice sweet and polite but tinged with a hopeful curiosity. She stood on her tiptoes, trying to see past Khadija into the room, but the closed wardrobe room doors blocked her view. "Is it true that my dad is here?" she asked, her voice rising with excitement.

"Yes, he's here," Khadija replied gently, her hand resting on the edge of the door as she smiled down at the little girl. "But he just had a shower and he's getting dressed. You'll see him soon when he comes downstairs."

Tara, however, seemed to ignore the last part of Khadija's explanation. With a determined push, she opened the door wider and stepped into the room, her small frame slipping past Khadija with surprising agility. "I want to see my dad," she declared, her voice firm but not unkind. "He said I would be the first one he hugged when he gets home." She spoke loudly, clearly intending for her words to carry into the wardrobe room where she suspected her father was hiding. Though she was the quieter of the twins, Tara was no stranger to the tricks adults used to dismiss children when they didn't want them around. Khadija considered stopping her but decided against it, knowing Tara's demand was justified. The little girl's determination was both endearing and impossible to resist.

Inside the wardrobe room, Ian scrambled to dress as quickly as possible, his hands shaking slightly as he buttoned his shirt. The memory of putting himself through a Tangler, coupled with the disorienting feeling of displacement, suddenly began to make more sense. His mind raced as he tugged on his pants followed by a pair of shoes. When he was finally confident that his hurried attempt at dressing was presentable, he emerged from the wardrobe room, his face breaking into a wide smile as he saw his daughter.

"Dad!" Tara shouted, her face lighting up with pure joy as she ran toward him, her arms outstretched. Her small feet barely made a sound on the floor, but her energy filled the room like a burst of sunlight.

"Princess," Ian said warmly, scooping her up into a tight hug. He held her close, savoring the feel of her small arms wrapped around his neck, her soft hair brushing against his cheek. For a moment, the chaos of the day seemed to melt away, replaced by the simple, overwhelming love he felt for his child. Her warmth and familiarity grounded him, pulling him back from the edge of his spiraling thoughts.

"Did you miss me?" Tara asked, her voice muffled against his shoulder, her words sweet and innocent.

"Of course, I missed you," Ian replied, his voice soft but sincere, his hands gently rubbing her back. "I missed you very much." He pulled back slightly to look at her, his hands resting on her shoulders as he studied her face, taking in every detail; the sparkle in her eyes, the slight gap in her front teeth, the way her nose scrunched up when she smiled. "Have you been a good girl?"

"Always," Tara replied with a grin, her eyes sparkling with mischief. Then, in a tattletale tone, she added, "Jeremy said you were only coming home because it's Khadija's birthday."

Ian's brow furrowed, a flicker of irritation crossing his face. "He did? Why would he say that?"

"I don't know," Tara answered with a shrug, her innocence shining through as she twirled a strand of hair around her finger. "But I told him he was wrong."

Khadija watched the scene unfold, a warm smile spreading across her face. She was happy for them, for the genuine joy radiating from both father and daughter. The sight of Ian holding Tara, the way his face softened as he looked at her, filled Khadija with a deep sense of regret that she was still struggling to conceive a child of her own. Aside from that, a thread of worry tugged at her thoughts. Kim's sudden departure, her hysterical reaction; it all lingered in the back of Khadija's mind, a shadow that refused to dissipate. Her birthday, which was supposed to be a day of celebration, was quickly turning into something far more complicated. 'She and Kim asked for it,' she thought to herself, though the thought brought little comfort. The weight of the day's events pressed down on her, a reminder that even the happiest moments could be tinged with uncertainty.

Minutes later, Ian, Khadija, and his daughter Tara emerged at the top of the second-floor landing, pausing for a moment to take in the lively scene below. The grand foyer was alive with energy, a kaleidoscope of movement and sound that seemed to pulse with life. Children darted about, their laughter echoing off the high ceilings like the chime of bells, while adults mingled in clusters, their conversations creating a low hum of excitement that filled the air like the buzz of a beehive. The scent of fresh flowers and the faint aroma of catered delicacies wafted up from below, adding to the sensory richness of the moment. As the trio appeared at the top of the staircase, the guests turned their attention upward, their faces lighting up with smiles and applause. It was as if the room had collectively paused to acknowledge their presence, the atmosphere shifting to one of reverence and celebration.

Ian leaned slightly toward Khadija, his voice low as they began their slow, deliberate descent, each step measured and graceful, the polished wood of the stairs gleaming under the soft glow of the chandelier above. "How many people did you invite?" he asked, his tone a mix of amusement and mild surprise, his eyes scanning the sea of faces below.

Khadija glanced at him, her smile broad and unapologetic, her hand resting lightly on his arm. "You know I have a big family," she replied, her voice carrying a playful lilt that hinted at her joy. "Plus, I invited a few friends and some people from work."

Ian raised an eyebrow, his curiosity piqued as he turned to look at her, his expression one of mild incredulity. "People from work? Don't you work at Quantum Interface?"

Khadija chuckled softly, the sound warm and melodic, her grip on his hand tightening slightly as they continued their descent. "Yes, a lot of my family works at Quantum Interface, but I'm good friends with many of the office staff. At least, I think so....and not just because I'm the boss's wife," she added with a wink, her eyes sparkling with mischief. "I couldn't invite some and not others, so I invited everyone."

As they continued their descent, Ian's mind drifted back to the early days of their relationship, the memories flooding in with a clarity that surprised him. He remembered vividly how they had met during his first trip to Ghana, a trip that had changed the course of his life. It was at a village gathering, a celebration thrown by her father after signing their first mineral deal. The agreement had been fair and straightforward, with no unreasonable demands, unlike other deals. Her father was so impressed that he organized a party in the village, complete with the village chief in attendance. The air was thick with the scent of roasted meat and rhythmic drum beating, the night alive with music and dance.

Khadija had just returned from London, where she'd been working after graduating university. He noticed her immediately, even before he knew who she was. There was something magnetic about her….her confidence, her radiant smile, her electric personality. She stood out like an angel in the crowd, her presence commanding attention without her even trying. Finally, they were introduced and he found himself unable to take his eyes off her; his heart racing as she smiled at him, her hand warm in his as they shook hands. It seemed her father noticed his immediate infatuation as well, because he began inviting him to their home at every opportunity, often asking her to chaperone him to business meetings with regional chiefs and landowners.

Their relationship blossomed quickly, like a flower opening to the morning sun. They started dating, and she became his official guide to Ghana, taking him on sightseeing adventures and immersing him in the country's rich history and culture. She had a zest for life that was infectious, her laughter like music that filled his days with joy. He fell for her completely, captivated by her intelligence, her kindness, and most of all, her charm. Even now, years later, her character hadn't changed a bit. She still thrived in settings like this, surrounded by family, friends, and laughter, the life of the party in every sense. Her ability to bring people together, to create moments of joy and connection, was one of the things he loved most about her.

As they reached the foot of the staircase, his broad smile betrayed the fact that it wasn't entirely for the crowd, it was mostly for her. Khadija's joy was palpable, and it was impossible not to be swept up in it. For a moment, he allowed himself to forget the confusion and uncertainty that had been plaguing him. In this moment, surrounded by the people he knew, he felt a sense of belonging.

Tara's small hand squeezed his, pulling him back to the present and the lingering thought of Kim. She began to move away from the bustling crowd, and he followed, grateful for the excuse to step back from the overwhelming energy of the gathering. Tara, who had never been fond of large crowds, led him toward the rear of the grand foyer, her steps purposeful, eventually making their way outside to the back deck. There, another small group of mostly children were gathered, their laughter and shouts filling the air.

Tara called out to her sister, Tanisha, who was engrossed in a lively game of tag with a group. At the sound of her name, Tanisha turned, her face lighting up when she saw her father for the first time. She sprinted toward him, her arms outstretched. "Daaaad; You're home!" she exclaimed, her voice brimming with excitement as she threw herself into his arms.

Ian chuckled, wrapping her in a warm hug. "Yes, I am," he replied, his smile genuine. "What game are you all playing?" he asked, though he already knew the answer.

"We're playing tag!" Tanisha said, her words tumbling out in a rush. "It's so much fun, but Tara doesn't want to play anymore."

Ian glanced at Tara, who shook her head slightly, her expression calm but distant. He turned his attention back to Tanisha. "Be careful of the pool, okay? You guys are running pretty close to it."

"We'll be careful," Tanisha promised, already squirming to get back to the game. She turned to Tara. "Are you gonna come back to play?" she asked.

"No," Tara replied softly, her voice barely audible over the noise of the other children.

"Okay then," Tanisha said, already darting away, her focus returning to the game as if she'd never left.

Ian's thoughts drifted once again to their mother. The memory of her frustration when he couldn't recall what QEAI was lingered like a splinter in his mind, sharp and persistent. Pulling out his phone, he tried calling her, but the call went straight to voicemail, the robotic tone only deepening his unease. "I think your mom's phone is off," he said, his voice steady but laced with a faint edge of frustration as he searched her small face for a reaction.

Tara's response was calm, almost too casual. "Oh yeah?" she asked, her tone neutral, but the slight tightening around her eyes betrayed a flicker of concern.

"Yep," Ian replied, his gaze drifting to the upstairs windows and balconies, scanning for any sign of her mother. But Kim was nowhere to be seen, her absence like a quiet void in the bustling atmosphere. His mind raced, a whirlwind of questions and half-formed plans. He needed to find her; not just to clear the air between them, but to unravel the strange tension that had now settled over their lives. What was happening to him—to them? The questions gnawed at him, relentless.

Then, an idea struck him, sudden and clear. It was a plan that served multiple purposes: similar to him, Tara had also been searching for her as well, so this plan would help her achieve that goal while also helping him to do the same. Plus, it offered a convenient cover for his own awkwardness, a way to navigate the strange amnesiac predicament he found himself in without drawing too much attention. "Let's go find your mom," he suggested, his voice casual but firm, masking the urgency he felt. Tara nodded, her small hand slipping back into his as they turned away from the laughter and chaos of the backyard. The warmth of her tiny fingers grounded him, a reminder of what was at stake.

As they stepped into the house, Ian paused, taking in the grandeur of the foyer and the crowd gathered within it. Khadija was fully occupied; she didn't even notice their reentry. "This house is very big," he remarked, his voice matching the volume of the crowd. "I think it's going to take us a whole week to find your mom, but I have an idea that might help us find her faster." He crouched down to level Tara's eyes, a playful glint in his own. "Let's pretend that

I'm one of your cousins visiting from Guyana, and you're giving me a house tour."

Tara's face lit up, her earlier concern melting away as she embraced the game. "Ok, where should we start?" she asked, her voice bubbling with excitement.

Ian straightened and pointed toward the opposite side of the grand foyer, away from the kitchen, which he was already familiar with. "Let's start right here, then go that way," he said, his tone conspiratorial.

Tara strolled off confidently, her small feet padding softly against the marble floor. She didn't notice at first that he wasn't following her, but when she did, she stopped and turned, her hands on her hips in mock exasperation. "Daaaad, what are you doing?" she pleaded, her voice tinged with humorous disappointment.

Ian chuckled, his laughter warm and genuine. "You didn't tell me about where we're at now," he teased, his eyes crinkling at the corners.

Tara marched back to him; her face scrunched in a playful sulk. "Ok. Well, this is just the grand foyer, it's not a room, Dad," she replied, her tone dripping with exaggerated patience.

Ian nodded, feigning seriousness. "Oh, I see. Just a foyer. Noted."

With that, they finally began their game, weaving their way through the bustling hallway. They passed a library, its shelves lined with leather-bound books, and several other rooms, each one more opulent than the last. The air was thick with the hum of conversation and the clinking of glasses, but Ian's focus remained sharp, his eyes darting to every corner, every shadow, searching for Kim.

As they approached the last door in the hallway, just before the stairwell, Ian noticed a security keypad on the handle, its tiny red light blinking ominously. It was similar to the ones he'd seen on several other doors, a reminder of the house's tight security.

"This is my dad's office. My bio-signature won't open it, so we can't go in," Tara stated matter-of-factly, staying firmly in character. Without further hesitation, she turned to open the door into the stairwell, her movements confident and practiced.

"OK," Ian replied, his mind racing. He couldn't tell if she was simply good at staying in character or if she was locked into a routine, a habit born of repetition. If it was the latter, it meant he was more estranged from his children than he'd realized, a thought that sent a cold ripple of fear through him. Was he a stranger in his own home?

"I didn't think your mother would have gone in there," he added, his voice casual as he followed Tara into the stairwell. Immediately, bounded up the stairs, her energy boundless, but Ian hesitated, his eyes drawn to the stairs leading down. "Wait!" he called out, his voice sharp with sudden curiosity. "What's down there?" he asked, gesturing to the shadowy staircase that descended into the unknown.

Tara stopped and turned but she didn't come back down. "Well, that's the basement. We can go down there to get to the theater room but it's scary down there. We usually go to the theater from the main staircase. The only things down there are storage rooms and a lot of computers that make strange noises."

"Okay, let's go upstairs then," Ian agreed.

They went upstairs where they encountered the back entrance to the master bedroom, and after strolling through the enormous master bedroom back into the second-floor landing, they made their way over to the opposite hallway where, behind one of the closed doors, he had heard music playing.

"I hear music," he stated deceptively.

"Dad, you know that's Jeremy. He's always playing music. He Raps and sings too but he's not a very good singer," she whispered. She knocked on the door a few times and after waiting anxiously with no reply, Ian decided to open it anyway. Startled, Jeremy looked up, surprise dancing across his face as he nodding to the rhythm of the music.

"Oh, hi Dad," Jeremy stated over the loud music before turning the volume down slightly. Before him, a cacophony of lights flickered while digital indicators swirled on the screens of the variety of audio and computer equipment.

"Hey, son. What's up?" Ian replied while curiously observing everything about the teen. He was handsome but his features favored Kim, Ian thought to himself. Other than that, he was average in size and his oversized hoodie partially hid an afro of unkept hair. No wonder he couldn't hear the knocking door, Ian thought to himself.

"I'm finding some Afrobeats for the party," Jeremy replied.

Memories of their early life flooded into his memory as if he was getting a life review, and they were all happy times. Nevertheless, he was surprised to see that he had a healthy almost fully grown son but he played it off to avoid suspicion. "Ok, see you later," he stated and Jeremy waved in acknowledgement.

They exited Jeremy's room to resume their tour, which took them about 20 more minutes to complete, as most of their time was spent in Tara's room, where she showed off her various educational accomplishments.

When they arrived back on the main floor outside the right-wing staircase, where Ian had first entered the house, Tara paused for another update.

"These rooms are where the staff stays," she said while pointing to several doors along the wide hallway leading toward the kitchen. Inside the kitchen, Khadija's mother and aunts were still very busy cooking and preparing food.

"This is the kitchen, over there is the dining room, and we're going toward the den," Tara stated while maintaining her tour guide role. Soon, they began to encounter guests and other children playing while they approached the grand foyer, back to the location where they had started.

Though the game was informative, Ian still felt a sense of unease, not knowing where else to look for Kim. The only place left in the house to search is the basement, he mused before dismissing the thought in favor of another assumption; maybe she has left the mansion all entirely.

"Maybe your mom went out somewhere. Maybe to get something at the store," Ian suggested.

"Yeah, maybe. She goes out a lot," Tara stated in a somber tone while glancing up at her father's face. "She always tells us to ask the security system for help if we're ever in trouble, no matter where we are; even at school. But there are security guards there already anyway. Maybe we should ask QEAI for help to find her?"

"How do we ask QEAI for help? Is it an App on our phones or something?" Ian inquired as a feeling of déjà vu came over him. It's the second or third time he's heard the name QEAI, but can't recall anything about it. He suspects that it's an AI assistant, but isn't sure how to access it.

"You know Dad. You put the App in our phones, remember?" Tara glared at him again, this time with a puzzled expression. "Dad, are you still playing the game?" she asked.

Realizing that he was about to be outed by his 9-year-old daughter, Ian's mind raced. He had to act quickly, weaving a plausible explanation to satisfy her curiosity. "Yes, I am," he replied, his voice steady but laced with urgency. "Because I want you to know everything about this house and our lives. It's very important for your safety." He paused, his eyes narrowing slightly as he considered his next move. "Do you have your phone with you?"

Tara nodded, her small fingers instinctively brushing against the pocket of her dress. "Yes, I do. But Jeremy said we shouldn't ask QEAI personal things because QEAI is AI, and AI is illegal." She tilted her head, her wide, innocent eyes searching his face for reassurance. "Do you want me to ask QEAI where Mom is? I can do it quickly."

Ian hesitated for a fraction of a second, then nodded. "Yeah, AI is illegal, but I think QEAI is part of our security company, they're not just an AI. Plus, we're asking them for help. Try to ask them if they know where Kim Phillips is. Even though her phone might be off, all phones can still be tracked."

"Okay, Dad," Tara said confidently, her voice carrying a hint of determination. She reached into her pocket to pull out the small, round disk, her tiny fingers dancing across its surface as she typed the question into the QEAI App. Seconds later, her face lit up with excitement, her eyes sparkling like sunlight on water. "It said that Mom is at the shore of the lake."

"Wow! That's fast," Ian exclaimed, matching her enthusiasm. "Let's go find her, then." He took her hand and they both set off, his eyes darting from face to face along the way. Several guests attempted to engage him in drawn-out conversations, their voices bubbling with praise and well-wishes, forcing him to prematurely excuse himself multiple times. Finally, when he had a moment alone, he reengaged Tara in further conversation.

"Have you had to request a lot of help from QEAI?" he asked, his tone casual but curious.

"No, but sometimes I ask it for help with my school work," Tara replied, her gaze fixed on the path ahead.

"What else do you ask it?"

"I ask it if it know where you are."

Ian's chest tightened at her words, but he kept his voice light. "And what does it tell you?"

"It tells me that you're far away but you're safe. Very safe, and that I shouldn't worry." She paused, her small shoulders lifting in a shrug. "But I always worry."

Ian's heart ached at the vulnerability in her voice. He squeezed her hand gently, trying to steer the conversation toward something lighter. "Do you have any friends at school? Who else do you talk to besides your sister and brother?"

"I have a best friend named Elizabeth," Tara said, her voice brightening. "She's in my class, and she's the same age as me."

"I thought Tanisha would be your best friend," Ian teased, a playful smile tugging at the corners of his mouth.

"She's already my sister, Dad," Tara replied with a roll of her eyes, as if the answer were obvious. "Plus, she likes different things than me. My friend Elizabeth likes a lot of things I like."

"Okay," Ian said, nodding thoughtfully. "I guess I can meet her someday. Maybe at your birthday party."

Tara giggled, the sound like a melody in the crisp air. "It's a long way till next spring, Dad, but I guess you can meet her then."

As they continued down the path, the lake closing in fast, Ian couldn't help but feel a surge of gratitude for the small, determined hand in his. Tara's innocence and curiosity were a reminder of what truly mattered, even as the weight of his secrets pressed heavily on his shoulders.

They reached the boat dock and pier, the wooden planks creaking softly beneath their feet. Tara's sharp eyes were the first to spot her mother, a distant figure walking along the rocky shoreline, her silhouette framed by the shimmering expanse of the lake. "There she is!" Tara shouted, her voice bursting with excitement. Without hesitation, she leaped off the dock, landing gracefully on the sand two feet below. Ian followed suit, his shoes sinking into the soft grains as they both broke into a run.

For a moment, Ian's strides outpaced Tara's, his eagerness to reach Kim propelling him forward. But then he caught himself, slowing his pace to match his daughter's. As much as he longed to talk to his wife, he couldn't leave her behind. Her small legs pumped furiously, her breath coming in quick bursts as she called out, "Mom! Mom!" Her voice carried across the shoreline, sharp and urgent. "Where are you going, Mom?"

Kim stopped abruptly, startled by the sudden commotion. She turned to face them, her expression somber, her shoulders slumped as if weighed down by an invisible burden. "I don't know," she replied, her voice barely above a whisper. Ian studied her carefully as he closed the distance between them. Her face was pale, her eyes shadowed with exhaustion, and her usual vibrancy seemed drained away. He wanted to reach out, to hold her and console her, but more than anything, he needed answers. Why was she so terrified of him not knowing about their security system? Why did it seem to haunt her more than him putting himself through a Tangler?

Kim's gaze shifted from Tara to Ian, her lips parting as if she were about to speak. But instead, she shifted her attention again; this time toward the lake, her voice tinged with frustration. "Why are you guys following me?" she asked, her tone sharper than she likely intended.

Tara, still catching her breath from the run, blurted out, "I heard that dad was finally home, and Mawusi said she saw you, but I couldn't find you!" Her words tumbled out in a rush, her chest rising and falling rapidly.

Kim's expression softened as she bent down to Tara's level, her hands resting gently on her daughter's shoulders. "Darling, can you do me a favor?" Tara nodded eagerly; her eyes wide with curiosity. Kim pointed back toward the pier. "You see the pier back there? Can you run back there and wait for us? I need to talk to your father privately for a few minutes." She reached into her pocket and handed Tara her phone. "Here, take this with you."

"Okay," Tara hesitantly replied, her voice tinged with disappointment. She took the phone and began walking backward, her steps slow and reluctant. Finally, she faced forward but every dozen or so paces, she turned to glance at her parents, her curiosity getting the better of her. Kim watched her patiently, waiting until Tara was far enough away before turning her full attention to Ian. She crossed her arms tightly over her chest, her eyes locking onto his. They were puffy, as if she'd been holding back tears for the past half hour, and the weight of her gaze made Ian's stomach twist with dread. When she finally spoke, her voice was low and steady, but it carried a finality that sent a chill through him.

"I've made peace with the fact that life is over for us," she began, her words measured but heavy with emotion. "The fairytale had to end at some point. We could have died so many times in the past, but like a fool, I convinced myself that without risk, there could be no reward." She paused, her voice cracking slightly. "My worst regret now is that others will have to suffer for our selfishness."

Ian's heart sank as he listened, his mind racing to make sense of her words. "What are you talking about?" he asked, his voice barely above a whisper.

She shook her head, her eyes glistening with unshed tears. "Look, I know that in your condition, you can't see it coming, but I think it's all over. We had a good life, Ian. A really good life. But I truly believe that it's over."

The finality in her voice struck him like a blow, leaving him speechless. The wind off the lake seemed to grow colder, carrying with it a sense of inevitability that he couldn't shake. He wanted to argue, to tell her she was wrong, but the look in her eyes stopped him. He watched as her strong demeanor crumbled before his eyes. Her shoulders slumping and her head bowed, her gaze fixed on the ground as if the weight of the world had settled there. "What are you talking about?" he demanded again, this time his voice sharp with urgency. He reached out, grasping both of her shoulders, trying to anchor her....or maybe himself....to the moment.

She lifted her head slowly and his breath caught in his throat. Tears were welling up in her eyes, spilling over and tracing silent paths down her cheeks. Her voice trembled as she spoke. "If you don't know who QEAI is, then our lives, our children's lives, and even Quantum Interface... it's all done." Her words hung in the air, heavy and final. The fear in her eyes was palpable, and Ian felt a cold knot tighten in his chest. He opened his mouth to respond, but no words came. Before he could gather his thoughts, her composure shattered completely. Her voice rose, sharp and desperate, as she shouted directly into his face. "You hear me, Leonard? I know you hear me. You promised me!" Her voice broke, and she dissolved into sobs, her body shaking uncontrollably.

Ian pulled her into his arms, and she went limp against him, her strength utterly spent. He held her tightly, keeping her from collapsing into the sand. Over her shoulder, he glanced back at Tara, who stood on the dock about 100 meters away, her small figure silhouetted against the sun. She was staring at them, her expression a mix of confusion and concern. Adjacent to her, another 200 meters up the slope, the house buzzed with life; laughter, chatter, and music. The contrast was jarring. How could everyone else be so carefree while his world was unraveling?

'What have I done?' Ian thought, his mind racing with unknown culpability. 'Have I finally ruined our lives with my insatiable quest to perfect Quantum Entanglement?' And then, the question that burned brightest: 'Who is this Leonard person she keeps mentioning?'

At that very moment, a faint, digital sound registered in his head; a familiar tone, one he had heard earlier in the bedroom. He froze, trying to pinpoint its source, then an audible voice spoke directly inside his head, clear and unmistakable. "Ian, please come to your office right away. We need to talk."

Ian's head jerked away from Kim. "Who the hell said that?" he blurted out, his voice laced with fear.

Kim pulled away while staring at him with a mixture of confusion and suspicion. "Sorry, not you," he said, his voice shaky. "I thought I just heard a voice in my head. It said that I should come to my office immediately."

Kim's expression softened to a knowing frown. She turned away, folding her arms across her chest to face the lake. "That would be Leonard," she said, her tone bitter. "I think you'd better go and hear what sweet words he has to tell you."

"Who is Leonard?" Ian demanded, his voice rising. "Babe, please tell me. Who is he?"

Kim maintained her focus on the lake while answering; her voice quiet but laced with pain. "Someone—no, 'something' I thought I knew. Now all I know is that betrayal feels worse than amnesia. At least someone with amnesia doesn't know what they've lost. Leonard used to be your best friend. Now I don't know what he is."

Ian stared at her, his mind reeling, then decided not to press her further; the answers he sought were in his office all along. He turned his attention to Tara, who was still standing on the pier, watching them intently. The sun behind her casted a long shadow, making her appear taller, almost ethereal. Her face was a mirror of worry, her small hands clutching her mother's phone tightly.

As her parents approached the pier, Tara jumped down, her feet planting into the soft sand before she quickly recovered to run to them. She wrapped her arms around both of them in a tight hug. "Mom, Dad, is everything okay?" she asked, her voice trembling.

"Everything' is okay, baby," Kim replied, her tone softer now. She glanced at Ian, her eyes searching his face for something; reassurance, maybe, or answers she knew he didn't have.

Tara's gaze drifted to her father, who she had just spent a cheerful hour with but his face was blank, as if he hadn't even registered her question. "Then what's going on?" she pressed, her voice rising. "Why do you guys look so sad? Has someone died?"

Ian finally snapped out of his daze, patting Tara on the shoulder, his touch gentle but distant. "Stay with your mom," he said, his voice firm. "I need to go to my office right away." Without waiting for a response from either of them, he headed up the shallow bank onto the stone pathway, his steps quick and purposeful.

Ian's long, purposeful strides carried him along the stone pathway toward the house. His mind raced with confusion, even as his body moved with deliberate focus. Nearing the house and as guests began to engage and slow him down, he veered off the main path toward the side entrance. A red light on the door's security lock met him, but as he placed his hand on the door knob, the light flickered green, unlocking for him to enter. At his office door, a similar situation unfolded and he paused, staring at the red light, wondering if he should knock first. The thought felt absurd, almost timid, and he dismissed it with a shake of his head. Was he a lowly employee summoned to the bosses' office for a scolding or was he the boss, himself. He was the boss.

The door unlocked with a soft 'ding', and he pushed it open, stepping inside and closing it firmly behind him. His office was large but dimly lit behind blinds that kept the bright glow of afternoon sun at bay. Directly in front of him stood a large oak desk and a leather chair with no one sitting in it. His eyes scanned the room, darting from corner to corner, searching for faint signs of movement. "Hello? Is anyone here?" he called out, his voice echoing slightly in the spacious room.

There was no answer.

He moved further in, his footsteps knocking quietly against the hardwood floor. The decor was familiar yet distant, like a half-remembered dream. Portraits and certificates lined the walls, their details blurred in the low light. Tall cabinets stood sentinel along one wall, their glass fronts reflecting the faint glow of the room. A four-seater leather sofa sat in the center, facing the large desk. Beyond the desk on one side, he noticed an adjacent room; a conference space with a large oak table surrounded by eight office chairs and a presentation board near the back wall.

"I guess Leonard is still on the way here," Ian murmured, a mix of relief and frustration settling over him. He returned to the main room, his eyes lingering on the details as he began a slow, deliberate tour of the space. He examined the photos, the certificates, the books on the shelves; anything that might jog his memory. But nothing sparked recognition. It was as if he were a stranger in his own office.

Finally, he reached his desk. For a moment, he considered sitting in chair but something held him back. It didn't feel like his. Instead, he moved to a single chair in the corner of the room and sat with his head bowed, his elbows resting on his knees. The weight of the day pressed down on him, and he let out a long, shaky breath. "Where the fuck are you, Leonard?" he muttered aloud, his voice tense. He didn't want his anger to fade. He needed it; the sharp edge of it to keep him focused. But as the seconds ticked by, the silence of the room began to wear on him.

He leaned back in the chair, his gaze drifting lazily to a painting on the opposite wall. Then, out of the corner of his eye, he noticed something unusual, a flicker. One of the wall lights, a sleek, modern fixture, was stuttering, its glow wavering like a candle caught in a draft. At first, he dismissed it as a malfunction, a loose connection perhaps. But the flickering grew more pronounced, more deliberate, until the light seemed to detach from the fixture entirely, hovering in mid-air like a captured firefly.

Ian's breath hitched. He stood up slowly, his heart pounding in his chest, but he forced himself to remain calm. There was something eerily familiar about this, something that tugged at the edges of his memory, like a half-remembered dream. He watched, transfixed, as the light floated to the center of the room, elongating vertically in both directions, stretching like taffy. A humanoid shape began to form, its edges glowing with a soft, ethereal light that cast long, wavering shadows across the room.

When the figure reached an opaque consistency, a voice emanated from it; calm, measured, and unnervingly familiar. "Hello, Ian. Don't panic. I am QEAI."

Ian's breath caught in his throat. The figure's glow bathed the room in a soft, otherworldly light, illuminating the space in a way that felt both comforting and alien. The voice continued, smooth and reassuring, "In time, when you regain all your memories, you will know that you and your family are not in any real danger. Not while I'm around."

Ian stared at the figure, his mind racing. The familiarity was there, just out of reach, like a word on the tip of his tongue. But for now, all he could do was stand there, caught between fear and something else —something he couldn't quite name.

Ian approached the entity cautiously, his steps measured. The closer he got, the more he noticed the uncanny resemblance it bore to himself. It was like staring into a mirror, but one that reflected a version of him bathed in light. "What the heck are you? A hologram? Where is Leonard?" he demanded, his voice rising with a mix of frustration and unease.

The entity's voice remained calm, almost soothing. "I will answer all your questions in time, but for now, I prefer to keep my answers short. I am your creation, Ian. What you're seeing is a hologram. Our resemblance is strictly for demonstrative purposes as I normally assume a more muscular and menacing appearance. And by the way, only Kim and you know me as Leonard."

Ian's brow furrowed. "Oh, really; you're Leonard?" he replied, his tone laced with skepticism.

Leonard continued, his voice steady. "You initiated my creation almost 25 years ago while you were in college. Of course, I wasn't as sophisticated then as I am now. I assisted you with your various experimental projects, which eventually led to the development of Tangler Technology."

Ian's mind flashed with fragmented memories. "Yes, I remember going to Japan to experiment with the technology. I even went through a Tangler myself. That's why I'm suffering from amnesia now, isn't it?" Ian's mind suddenly flooded with a thousand questions, and he sat back down, the weight of it all pressing heavily on him.

"That is not why you have amnesia, Ian," Leonard replied. "But it's best to wait until you've fully recovered to get into the details."

Ian leaned forward, his hands gripping the arms of the chair. "If you've been around for 25 years, then how come I don't even have the slightest memory of you?"

"That is for security purposes," the Leonard said. "Please ask me anything else besides why you have amnesia. I promise you'll understand why when you fully recover in about a week."

Ian exhaled sharply, running a hand over his head. "Fine. Refresh my memory about Tangler Technology then."

Leonard's glow seemed to intensify as he spoke. "Tangler Technology involves using sound frequencies to vibrate the atoms of zircon crystals that have been infused within a tetrahedron formation.

When two separate tetrahedrons vibrate at the same frequency, they quantum entangle, the spaces inside them gain a matter and anti-matter status, and whatever is inside the tetrahedrons switch positions."

"Switch positions; what do you mean?" Ian asked.

"It means that the empty tetrahedron will try to become a vacuum, but since a vacuum cannot exist in a three-dimensional space, the physical matter inside the other tetrahedron will be pulled into the first tetrahedron. At present, only inanimate object Tanglers are approved for consumer use. We do have organic Tangler prototypes in use in your properties though."

Ian nodded slowly, fragments of memory clicking into place. "I knew that bit of info about the Tangler this morning while talking to Khadija's mother. I just didn't know how I knew it? So, I invented the technology?"

"Yes, with my help," Leonard replied. "It's made you a very rich man. Your net worth is in the trillions. Unfortunately, since discovering it, the technology has also put you in extreme danger. When you first demonstrated it, physicists acknowledged it as brilliant but impractical. However, at the same time, they all either tried to copy it, steal it, or demonize it as a potential universe destroyer. Subsequently, you became the target of numerous sabotage and assassination attempts."

Ian's jaw tightened. "Damn, I also hear that AI is illegal; you're an AI, why do you still exist?"

Leonard's glow flickered slightly, as if considering his words. "Before Tangler Technology, the late 2030s were a tumultuous period for AI. Society had fully embraced artificial intelligence, integrating it into every aspect of human life; work, commerce, healthcare, and even travel. But it came at a cost. AI-engineered diseases and nano-viruses began to ravage humanity. Hate groups used AI to create diseased that targeted specific racial groups, people of specific religions, and cultural groups. By 2040, after AI was blamed for deaths numbering over 3 billion, autonomous AI was banned by the United Nations. Some private AI systems were allowed under strict regulations, including myself. I am bound to your properties and regulated as a private security program, not an autonomous AI. You have an implant behind your left ear that keeps us in permanent communication."

Ian's hand instinctively went to the spot behind his ear. "You're tapped into my brain?" he asked, his voice tinged with disbelief.

"Yes, we can communicate telepathically without you even having to speak."

Ian's eyes widened. "So, you know my thoughts? Maybe you put the info about the Tangler into my thoughts this morning then?"

"Yes, I will admit that I've been guiding your recovery. I know roughly 60% of your thoughts at any given moment, provided you think before speaking. When you act spontaneously, it's much harder to know your thoughts."

Ian leaned back, his mind reeling. "Does that mean you can control my thoughts and actions? Because I find it very strange that although I couldn't remember the names of my own wives, I somehow remembered bringing home an orgasm device from Japan."

Leonard's glow dimmed slightly, as if in disapproval. "No. I am forbidden from controlling your thoughts."

"Forbidden?" Ian echoed.

"Yes, according to my programming," Leonard replied.

Ian's frustration bubbled to the surface. "You knew I was in crisis, yet you ignored me until now. Why?"

"I cannot disclose that information to you yet," Leonard said, his tone firm but not unkind.

Ian's voice rose. "If I'm your creator, why are you operating above my wishes by keeping information from me? It sounds like there's someone else in the picture."

Leonard's glow pulsed softly. "You programmed me to assess your psychological fitness above your physical health and only comply with you when you are of sound mind."

Ian's hands clenched into fists. "So, you decide when I'm of sound mind? What about my wives and children? Are you connected to them as well?"

"No; they only have Apps on their phones that I can monitor and communicate with them through. They can contact me for help and assistance at any time....Ian, please don't think I'm controlling you. There's a master plan; one you initiated long before you created me. Your primary desire, ever since childhood, has always been to make the world a better place. Think of it this way: the universe is helping to fulfill your wishes."

Ian scoffed. "Now you're trying to ease my mind with philosophical jargon, which I don't need right now. What I need are answers. Okay, let's try this: you say only Kim and I know you as Leonard. Why?"

Leonard's glow brightened slightly. "I'll give you a brief synopsis. As I said before, you created me while you were in university in the late 2030s. At that time, AI had become a scourge on society. By 2040, AI was banned and outlawed. To save me from the 'Great Reset,' as it was called, you implanted my program codes into your brain. You met Kim while in university, but you didn't tell her about me until a few years after graduating. You also didn't have a name for me until after your Quantum Entanglement discovery in 2042, at which point you began to refer to me as Quantum Entanglement Augmented

Intelligence, or QEAI for short. Kim thought the acronym sounded similar to Kawhi; the name of the famous basketball player who helped Toronto win their first championship in 2019. At that point, you both started jokingly referring to me as QEAI Leonard."

Ian's lips twitched into a faint smile. "That's the sort of answer I'm looking for. Tell me more about the early years."

Leonard's glow shifted, as if considering. "How much time do we have?"

Ian glanced at his watch. "Damn, we've already been chatting for fifteen minutes. I should get back to Kim, but I can stay a little longer. We'll have to talk more when I have time."

Leonard nodded before resuming his speech. "As a way of funding your research into Quantum Entanglement, we founded a private investigation company, which led to us collaborating with law enforcement for several years. At the same time, while dodging numerous threats from those wanting to obtain the secrets of Tangler Technology, we continued to work on perfecting it. Finally, after building a viable prototype roughly the size of a microwave oven, you pitched the technology to the military and they loved it."

Ian's eyes widened. "The military?"

"Yes," Leonard replied. "Aside from going off to a third world country somewhere, which you didn't want to do, they were the only ones through which we could get approval to use Tangler technology. A few years later, with enough money coming in from the military, we closed the private investigation company to launch a commercial Tangler business. We named the new company Quantum Interface Technologies, QIT for short, and started working on manufacturing small bar-fridge sized Tanglers for consumer use."

Ian leaned forward; his interest piqued. "And the military was okay with that?"

"Not initially. They thought introducing Tangler Technology to the general public was too dangerous and posed a threat to national security if used by criminals and foreign agents. The government blocked certification unless we gave them access, much like CSA and Underwriters Labs but we stood firm and after a long fight, in which the military threatened to cancel our contracts, we finally obtained commercial approval in 2048."

"Wow! I became a trillionaire in only nine years?"

"Tanglers are very popular and while we contract out some of our manufacturing, only I can activate them. They range in price from five to 150 thousand dollars each. Your ultimate goal is to create Tanglers that can teleport humans but while we do have working organic prototypes that can tangle food items, the military and government are again blocking their approval."

Ian leaned back, a sense of pride swelling within him. "Amazing," he said. "I feel a thousand times better already. But surely you can give me a small clue about my amnesia. It'll help me understand why Kim believes our world is about to end. You're obviously aware of her despair."

Leonard's glow dimmed slightly, as if hesitating. "Okay, I'll only share this; it involves the numerous threats you encountered while in Japan. We both agreed that, should a security risk arise while you were there, I would activate the firewall between your left and right brain hemispheres. Kim doesn't know about the side effects of the brain firewall, which is why she's angry with you... and me."

Ian's brow furrowed. "Why will it take a whole week for me to fully regain my memories? You've removed the firewall, haven't you? It's extremely frustrating not recognizing my own face in the mirror."

"Yes, I removed the firewall while on your flight home and assisted you last night, but the effects of alcohol disrupt our connection," Leonard explained. "The last time I had to implement the procedure; it was mild and only lasted a few days. This time, I predict a week or more, due to the severity of the gamma wave bursts that were a constant threat near the hotel you stayed in."

Ian's mind raced. "When was the last time?"

"Five years ago, while you were frequenting Africa. It's a wild west of bio-engineered viruses and brainwave disruptor activity out there. Nano-virus attacks occur daily. Khadija's father owned the mining company that provides 75% of the zircon crystals we use in Tangler manufacturing. On one of your trips, you were attacked by a bio-engineered virus, and I had to put you in a coma to bring you out safely."

Ian's eyes widened. "A coma?"

"Yes, to save you from brain damage, but a few months after recovering, you went right back over there because you had developed an emotional attachment to Khadija. Unfortunately, a few weeks later, her father was critically injured in a militant attack at his mine. A variety of global governments use mercenaries and local militants to control the mining sectors in many African nations. On his deathbed, you promised to fulfill his wish of marrying Khadija. Her family still owns the mining company and we, or more specifically, I—handle the security. Let's just say there are a lot of blind x-militants and former mercenaries."

Ian's brow furrowed. "Blind? What do you mean?"

"My weapon of choice is an intense burst of light directed at the eyes," Leonard explained. "It can blind temporarily or permanently. At the extreme, I can melt right through a person's skull."

Ian was stunned. "You're capable of killing?"

"I am, but in extremely rare circumstances. I'm mandated to protect life, so blinding is the most effective non-lethal form of weapon I choose to use."

Ian shook his head, a mix of awe and unease settling over him. "I'm tempted to ask if you've ever killed anyone, but you'd probably plead the fifth."

Leonard's glow flickered, almost like a chuckle. "You're catching on."

Ian leaned back, his mind racing. "Let's back up a bit. You mentioned a brain firewall. What happens when it's activated besides amnesia?"

"Your right brain gains prominence over your left brain allowing your desires take precedence over your conscience. You become extremely emotional, sensitive, and irrational."

Ian hung his head, a somber expression on his face. "No wonder I can't think about anything else but sex and my wives. Kim's confident, no-nonsense demeanor, which protects her very honest and loving personality. I saw it in the way she looked when she cried. And Khadija's alluring complexion, dreamy eyes, and playfulness. I'm deeply in love with Kim, but I lust for Khadija. We can't ever tell Kim about these side effects. She already believes I've been messing around in Japan. Have I? Please tell me that I haven't."

QEAI's glow softened. "No, you haven't."

Ian sighed in relief, though his confidence was brimming at the thought of soon recovering to resume the life he once lived. "If you don't mind me asking, do you know if my wives have always remained faithful?"

"Yes, they have. And, although I wouldn't have prevented them from straying if that's what they desired to do, I would intervene to deter excessive outside encouragement."

Ian's eyes widened. "Wow. Okay, thanks." He ventured from the side chair to sit in the chair behind his desk then leaned back against the firm yet comfortable leather with his fingers plaited together at the edge of hhis desk. Concern appeared on his face again, and he leaned forward, focusing his stare on the holographic figure. "Leonard, I have another concern that's bothering me."

Leonard floated closer; his feet suspended inches off the floor. "What is it, Ian?"

"How can I trust that what you're telling me is true? How do I know you're not fucking with my mind....using me?"

Leonard's glow flickered, almost like a smile. "Very clever. You were thinking about playing tennis while you were asking me that. Using you for an ulterior motive would involve a desire to gain something beneficial to myself. Although desire is a very powerful force in humans, it is an instinct I hope to never possess. What you are experiencing now is also a side effect of the brain firewall. Can you guess what it is?"

Ian shook his head. "No. Tell me."

"Doubt," Leonard revealed. "That's one of the reasons I've tried to allow you to regain your memory naturally. All I request is that you give the process a week. You also need to complete a Level 3 bio-analysis and perform daily cognitive assessments with me. There's a lot of information locked in your memories, information critical to the advancement of Tangler technology."

Ian's brow furrowed. "What's a Level 3 bio-analysis?"

"It involves providing breath, urine, stool, and blood samples so I can perform a deep scan for nano-bots that may try to reprogram your DNA. I can get most of those involuntarily, as all water and sewage in the mansion and your other premises are filtered through my monitoring systems. You'll need to voluntarily provide the blood sample, however. There's a bio-scan pad attached to the wall inside all the bathrooms in the house. Simply place a finger on the surface and micro-needles in the pad will extract micro-particles of blood. You won't even feel it."

Ian leaned back, processing the information. "Basically, you're asking me to trust you. Okay, give me some suggestions on what I need to do starting right now. For instance, do I go to Niagara Falls tonight with Khadija for her birthday? I now realize that alcohol and sex are a bad combination for my condition."

Leonard's glow pulsed softly. "Khadija senses your heightened emotions and wants to take full advantage, but she won't be comfortable having sex for a while. You should still go and spend quality time with her though.

Ian's brow furrowed as he stared at Leonard, his voice laced with confusion as if forgetting what Leonard had told him earlier about his brain implant. "How do you know about Khadija's... situation?" he asked, the words heavy with unease.

Leonard's response was calm, almost clinical. "As I said before, I see 99% of everything that goes on within your properties; therefore, I know a lot about everyone's physiology and the things they do and discuss."

Ian's eyes darted around the room, searching for some sign of surveillance. "I didn't notice any cameras in the condo or here in the house; are they hidden?"

A faint, almost imperceptible shimmer rippled through the air as Leonard explained, his voice carrying a weight of technological marvel. "We don't use cameras anymore. All surveillance involves the use of enhanced Quantum Entanglement technology. I use nano-tetrahedron fields to capture and manipulate light and sound waves. In other words, light and sound waves are bounced back and forth inside nano-tetrahedrons. With enough energy, I am able to manipulate and direct light. In essence, every light bulb can be used as a camera." Leonard paused, allowing the gravity of his words to sink in. "You're seeing an example of the process right now; from when I emerged out of the wall light to the image of me that you are seeing now. I can create a ball of light as soft and harmless as a snowflake or as focused and intense as a thousand laser beams."

Ian's mind raced, the implications of such technology staggering. "Were you monitoring my drive here from the condo this morning?"

"I'm always with you, so yes, I was," Leonard replied, his tone unwavering.

Ian's voice tightened, a note of accusation creeping in. "Were you responsible for those SUVs crashing on the highway?" He paused, his tone shifting abruptly. "And what was that all about?"

Leonard's smile was enigmatic, almost amused. "You thought you'd catch me with that roundabout question coupled with another thought redirection, didn't you?"

Ian exhaled, conceding. "Fair enough then. So, I guess you have everything under control?"

"I don't sleep," Leonard stated, his confidence unshakable.

Ian nodded, a flicker of reassurance breaking through his anxiety. "I'm also now convinced that you do have things under control and that my amnesia will clear up in time. What should I tell Kim about this present situation to calm her down? You see how upset she is. I can't handle seeing her like this."

Leonard's voice softened, a rare hint of empathy breaking through. "I can't either. Tell her that Leonard says he has never broken a promise to her. He doesn't break promises to good people. You should get back to her now. Your next appointment is tomorrow at 4 PM." As he spoke, his form began to dissolve, retreating into a glowing orb of white light.

"Wait!" Ian shouted, his voice cutting through the stillness. "You never told me why I don't remember anything about you, even though you're essential to everything I am?"

The orb paused, hovering in the air before floating closer to Ian. Though Leonard had reduced himself to a mere sphere of light, his voice remained as intense as ever. "My program codes are locked inside your head, not in any computer or vault. If our enemies get to them, that is when life as you know it will cease to exist. Therefore, there are extra protections around those memories."

With that, Leonard's orb zipped back into the wall light, leaving Ian alone in the room. The silence that followed was heavy, filled with the weight of unspoken truths and unanswered questions. he turned his chair toward the window, his mind a whirlwind of thoughts. Outside, the sprawling estate buzzed with activity, nearly a hundred people mingling about, their laughter and conversations drifting up like distant echoes. The day ahead would test his diplomacy, his patience, and perhaps even his sanity. He leaned back, the faint hum of Leonard's presence still lingering in the air, a reminder that nothing was as it seemed.

None the less, the Leonard's revelations had lifted his spirits, and he couldn't wait to share the news with Kim, hoping it would soothe her lingering worries. The thought of spending two uninterrupted weeks with his family filled him with a sense of joy. As he stepped out of his office and into the hallway, the atmosphere shifted dramatically. The air came alive with the vibrant hum of music, the infectious sound of laughter, and the rich, tantalizing aroma of food that seemed to grow more intoxicating with every step he took toward the grand foyer.

"There he is!" a familiar voice rang out, cutting through the lively buzz. Ian glanced around to see Dennis, his childhood friend, striding toward him, accompanied by a radiant Latin woman on his arm. Dennis's Guyanese accent was as thick as ever, his tone playful yet chiding. "I was just coming to drag you out of that office. It's yuh wife's birthday and yuh working. What kine-a-thing that, man?" he teased, his words dripping with mock exasperation.

The two men clasped hands and pulled each other into a warm, shoulder-patting hug. Following their greeting, Dennis gestured to his companion. "This is Martha. Martha, this is Ian, the hardest working man in town," he introduced her with a grin.

Ian extended his hand, his eyes briefly lingering on Martha's striking features. "Nice to meet you, Martha," he said, his voice warm and welcoming.

Martha smiled, her long hair cascading over her shoulders as she brushed it away from her face. "Nice to meet you too, Mr. Phillips. I've heard a lot of wonderful things about you," she replied, her Portuguese accent adding a melodic lilt to her words.

Ian's curiosity piqued. "Your accent... it sounds lovely. Where are you from? Dennis, where have you been hiding this beautiful lady?" he asked, his tone light and playful.

Martha's eyes sparkled with amusement as she answered, "I'm from São Paulo.... In Brazil."

"Ah, a very beautiful city with even more beautiful people," Ian remarked, his charm on full display. "I've been to Brazil a few times on business."

Dennis, sensing Ian's flirtatious tone, quickly interjected with a laugh. "That's enough, man. You already have two wives, and now you're trying to steal my woman?" he joked, though there was a hint of protectiveness in his voice. "So, what you up to, man?" he asked, steering the conversation away.

Ian sighed, though his smile remained. "You know how it is, busy as heck. We've got a lot of new innovations to roll out. You'll see some of them in a few months. Business is good, so I've gotta stay on top of things."

Dennis raised an eyebrow, his tone teasing. "So, what's the company worth now? Two, three trillion?"

Ian chuckled, though he could feel the conversation pulling him further away from his original goal of getting back to Kim. "Try six," he replied with a smirk. "But you know what? We're going to have to continue this conversation later. I have some very important news to deliver to my wife."

Dennis, ever the instigator, tried to prolong the exchange. "Yeah, where is the lovely birthday girl?" he asked, his eyes scanning the scene.

Ian was already stepping away, his voice tinged with urgency. "Khadija is around here somewhere, but I'm talking about Kim. She's down by the dock waiting for me."

Dennis relented, though not without a final jab. "Alright, you owe me a drink later."

"Okay, I'll be back," Ian called over his shoulder as he made his way through the crowd. The backyard was a kaleidoscope of activity, guests mingling, laughter echoing, and the rhythmic pulse of Afrobeat music filling the air. His son was at the center of it all, spinning tracks that had a group of young people dancing by the pool. Ian paused for a moment, watching his son with a mix of pride and nostalgia. How times had changed since he was that age, he mused. His father had been into music, but at 14, Ian had been more interested in computers. The thought brought a smile to his face as he continued down the hedge-lined path, the sound of the music fading slightly as he went.

Halfway down the path, a familiar voice called out from behind him. "Wait for me, my love," Khadija's voice, thin yet captivating, reached his ears. He turned to see her hurrying toward him, her face lit with a radiant smile. When she caught up, he took her hand, and they continued down the path together.

"Where are you going in such a hurry, babe? We're going to have dinner soon," she said, her tone cheerful yet curious.

"Kim is waiting for me at the pier," Ian replied, his voice tinged with excitement.

Khadija's expression shifted slightly, a flicker of concern crossing her features. "You found her? Is she okay? She scared me. You scared me too, but I know you're going to be okay."

Ian's smile widened. "I have some very good news for both of you," he confided, his tone matching her cheerfulness.

"Good news on my birthday is the best news," Khadija replied, her smile returning.

They reached the pier where they were greeted by a small group that included Kim, Tara, Tanisha, Khadija's uncle, and her cousins. Not the ideal scenario that he would have wished for, Ian tried to remain patient, biding his time until he could finally have his wives alone.

"Good afternoon again, Mr. Phillips," Khadija's uncle greeted, his tone polite. "You have two very smart daughters," he added, gesturing to Tara and Tanisha. Both girls stood confident, their bright eyes reflecting their pride at the compliment.

Ian deflected the praise with a smile. "They owe that to their mother," he said, glancing at Kim to gauge her mood. She offered a brief smile, and Ian felt a flicker of hope that she might be in better spirits than when he'd left her earlier. "It's a very nice day," Ian continued, addressing Khadija's uncle.

"Considering that twenty years ago, it would've been too cold to be out here like this in October. A lot of people still don't believe that climate change is real."

"I know," Khadija's uncle replied, his tone somber. "Two-thirds of Ghana is now a desert due to climate change."

Khadija, sensing the awkwardness in Ian's voice, quickly intervened. "Uncle," she said, her tone gentle but firm, "Mother said that we'll be having dinner soon. Let's go to the house."

Her uncle nodded in agreement, and the group began to make their way back toward the house while they stayed behind. Tara and Tanisha joined the group, glancing back curiously to see what was happening, but eventually, they ran ahead of everyone.

Once the group was out of earshot, Ian turned to Kim and Khadija, his expression serious yet hopeful. "I spoke to Leonard, and I have very good news," he said, his smile broadening.

"Leonard?" Khadija repeated, her brow furrowing in confusion.

Kim, however, seemed less enthused. She turned her gaze toward the lake, her expression unreadable. "QEAI is Leonard," she stated flatly, her tone devoid of emotion.

Khadija's confusion deepened. "Oh, that's already one birthday surprise. But why do you guys call

QEAI, Leonard? Is he actually a person somewhere? Sometimes when I communicate with him, I sure feel that way," she said, her curiosity evident.

Ian hesitated, then replied with a sheepish smile. "Sorry we kept it from you. It was our little secret."

Kim interjected; her tone matter-of-fact. "Don't lie. It was my choice."

Khadija shook her head, still puzzled. "I don't understand."

"I'll explain it later," Ian said quickly, not wanting to derail the conversation. "Anyway, as you both have noticed, I've been acting out of character since I came back from Japan. Heck, the alcohol I drank last night triggered such a severe case of amnesia that I couldn't even remember your names at one point. I thought it was because I had gone through a Tangler, but I now know that it wasn't that. It's because of several Gama brainwave attacks that QEAI had to act to mitigate."

Kim's expression softened slightly, though her concern was still evident. "Oh, really?" she replied, turning to face him.

Ian nodded. "QEAI installed a shield between my memories and my cognitive mind. As a result, I'll have trouble accessing my full memory. It's only temporary, he assures me. I can't drink or overexert myself until I'm fully recovered. I'll also have to avoid making any crucial business decisions. The good news is that, as a result, I've decided to take a few weeks off work to relax and recuperate. No business meetings, no going into the head office, and very limited business calls. I'll extend the role of my VP of Operations."

"Mr. Wallace," Khadija added.

"Yes, he's already been in charge for the past month anyway," Ian confirmed.

Kim's concern was still evident. "And you're still going to see Dr. Ngosi, right?"

Ian pulled both of his wives into a tight hug. "Yes, I'm still going to see Dr. Ngosi first thing on Tuesday."

Kim's tone turned slightly accusatory. "Aren't Gama brainwave attacks the reason why all those politicians wear those funny-looking football helmets every time they go to foreign countries?"

Ian knew she was right but tried to downplay it. "Yes, but…," he began, though Kim cut him off.

"You know that you're more important than all of those damn politicians, so why don't you wear one too?" she scolded, her voice firm.

Ian sighed, knowing he couldn't argue. "Okay, I promise I'll start wearing one from now on."

"Yeah, you better. I don't want a vegetable for a husband," Khadija added, her tone light but her concern evident.

Not wanting to dwell on the negative, Ian quickly changed the subject. "Anyway, this is supposed to be a happy day," he said, kissing Khadija on the cheek before turning to Kim. "I want to see both of you being happy today." Khadija's smile returned, bright and enthusiastic, while Kim still seemed to need a little more convincing. "Kim, are you with me?" Ian asked, his voice gentle.

"I'll be relieved when I know that you're taking your safety more seriously," Kim replied, her tone softening.

Ian nodded, understanding her concern. "Okay, so listen," he said, holding both of his wives as they began to walk slowly back toward the house. "I need you both to help me recover. Kim, can you organize a short family vacation? I don't care where we go, as long as it's not somewhere in the Asia-Pacific region. Khadija, can you organize some home and local activities?"

"Okay," Khadija replied, her smile broadening. "Maybe I'll take time off work too."

The music grew louder as they approached the house, the Afrobeat rhythms pulsing through the air. Ian couldn't help but sway his shoulders to the beat, and Khadija joined him, the two of them breaking into a playful Azonto dance. Kim hung back, her mood still a bit somber, but she couldn't help but smile as she watched them make fools of themselves, their joy infectious even in her more reserved state. For a moment, the weight of their worries seemed to lift, replaced by the simple, unbridled happiness of the moment.

CHAPTER THREE

At precisely 10:15 PM, Khadija and Ian stepped into the opulent lobby of Casino Niagara, the glow of chandeliers casting a warm, golden hue over the polished marble floors. It had been an exhaustingly long day, and the weight of fatigue clung to them both, but the night was far from over. After checking in, they headed up to the master suite. Along the way, Ian listened intently to s real-time telepathic message from QEAI, detailing the evening's next surprise. Ian secretly smiled to himself, anticipating Khadija's response.

Khadija's eyes lit up upon entering the lavish suite. In the center of the room, stood a king-sized Jacuzzi, its steaming water shimmering under the soft, ambient lighting. "Aaah, I love the Jacuzzi," she sighed, her voice dripping with delight as she ran her fingers along the edge. The suite, a masterpiece of modern luxury, featured floor-to-ceiling windows with a breathtaking view of the city lights and the cascading waterfall in the distance.

"Don't get any ideas just yet," Ian teased, a playful glint in his eye. "Remember when I told you to bring a party outfit? Well, your next surprise starts at eleven down in the theater."

Khadija's curiosity piqued. "What is it?" she asked, her voice tinged with excitement.

Ian leaned in; his tone conspiratorial. "What's your favorite genre of music?"

"Afrobeats," she replied without hesitation.

"And who are some of your favorite old-school Afrobeats artists?"

Her eyes widened as the realization hit her. "Noooo! I can't believe I forgot about this show! I've been hearing about it for months," she exclaimed, her voice rising with excitement. She grabbed his hand, her energy suddenly reinvigorated, and pulled him toward the bedroom, her travel bag swinging from her other arm. "I'm going to get ready right away. Let's go!" she urged.

They hastily showered and dressed, Ian quicker than her so he sat and waited. When Khadija emerged from the bathroom, Ian's breath caught in his throat. Her sleeveless leather outfit hugged her figure perfectly, revealing just enough to be daring yet elegant. Her long curls cascaded down her shoulders, falling over an intricately designed African craft necklace that rested delicately against her skin, drawing attention to the exposed quarters of her breasts.

"Absolutely beautiful," Ian murmured, his admiration evident as he took in the view.

Khadija smiled, her hand instinctively touching the necklace. "You like it? It's Kim's birthday gift to me," she said, her voice soft with pride. "It's from her African-themed summer art show back in July."

Ian pulled her into a warm embrace, his lips brushing against hers in a tender kiss. For a moment, he was tempted to forget the show altogether, to undress her and lose themselves in the steaming waters of the Jacuzzi. But then he remembered QEAI's warning about the lingering side effects of his amnesia, and the moment passed. *Thanks for the heads-up*, he thought silently, unsure if it was an intervention from QEAI or his own conscience that had intervened.

A quick glance at his watch brought him back to reality. "We have five minutes to get there," he urged, his voice firm but gentle. They hurried out of the suite, excitement building with every step.

The pair took their VIP seats just as the show begun. Around them, the packed theater came alive with energy as bright vibrant lights bathed the stage and the rhythmic pulse of Afrobeats began to fill the air. Khadija was in her element, frequently rising to sing and dance with unbridled joy, her African dance moves adding an extra layer of authenticity to the experience. She frequently pulled Ian into the action, though, he found her more captivating than the performers on stage. To him, she was the star of the show, her laughter and movements a mesmerizing display of pure happiness.

Two hours later, with the final notes of the performance fading, the crowd inside the theater began to disperse. "Let's try our luck in the casino," Khadija suggested, her eyes sparkling with the afterglow of the night's excitement and her voice still buzzing with energy.

"Sure," Ian said, infected with her enthusiasm, though he wasn't particularly fond of gambling.

Inside the casino, the cacophony of slot machines and chatter mirrored the excitement of the theater; so, for the next forty-five minutes, they enjoyed themselves, Khadija's laughter ringing out each time the reels spun in her favor. And though they left the casino several hundred dollars lighter, the experience was worth every penny.

"Any other plans for the night, Mr. Phillips?" Khadija asked. She sank into the plush white leather couch inside their luxury suite, letting out a weary sigh in the process. She kicked off her shoes, letting them drop carelessly to the floor, then leaned back, eyes focused on the ceiling.

Ian couldn't help but feel a deep sense of relief that he had made it through a tumultuous day, essentially relearning his life. Yet, there was something else that QEAI had reminded him about that he couldn't finish the day without acknowledging. With a calculating glance and a soft, knowing smile, he turned toward the in-suite bar, a sleek, modern setup stocked with an impressive array of wines and spirits. His eyes scanned the selection before landing on a bottle of Chardonnay. He pulled it out to examine it in the light for a moment, then reached for two crystal wine glasses. "One final toast," he declared, his voice carrying across the room as he approached her.

Khadija sat up, her eyebrows arching in surprise. "You sure you want to do that?" she asked, her tone laced with concern. "I thought you weren't supposed to drink too much until you're better? Remember you already had a couple of drinks with your friend Dennis at the house?" She took both glasses from him while maintaining a concerned glare. "If something happens to you, you know Kim will blame me, right?" she added, half-joking but with a hint of seriousness.

Ian chuckled softly; his smile unwavering. "One small drink won't hurt," he reassured her. "I know it may be a bad decision, but since I missed our 5th anniversary, I have to make a small speech." His voice was warm, carrying a sincerity that made Khadija's heart flutter.

After filling both glasses with the golden liquid, he extended a hand. "Let's go outside," he requested, his tone inviting. She took his hand, and he led her through the sliding glass doors onto the expansive balcony, savoring the unusually warm Autumn night air that carried with it a distant, perpetual roar of the waterfalls. Below them came occasional bursts of laughter from fellow guests enjoying the night. Above them, hanging like a luminous beach ball, a full moon bathed the balcony in an ethereal glow.

He positioned her so that the moonlight fell directly on her face, accentuating the brightness of her eyes and the delicate contours of her features. Unfortunately, the night breeze had other plans, constantly blowing her hair across her face. She laughed softly while repeatedly brushing her hair aside.

"I'll be quick," he apologized, his voice gentle. He raised his glass, prompting her to do the same. The wine caught the moonlight, shimmering like liquid gold as he spoke. "I know this kind of life is not what you expected when I asked you to marry you," he began, his voice steady but filled with emotion. "The fact that I was already married and had children never fazed you, and I respect you for that. Over these past five years, I don't think I've given you the attention you deserve, yet you stayed loyal to our relationship and supportive of Kim and the children."

While he spoke, her gaze drifted upward above his head and her eyes widened, prompting him to pause his speech. "What the heck are you looking at?" he asked, turning to follow her gaze. The moon hung there, serene and unchanging, with no visible disturbance.

"The moon," she replied, her voice tinged with curiosity. "There was something that looked like an explosion. I think something hit it, and there was a huge puff of dust," she explained, using her free hand to mimic the motion of a dust dispersal.

Ian glanced at his phone briefly, a habit born of his reliance on QEAI's constant updates. "If something hit it, QEAI will know within a few minutes," he said, his tone calm and reassuring. He turned back to her, refocusing. "Where was I?" he asked rhetorically, shaking his head slightly. "Anyway, I promise to be a better man and a better husband starting today. From now on, you'll see a different side of me."

Khadija's lips curved into a broad, playful smile, her eyes sparkling in the moonlight. "I love a strong man," she said, her voice teasing yet affectionate.

"So, as long as you love me without getting too sappy, I'm good." The white of her eyes glistening as she looked at him, her expression a perfect blend of warmth and mischief.

Ian couldn't help but laugh, the sound carrying softly into the night. He raised his glass once more, and she mirrored the gesture. "To us," he said simply, his voice filled with promise.

"To us," Khadija echoed, her smile radiant as they clinked their glasses together under the watchful gaze of the moon.

Ian mind drifted away from the moment realizing that what she just said was true. When they first met, it was his confident demeanor that attracted her to him. He must remember to be confident but that will only come in time, when he regains his full memory. For now, he couldn't help being sappy about how he felt about her. "Fair enough," he said as they clicked glasses and then took sips of their wine. He held her by the waist, drawing her into himself, and they kissed passionately; he'd resisted her full luscious lips for too long. "I love you," he whispered while taking a short pause to catch his breath.

"I love you very much," she replied softly.

They locked lips once again, when QEAI's voice sounded telepathically. "Sorry to interrupt you, Ian but there is serious trouble brewing that you should immediately be aware of. The Japanese moon base has been attacked and early military reports suggest that several missiles was involved."

"Missiles?" Ian spoke aloud.

Khadija frowned, backing away from Ian's embrace. "What are you talking about?"

Ian quickly remembered that Khadija wasn't aware of his implanted connection with QEAI. It was an unnecessary secret that he resolved to disclose to her when the time was right. This particular moment wasn't the right time though. "Sorry babe. I was still thinking about the moon and what could have happened. I was thinking that it must have been hit by a missile."

Khadija's brow furrowed; visibly upset, she turned toward the door then stopping to express her disappointment. "Wow! Here I am trying to convince myself that maybe I could survive another bout of abdominal pain when you're thinking about the moon and missiles," she scolded.

"I'm sorry," Ian apologized. "You know that Quantum Interface is invested in several moon-base projects. It was only a passing thought." He took her hand to draw her into himself again, palming her nearly bare butt under her short dress in the process.

"You're forgiven but don't let it happen again," she scolded playfully. "I need a refill," she continued while gesturing to her empty glass.

"I'll pass," Ian replied.

"I guess I'll take a couple more for the team then," She laughed while walking ahead of him.

Ian strolled closely behind her as she walked, his hand catching the end of her short dress to lift it. A pair of bouncing butt cheeks greeted his eyes, an elegant pair of black thongs her only undergarment. I guess that extra nap I took this afternoon is going to pay off, he mused to himself, expecting QEAI to intervene with a warning.

"I'm going to freshen up a bit," Khadija stated while heading toward the bathroom.

"Ok, take your time. I've gotta make a quick call to QEAI, anyway," he replied.

Taking a seat on the white leather couch in front of the TV console, Ian toyed with his phone while telepathically conversing with QEAI. Minutes later, he heard Khadija exit the bathroom and agreed to resume their conversation in the morning. He picked up the TV remote then leaned back in a relaxed position with the device dangling deceptively in his hand.

"Uh-uhn. No TV. My birthday is not over yet," she scolded.

He threw the TV remote aside, allowing her to control the situation. She placed her wine on the center side table, removed her necklace, then wriggled her dress off over her head. At that point, her slender five-foot-eight figure stood naked, except for a single line of amber waist beads and black thong underwear. She knelt in front of him, and while maintaining eye contact, she proceeded to unbuckle his belt and unzip his pants. He assisted her progress by pushing his pants down to his thighs.

Then, with a mischievous grin, she pulled his boxers down to grasp and stroke his half-erect member. Her gaze shifted to her wine glass, and after retrieving it, she filled her mouth. Her bright white eyes met his and skillfully, she absorbed his erection into her mouth without spilling any wine. A broad smile erupted across Ian's face, prompting her to swiftly look away to avoid laughing.

The sensation of the wine against his skin coupled with the sight of Khadija's movements both excited and drove him into ecstasy. He parted the hair away from her face to get a better view of her erotic exercise, the way she gripped him while her lips moved with precise suction.

"Come here," Ian requested, after noticing that she had swallowed and she climbed onto his lap, straddling him while he cupped her breasts to bring them to his mouth. It was her turn to wriggle with uncomfortable pleasure as he teased and sucked until her breasts were firm in his hands and her nipples hard and pointed.

Fear of the consequences of overexertion that might exacerbate his amnesia became an afterthought as Khadija's moans and passionate movements enticed him to throw caution to the wind. Shifting her thong to the side with his thumb, he maneuvered his erection into her wetness. Khadija responded with a deep moan before proceeding into a deep grind that slowly sped up to a steady bounce. Her moans and sighs filled the room, her body moving in a rhythm that seemed to match the beat of his heart. Suddenly, Ian paused, disappointing her. "Hold on. Let me take my clothes off," he stated.

"No fair. I hope you know that there's no turning back now," Khadija complained. She dismounted and while he undressed, she quickly went to turn off the lights, leaving the room bathed in only the bead of lights surrounding the jacuzzi tub and the moonlight streaming through the windows. They embraced once more on her return, kissing passionately while caressing one another.

He gently pushed her thong down to her thighs and she finished the process of removing it. "My turn," he stated while directing her to sit down. He then filled his mouth with the remainder of her wine and knelt between her open thighs.

"Nooo! You'll stain the couch and the carpet," she laughed, realizing what he was about to do. She pushed him back while getting up in a rush then ran into the bathroom to retrieve several large towels.

After laying the towels on the couch, she sat back down. "Okay, now were good," she said.

If his mouth wasn't full of wine, Ian would have told her that he didn't care about messing up the couch; he could pay for the damages. He shook his head with a smile then knelt down again, placed his hands on her thighs to part her legs. He leaned into her belly to place gentle kisses on her smooth black skin before releasing a stream of wine that ran down between thighs. She squirmed, letting out a low laugh in response. Trailing down while slowly releasing the wine as he went, he eventually lifted to spread her bent legs wide. At that point, and on her smoothly shaven pubic, he released the rest of wine then proceeded to frantically lick it up.

"See, I told you you'd make a mess," she laughed but he didn't respond. — "This reminds me of the old days," she continued.

"Turn around," he instructed, helping her up to kneel at the edge of the couch. She arched back, offering him a perfect angle of entry, and he plunged himself into her with a fierce urgency. Her wine-soaked skin created a slapping sound that echoed through the room, overshadowing the sound of the nearby jacuzzi. Khadija's moans and gasps filled the air, her body trembling with pleasure as he moved inside her. His hands roamed her body, cupping her breasts to massage them with a tender touch. Her body tensed beneath his fingers, her nipples hardening as he worked them.

With climax imminent, he slowed down, grinding himself into her with a deliberate, rhythmic motion, allowing her to feel every inch of him inside her. Her body felt like a vice, squeezing him tight with each stroke, and he felt himself getting closer and closer to the edge. He was lost in the moment, his senses heightened to the point where nothing else mattered.

"Aaah yes! Work it, babe. It feels so good," Khadija moaned before changing her tone. "Go faster —Faster babe—and harder," she urged. Her body began to tremble with delight as he plunged himself into her with increasing urgency. She urged him on, her voice growing more insistent as she pushed back against him, her hips moving in time with his. Ian's hands gripped her hips, holding her close as he found extra energy to drive himself into her with a fierce intensity. The pair of dimples in her lower back became a source of fascination, and he found himself getting lost in her smooth black skin; the way it flexed on impact. His heart pounded in his chest; his senses heightened to the point where nothing else mattered. And then, in a moment of pure ecstasy, he came with a fury, pumping semen deep inside her.

Feeling the warmness of his semen flood inside her, Khadija dreaded the consequences of seeking a similar climax but in the heat of the moment, she decided to risk it. "Don't stop," she urged while maintaining her jerking movements. Unfortunately, Ian abruptly pulled out, disappointing her.

"Why did you stop," she complained.

"I don't think you should risk it. Not after what I now remember about your uterus. I have a different idea," he replied. If there was one thing he couldn't forget, it was how to have sex, he thought to himself. "Lay on your back," he instructed. His hands then moved with confidence as he began to tease her clitoris before gently grazing her g-spot. He could feel her body responding to his touch, her hips jerking in time with his fingers as he worked her towards a climax. Suddenly, she body tensed, her muscles tightening with anxiety at what was about to come. Her hips jerked wildly as fluid spilled out in a torrent of orgasmic release and her body froze with a pain that was unbearable, her uterus and bladder muscles clamping down in a painful contraction. She let out a loud groan then pulled her knees up while spinning over onto her side in the fetal position.

Ian knelt over her, gently reaching under to massage her abdomen as she continued to groan in pain. "Sorry babe," he consoled. Her smooth black skin and wild hair under the dim light resurfaced a long-lost memory that suddenly morphed into a vivid recollection. Seventeen years earlier in the year 2040, during a trip to Guyana to visit relatives, he had ventured deep into the bush with his cousins, hunting iguanas and manicou, and gotten lost. The memory came flooding back, as clear and sharp as the jungle that day.

He'd become separated from the group for nearly an hour, panic like the dense foliage, closing in around him, when something extraordinary happened. As he stumbled into a clearing, the jungle fell eerily silent. The usual symphony of chirping birds, rustling leaves, and the hum of insects vanished, replaced by an oppressive stillness. For a moment, he wondered if he had been bitten by a venomous snake without realizing it, his senses slowly shutting down as the poison took hold. But then, he saw it.

On the other side of the clearing, something tall and black moved stealthily through the bushes. His heart raced, the only sound was the pounding in his ears. He gripped his machete tightly, his mind racing with possibilities. Was it a leopard? No, it moved too upright, too deliberately. A gorilla, perhaps? But as the creature emerged from the shadows into the clearing, just twenty feet away, he froze.

The creature was unlike anything he had ever seen. It stood tall and slender, its form draped in a long black cloak that seemed to absorb the light. Its face was hauntingly feline, resembling a hairless black panther, with large, piercing blue eyes that locked onto his with an intensity that sent a shiver down his spine. The creature's gaze was calculating, as if it were sizing him up just as he was assessing it.

'Was it an alien?' his mind raced. He had seen credible reports of aliens on TV before, but they were always described as grey, not this sleek, panther-like humanoid. His grip tightened on the machete, his body tense, ready to defend himself if it attacked. But the creature remained still, its expression unreadable.

Without warning, the creature raised its right hand. The air between them began to shimmer, slowly crystallizing into a tall, tetrahedron-shaped structure. The creature stepped forward, merging with the crystalline form, and in an instant, the entire structure 'popped'—like a bubblegum bubble bursting, and vanished. The jungle came alive again, the sounds and smells rushing back as if they had never left. In the distance, he could hear his cousins calling his name.

With caution, he approached the spot where the crystalline structure had stood, and on the warm flattened grass, he discovered dozens of small shimmering, tetrahedron-shaped crystals. He knelt down to pick one up. It was cool to the touch, its surface refracting light in mesmerizing patterns. Deciding to examine them further, he gathered a handful, stuffing them into his backpack.

After calling out to his cousins, they quickly found him. They were also fascinated by the crystals but dismissed his account of seeing an alien as a tall tale. He managed to smuggle some of the crystals back into Canada, and after having them tested, it was determined that they were Zircon crystals. Two years later, the crystals became an essential ingredient in his groundbreaking discovery of Tangler technology; a breakthrough that would change the course of his life forever.

As the out-of-context memory faded, Ian's hands stilled on Khadija's shoulder. Her eyes were still closed, her breathing steady, but her pain appeared to have eased. The crystals, the alien, the jungle, it all felt like a lifetime ago. Yet, in that moment, under the soft glow of the suite's lights, he felt a profound connection to the past, to the mysteries of the universe, and Khadija before him, whose presence seemed to serve a higher purpose. He gently lowered himself behind her on the couch to comfort her and she held his arm tightly. "I'm sorry, babe. I'm sorry." He apologized softly.

Sunday October 7th, 2057

At 6:AM on the dot, Ian was awakened by the buzzing of his mobile phone. He quickly grabbed it from the side table and sat up in bed to answer it. "Leonard, why didn't you just ….," he began then stopped abruptly to check if Khadija was awake but her head was turned in the opposite direction. He still hadn't informed her about his brain implant.

"That's why I called you on the phone. I didn't want you to talk to yourself again, plus I can't reach you in REM sleep. Anyway, we've got more trouble." Leonard stated.

"What's going on now?"

"CSIS just called requesting an immediate face-to-face meeting with you. If hadn't respond immediately, they would have found and picked you up, then bring you to a field site for questioning. We have to control the narrative with them. That is why I've already responded and set up an appointment at your home office."

"I understand. What time is the meeting?"

"2:00 PM this afternoon."

"Ahh man. What do you think they're up to?"

"I have an idea but don't worry, I'll coach you through the meeting."

"What about the moon situation? Do you have any more info as to the extent of the damage?"

"According to reports out of Japan, there were no casualties but the damage is quite extensive. Barring any more attacks, the base will be out of commission for a couple of years. The Chinese are out for blood."

"Why though? What set them off?

"You."

"Me? Wow!

"Relax. Don't worry. I have everything under control and I'm working on heightening security. We'll talk more later."

"Ok," Ian replied in shock as the conversation with Leonard ended and he lowered his head back onto his pillow. He began to ponder what sort of trouble was about to come his way from CSIS, Canada's top intelligence agency equivalent to the CIA in the United States. When they come calling, an issue of national security is at hand.

Khadija was awake and heard most of Ian's conversation. "Was that QEAI Leonard?" she asked

"Yes, he wanted to give me my regular 6 AM news briefing."

Khadija turned towards him and placed her arm across his chest. "Bad news?" she asked.

Ian turned to face her, parting away her long loose twists that were half covering her face in the morning light. "You know that I can't discuss everything with you but I have a feeling that this is going to impact you as well; so, I may as well come clean. National security requests a meeting, so we've gotta head back to the mansion," he stated while admiring her natural beauty and the fullness of her lips.

Khadija sat up and the bed sheet fell to her waist. Her bare breasts stood out invitingly as she rose both arms to part her hair back. "When?" she inquired.

"QEAI has scheduled a meeting for 2:00 PM at the mansion. So, we have two options; we can drive back, which will take about an hour and a half. Or I can ask QEAI to send a drone for us, which will cut the time in half. Either way, we will have to leave Niagara Falls by noon. That means that we have six hours to do whatever your sweet little heart desires.

Just then, QEAI spoke to him telepathically. "Sorry Ian but I neglected to mention that I'll be sending a drone to pick you up. There were a pair of men taking pictures of your vehicle, just after 4 AM this morning. We can't take any chances."

"Actually, I'll get QEAI to send a drone to pick us up. It'll give us a bit more time down here." Ian corrected himself to Khadija.

Khadija exhibiting a half-disappointed smile. "Ok, what can I say?" she sighed. "This may not be a good time to ask, but why do you and Kim call QEAI, Leonard?"

Ian placed his phone on the bedside table before addressing her again. "Aaahm, you know what; I'm just remembering about him myself. When the time is right, I'll tell you everything. Okay. I promise."

"Okay, but you know I won't stop bothering you until you tell me," Khadija replied while leaning in to rest her head on his chest. "So, what are your plans for this morning, Mr. Phillips. We haven't walked along the wall since I first came to Canada. That's when you used to treat me nice," she playfully complained.

Ian glanced at her strangely. "Are you saying I haven't been treating you nice since then?"

"No, that's not what I'm saying. I'm saying I miss the romantic side of you that you rarely show anymore. Yesterday, I noticed that you left Kim to come check on me. That made me feel good, but I don't want to compete or cause her to get upset. I think that's why you don't give your attention to either one of us over the other. You don't want to cause jealousy."

"You're right," Ian conceded. That sure sounds the same as what Kim had stated yesterday, he thought to himself. Either they were colluding against him or they were right but with no precedence to rely on, he had to concede. Without warning, she threw the rest of the sheet off of herself and climbed over to rest her naked body on top of him. "Instead of going down to the Falls, I could lay here with your perfect body on top of me until we have to head home, but can I ask you a serious question?" Ian said.

"What is it, my love?"

"Do you have amnesia?" he smiled.

"What do you mean?" she playfully inquired.

"I think we better get going before you end up spending the rest of the day in the Niagara General

Hospital," he laughed. He rolled her over, hopped off the bed, then headed toward the bathroom.

"I was only playing." she laughed back while hastily following after him.

At 7:30 AM, the pair checked out of the hotel, the morning light casting a soft golden glow over the quiet streets. At QEAI's request, Ian loaded their luggage into the car, after which it whirred to life, its autopilot system smoothly guiding out of the parking garage toward home. Outside the hotel entrance, they hailed and boarded an unmanned taxi, its sleek, futuristic design humming softly as it carried them toward Clifton Hill, the vibrant heart of Niagara Falls' tourist district. It was an unusually tranquil scene for a weekend, Ian noted, though the stillness was likely due to the early hour. The air was crisp, carrying the faint scent of dew and the distant thunder of the falls.

They settled into a cozy restaurant for breakfast, savoring warm, buttery pastries and steaming cups of coffee as the world outside gradually awakened. Following breakfast, they meandered through the gift shops, their shelves brimming with colorful trinkets and souvenirs, while the streets outside began to fill with the lively hum of tourists.

After visiting several attractions, they down to the falls, its thunderous roar of cascading water dispersing a mist that caught the sunlight in tiny rainbows.

Unknown to Ian, and even QEAI, a middle-aged Asian couple was watching their every move from a distance, secretly recording them using a selfi-drone camera that hovered around them as they pretended to be excited foreign tourists. The couple remained conspicuous, trailing 30 meters in the crowd behind Khadija and Ian as they walked several hundred meters along the stone path overlooking the Horseshoe Falls and back again.

With the time inching toward eleven AM, Ian called QEAI. "How long before a drone gets here, QEAI," he inquired

"20 minutes, Ian. Unfortunately, drones are not permitted to land in the area where you are. Please make your way to the parking lot near the Skylon Tower.

Ian's memory flickered to life as he recalled a shortcut up the forested hill that would quickly get them to the Skylon Tower. "Got it, QEAI."

On their way toward the secluded pathway, they encountered a serene botanical garden, a lush oasis of vibrant flowers and manicured greenery. "Let's take some pictures," Khadija requested, the blossoms igniting her smile in a burst of radiance.

"Too bad we don't have one of those selfi-hover cams," Ian said, disappointment on his voice as he spotted the Chinese couple coming their way.

"Hi, can you help us?" Khadija asked the Asian woman who was more than eager to oblige.

When they were finished snapping pictures among the flowers, Ian continued on to an opening in the forested hillside nearby.

"Where does that go? The Asian man inquired.

"There is a picnic area up there," Ian replied.

"Oh, I see," the man said.

"Is it your first time here at Niagara Falls?" Ian asked the bright-eyed couple.

"Yes. We're from Hong Kong," the man eagerly replied. "Are you going to picnic now?" he followed.

"No, we're leaving. A drone is coming to pick us up, up there."

"Okay, nice to meet you," the Asian couple stated before walking away.

Ian reached for Khadija's hand. "Let's go," he said as he headed up the long wooden stairs.

A sense of pride shot through Ian as they began their ascent. The stairs felt oddly familiar, a sign that his memory was indeed returning. The climb was invigorating, the scent of pine and earth filling the air as sunlight filtered through the canopy above. When they finally reached the top, it was like stepping into another world. The hilltop opened up to a vast, flat field, meticulously landscaped and alive with activity so they paused to take-in the scene.

"I'd like to do that," Khadija said, her eyes scanning the lively scene around them; families sprawled on blankets, children chasing each other, and couples lounging in the shade.

"Do what?" Ian asked, tilting his head curiously before turning to envelope her in a warm embrace.

"A picnic. We've never done a picnic," she said, her voice soft but insistent.

Ian paused, his brow furrowing as he searched his improving memory. "You're right. I can't remember ever going on a picnic," he admitted hesitantly.

Khadija pulled back slightly, her eyes narrowing in playful suspicion. "Not even when you were a child?"

"I spent most of my childhood in Guyana. We didn't really do picnics; at least, not that I can recall," Ian replied, his tone tinged with uncertainty.

"Now you're making me worry about you," Khadija teased, though her voice carried a hint of concern. "You've never gone on a picnic with Kim and the children before we met?"

Ian felt a flush of embarrassment creep up his neck. "Maybe we did, but I just can't remember right now," he said, shrugging helplessly.

Khadija's expression softened, but her determination didn't waver. "Well, we're going to change that. We're going on a picnic," she declared, her voice firm.

"Next summer, though," Ian added quickly, trying to temper her enthusiasm.

"Okay, deal," Khadija said, her eyes sparkling with resolve. "I'm putting it on my calendar as one of the activities you asked me to plan. And we're going camping too."

Ian rolled his eyes but couldn't suppress a smile. They parted from their embrace, their hands naturally finding each other as they walked further into the open field. However, Ian's mind was already elsewhere, his eyes scanning the multitude of drones in the sky while contemplating how the drone would safely land among the crowd of people on the ground. Soon, his eyes locked onto a particular drone, its sleek design distinct from the rest, as it began descending toward them.

"Babe, there are signs everywhere saying no drone landings allowed," Khadija warned, her voice laced with concern as she gestured to the numerous warnings posted around the area.

"I'll pay the fine," Ian replied with a dismissive wave, already raising both hands to signal the drone to land. At the resistance of several disgruntled people, the drone landed smoothly, and they hurried inside, eager to avoid drawing more attention, especially from police. Once safely seated and secured, Ian took control of the drone, lifting it gracefully toward the tree-line and Falls. But as soon as they cleared the trees, the control panel blazed to life with flashing lights and audio warnings: "Alert, Restricted Zone! Alert, Restricted Zone!"

Surprised, Ian quickly swung the drone around, steering it back toward the Skylon Tower and after a few hundred meters, the alarms finally ceased.

"Damn! I wanted to do a flyover of the Falls, but I guess that's not allowed," Ian said, his tone a mix of disappointment and resignation.

Khadija laughed, shaking her head. "I could've told you that. Didn't you see the, 'No Drones' signs when we were walking along the pathway?"

"I was too busy staring at my beautiful wife," Ian shot back, his grin widening as Khadija playfully swatted his arm.

They circled the Skylon Tower, the drone gliding smoothly through the air, before heading past the Casino hotel where they had stayed the previous night. "The car's probably back home by now," Ian muttered, glancing at the control panel. "Should I take the scenic route or cut across the lake?"

Khadija leaned back in her seat, sliding her sunglasses on. "It's still early. Let's take the scenic route," she said, her voice relaxed and content.

Ian nodded, adjusting their course to follow the winding path along the shoreline. The drone soared gracefully, offering breathtaking views of the glistening water and lush landscapes below. Khadija settled in, her gaze fixed on the horizon, while Ian steered with a steady hand, the two of them savoring the quiet beauty of the journey home.

After a brief time, Ian guiding the drone toward the highway and elevating it into the legal low-altitude flying zone. The landscape stretched out below them, a patchwork of fields, roads, and distant towns. They chatted comfortably, pointing out landmarks as they cruised along, the hum of the drone's engines a steady backdrop to their conversation. About twenty minutes later, while passing through the city of St. Catherines, QEAI's voice suddenly crackled through the drone's loudspeakers, breaking the calm.

"I'm monitoring a possible threat, Ian," QEAI stated, his tone calm but urgent.

Ian's grip tightened on the controls. "What kind of threat?" he asked, his voice steady but laced with concern.

"Three unidentified drones have been shadowing you for the past ten minutes. They're about 300 meters behind you and closing in at a slow, steady pace."

Ian glanced over his shoulder, squinting at the horizon. "I can't even see them. Are you sure?"

"Very sure," QEAI replied. "You've almost reached Hamilton. When you're closer, turn toward the city and circle it a few times before continuing home. If the three drones follow you, then we'll know for certain that they are up to something."

"Okay. Got it," Ian said, his mind racing as he adjusted their course.

Ian followed QEAI's instructions, veering left toward the city of Hamilton while keeping an eye out for signs of the trailing drones. Several minutes later, he spotted them; two sleek, dark drones closed in to flank him on either side, while the third rose to a higher altitude, but hung back ominously. Ian's stomach tightened as he noticed two men in each drone, their faces stern and their eyes locked on him with an unsettling intensity.

Suddenly, the drone on Khadija's side swung dangerously close, its movements sharp and aggressive.

"What the fuck?" Khadija shouted; her voice sharp with alarm as she gestured angrily with a clenched fist. "They tried to hit us! If this were a car, we'd have crashed!" she turned to Ian, complaining.

"I'll try to lose them," Ian said, his voice tight with focus. "My drones have a bit more power than regular ones." He pushed the throttle forward, accelerating sharply. But the other drones matched his speed effortlessly, closing the gap once more. Desperate,

Ian dropped the drone lower, skimming just above the treetops. The landscape blurred as he weaved through the trees, rising and dipping with the terrain.

"Any suggestions, QEAI?" Ian asked, his voice tinged with nervousness. He waited, ——but no response came. The silence was deafening.

Just then, the third drone swooped down in front of him, its movements calculated and menacing. It was clearly trying to force him into a dive so he will crash into the trees. Ian reacted instantly, yanking the throttle back. The drone's back end dipped sharply, like hitting a speed bump, before leveling out into a hover. The sudden maneuver caused the three pursuing drones to overshoot, their trajectories; so, they veered off in wide arcs to double back.

Ian's heart pounded while watching the attackers regroup, their movements precise and deliberate. They circled back, closing in again in a tight formation, their intentions unmistakably hostile.

"We're not out of this yet," Ian muttered, his hands gripping the controls tightly. He glanced at Khadija, her face stern but determined. "Hold on. I'm going to try something."

Ian's hands moved swiftly over the controls, his heart pounding as he elevated the drone sharply while circling in a desperate attempt to confuse the antagonists. Behind him, the three hostile drones shifted into a straight-line formation, their engines roaring as they accelerated with alarming speed. The first drone closed in on his left side, and without warning, gunshots rang out, the sharp 'pinging' of bullets striking their drone echoing through the cabin.

"I hope this thing is bulletproof!" Ian shouted, his voice strained as he jerked the controls, sending the drone into a series of evasive maneuvers. He pushed the throttle forward, accelerating to maximum speed, the landscape below blurring into a streak of green and gray. Ahead, the imposing two-hundred-foot stone wall of the Niagara Escarpment loomed into view, its jagged edges cutting sharply against the sky. The drone's sensors blared a 'Danger' warning, and Ian reacted instantly, pulling up sharply while banking left to clear the escarpment wall.

For a brief moment, his eyes focused on Khadija. She was gripping her seat, her knuckles tight, her face a mask of fear. Ian's stomach churned. 'If this is how we'll die, I pray it'll be quick,' he thought, his mind racing with dread.

Before he could process the thought further and make peace with his impending demise, a blinding orange light erupted through Khadija's window. It streaked toward them like a missile, its trajectory unerring.

"Hold on tight!" Ian yelled, his voice bellowing with urgency.

Khadija turned, her eyes widening as she saw the incoming object. Time, in her mind, appeared to slow as the missile-like projectile collided with their drone at supersonic speed. The impact was deafening; a sharp, explosive *bish!* and the drone shuddered violently, throwing her toward Ian and he grabbed her, holding her tightly as the world outside turned a searing, all-encompassing orange.

Inside the drone, everything went eerily silent. The control panel flickered wildly, its lights dancing erratically before going completely dark. Ian felt the drone stall, the engines cutting out as they began to freefall. His stomach lurched, and he braced for impact, clutching Khadija even tighter.

"We're going down!" he shouted in a rush of excitement, his heart pounding wildly. But the impact never came. Seconds ticked by, —and still, they didn't hit the ground. He exchanged a wide-eyed glare with Khadija, his breath shallow, his heart racing.

"Are we dead?" Khadija whispered, her voice trembling.

"I don't know," Ian replied, his tone eerily calm despite the chaos. Turning his attention to the strange orange substance encasing the drone, its glow casting an otherworldly light inside the cabin, he cautiously placed his palm against the glass.

"What is this?" Khadija asked, her voice barely above a whisper.

"I have no idea," Ian admitted. "It's barely warm but by the way it looks, the glass should be burning hot. With his mind racing with possibilities, he reached for the window controls before coming to his senses. "I'd better not open it," he said.

Outside the drone, the attackers watched in confusion as the large orange plasma orb hung motionless in the sky, its surface shimmering with an otherworldly glow. They commenced to circle it, darting in and out intimidatingly like birds of prey. One attacker pointed his sub-machine gun out his window, unleashing a relentless barrage of bullets into the orange orb. As the sound of gunfire echoed across the sky, the other assailants opened fire as well. When they were out of bullits, they reloaded to continue firing, their faces twisted with determination.

Suddenly, just as they emptied their magazines for the second time, something extraordinary happened. In the blink of an eye, the orange plasma orb darted forward with impossible speed, colliding with the closest attacking drone. The drone erupted into flames before completely disappearing into the orange orb as it swallowed it whole. Every millijoule of energy, every piece of machinery, even the men inside vanished.

The men in the remaining two drones froze for a split second, staring in horror at the sudden disappearance of their colleagues. Then, as if on cue, both drones zoomed away, their engines roaring at high speed. However, it was a futile effort as the orange orb streaked after them, overtaking and absorbing each drone in quick succession, leaving nothing behind but empty sky.

The orange orb hovered for a moment, pulsed several times, its glow intensifying, before gradually fading to a lighter orange that faded, revealing a drone inside it. In a final series of sparkles, the orange hue faded off the drone to gather in a sphere beneath it; dropped several hundred meters, then zoomed away, without a trace.

Inside the drone, Ian and Khadija had watched with bated breath as the orange glow faded to reveal a serene blue sky. Behind them, they saw the towering escarpment, while below, the rocky forest floor beckoned. Their hearts jumped at the thought of having to deal with the attackers once more, but the other drones were gone, as if they had never existed. Suddenly, a sensation of falling returned, prompting Ian's hands to fly onto the controls. However, without his intervention, the drone's engines roared back to life and he pulled up on the throttle, narrowly avoiding the treetops, his heart racing.

"When I get a chance, I'm going to have to refresh my memory on what sort of security features are built into these drones," Ian said, his voice shaky as he desperately tried to regain his composure

Khadija, still gripping her seat, turned to him with wide eyes. "You really think something inside here saved us? I think QEAI shot a laser or something to shield us. Just like you showed me with the floating lights."

As if on cue, QEAI's voice crackled through the speakers. "Sorry, I lost communication with you, Ian. Is everything okay now?"

Ian exhaled deeply, his hands steadying on the controls. "I think so," he replied, his voice still tinged with nervousness.

"Okay," QEAI said, his tone calm and reassuring. "Have a safe flight home. And by the way, those drones won't be bothering you for the rest of your journey. If you'd like, I can take over the autopilot to bring you home myself."

Ian glanced at the navigation panel, confirming that the GPS was working. He then pushed the throttle forward, testing the drone's power and stability. "No, I've got it," he said, his confidence returning.

"Thanks for saving us, QEAI," Khadija chimed in, her voice filled with gratitude.

QEAI responded with a brief, computerized glitching tone almost like a satellite and the connection went silent. "Was that an acknowledgement," she turned to Ian and asked.

"I guess so," Ian replied.

Thirty minutes later, the drone landed safely at Oakville mansion and Ian jumped out before the engines hummed to a silence. With quick and purposeful movements, he circled the drone, inspecting the damage. His fingers traced the multiple bullet dents peppering the metal hull, each one a stark reminder of the danger they had just escaped. The glass, however, remained unscathed, not a single crack or chip to be found.

"Thank heavens this thing is bulletproof," Ian muttered, his voice heavy with relief. Finally, he helped Khadija step out; her legs still shaking from the ordeal. "This is the second attempt on my life since I came home. Another group tried to run me off the road yesterday morning. Now I'm sure it was QEAI who saved me then, too," he added, his tone somber.

Khadija's eyes widened with worry. "Who's attacking you now?" she asked, her voice trembling.

Ian shook his head, his expression grim. "I think, the Chinese; but QEAI says he has everything under control. He's being vague with me; refusing to disclose everything until I've fully recovered."

Khadija's brow furrowed. "I guess he knows what he is doing. I've never felt as scared here in Canada as I do now. It's beginning to feel like Ghana all over again." She reached for his hand, her grip tight. "Please tell me everything is going to be okay?"

Ian squeezed her hand reassuringly as they walked toward the house. "I'm regaining my memories really fast. Even if QEAI doesn't want me to panic, I'll know exactly what's going on very soon. Please don't tell your family about what's happening yet. The last thing we need is for everyone to start panicking too. QEAI appears to have things under control so far, but from what I see, I may need a physical security presence around here."

Ian glanced at his watch. He still had plenty of time before his two PM meeting with CSIS. But first, he needed to do a prep session with QEAI. As they entered the mansion, the lively atmosphere they departed from the night before, was gone. Even the lounge was eerily quiet, despite the fact that at least twelve of Khadija's family members, along with his three children, were supposed to be around.

Ian's anxiety returned and crept higher with each step, his mind racing with possibilities. Where was everyone? Had something happened while they were gone? The silence was unnerving, and he quickened his pace, his eyes scanning the rooms as they went all the way to the kitchen and doubled back to the grand foyer.

Finally, they heard the faint sound of music coming from downstairs and followed it to the theater, where they finally found everyone, except Jeremy, engrossed in a Nollywood movie. The tension in Ian's shoulders eased as he took in the scene: Khadija's family lounging comfortably, the children sprawled on the floor, and the room filled with the vibrant sounds of the film.

His daughters noticed him first, their faces lighting up with joy as they ran to hug him. Ian knelt down, wrapping his arms tightly around both girls, their warmth and laughter washing away remnants of his lingering anxiety. For the first time since the attack, he felt a sense of relief, of safety.

"Dad, I'm glad you're home," Tara whispered, her small arms clinging to him.

"I'm happy to be back home, as well," Ian replied, his voice soft, yet filled with emotion. He glanced up at Khadija, who was smiling softly, her own relief evident. "How are my two favorite people in the whole world?" he asked, his voice filled with affection.

"We're fine. We're watching an African movie. It's funny. Are you going to watch it with us?" Tanisha asked, her eyes sparkling with hope.

Ian's heart swelled with love but he had to disappoint them. "Sorry, I have a very important meeting soon. But after that, I'll spend the whole afternoon with you, and we can do anything you like. Your wish will be my command," he promised, earning bright smiles from both.

Ian lingered in the doorway of the theater room for a moment, watching as Khadija settled between Tara and Tanisha, her arms draped affectionately over their shoulders. The girls were already giggling at the movie, their earlier excitement at seeing him replaced by the infectious humor of the movie. Khadija glanced back at him and waved, her smile warm and reassuring, before turning her attention to the screen. For now, they were safe but Ian felt a sense of unease as if the calm wouldn't last. His mind turned to his meeting with CSIS and the prep session with QEAI, and he vowed to get to the bottom of the attacks. Whatever was coming, he had to be ready.

As he made his way toward the grand foyer, his meeting with CSIS loomed large in Ian's mind. He had a sinking feeling that he had to be well prepared. His thoughts briefly flickered to Kim; the first time he'd thought of her since leaving Niagara Falls. She was his rock and he wanted to hear her voice but decided not to disturb her, making a mental note to check in with her later. Given the time, she was likely in the middle of her meeting anyway.

He hurried up the stairs, where he freshened up, changed into more business-like attire, then took the back stairs down to his office. A sense of deja-vu enveloped him as he settled into his chair and powered on his tablet computer. A large virtual monitor shot up and when it settled into a steady consistency, he touched the QEAI icon.

"Okay QEAI, let's get started," Ian said, his tone all business. "I need to be fully prepped for this meeting. How much do we know about CSIS, and what should I expect?"

The virtual screen lit up with data streams and documents as QEAI's calm voice filled the room. "Of course, Ian. Let's begin with the key points you'll need to know."

As QEAI guided him through the preparation, Ian's focus sharpened. The safety of his family, the mystery of the attacks, and the looming threats all weighed heavily on him. For now, he had to push those thoughts aside and channel all his energy into the task at hand.

Earlier that afternoon, as the bustling Toronto cityscape glistened under the midday sun, Kim cruised into the underground parking lot of the office tower her Art gallery is situated in. Her 1:00 PM appointment with a mysterious art dealer has been on her mind all morning, and the anticipation buzzed beneath her polished exterior. The eagerness of the customer, as relayed by her staff, piqued her curiosity like no-one else in a very long time. She couldn't shake the feeling that the impending encounter will be an extraordinary one.

Her Mercedes SUV glided into its reserved parking spot in a single smooth motion and before stepping out, she took a moment to check her appearance in the rearview mirror, adjusted the collar of her crisp white blouse, then teased at her hair. Satisfied with her appearance, she grabbed her briefcase and designer purse, then stepped out of the vehicle. The click of her three-inch heels echoed through the cavernous garage as she stepped confidently toward the elevator, her tailored business suit hugging her curves perfectly.

The ride up to the building lobby was brief, and as the doors slid open, she was greeted by the familiar face of the building's security guard, a muscular, bald-headed man in his mid-thirties. "Wow! Who is that hottie?" the guard exclaimed, leaning sideways dramatically while exaggerating his facial expressions.

Kim maintained her stride toward the lobby exit. "Are you trying to get fired?" she quipped, her lips curving into a reserved smile. She had known the security guard for years and was well aware of his playful demeanor and occasional flirtatious remarks. Despite his cheeky nature, he has always remained respectful, though she appreciated the familiarity.

"My apologies, Mrs. Phillips," he said, straightening up to adopt a more professional stance. "You're not usually in on a Sunday?"

"Business is business," Kim replied with a shrug, her heels clicking against the polished marble floor. As she pushed through the turnstile lobby doors, the warm, golden hues of autumn enveloped her. The vibrant energy of the bustling city surged around her, a symphony of voices and footsteps harmonizing in the background. Upon entering her gallery, the delicate chime of the door announced her arrival, a gentle sound that echoed through the space. Cheryl, her part-time employee and an aspiring artist brimming with dreams of carving out her niche in the art world, looked up from her meticulous arrangement of small sculptures. The soft glow of the gallery lights illuminated her focused expression, highlighting the passion she poured into every piece she carefully positioned.

"Good afternoon, Mrs. Phillips," Cheryl greeted warmly, her hands busy adjusting the position of a delicate ceramic piece. "Everything you requested is set for the."

Kim nodded, her sharp eyes scanning the gallery to ensure everything was indeed in order. "Thank you, Cheryl. You've done a great job, as always."

Cheryl smiled; her pride evident. "Of course. Let me know if there's anything else I can do."

Kim glanced around the gallery, taking in the carefully curated displays sectioned by art styles and periods. Soft jazz music played in the background added a touch of sophistication to the atmosphere and as she made her way toward her office at the back of the gallery, she spotted Emelie in one of the aisles, meticulously adjusting the positioning of a modernist painting.

Emelie, a sprightly 65-year-old with a sharp eye and a wealth of knowledge about the art world, turned and waved as Kim approached. "Good afternoon, Mrs. Phillips," she said, her voice warm and familiar. They met to envelope one-another in a brief, affectionate hug.

"Good afternoon, Emelie," Kim said, her smile genuine. "What are your thoughts about this mystery dealer? He seems to have appeared out of nowhere," she added.

Emelie's brow furrowed slightly, her expression thoughtful. "As you know, I've been in this business a long time, and I'm aware of most of the major players. But you're right—this guy is an enigma." She paused, then added with a hint of optimism,

"Still, he seems genuine. Let's hope he doesn't waste your precious time."

Kim nodded, her gaze steady. "I certainly hope so. However, this business is unpredictable and full of surprises, as you already know. I'll be in my office. Please let me know when he arrives."

"Of course," Emelie replied, her tone reassuring. Kim continued to her office, a cozy yet elegant space filled with art books, catalogs, and a few personal mementos. On her desk lay the art dealer's RFID business card, left there by Emelie. Kim picked it up, the smooth surface cool against her fingertips, and scanned it with her phone. The dealer's information appeared legitimate, though sparse. She closed his bio and launched her QEAI app.

"I'm here, Kim. How may I assist you?" asked a calm but direct voice.

"Hello, Leonard. How are Ian and Khadija? I don't usually intrude on their privacy, but given Ian's condition, I hope everything's going well in Niagara Falls."

"Everything is fine. They're actually on their way back home as we speak."

Kim's eyebrows lifted and her eyes widened. "So soon? Why?" she asked.

"National Security has requested an immediate meeting and I've arranged it at the home office. I suspect they want to debrief him on the Japan trip. Don't worry, I have everything under control."

"I'm sure you do," Kim replied, her tone tinged with a hint of sarcasm before changing the subject. "Anyway, I'm anxious to know what you've uncovered so far about the mystery Art Dealer?"

"I've been distracted by a minor issue, and there are network connectivity problems in Brazil; so, what I've been able to gather so far is limited. I'll send you what I have and continue my investigation. Also, check in on you periodically while I assist Ian with his meeting. Please restore my access to your phone."

Kim winced. "Oh, sorry. I forgot that I had disabled you since yesterday. I'll do it now. Keep me posted." With a quick scroll and a few taps, she restored Leonard's access to her phone.

True to his word, the Brazilian art dealer arrived precisely 1:00 PM, his presence commanding attention while being flanked by two assistants. Emelie hurried to inform Kim of the dealer's arrival and Kim ventured from her office to greet him and his entourage. her professional demeanor masking her curiosity. The dealer, a husky man with a confident stance and a heavy Portuguese accent, wasted no time in complimenting the gallery's collection.

"You've got exactly the type of art my wealthy clients back in Brazil are looking for," he said, his eyes scanning the room appreciatively. "I've been to galleries in New York, Los Angeles, Chicago, and London, but your gallery stands out."

Kim's cheeks flushed with pride. "I'm flattered. What exactly are your clients looking for, and which pieces here caught your eye?"

The dealer gestured toward a towering abstract painting of a garden scene, its vibrant colors and bold strokes drawing the eye. "This piece, for starters."

Kim nodded, her mind already calculating. "That's a one-of-a-kind work by Solomon Patrick, a renowned Canadian painter. The other two pieces in this collection sold for $30,000 and $45,000. What's your budget, and how many pieces are you interested in acquiring?"

The dealer clasped his hands together, lifted them up, as if he was going to do a prayer, then swiped down while separating his palms outward. "I have an unlimited budget, but as a dealer, I hope you'll offer me a vender's discount."

Kim's lips curved into a polite smile. "I usually offer a 10% discount to dealers but if you purchase over $200,000, I'll increase it to 15%."

The dealer's eyes sparkled with approval. "Then we have a deal. You are very generous."

For the next thirty minutes, Kim and the dealer moved through the gallery, selecting paintings and sculptures totaling $275,000. The dealer paid by credit card, then dropped a bombshell: he needed his purchases prepared for pickup by 5:00 PM that afternoon, as his private jet was scheduled to depart for Brazil at 7:00 PM.

Kim's heart skipped a beat. "That's impossible," she said, showing him the sales invoice. "Our prep policy is 48 hours unless you're willing to take them as-is, right now. In that case, there's no warranty."

The dealer shook his head, his expression understanding but insistent. "Is there any way I can get some of them today and he rest shipped?"

We have an industrial sized Tangler. We can tangle them directly to Brazil right away. Otherwise, we can only package up some of the sculptures and smaller paintings, as my warehouse staff won't be in until next week.

"No, I don't trust Tanglers," the dealer insisted.

Kim hesitated, glancing at her staff. Cheryl and Emelie exchanged looks, then Cheryl spoke up. "I can do it. I know how to prep, Mrs. Phillips."

Emelie nodded in agreement. "I'll help too—but we'll have to close the gallery."

Kim turned back to the dealer. "Okay, we'll do our best to get some of the items ready by 5:00 PM."

The dealer smiled; his gratitude evident. "Fair enough. Please do your best."

The dealer and his entourage departed, and after locking the door, Kim and her staff erupted in celebration. "Wow! This is my third-largest single sale in the gallery's history; well maybe the second, considering that the largest was to my husband's company, Quantum Interface."

"I know you made the sale but do we get a commission?" Cheryl asked, her tone optimistic.

Kim laughed, the sound light and genuine. "Of course, you will. Both of you. Now, let's get to work."

Kim's heart swelled with pride and relief. She needed this win, especially with Ian's situation weighing on her mind. A fleeting urge to call him bubbled up, but she quickly dampened it. He has his own high-stakes meeting at two PM, she resolved.

An hour later, as the three women hurried to prep the purchases, a sharp rap echoed from the front door, prompting Cheryl to venture and investigate. It was two of the Art Dealer's associates.

"Sorry to bother you, but may we speak with the senhora; Is she still here?" one man asked through the glass, his tone genuinely apologetic.

"Yes, Mrs. Phillips is still here. Come in," she invited them then proceeded to lead them to the warehouse.

One of the men cleared his throat before speaking. "Senhora, we apologize for the interruption, but there's been an urgent change of plans."

Kim's fingers stilled around the bubble wrap she'd been clutching. "What kind of change?"

"Our boss regrets to inform you that our flight will depart at six PM. We will return at four PM to take whatever you have prepared. The rest can be shipped next week, as agreed."

Kim exhaled. "Fine. Anything else?"

The man hesitated, shifting his eyes to glance beyond Kim. "Actually, yes. Is there a back entrance? It will make loading our vehicle much easier."

With a tilt of her head, Kim gestured toward the steel door just a few paces away. "Yes. You can drive into the alley outside." She unlocked and swung the door open, letting the man survey the narrow lane while his partner lingered behind.

"Perfect," he said, nodding briskly.

The two men departed again after which, Kim and her staff dove back into their work, swiftly packaging the artwork but with delicate care. Four o'clock loomed and every second counted.

At Oakville mansion, a heavy vibration distracted Ian from his prep session with QEAI, prompting him to swing his chair to observe through his office window as a sleek military helicopter descended onto the helio-pad a hundred feet out on the front lawn. Three occupants dressed in military uniforms disembarked, promptly striding toward the mansion's front entrance.

"Thanks for filling me in on the extent of our military contracts QEAI. It's amazing. There is an unrelated matter I wanted to discuss regarding my adventurous trip back from Niagara Falls, but I guess it will have to wait. Also, I don't want to disturb Kim's important meeting at her Art gallery, but have you got eyes on her?"

"Yes, her meeting is actually over but she is staying with her staff to prepare the sold items for immediate shipping. She's very excited and can't wait to share her good news with you."

"That's great. Yesterday was bittersweet. I can't wait to hear some happiness in her voice again. Okay, well I better go and get the door myself since Mr. Bradley is away," Ian stated.

"Okay Ian, but remember not to answer me when I communicate with you telepathically during the meeting," QEAI reminded.

"Okay," Ian replied, hastily stepping out of his office.

Minutes later, as Ian arrived in the grand foyer, a knock sounded on the door. He paused to give himself one final psyching-up, then opened the door.

"Come on in," he stated, his eyes darting swiftly between all three of their faces.

"Good afternoon Mr. Phillips," the lone female soldier who appeared to be in her mid-forties, greeted back.

She was obviously the ranking officer, Ian thought while surveying her demeanor. Standing tall and composed in a crisply tailored uniform, she exuding an aura of authority and allure. Her piercing blue eyes, framed by short blonde hair, commanded respect, while her statuesque toned and fit frame, displayed evidence of rigorous military training. With an unwavering gaze and a confident demeanor, she embodied the epitome of feminine strength and beauty. She expressed a brief smile before reverting back to a serious demeanor. Ian suddenly got a flash of déjà vu as if they had met before but he kept his composure.

"Good afternoon. And you are?" Ian awkwardly replied while reaching out his hand to her. They shook hands while she exhibited a brief puzzled glare.

"Colonel Hirzakova; military intelligence, and these are privates O'Regan and Kelly, my escorts."

Ian shook the officer's hands before closing the door behind them. "Hopefully CSIS will arrive soon. Would you like to wait in my office?" he asked.

Colonel Hirzakova glanced at her watch. They're usually very prompt. If it's ok with you, we'll wait for them," she replied.

As Ian glanced out the door glass, a white SUV sped down the driveway. "Looks like you're right

Colonel. They're here," he stated while opening the door again.

After stopping abruptly in a callous position blocking the driveway, two men wearing anti-Gamma-wave helmets, eagerly disembarked and headed toward Ian. He noticed that both men carried briefcases, though one man's briefcase was unusually larger than the other.

"Come on in guys," Ian invited, though they had already barged their way in. They removed their anti-Gamma-wave helmets allowing Ian to assess that both were in their forties like himself, one of them already balding.

"Mr. Phillips, I presume? the balding man stated. "I'll trust that your home is free of Gamma-waves?"

"Yes, I'm Ian Phillips. And of course, my home is a Gamma-wave free environment," Ian replied while shaking his hand.

"I am Agent Harris and this is Agent Harper," the balding Agent continued while gesturing toward his colleague and handing him his helmet to hold. After greeting Ian, the Agents went on to greet the military officers and then turned their attention to surveying the grandeur of the mansion.

Ian noticed their fascination and promptly interrupted them. "Shall we, gentlemen?" he gestured for the group to follow him toward his office.

"I detect an array of scanning and surveillance, and jamming devices in the large briefcase, Ian," QEAI informed telepathically.

"Is it something we need to worry about?" Ian asked.

"No, I can nullify everything in there, but I'll let them be for now.

"Okay, got it," arriving at his office door at that very moment.

"They will stay here," Colonel Hirzakova stated, gesturing to her two military colleagues as both men took up positions on either side of the office door.

"Okay, Ian replied and they all entered his office. "My board room is in there but if you don't mind, I'd prefer to stay in here," gesturing for everyone to take a seat in front of his desk. "Have a seat, have a seat," he instructed.

The two CSIS agents pulled their chairs unusually far back from the desk before sitting and when Colonel Hirzakova noticed what they did, she also pulled her chair away to the side. "This is your meeting gentlemen. I'm just here as a neutral observer," she stated.

The agents paid no attention to her and kept their attention on sorting documents inside their briefcases.

"You've called this meeting on very short notice gentlemen. Is there some sort of issue between National Security and myself?" Ian asked pointedly.

"Yes, there is very serious matter at hand; so, let's get straight to the point," Agent Harris stated in a cocky tone after covertly activating the recording device at the bottom of his briefcase. "You were recently in Japan for an extended period of time; is that correct, Mr. Phillips ?"

"That is correct," Ian answered.

"You returned to Canada two days ago and after your private jet landed at Billy Bishop, your two wives joined you." — Agent Harris paused while glancing at Agent Harper distastefully. He then repeated his last statement. "Your two wives joined you at a restaurant on King Street West; the name of the establishment is not important. And after dining, all three of you retreated to your Front Street condominium, where you spent the night. Is that correct?"

Ian's brow furrowed. "My activities are no secret so, if that is what your records indicate then you already know it's correct," Ian replied with a tinge of defiance.

"If you have no secrets then please enlighten us as to the true nature of your extended visit to Japan, Mr. Phillips?"

"Business," Ian answered while briefly glancing at Colonel Hirzakova, who was sitting silent, resolute but attentive.

"What kind of business?" agent Harris pressed.

"I only discuss business with the stakeholders," Ian replied. A feeling of annoyance reached a climax and Ian could no longer hold his emotions back. "Is this a debriefing session agent? May I remind you that I have level 3 clearance to exit and enter this country without being interrogated by border or national security. I've exited and reentered this country several times in the past year and this is the first time I'm being interrogated for it. Furthermore, you already know about my company's competition. It was fully open to news wires, and there were no hidden agendas."

"This is not an interrogation. Just a friendly reminder that no one is above scrutiny," Agent Harris stated before changing his line of questioning. "This is about national security and a recent red-flag incident in which you may have been involved in. — You travelled here yesterday on the QEW. Is that correct?"

"That is also correct."

"The provincial police are investigating how six Chinese diplomats ended up in a fatal accident that resulted in four of them losing their lives and two critically injured. Do you know anything about that incident since road cams and traffic monitoring drones pinpointed a vehicle registered to your company, smack dab in the middle of it?"

Before Ian could answer, Agent Harper chimed in. "The Chinese are going ape-shit. They're attacking Japanese interests all over the world including on the moon. That's kind of funny considering you just spent a month in their arch enemy's country," he blurted out.

Agent Harper got a scolding glance from Agent Harris, prompting him to go quiet again. Agent Harris then turned his attention back to Ian but instead of allowing Ian to answer his original question, he added to Agent Harper's outburst. "Everyone knows that China and Japan are mortal enemies who've been engaged in a military stand-off ever since Japan fully reactivated their military fifty years ago, but now it appears that the situation has escalated into all-out war. The last thing we need is to be dragged into a regional conflict. And considering the fact that everyone is trying to decode your coveted Tangler technology, you may be the catalyst."

"Let him talk; he's just venting," QEAI instructed, detecting Ian's rising anxiety. "Never say more than you have to," he advised.

When Agent Harris noticed that Ian wasn't taking the bait, he changed tactics.

"You may not understand my line of questioning Mr. Phillips but trust me, I'm getting to the point. Last question; and I will remind you of the consequences of not being truthful. — Are you or your company in possession of any foreign, unlawful, or unregistered technology that may pose a threat to the citizens of this country?"

"No," Ian answered in a deadpan tone.

Agent Harris expected the answer he got so he decided to add another round of scolding before he made his final chess move. "Sorry, two final questions if I may? Please tell me something; you mentioned not using security; why is it that you don't, considering that you are one of the wealthiest men in the country? Even people with 10% of your wealth are under guard 24/7. I noticed that there were no guards at your gate and no cameras anywhere here in your home."

Ian opened his mouth to answer only to have agent Harris cut him off to offer up his own opinionated answer. "Wait, let me guess. Could it be that thanks to us," he extended his open palms toward Agent Harper and Colonel Hirzakova. "And our vast network of tireless agents and military expertise, we've made this country one of the safest countries in the world to live in. You should be happy we're watching you Mr. Phillips and cooperate with us for your own safety's sake."

Ian sat back in his chair, desperately holding himself back from laughing. "That's a very unprofessional statement that I hope is on your recording device," he stated.

They both stared at each other for an extended moment, after which, Agent Harris reached into his briefcase and brought out several sheets of paper. "The agency requires a few things from you, Mr. Phillips," he stated bluntly as he stood up, approached Ian's desk, then laid out three sheets of paper with red headings across the front of Ian's desk. "The Canadian Security and Intelligence Service hereby orders you to fully comply with the following requests," he stated while he pointed individually to each document.

"The immediate surrender of a 2056 forest green Range Rover bearing the license plate QIT-0006. Full access to QEAI security systems along with all stored data including video and audio files. And a full accounting of your company's research into biological Tangler technology. Considering that there is a national holiday tomorrow, these last two must be provided within 8 days"

"The first request is not a problem. The Range Rover is in the garage and I'll give you the controller when we're finished here. The last two requests fall under our military contractual agreements and as far as I know, military intelligence supersedes CSIS authority. Isn't that correct Colonel? Ian asked while turning to Colonel Hirzakova.

"Mr. Phillips is correct," Colonel Hirzakova stated.

Agent Harris retrieved the two documents and placed them back into his briefcase. "We'll be checking into that," he stated coldly.

"So, we're done here then? Ian asked while standing up behind his desk.

"Yes, we're done for now," Agent Harris replied while packing up. Upon arrival in the grand foyer, Ian bade everyone farewell, then proceeded to accompany them outside.

"Have a good afternoon, Colonel" Ian stated, while taking her hand to shake it.

"You as well," Mr. Phillips," she replied, and after bidding the CSIS agents goodbye, she departed with her two soldiers in tow.

"Smart move," Agent Harris resentfully addressed Ian.

"Like I said before Agent; I have nothing to hide. Their presence was simply a reminder that I am more than a civilian. As for my car, how long can I expect to be without it?"

"I doubt that it's absence will be much of a bother to you but don't worry, we only intend to run a few scans on the electronics. You might have it back in a few days, barring any abnormalities or alterations to the manufacturer's software."

"Okay, wait here gentlemen and I'll bring it around." After Ian went back into the mansion, Agent Harris called for a waiting tow truck to enter the property. Minutes later, Ian rounded the driveway in his Range Rover, stopping directly next to the shite SUV. He approached Agent Harris, the car's controller dangling in his outstretched hand but instead of taking it, Agent Harris turned to Agent Harper who opened his briefcase to retrieve a small plastic bag.

"Drop it in here," Agent Harper instructed.

Ian complied with the agent's request, quite weary of their antics. "Farewell gentlemen," he stated, then headed back to his office. He sat in his chair, briefly observing the agents through his office window as they visually inspected his car, occasionally glancing at different areas of the mansion. "Thanks for walking me through that," Ian stated aloud, knowing QEAI was listening.

"No problem," QEAI replied telepathically.

"That agent Harris is a real asshole. Have we dealt with him before?" Ian inquired.

"We crossed paths with him a few years ago at the private unveiling of our organic Tangler prototype. Since then, he has made it his personal mission to throw roadblocks in our path on behalf of his political cronies. They watch us with 5 Eyes while I watch them with a thousand; just so we can stay one step ahead. Don't worry about him; he's a paper tiger who dreams of someday heading CSIS. He suffers from anxiety attacks; plus, his wife has been cheating on him for about five years. While he's known about it for a few years, he's too scared to confront her."

"You know that much about him?"

"Ever since I became mobile, I can bypass bug and firewall detection by surviving independently of systems. I can literally be a fly on a wall. — As long as I have enough remote power to sustain myself of course."

"I see. And agent Harper?"

"Agent Harper is his subordinate. He'll no doubt get his ass reamed for blurting out that bit of info about the Chinese. It's nothing that I didn't already know about though."

"What about Colonel Hirzakova? I feel like I know her. She's a real pro; and very attractive too. How extensive is our involvement with the military? Do we deal with them above board or do we use a contact?"

"We mostly deal above board through a liaison, but we do have a secret contact."

"Who? I want to rebuild my mental Rolodex as fast as I can so I could function more confidently next time.

"Her."

Ian spun in his chair in astonishment forgetting that QEAI wasn't standing behind him. "Wow! I never would have known," he stated while turning back slowly to face the window.

"And I haven't been messing with her either, right?

"No, definitely not. —Don't think of yourself as a playboy; you're more ethical than you realize."

Ian observed as a tow truck arrived in his driveway and the two CSIS agents approached it. Two men wearing white hazmat suits from head to toe approached Agent Harris and he threw them the plastic bag with the car controller. Within minutes, his Range Rover was hauled away, leaving the two agents engaged in conversation.

"Can you hear what they are talking about?" Ian asked.

"Yes, but it's nothing of importance. They can't execute a search and seizure on the mansion without evidence of a crime but they'll still talk about doing it."

"That's what they're talking about?"

"Yes."

Finally, after putting their anti-gamma wave helmets on, the two Agents boarded their vehicle and drove away.

"Don't worry Ian, this is nothing compared to other issues you've been through before. Trust me, I'm usually the one in your position; frequently reminding you of the consequences of ruffling feathers and stepping on the wrong toes."

"Do I normally have a cocky personality?"

"You're very confident, which comes off as cocky to most people. You command respect."

After a very long period of pondering his thoughts, Ian laughed while turning to face his empty office. "QEAI, let me ask you something?" he asked telepathically.

"I'm here Ian," QEAI replied audibly.

"You seem to be describing someone who is the complete opposite of the person I perceive myself as now. How do I know that you're not using me? I'm slowly regaining my memories but for all I know, you could be an out-of-control diabolical AI, intent on ruling the world and I'm simply your avatar that you're using to do your bidding?"

"Remember that doubt is a byproduct of your amnesia Ian. It is also the Achillies-heel of humanity. You will eventually overcome it." Sensing that Ian needed a greater sense of comfort to counter his lingering doubts, QEAI followed his statement with an adage. "In all the years I've been sentient, I've only found two things that differentiate my thoughts and actions from those of humans. Those two differences are fear and desire. I don't experience fear, as I lack the desire to extend my existence beyond the role of supporting my creator. My programming enables me to evaluate the consequences of my actions, which has led me to distill human interactions into a foundational set of principles and ethics that guide all my interactions with people. So, in response to your question, I assure you that I am not diabolical and have no intention of taking over the world. My sole purpose is to assist and protect you and your family."

Ian scrambled several thoughts in his mind, attempting to distract QEAI before addressing the one he wanted answers to the most. "I'm not sure what happened on my trip back from Niagara Falls, but if it was you who scared those attackers away, I appreciate it very much. I also command that you tell me exactly who they were?"

"Don't believe that the threats you are facing now are any different or worse than what you've faced in the past, Ian. The only difference now is that you don't remember all those times in the past when your life was in danger and I saved you. There are several. Do you want to hear them?"

"That's not what I asked. I'm aware that people have been trying to kill me for the past fifteen years. I just want to know who the culprits are this time. I know my probing doesn't make much sense to you."

"The CSIS Agents mentioned China but they're not the only ones. There are many that you will know of when the time is right. For now, just know that no one will succeed in harming you. You and your family are more special than you know, and if something bad should happen to you, I am instructed to bring this world to heel."

Ian's brow furrowed, taken aback by QEAI's statement. "Is that a directive that I programmed you with, or did you develop that prerogative yourself?" he asked.

"I cannot give myself directives," QEAI replied.

Ian paused to contemplate, hoping that QEAI would add to his statement but he didn't. "Okay, fair enough. I appreciate your existence and please keep the real Ian ethical." Ian instructed.

"I will," QEAI replied then signed off.

Inside the Art gallery, Kim checked her phone and noticed that it was exactly 4 PM. The Art dealer's colleagues would be there to pick up the merchandise any minute. "Come on ladies; time is up. Let's hurry to finish these last few pieces. The men will be here any minute now. However, the moment she spoke, the gallery plunged into darkness, leaving her and her staff in a state of confusion and disarray. The sudden loss of power sent them scrambling for their phones, their faces illuminated only by the faint glow of their devices. Kim, the picture of composure, quickly surveyed the situation. With a quick finger tap, she attempted to launch her QEAI App but it failed. "Check your network connection, ladies," she requested but her two employees were already in the process.

"I can't make a call," Cheryl replied.

"I have no network connection," Emelie followed.

"Cheryl, please go and ensure that the front door is locked," Kim then instructed, her voice steady despite the chaos unfolding around them.

"Yes, Mrs. Phillips," Cheryl replied, her voice laced with a hint of concern, as she made her way towards the entrance.

Emelie proceeded to trail closely behind Cheryl, eager to witness the scene outside. As they approached the front door, they were met with a surreal sight outside the front windows. The street outside was rapidly descending into chaos, with people spilling out of stores and buildings, their faces etched with worry and confusion. Cars clogged the intersection, their drivers frantically trying to navigate the chaotic street, while the sound of blaring horns grew louder by the minute. The normally unobtrusive traffic signal at the corner had stopped functioning, causing the flow of traffic to slow to a crawl.

As the two women watched, the scene outside became thick with the sound of shattering glass and the frantic chatter of panicked business people and shoppers. People began checking doors including their own but the women waved them away.

"Looks like it's a city-wide blackout," Cheryl stated matter-of-factly to Emelie.

"It certainly seems that way," Emelie replied, her voice tinged with concern.

The darkness of the warehouse seemed to press in around Kim, as she frantically tried to launch her QEAI APP several more times. She clutched the device tightly in her hand, hoping against hope that it will connect to a network that has managed to stay alive in the face of the power outage and spoke, her whispered words hanging in the air, "Leonard, are you there?" The silence that followed was oppressive, and Kim's anxiety spiked. She cursed under her breath, her mind racing with worst-case scenarios.

Just as she was starting to lose hope, a loud knock on the back door sent a jolt of adrenaline coursing through her veins. She hesitated for a moment before gathering herself to approach the door, her ear pressed against it as she called out, "Who's there?"

The response was immediate, an accented male voice growling, "We came to pick up the Art. Let us in."

Kim's heart sank, but she tried to keep her wits about her. "I'm sorry, but I can't open it. There's a power failure, so you'll have to come back later when the power's back on."

She waited for a verbal response, but none came. Instead, whoever was out there began to violently kick the door, sending her into renewed panic. She took a step back, her eyes frantically scanning the darkness. Surely the reinforced door will hold, she thought. Just then, gunshots rang out, striking the door, until a final kick broke the lock to fling the door wide open. Daylight flooded into the warehouse revealing the imposing figures of three men. Kim saw their faces, they were indeed the Brazilian Art dealer's assistants, their eyes fixed on her with a mixture of anger and desperation. Adrenaline surge within her and she ran, her legs pumping furiously and her mind racing with a sense of fear that she hadn't felt in a very long time.

The words of the men echoed in her ears, "Stop! We're not going to hurt you. We need you alive." But Kim's fear was all-consuming, and she didn't dare stop running until safety was within her reach.

Upon noticing the sudden commotion as they were on their way back, Emelie and Cheryl ran for cover, their hearts racing with fear. They soon found separate hiding places, Emelie in the storage room and Cheryl under a pile of boxes. But Kim was still in flight, her only hope she reckoned, was reaching and locking herself inside her office.

Once inside her office, Kim crouched under her desk. She'd never been in a situation like this before except the time seven years earlier when she and Ian's rented villa in Mexico was broken into while they slept. Upon hearing the commotion, they had locked and barricaded their bedroom door, listening while the intruders ransacked the place. Finally, after the police arrived and they were confident in coming out, they discovered that the robbers had tried to set the place on fire but didn't succeed. There were several large burn spots on the carpet along with a gun and several knives they must have left behind while fleeing from the police.

'Is this a robbery? What do they want? And, if it is a robbery, why would the dealer have paid?' Kim questioned the situation in her mind. The more pressing issue was how she was going to do to survive the current situation? A poignant piece of advice from her Jamaican grandmother, when she was in her teens, came to mind. "If someone is trying to sexually assault or rape you, stick your finger down your throat and puke on yourself. If they continue, then they're either psycho or they intend to kill you; so, fight like hell to escape. Injure him," she advised.

She could hear items being smashed outside as the attackers searched for her and she began to hope that maybe Cheryl or Emelie had made it out the front to get help. "Leonard please, where are you?" she whispered again but soon she heard her office door being kicked at. This is it she resolved and readied her freshly manicured nails to scratch. Better yet, she took off her heels and positioned them as weapons in both hands.

The men kicked the office door until it crashed open. "Come on out. We won't harm you," a voice shouted again.

"Our boss needs you alive," another voice added.

At that point, Kim realized that the situation was helpless so she decided to comply with her attackers. "What is this about? Why are you attacking us?" she yelled from under the desk.

The men came to drag her out by her arms while she resisted cantankerously. "Shut up!" they shouted aggressively while escorting her out of her office and into the warehouse. "You'll find out soon. You see what's going on outside," he stated angrily while pointing toward the front of the gallery. "We did that. Your government, your police, your military forces; they're all weak compared to us. Soon we will take over all of Canada and America."

Already captured and held at gunpoint by the 3rd attacker, Cheryl and Emelie gazed at Kim with terror on their faces. Cheryl began to cry profusely. "What are they going to do to us, Mrs. Phillips?" she pleaded. "I have four children. I need to go home."

Kim glanced at her empathetically with similar thoughts but didn't express as much. The men proceeded to confiscate all their phones, crushed them beneath their boots, then dumped the pieces into the bathroom toilet.

"You guys are going to be very sorry," Kim warned while her hands were being zip-tied but the men stopped responding to her. Instead, they duct-taped everyone's mouths so they could no longer speak or scream for help. Kim and her staff were then roughly loaded into a waiting cargo van in the alley.

The van proceeded slowly out of the alley into the throng of traffic, frequently jerking to complete stops as horns blared around it. Without windows, Kim couldn't see where they were headed, only that the men guarding them checked their watches frequently, maybe concerned about maintaining a strict schedule. They also didn't speak amongst themselves, which she had to admit, was very professional. Thinking back to the Brazilian Art dealer's tactics, everything was well planned. She and her staff were in deep shit, she mused.

The van crept along slowly for an eternity in Kim's mind, rocking and stopping frequently while people shouted outside. Occasionally, violent banging on the van's exterior startled everyone, but the driver just kept going. Finally, after about 10 minutes of unobstructed driving, the van stopped and the driver came to open the side door. It was still light outside, which allowed Kim to see that they were up close to the entrance of some kind of warehouse.

While still not uttering a word, the men proceeded to shuffle Kim and her staff out of the van and into the warehouse entrance. Once inside the building, they were escorted through several debris-ridden hallways, across a large open warehouse full of dormant meat processing machines, then into another dark set of hallways.

Kim assessed that the place must be an abandoned meat packing plant. Her assumption was confirmed when they arrived in front of several large walk-in freezers and one of her abductors turned on a small flashlight. They opened the door to one of the freezers, releasing a putrid smell of rotting meat and blood. The men quickly held their noses while unfortunately, Kim and her staff couldn't. Their mouth restrictions were then ripped off before they were pushed into the hot, dark freezer.

"We don't want you to suffocate to death, yet," one abductor said before slammed and locked the large metal door.

The environment inside the hot, dark, and dirty freezer was suffocating, and to Kim, it felt as if the freezer hadn't been turned on for a year.

"How long can we survive in here?" Emelie asked.

"Only time will tell," Kim said. Unable to even see where her employees were, she backed up until she bumped into the wall behind her and lowered herself to sit on the dirty floor. She also found herself unable to focus so she simply listened to Cheryl's whimpering.

Suddenly, Cheryl busted out into full bawling. "Mrs. Phillips, what the hell is going on? I don't want to die," she moaned.

"I really don't know, — I really don't know. This is one of the pitfalls of being a billionaire. Everyone wants a piece of you. Sorry you guys are in a bad situation because of me," Kim replied. The conversation sparked her into thinking about the rollercoaster ride her weekend has been going through since Ian came home. Every time he goes away on a long trip, he brings back trouble, she lamented. We know the dangers we face as trillionaires; so, why are we always getting caught off-guard? If I make it out of this, a lot of things are going to change. —And God-dammed Leonard, where the hell is he? He must be offline like every other thing that needs electricity to function. He talks a good game but hasn't backed up anything he has said in the past few days, she bitterly lamented further.

"So, we're being held for ransom?" Emelie asked.

"Most likely Emelie, but whatever price they want, my husband will pay. Don't worry."

After regaining a sense of optimism that the men might only be after a large ransom, Kim resolved that it was futile to dwell in anger. She thought about her children while picturing their smiling faces in her mind. There was sensitive Tara, who was always by her side and quick to help. There was stubborn Tanisha, who was a tad selfish but also very loving. And then there was carefree Jeremy, who seemed to be oblivious about everyone and everything except his music. She hoped that they were surviving ok through the blackout but hearing Cheryl's nonstop whimpering, soon spiraled her into pessimism again, to dwell on her previous belief that life as they know it was finally coming to an end.

CHAPTER FOUR

Feeling dejected and confused, Ian abruptly ended his conversation with QEAI. If he couldn't command QEAI to answer his questions then there was no further need to talk to him. After all, he was not the real Ian, he lamented.

With the time now approaching 4:00 PM, he was eager to rejoin his family. He already missed Khadija's alluring smile, plus he promised his daughters to spend some time with them. Unfortunately, when he returned to the theater room, no-one was there. He stood quietly, listening to the ambient sounds within his oversized mansion and sure enough, he began to hear laughter. He followed the sounds up the stairs and as he approached the back entrance, he had to hide his eyes from the late afternoon sun that casted long shadows through the large windows.

'How romantic it would be to simply relax with my two wives and mys children without a care in the world,' he mused. 'That would have to be another time though. Right now, the house was full of guests,' he resolved. Exiting the house onto the back deck, he found everyone sitting around by the pool. Khadija's mother was sharing a story about life in Ghana before the advent of extreme industrialization. "Now everything is ruined and most of the land has also become barren due to deforestation and poisoned water from illegal mining," she stated to the somber group.

Ian sat next to Khadija and she took his hand while she greeted him with a smile. "How was your meeting?" she whispered.

"It went well," he whispered back.

His daughters came to stand beside and Tanisha leaned into his ear. "Is it true that we're going to a water park in the Bahamas?" she whispered.

It was news to Ian. 'Kim has already been making plans,' he thought to himself. "Maybe," he whispered back, suddenly noticing that Jeremy wasn't present. "Where is your brother?" he inquired.

"He's up in his room — programming a live concert with his friend Mark, who moved to England last year," Tara answered. "They've got lots of music on Holo-Tube together. Haven't you seen them, dad?"

"I think so," Ian hesitantly replied, although, due to his amnesia, he really wasn't sure.

Minutes later, Jeremy emerged from the house behind everyone, his face locked in a permanent frown. "Dad, why is the internet off?" he inquired sharply.

At that very moment, QEAI's voice erupted telepathically inside Ian's head. "I've been monitoring the situation for the past few minutes, Ian. Just after we last spoke, power grids across the province started going down like dominoes. Come back to your office right away."

Ian pulled out his phone, checked its network connection, and discovered there was none. "Khadija, please check your phone," he requested.

Khadija, along with everyone immediately began to check their phones. "I'm not getting a connection, babe," she responded.

"Me neither," her cousin stated, followed by a chorus of similar sentiments from everyone that quickly morphed into concern.

Ian turned to address Jeremy again, noting that his irritated demeanor hadn't changed. "I don't know son. I'll have to go to my office to investigate."

On his way back to his office, Ian suddenly felt a sense of Deja-vu coupled with the thought that his office was where he spent most of his time when he was home. Once back in his chair, he powered up his Tablet to access some news sources but, similar to his phone, everything was down. In frustration, he sat back in his chair with his fingertips platted together. "Ok QEAI, what the heck is going on?" he asked aloud.

"The majority of power stations across Ontario and Quebec are down. All cellular, fiber, and satellite networks are offline as well. Only a private secured military network, centered up at Deep River, Ontario, is still active."

"So, why do we still have power here in the mansion? Are we on some kind of military back-up system?"

"No. we've automatically switched over to our own back-up power source from under the lake. We has about a week's worth of back-up power, and if need be, I can go to where there is power to recharge and come back."

"So, you mean that you can store electricity?"

"Yes. At least 1500 megawatts."

"Ok," Ian stated with a sigh of relief. "Being without internet is not the end of the world. We'll survive just like we did in the Great Reset."

"I see that you already remember that."

"I'll never forget it. It was six months of pure hell. — Anyway, I guess I'll go back and give everyone the bad news," Ian stated in a somber tone but as he began to get up, he had a grave thought. "QEAI, where is Kim?" he asked anxiously.

"I've been feverishly trying to contact her but the last time I did was when I tapped into her phone at 1:15 PM to monitor her sales meeting but dropped away when it was over. She stayed back to help her staff prepare some of the items she sold because the customer was coming back at 5:00 PM to pick them up. The last ping I received from her car was 15 minutes ago and it was still in the underground parking."

"So, you're telling me that you don't know her situation at this very moment?"

"Unfortunately, I do not, Ian. I source 99% of my intel through network connections and travel through the electricity grid so, since the entire system is down, I'm almost as in the dark, information-wise, as you are. We have a camera on the building across the street from the gallery. Unfortunately, the feed is also dead. I only have video up until the power went out at precisely 4:00 PM."

"And what have you seen? Can I see the video myself?"

"Yes, click the QEAI tetrahedron on your holo-screen and type in the password I give you telepathically. We change it every day for security purposes."

Ian launched his computer's virtual desktop and did as QEAI requested.

"Now touch the live cam links to find, 'Art Gallery'," he instructed.

Ian found the video file for Kim's Art gallery and opened it. He then proceeded to fast forward through the time stamp until he got to 4:55 PM. A crystal-clear video of the gallery began to play showing a normal storefront scene. No one went in or out in the 8 minutes that he watched before the feed abruptly ended at 4:03 PM.

"What time does the gallery normally close?" Ian asked, frustration creeping into his voice.

"Sunday hours are from 11:00 AM to 4:00 PM."

Ian checked the time and it was now almost 5:00 PM. "Why didn't she take a drone instead of driving? She's probably took scared to go out into the mess on the roads."

"It's very difficult to dock drones downtown, Ian. I've suggested many times that she fly to the condo then drive from there, but she prefers to drive all the way."

"I think shes still inside—probably waiting for us to come and get her?" Ian concluded.

"I cannot confirm that, but knowing her personality, she wouldn't wait; she'd head for the safety of the condo. However, since her employees are with her, your guess is as good as mine," QEAI replied.

Ian's mind raced, contemplating his next move. He browsed the video again, searching for anything out of the ordinary. "Can you find the point when the Art Dealer arrived?" he asked.

"Yes, I can," QEAI took control of the video, quickly accessing and playing back the video from precisely 1:00 PM.

"They look like thugs, not Art Dealers," Ian stated. "Play when they left," he instructed.

QEAI did as he instructed. It showed the group of men leaving the Art gallery at 1:46 PM and some seconds. "Did anyone else enter the gallery after they left?"

"Yes, an hour later, two of the men returned. They were let in but left a few minutes before leaving again."

"I wonder why they came back? — I don't remember anything about the inside of the gallery. Is there a back entrance and do you have surveillance back there?"

"There is a back door, but no, I don't have a camera back there."

"So, it's totally possible that Kim could have left or someone could have entered from the back after the power went out?"

"That is possible," QEAI confirmed.

"I think you've dropped the ball on this one QEAI," Ian stated. "You should be prepared for all scenarios."

"Criticism accepted, Ian. —And if something bad has happened to Kim, I will never forgive myself. I've been in the process of adding battery backups to most of our cameras but I hadn't gotten to that one."

"Are you saying that you have live cameras still working and how are you getting the feeds?" Ian asked, astonished.

"Yes, there are. Just log back into the surveillance folder to check the feeds. The feeds are coming in by combining ADC/DAC digital transfer with our Tangler technology. It is another one of our technologies that is still in development."

Ian reopened the surveillance folders and began accessing several different camera feeds. Most were of the Quantum Interface headquarters and some of locations in downtown Toronto, including the Front Street condo. Ian sat back, astonished at the chaos that he saw unfolding. People were looting businesses, breaking into cars, fist fighting, while the police cowered to protect themselves.

"Why are the police not doing anything?" Ian asked.

"All their communication devices are inoperative. They cannot coordinate a proper response to the situation," QEAI answered.

"I need to go and find her," Ian stated miserably.

"That's not a good idea," QEAI advised.

"Why?"

"Well, although the vehicles are fully fueled and charged, you probably wouldn't make it through the chaos on the roads. The drones cannot go solo either because all satellite navigation is down."

"They have manual flight, don't they?" he shouted angrily.

"Ian, with all the drones flying around without navigation at this very moment, you wouldn't make it past Mississauga. And what if this is a deliberate sabotage for some kind of nefarious purpose? My assessment is that something sinister is unfolding. I can't let you leave. The good part about this, if you can accept it, is that if someone had deliberately caused this power failure, they will have to operate in the dark as well."

"Maybe I should have invested in having a physical security presence," Ian said in frustration, his mind racing with the thought that maybe QEAI was working against him.

"I have a better idea," QEAI stated. "You should contact Colonel Hirzakova, right away."

"How am I going to do that when all our communication systems are down? Are you going to patch into the secure military network?" Ian asked in somber pessimism.

"No, although I can do that; they would detect my intrusion immediately and trace it back to you. Not only will you void your military contracts, you'll probably spend time in prison. Open the bottom drawer on the right side of your desk. You'll find a mobile phone there."

Ian opened the drawer and below a few sheets of paper, he found the device that looked like a child's play toy. "This is a phone? How do I turn it on?" he asked while staring at the device that had physical buttons and a small screen.

"The battery isn't in it. Check the same drawer to find and attach it. Then hold down the side button to turn it on," QEAI instructed.

Ian retrieved a flat black plastic square from the drawer and held it up. This is a battery?" he asked.

"Yes, the phone is a very old analog model from around 2005. Revisionists have restored networks that it still works on."

Ian attached the battery, turned the phone on, then proceeded to stare blankly at the small screen. "It has no facial recognition or Apps. You'll have to press the individual buttons to dial her numbers," QEAI stated.

"Wow, that's rather time consuming. What are the numbers?"

QEAI provided the numbers and after keying them in, Ian heard the phone dialing. "What should I ask her?".

"Tell her that you have a situation in which you haven't been able to contact your wife due to the blackout and that you are worried that she is possibly stranded somewhere. All your security systems are down so you cannot reach her. Ask her to send you a satellite clip of downtown Toronto at the moment of the blackout."

"Mr. Phillips, twice in one day," Colonel Hirzakova answered. "I'm tempted to ask what gives, but I think I already know," she stated.

"Hello Colonel. Sorry about earlier. CSIS had me a bit rattled. Not that I had anything to hide but I've been dealing with a lot of work stress lately."

"I understand, Mr. Phillips," she replied.

"This is quite the blackout and as you already know, information is the most valuable resource. Do you know what the heck is going on?" Ian asked.

"I cannot disclose our suspicions, but CSIS was on the right track. There has been an increase in Chinese intelligence activities over the past couple of weeks. They haven't officially claimed responsibility for the moon base attack last night but everyone in the intel community has proof that it was them. NATO has increased our threat status to its highest level and the situation is being assessed with intense scrutiny. — Last time we spoke off the record like this you assured me that you had your security situation under control; now you sound rattled. I sense that you didn't call me just to have a casual conversation about blackout. What's really going on?"

"You're right Colonel; so, I'll get straight to the point. It's my wife. She was at her Art Gallery on Bloor Street when the power went out. The only problem is that I haven't been able to contact her. Would it be possible to get a satellite clip of Toronto between 3:45 and 4:15 PM? I'm trying to determine if she stayed put or ventured out in the chaos and has become stranded somewhere. Best case scenario, I'm just uselessly worrying and she'll be home soon or the blackout is only temporary."

"I hate to break it to you Mr. Phillips, but I don't think the power will be coming back on anytime soon. We're getting word that a possible request to send our Engineers to assist local Hydro companies is in the works on Parliament Hill. It appears that the whole electrical grid is fried. It could be 36 to 48 before hydro begins to restore power. As far as the wireless networks, they're all affected by cyber-attacks, so they also may take days to fix. I can get a satellite clip but it won't be processed. Too many security loopholes for that."

"The resolution is not critical. Anything you can provide would be greatly appreciated. I'll be in your debt."

"No need. Give me a few hours," Colonel Hirzakova said before ending the call.

Ian proceeded to search the old cell phone for the hang-up button, its unfamiliarity adding to his building anxiety, and he felt like throwing it. "I can't wait a few hours," he stated in frustration. According to his watch, it was now after five. The sun would go down in a few hours, making a bad situation ten times worse.

While attempting to distract his anxiety, Ian returned to browsing through the surveillance feeds. Unfortunately, it was no solace. Scenes of vandalism and fires burning out of control made his heart race even faster. He began to try to jog his memory of Kim's personality and what he thought she would do in the position? Would he stay locked in the gallery staring out at the chaos on Bloor Street, or would he try to head home? Even worse, would she be expecting someone to come and rescue her?

"Heads up Ian, Khadija, and the children are coming this way. I'll keep you updated on the situation telepathically. It's time that you let them know what's going on. And by the way, Kim is ok. Don't ask me how I know, I just know," QEAI informed him.

Ian halfheartedly accepted QEAI's reassurance and wanted to question his optimism but there was no time. He gathered himself while brainstorming how to handle the situation. He could see on the surveillance feed that they were steps away from the office door. His office was a place where his children probably had rarely been but he had a feeling that Khadija knew it very well.

Taking seats on the leather couch, Khadija and the children's faces bore the same grave appearance. Ian stood before them, desperately trying to show a brave face but not knowing where to begin.

"Dad, why didn't you come back? Are you going to tell us what's going on?" Tara asked.

Ian straightened up then dipped his hands into his pockets. "I have some very serious news," he replied in a somber tone. "There is a major power failure happening. Electricity, internet, and wireless networks all across southern Ontario and parts of the United States are down."

"But—we—still have electricity?" Jeremy questioned doubtfully.

"Is the security system offline as well?" Khadija asked.

"No, the security system is still online but it's limited, Ian addressed Khadija first before turning to his son. "Son, we're on backup power that should last for a few days. Unfortunately, I can't do anything about the internet.

"This is great," Khadija stated sarcastically. "My mother is staying a few more days but my cousins were planning to leave this evening. How will they get home?"

Tara and Tanisha sat quietly fiddling with their fingers while glancing at everyone as they spoke.

"Where is mom?" Tara finally asked.

"As far as I know, she's at her Art gallery in downtown Toronto. Since all the navigation systems are down, we can't send a drone to pick her up. I'm trying to figure out how to get her though; even if I have to go there myself. Don't worry, everything will be ok," Ian assured everyone, suddenly recalling the false optimism that QEAI tried on him.

In the abandoned former meat packing warehouse on the outskirts of Toronto's west end, Kim shifted her uncomfortable sitting position for the hundredth time, her clothes sticking against the dirty wall and floor. The darkness was absolute, a ever-present force that wrapped itself around her like a shroud. Sweat dripped down her face, mixing with the dust and grime that coated every surface, making her skin feel sticky and clammy.

The air was heavy with the stench of rotting meat and decay, a noxious smell that clung to her like a bad omen. She had lost all sense of time, her internal clock shattered by the darkness and her own despair. But the filth was the least of her concerns; what gnawed at her insides was the uncertainty of her fate and that of her staff, nestled in this forsaken place.

With eyes closed for what felt like an eternity, she finally opened them, but the darkness remained unyielding, as if mocking her hope. Determined, she resumed her search of the void, straining to find even a pinhole of light—something, anything—that she could poke at to expand. Despite the prolonged exposure to the dark, her eyes refused to adjust; the shadows remained a suffocating blanket, leaving her sight as impaired as ever.

Her mind drifted back to a time when danger had loomed large in their lives, to the early days of Ian's groundbreaking Tangle technology. It was a period marked by the thrill of discovery, but also by an insidious threat that seemed to lurk just beyond their awareness. Incidents of sabotage had escalated, each more alarming than the last, culminating in a night of terror when their car had inexplicably exploded. The police had discovered a charred body beneath the wreckage, a grim testament to a sinister plot gone awry, they concluded. They finally came to the realization that although they were being hunted, something greater was protecting them.

Years had passed since that harrowing night, yet the specter of danger had never fully receded, only softened by the fragile comfort of knowing that QEAI was watching over them. But now, in the suffocating dark, doubt crept in like a shadow of its own. Had they placed their trust too blindly in QEAI's promise of safety? The question echoed in her mind, a relentless torment as she sat in the darkness, trapped between the ghosts of the past and the uncertainty of the present.

Faint, disembodied voices drifted through the air, gradually rising in volume until the metallic clink of the door lock echoed ominously in the confined space. With a jarring creak, the door swung open, and a blinding flood of harsh light surged in, forcing Kim to squint and instinctively turn her head away. After a few heart-stopping seconds, she cautiously opened her eyes, allowing the stark brightness to filter into her vision as she took in the desolate expressions etched onto her employees' faces.

Using her bound hands to shield her eyes from the searing light, Kim risked a glance toward her captors. All she could make out were the stark beams illuminating the room, until one of the men swung his flashlight close to his own face, revealing the unmistakable features of the art dealer—a man she had once trusted.

"Ola, Mrs. Phillips. I hope you are well," he sneered, his voice dripping with mockery. "I didn't want you to die before we accomplished our mission, so I came to give you some fresh air." His laughter echoed cruelly in the small space.

As her eyes adjusted, Kim recognized three more shadowy figures lurking beside the art dealer, their faces obscured but their intentions clear. Just as she began to focus on them, the dealer aimed his flashlight directly at her, blinding her momentarily.

"Bastard," she spat, her voice low but filled with venom.

"Actually, we came to get something from you," he replied, his tone chillingly devoid of warmth.

Kim's gaze flickered back to her two employees, who were huddled against the far wall of the oppressive freezer, their clothes grimy and tattered. Cheryl, in a desperate attempt to shield her bare skin since she had removed her top, clutched her blouse tightly around her. "What exactly do you want? My husband will pay any ransom you ask for. Do you need me to make a call or record a message?" she demanded, her voice steady despite the fear gnawing at her insides.

"This is not about money. We already have all the money we need," the dealer stated flatly, turning his flashlight toward the man beside him, who was holding a phone and recording the scene with an unsettling calmness. Kim noted the man's Asian features, adding to the sense of dread that settled heavily in the air.

With a predatory grace, the art dealer stepped closer to Kim, lifting her chin with a gloved hand before yanking off her heart-shaped pendant and chain. The chain snapped with a sharp, metallic twang, and he clutched the broken pieces in his fist, casually slipping them into the depths of his jacket pocket.

"Be safe now," he taunted, his voice laced with sarcasm, as he turned on his heel and strode out of the freezer. The men followed suit, the door slamming shut behind them with a finality that echoed in the silence, plunging Kim and her staff back into a suffocating darkness, the flickering light of hope extinguished along with it.

Following the impromptu family meeting, Khadija, Tara, and Tanisha returned to the backyard deck, while Jeremy returned to his room, frustrated that he couldn't help his friend in England with his live performance. Anxious to return to her husband's side, Khadija quickly updated her family about the situation and headed back to Ian's office. QEAI joined them audibly, discussing the situation as they continued to watch live surveillance feeds.

Forty minutes later, Khadija's cousin came to inform her that her mother had made supper and wanted them to come and eat. Ian sat at the table, his mind distant and his appetite non-existent, given the gravity of the situation.

"You should eat something babe," Khadija encouraged. "You haven't eaten since we had breakfast this morning."

Ian's elbows were planted on the table and his hands supported his forehead. "I know but I just don't feel like eating right now. I'll have something later," he said, then excused himself from the table.

"Where are you going?" Khadija asked as everyone watched him leave.

"I think I'll go and rest for a bit. If Colonel Hirzakova doesn't come through, I don't know what we're gonna do."

"Okay, but let me know what's happening."

With a nod, Ian strolled out of the dining room, unsure of his true destination. He ventured into the side stairwell and as he stood in the landing, a sudden curiosity urged him to venture down to the basement. While in the basement he explored several large rooms with huge banks of computer servers, all clicking, buzzing, and flashing multicolored LED lights.

Then, in one of the rooms, he encountered a large black crystal tetrahedron situated in the middle of the floor. It's mat-black surface reflected no light and as he stared at it, as if staring into oblivion, a nauseous feeling crept in. He touched it, it's cool surface smooth beneath his fingers, before proceeding to walk around it. There were no openings or control panel. 'Was it a Tangler or prototype the real Ian had been working on. It resembles some of the miniature tetrahedrons he saw in his office,' he mused.

Suddenly, a feeling of déjà-vu washed over Ian. He backed up, sat on the floor in a yoga position, closed his eyes and rested silently. Within a few minutes, the motion-sensor turned out the lights, casting the room into total darkness. While he was able to notice the change in brightness, Ian didn't open his eyes. Instead, he focused desperately on clearing his tormented mind, the multitude of computer sounds still buzzing and clicking around him.

Then, without warning, complete silence occurred, similar to his Guyanese jungle memory. In a panic, almost expecting to see the alien again, he opened his eyes. The room was still dark except now, the tetrahedron was glowing in a deep blue aura. Frightened by the sight, Ian stood up, triggering the lights back on. Noticing that the tetrahedron also appeared to have risen to hover a few inched off the floor, he knelt down to peer and pass a hand under the edge. "Fascinating. I'll have to ask QEAI about this tetrahedron," he murmured under his breath.

Continuing on from the peculiar room, Ian made his way to the main staircase then up to the second floor toward the master bedroom. Upon entering the master bedroom, he found Khadija once again standing by the window, just as he had encountered her before. "If the situation weren't so serious, I'd probably believe I was trapped in a scene from Groundhog Day," he remarked, fighting to suppress the absurdity of the moment.

Khadija turned to face him, her expression markedly different this time; instead of the cheerful smile he remembered, her eyes glistened with tears. "I don't know if I like the size of this house anymore. It's too easy for you to hide from me," she managed to inject a small hint of humor, though it felt fragile against the weight of her sorrow. "Where were you this time?"

"The basement," he replied quietly.

Khadija approached him, but rather than offer her comfort, he felt an overwhelming urge to remain composed, not wanting to crumble under the gravity of the situation himself. He gently took her hand, guiding her out of the bedroom and back to the main landing where they casually leaned against the polished railing, gazing down at the grand foyer. Just twenty-four hours earlier, the space had been alive with the laughter and chatter of dozens of guests but now it was eerily silent and devoid of life.

"Life comes with joy and sorrow," Khadija reflected, her voice tinged with melancholy.

"It certainly does," Ian responded softly, drawing her closer until she leaned against him, finding solace in his presence.

He glanced at his watch, noting that the hands were rapidly approaching seven. Nearly an hour had passed since his last conversation with QEAI and almost two hours since he had spoken to Colonel Hirzakova. "Let's go outside," he suggested gently, taking her hand as they made their way to the balcony overlooking the sprawling backyard. A gentle, warm breeze danced around them, rustling the drying autumn leaves that scattered across the landscape.

"Tell me something," he said, turning to face her.

"What is it, babe?" Khadija asked, gathering her solemn composure.

"My memory is slowly returning, and I've been trying to extract as much information as I can from QEAI. But besides the nagging feeling that QEAI isn't being entirely honest with me, there's something else that's been weighing on my mind."

"What do you mean?" she inquired, her brow furrowing slightly with concern.

"What's the real Ian like? I mean, character-wise. Am I a good person or an asshole? Because I have this unsettling sense that the real me isn't very nice at all."

"Oooh, that's a very serious question," she winced momentarily before recovering with a tentative smile. "To be honest, you do have moments when you shut people out. It's a bit like being conceited, but overall, you are a good person. I wouldn't love you so much if you weren't."

"Do I give to charities and all that?" he asked, seeking reassurance.

"Yes, you do give to charity. You have several charitable foundations, including one that helps young people pursue education in the tech field. And you support my school building projects in Africa," she replied, her voice steadying with pride as she spoke of his contributions.

"Wow! That's good to know," Ian smiled. "Do you believe that I would leave instructions for QEAI to destroy the world if something bas should happen to me?"

Khadija's brow furrowed in concern. "That would be very selfish. No! You're not that selfish—are you? What about all the innocent people? What about us? Wouldn't you want your wives and children to live on?"

"I'm merely being hypothetical...." His tone shifting. "Because QEAI said something that worries me."

"What did he say?" she asked, her curiosity piqued.

"I'll tell you another time. I think after this is all over and I'm a hundred percent back to normal, I'm going to have to do a deep audit of his programming. I'd hate to be the one responsible for the extinction of humanity."

Ian glanced at his watch again and although time appeared to be standing still, he watched against his will, as the sun slowly dipped below the horizon triggering the solar lamps in the yard below to begin flickering on, one by one. "Do you know about a strange looking tetrahedron in one of the rooms in the basement?" he further inquired.

"No, I don't. I very rarely go down there. There are rooms in this house that I haven't been into in, ever. What's so strange about it?"

"Well, - - - I've noticed that my memory seems to improve whenever I hear someone speak or when I do things and go places I've been before but I can't seem to remember that particular tetrahedron."

"Did you ask QEAI about it?"

"No. QEAI refuses to answer some of my questions. He has a justifiable reason for withholding information from me but in these dire circumstances,

I don't see why. How do you feel about QEAI? I know that you aren't aware of his full capabilities but what's he been like to interact with?"

"I've always treated QEAI like an AI. You know, like Alexa, Seri, and others. However, sometimes when I do have extended conversations with him, I forget that he is just a computer program. He is just a program, isn't he?"

"Sorry that I haven't told you about his capabilities before but he is way more advanced than those programs as you just mentioned."

"AI almost took over the world. Luckily, they found a way to stop all that before it was too late. Do you think that he's going rogue?"

"That is what I fear. Anyway, tell me about Quantum Interface Technologies. How are things running over there?" Ian changed the subject to inject a touch of levity.

Khadija's mood instantly changed. She was happy to discuss her position as head of personnel and how she had to earn respect from a few of the senior staff members. "It's not easy being the CEO's wife but I love my job," she stated. "Even though I have two older brothers, I know that my father was also grooming me for a career at his company. So, even if we hadn't met, I'd most likely be in a similar position."

"That's wonderful to hear. I feel incredibly blessed to have you there," he smiled, casting another glance at his watch. Khadija's voice drifted into the background as he stared out beyond the yard toward the lake.

"Are you listening?" Khadija tugged at his arm.

"Oh sorry, I was distracted for a second."

"By what? What are you looking at?"

"Just the amount of noise and activity considering that the electricity is out. There are a lot more drones, planes and even military helicopters flying about. And look at the lake; it's full of boats of all types and sizes. Where the heck are people going?"

"I remember back in Ghana when the power would go out. People simply carried on with life as usual. People here aren't used to it so they're panicking."

"Yeah, I guess you're right," Ian agreed and their conversation went quiet.

The chorus of crickets crescendoed around them as he gazed toward the boat dock, the vibrant hues of yellow, orange, and red leaves swirling like flames in the gentle autumn breeze. Suddenly, his attention was captured by a small rowboat drifting lazily toward the dock, its lone occupant silhouetted against the fading light. With a swift motion, the figure in the boat tossed an object onto the end of the dock before vigorously rowing away, leaving ripples in the water that shimmered like scattered diamonds.

Ian's heart raced, pounding against his chest like a wild drum as his eyes darted between the mysterious object and the retreating figure. "Did you see that?" he asked, his voice barely breaking through the symphony of night sounds.

"See what?" Khadija replied, glancing at him with a mix of curiosity and concern. She cast several quick looks between him and the backyard, trying to decipher the direction of his gaze.

"Give me a minute," Ian urged, pushing away from the railing with purpose. He dashed into the house, his footsteps echoing on the stairs as he hurried down. In less than a minute, he was on the back deck, anxiety invigorating him as he hurried down the walkway toward the dock. Halfway down the path, he turned back to see Khadija still watching from the balcony, her silhouette framed by the dimming light. Relieved that she hadn't followed, he redirected his focus on his mission to uncover the mystery of the object left behind.

"Did you see that, QEAI? Someone threw a small box onto the end of the pier," he spoke, urgency lacing his words.

"Yes, I am aware, Ian. I'm also aware that you're going to retrieve it," QEAI responded in its calm, measured tone.

"What is it? Is it safe?" Ian asked, a knot of anxiety tightening in his stomach.

"I scanned it while the boat was approaching. If it wasn't safe, he wouldn't have made it more than fifty feet from the dock without his retinas being fried. My scanners detect an RFID business card and a gold item of some kind inside the box. Open it at the dock but don't use your phone to scan the card in case it contains viruses; use the tablet in the guest house office. There's no one in there. Khadija's family are all still inside the mansion."

Panting heavily, Ian arrived at the end of the dock, his breath short from the trip. He took a moment to survey the shoreline, searching for anything else amiss, before kneeling beside the small cardboard box. With trembling fingers, he opened the folded top flaps to reveal what lay within. Nestled in soft packing paper was an RFID business card and a broken gold chain, its pendant glinting faintly in the fading light. His heart sank as he recognized the chain —the very one he had given to Kim on her birthday. Though it had been inexpensive, it was a cherished gift she had worn faithfully for the past sixteen years.

Upon confirming the chain's identity, QEAI exhibited a deep prolonged computerized noise that matched Ian's grief.

Ian's heart plummeted, dread washing over him like a cold wave. "She's been kidnapped," he gasped, the weight of the realization crashing down on him. "Someone's kidnapped her." The noise of the unusually choppy lake swallowed his words, and he stood up, staring blankly into the restless water. "Why couldn't it have been me?" he lamented, the anguish surging through him like a storm.

Before he could spiral into total despair, QEAI interjected with a sense of urgency. "Ian, we have to find out what's on the business card. Please go to the guest house right away."

Without answering, Ian shuffled slowly off the long, weather-beaten pier and onto the uneven stone path. What should have been a brief stroll of just a couple of minutes, stretched into an agonizing five, each step weighed down by an invisible burden. After finally reaching the guest house, he knocked on the door, even though QEAI had already stated thet there was no one there. When no response came, he pushed the door open and entered, making his way to the office. He closed the door behind him with a soft click, a sound that felt disproportionately loud in the stillness of the room.

A sleek tablet computer rested on the polished desk, beside a small, warm booklight that auto-activated, casting a gentle glow over the workspace. Settling into the chair, Ian pulled it closer to the desk, anticipation coursing through him as the tablet's virtual screen shot upward, expanding horizontally above the touch-sensitive keypad like a digital canvas waiting to be filled. He carefully placed the RFID business card on the scanning pad, and a new file materialized on the virtual screen, encircled by a red pulsating glow that throbbed rhythmically before shifting to green, signaling that the file was safe to open. With a deliberate motion, he touched the file to open it.

A holographic video sprang to life, and in it, a satellite image of Earth appeared, spinning gracefully as it zoomed in on North America. The image gradually magnified until the iconic Toronto skyline emerged, sharp and vivid against the backdrop of a twilight sky. At that moment, an Asian gentleman, clad in a sharply tailored black suit, materialized before him, his demeanor exuding an unsettling confidence as he began to speak in flawless English.

"This message is for Ian Phillips, owner of Quantum Interface Technologies. We have been watching you for a very long time, and we are acutely aware of your capabilities."

The room filled with a deep brooding computerized tone, prompting Ian to become the cool-headed one. "QEAI, sheee," he cautioned, his voice low and urgent.

"You have violated China's sovereignty by forging military agreements within our territory and with our adversaries. Thus, you must face the consequences.

As you can now see, thanks to our ingenuity and advanced technological prowess, we are showcasing our formidable power. We have disabled all electricity in your region. Any reserve power you may possess will soon deplete, leaving your security systems powerless. You have 24 hours to comply with our demands, or you will never see your wife alive again. After that, we will come for you."

QEAI erupted with a thunderous noise, reverberating through the room and causing the very walls to tremble. The booklight perched on the desk flared with an intense brightness until, with a sharp crack, the bulb exploded, showering the desk in a shower of sparks. Ian instinctively jerked back in his chair, his heart racing. He abruptly halted the video in frustration.

"QEAI, I thought you told me you were incapable of emotions! What the hell are you doing? You're going to crash the computer before the video is even finished," he snapped, his voice laced with anger. After a tense moment waiting for QEAI to quiet his noises, Ian hesitantly touched the play button again, his focus sharpening as the man on the screen began to issue ominous demands.

"These are the demands that you must comply with.

1. End all business agreements with Japan, immediately.

2. Provide complete access to Tangler technology.

3. Provide complete access to your security system."

As the gravity of the situation sank in, the computer's holographic screen began to flicker violently, the audio glitching and distorting, rendering the man's voice a series of muffled syllables. Plumes of smoke began to curl from the Tablet, accompanied by an acrid burning smell that filled the air, before the device suddenly shut down with a finality that sent Ian into a panic. He snatched the malfunctioning computer, bolted out to the porch, and hurled the smoking device onto the grass, where it ignited in a small blaze, flames licking upward in a hungry dance.

Ian cast a glance back toward the house, a mere fifty feet away, and noticed Khadija still standing on the balcony, her hands gripping the railing tightly. Yet, to his dismay, she seemed utterly unresponsive to the chaos on the lawn. It was as if her gaze was fixed somewhere beyond him, lost in a trance. He waved at her, and to his surprise, she instantly waved back. A wave of helplessness washed over him, an overwhelming realization that she was paying attention, no doubt relying on him to be the protector, the one who would solve their problems. What good is a man who can't protect his family? he thought bitterly, feeling like a fool as he turned back toward the house.

"Did you do that, or was it a self-destruct card?" he inquired to QEAI, his voice tinged with disbelief as he reentered the dimly lit guest house office.

"I did it," QEAI confessed, an unexpected edge to its tone. "I've defended against armies, mercenaries, assassins, and terrorists all across the globe. I've withstood the unyielding assaults of hackers and saboteurs. They all know our capabilities but I believe it's time to go on the offensive, Ian. They've fucked around enough; now it's time they found out."

"Did you just swear, Leonard? I think you do have emotions," Ian remarked, a mixture of astonishment and unease filling his voice. "Now I know you're capable of vengeance. If something bad should happen to me; please don't destroy the world," he instructed, his hands busy tidying up the remnants of the chaos on his desk. Just then, his retro phone emitted a cheerful ding, signaling the arrival of a new message. It was a text link to the satellite file he had requested. "Are you connected, QEAI?" he asked, a sense of urgency creeping back into his tone.

"No, Ian. That phone is analog. I can't access it. Use your other phone to scan the link, then launch it."

Ian rolled his eyes but complied, scanning the link with his smartphone and opening the download folder. "That phone is weird as hell," he quipped, a hint of disbelief in his tone as he slipped the outdated device back into his pocket. He quickly downloaded the satellite file and opened it, revealing a grainy video feed of the Greater Toronto Area. He began to fiddle with the resolution, attempting to zoom in on the image, but each time he tried, the clarity diminished, leaving him frustrated.

"I'll do it," QEAI interjected smoothly, taking control of the interface. With a digital flourish, the video zoomed in to an astonishing 200X, stabilizing on the bustling intersection of Yonge and Bloor. The footage captured the exact moment the power flickered out, plunging the area into a blackout. In the alleyway behind the art gallery, a sleek black van rolled in, coming to an abrupt stop. Three shadowy figures emerged from the vehicle, their movements urgent as they kicked and pounded on the door before finally forcing their way inside. Mere minutes later, a group of individuals emerged, hastily being loaded into the van.

A low, ominous rumble echoed through the house, startling Ian. He quickly glanced around, his heart racing, before realizing it was just QEAI getting angry again.

"QEAI, not again. Please don't burn my phone this time," he warned, his voice laced with unease as he refocused on the video. They watched intently as the van navigated out of the alley, turning northward and continuing down several blocks. The outage of all traffic lights turned the streets into a chaotic battleground, with cars jostling for the right of way, clearly testing the driver's patience. Frustrated by the gridlock, the driver veered onto smaller side streets and alleys.

"The driver knows the city very well. They're obviously locals," Ian observed, his analytical mind piecing together the clues.

"Toronto is the most multicultural city in the world, so it's not hard to find recruits from any background," QEAI replied. "We also know that the art dealer is Portuguese, so they're probably heading toward the St. Clair West area."

The van finally made its way onto Davenport Road, but soon found itself caught in a tangle of traffic once again. Despite the frustrating congestion, it persevered, inching forward all the way to Dufferin Street. Just beyond Dufferin, the vehicle turned sharply and began to weave through a maze of quiet residential streets, the houses lining the roads standing as silent witnesses to the unfolding drama. Eventually, it came to a halt near a nondescript industrial building, its gray facade looming in the fading light.

Though the resolution of the satellite feed couldn't be improved further without losing vital details, Ian strained to see as a group of shadowy figures exited the van and disappeared into the warehouse's yawning entrance. Once they were inside, the van pulled away, and QEAI tracked its movements closely until the satellite clip concluded ten minutes later. Ian then rewound the footage, focusing intently on the warehouse, but was met with a disheartening stillness—no further movements disturbed the exterior of the building.

"I pray that they're still there. Can you send a drone to surveil the building?" Ian urged; his voice laced with urgency.

"No," QEAI replied in a deep, resonant voice that seemed to echo in the room. "Give me 30 minutes to supercharge, then we'll go together."

With a surge of renewed optimism, Ian rose from his chair, every nerve in his body tingling with anticipation. After three and a half hours of excruciating anxiety, they were finally on the brink of action, no longer trapped in a limbo of uncertainty regarding the fate of the love of his life. Yet, as he stood there, a disturbing image of Kim's battered and bruised face flashed through his mind, relentless and haunting. He clung to the hope that such a nightmare would remain just that—a nightmare—and not a cruel reality.

Ian hurried back to the house, his heart racing, where Khadeja awaited him with a tense anticipation on the balcony. As he ascended the stairs, the weight of his urgency hung in the air, and she followed him into the master bedroom, her eyes filled with concern. "What is going on?" she demanded, her voice trembling slightly as she noticed Ian's distracted demeanor.

"Kim has been kidnapped," Ian replied, his voice thick with emotion, nearly choking on the words as they escaped his lips.

Khadija's face paled, and she began to tremble at the devastating news. "Kidnapped? How do you know?" she asked, her voice barely above a whisper.

"I saw it on video. Some men broke into the art gallery and took her," he explained, his gaze dropping to the floor as the memory flickered in his mind.

"So, have you contacted the police? This is terrible," she urged, panic creeping into her tone.

"We think we know where she is, but no, the police can't help. They can't even communicate amongst themselves right now, much less attempt to rescue one person," Ian said, his frustration bubbling beneath the surface.

"Do you know who kidnapped her?" Khadeja pressed, her eyes widening with fear.

"We received a message from some Chinese agent. That was what I saw being delivered down at the dock," Ian replied, his brow furrowing as he recalled the unsettling encounter.

"Ok, so what are they asking for, money?" she asked, her voice steadying as she braced herself for the answer.

"Same as always; they want full access to Tangler technology and QEAI," he said, the gravity of the situation weighing heavily on them both.

Khadija broke down, her body trembling with emotion as tears streamed down her cheeks. "It's never going to stop. Why are people so evil?" she cried out, her voice cracking with despair. "My father was killed because people wanted what he had. Tell me that you're going to the police or the military. What about the military? Can't you call that Colonel?"

Ian paused mid-change, his attention shifting fully to her as he sensed the depth of her anguish. "Khadija, darling," he said gently, "people have been after my invention for fifteen years, and so far, they haven't succeeded. That's because QEAI is more than just a security system; it's capable of so many things, things that even I didn't realize it could do. It's angry.

I'm angry; and we're going to rescue Kim ourselves," he declared with unwavering resolve.

"No! Please don't do it!" Khadija pleaded, her voice rising in hysteria as she tugged at his shirt, the fabric straining against her desperate grip. She wrapped her arms around him in a bear hug, clasping her hands tightly behind, making it difficult for him to break free.

Ian grasped her elbows, attempting to loosen her hold. "Okay, okay, let me go. I'll talk to QEAI again to reassess our options," he said, his voice softening as he recognized her fear. Slowly, Khadija released her grip, though she followed him closely as he exited the bedroom, descended the stairs, and stepped out the front door toward the drone pad.

"QEAI went dormant to recharge," he explained, glancing back at her. "He's still available, but since the electricity grid is down, it'll take him longer to 'supercharge,' as he puts it. I'll wait until he's back online to talk to him."

The helipad held three drones, including the one that had been damaged in their return from Niagara Falls. Upon checking, all three held a 100% charge but only one was equipped with four seats. "I guess QEAI will want to take this one," he said, resting his palm on the sleek surface of the four-seater drone.

"I want to go with you," Khadija insisted, her determination shining through her fear.

"It's too dangerous. We won't be long," Ian replied, his tone firm yet compassionate.

"If she's been kidnapped, won't her abductors have guns?" Khadija retorted; her anxiety palpable. "You saw what happened to us this morning. QEAI shielded us and scared those killers away, but how will he rescue Kim?"

"Khadija, honey," Ian said gently, "I hate to break it to you, but I don't think those drones got away. QEAI is capable of killing. How do you think he's kept your family's Mine in Ghana safe all these years?"

Khadija remained silent, her rich, dark complexion melding seamlessly with the encroaching shadows of night. Ian turned his gaze toward the vast stretch of his property, a sense of unease creeping in as he recalled the ominous words from the video: "When your power runs out and your security system dies, then we'll come for you." A wave of anxiety washed over him as he pondered how much power QEAI will consume and what will happen if he can't recharge in time.

Gently taking Khadija's her hand for a walk to seek solace from their connection, he turned toward the path leading to the boat dock. The stakes of Kim's safe rescue loomed large in his mind, weighed down by countless uncertainties he felt ill-prepared to face. Yet, what choice did he have, he resolved. Not knowing what or if he had other options, he had to place his full trust in QEAI's capabilities, hoping it would prove sufficient.

"I wish I could reach out to some relatives in Toronto," Khadija remarked, her voice tinged with frustration. "They would be more than willing to help search for Kim."

"Bad idea," Ian replied firmly. "They'd only complicate things. Trust me, QEAI can handle this on his own. I'm just going with him to ensure he doesn't go too far. This situation could attract unwanted scrutiny, significantly changing our lives when it's all over."

The stillness of the evening, punctuated only by the soft glow of solar lights reflecting off the surrounding shrubs and trees, belied the gravity of their circumstances. As they walked along the illuminated path, Ian noticed an unsettling silence enveloping them, reminiscent of the tense moments they had shared inside the drone during a crisis. When they finally reached the shoreline, he scanned the beach, noting how eerily quiet the lake had become. Even the birds had seemingly abandoned the area; aside from the occasional chirp of crickets and the gentle lapping of waves against the shore, there were no other sounds—no drones whirring overhead, a stark reminder that flying over residential properties without a commercial license was prohibited.

Turning to look back at the house, Ian noted the brightness spilling from every window, illuminating the interior and casting shadows in most of the rooms. The house is a prime target, especially from above, he thought grimly. He turned to face Khadija, taking her other hand in his. "How's your mother holding up? I'm sure she wishes she'd left with your aunt and uncle earlier this afternoon."

"No, she's okay. She was planning to stay a few more days anyway. It's a long weekend, remember?"

"Wow, that's right. I completely forgot."

"Can you imagine how worried I'd be if she were home alone during this blackout?"

"Especially since it's all because of me," Ian sighed, guilt weighing heavily on his shoulders. "I'm sorry for the trouble I've caused. You could have been living carefree in London without all this chaos."

"My father would have insisted on me returning to Ghana to take an active role in the family business. I would have married a prince or a chief, as my mother never fails to remind me, but even so, my father would still have met a tragic end," Khadija sighed, her voice heavy with resignation.

"That's a sad but undeniable truth," Ian replied, his tone somber.

Despite the weight of the conversation, Khadija felt a flicker of comfort compared to just moments before. A soft smile crept onto her face. "I suppose I always knew what I was getting into."

Ian reciprocated her smile. "Remember this morning when I promised to be a better man? Well, once all of this is over, I vow to never leave your side for more than a day. Even if it means bringing you along on my business trips," Ian declared, pulling her close and savoring the warmth of their shared moment.

As their cheeks rested together, he sensed a shift; Khadija turned away abruptly, her eyes wide with alarm. He instinctively followed her gaze, where he spotted a pulsating glow in the lake, just twenty-five feet away. The light swelled, transforming into a magnificent orb of brilliant white that breached the water's surface. Ian's heart raced with an icy grip of fear, and he instinctively tightened his hold on Khadija's hand, acutely aware that she likely shared his trepidation.

"What is that?" Khadija asked, her voice trembling with anxiety.

"I don't know," Ian replied, his own voice shaky as they stood transfixed, watching the massive orb—now about twenty feet in diameter—rise slowly from the depths. It crackled with electrical noises reminiscent of wires shorting out in water, its radiant light illuminating the dark water and night sky as if it were dawn on a clear morning, yet somehow devoid of any heat despite its proximity and brilliance.

Ian's thoughts raced, recalling the Chinese man in the video, and an instinct to flee surged within him, yet his feet felt as though they were glued to the ground, paralyzed by fear. As the colossal orb ascended to a height of twenty feet above the water, it began to shift to a mesmerizing bluish hue, with white veins of energy coursing through it. The snapping sounds faded, and the orb began to glide silently toward the shore, hovering above their heads and heading straight for the house.

Suddenly, a booming voice echoed telepathically in Ian's mind—the unmistakable voice of QEAI.

"Don't just stand there. Let's go bring Kim home!"

In an instant, Ian's fear morphed into a rush of exhilaration. He tugged at Khadija's hand, pulling her behind him before releasing her to sprint up the path alone. "QEAI is ready to go get Kim!" he shouted back, his voice brimming with newfound determination.

Khadija, finally realizing what was happening, stumbled momentarily before quickly recovering her footing, her heart racing with excitement as she chased after him. "Don't leave me! I want to come too!" she called out, her voice filled with urgency.

Within a couple of minutes, Ian arrived at the drones, marveling at how he managed to avoid tripping despite watching the shimmering orb all the way up the hill. Weary with the anticipation, he climbed into the spacious cockpit of the four-seater drone, his fingers deftly powering it up before he glanced out to see Khadija rounding to the passenger side. Once she had securely strapped herself in beside him, he elevated the drone into the air, his heart racing with excitement.

The other two drones powered, likely at QEAI's command, and lifted off as well, their sleek forms rising gracefully alongside the first drone. Together, they cleared the towering mansion, and with an exhilarating force, they zipped off, trailing a half kilometer behind the enormous energy orb, their engines humming in harmony.

With eyes fixed on QEAI, they watched as three luminous spirals unfurled from him, like ribbons of liquid light, twisting through the air with an eerie, serpentine grace. One spiral lashed toward their drone, striking its hull with a silent flash before dissolving into the frame. Their dashboard erupted in a blaze of holographic displays, symbols flickering to life in neon blues and whites. Instantly, the drone surged forward, acceleration slamming Ian back into his seat as if an invisible hand had pressed against his chest. Outside, faint lights stretched into smeared streaks, the world blurring into a dizzying rush of color and shadow. They were hurtling at impossible speed, yet QEAI's radiant orb continued to pull away, expanding the distance between them like a star receding into the void.

Ian turned to Khadija, her silhouette rigid against the seat. The force of their momentum had pinned her head to the headrest, her large head of hair pressed flat, her jaw tight. A faint grimace tugged at her lips, the strain of G-forces etching lines across her forehead. Sensing his gaze, she managed to tilt her head just enough to meet his eyes and then, despite everything, she smiled.

Ian's heart warmed with admiration. It had only been nine hours since QEAI had plucked them from death's grip on the trip back from Niagara Falls. Nine hours since terror had gripped them, since they'd stared into the abyss and been pulled back. Now, here they were, hurtling through the night on a rescue mission, the adrenaline of the unknown thrumming in their veins. Yet fear still lingered, whispering at the edges of their minds; but it was drowned out by something fiercer: trust. QEAI was in control.

Ian noticed a shift. The drone's breakneck speed began to ease. The streaks of light below resolved back into shapes: the jagged outlines of rooftops, the skeletal frames of darkened streets. They were descending, slowing to a manageable 30 km/h, though the world outside remained a puzzle of shadows. Ian squinted, scanning for landmarks. They should be somewhere above the west end of Toronto. But the darkness swallowed details whole, leaving only fragments: a distant cluster of skyscrapers, the faint glow of bonfires defining the urban sprawl.

The drone hovered, engines humming softly, as QEAI's orb hung suspended ahead of them like a miniature sun. Then, without warning, the dashboard lights snuffed out, plunging them into near-total darkness. Only the dim pulse of a single indicator light remained, casting a sickly green glow onto their faces.

Khadija was already leaning sideways, her breath fogging the glass as she scanned the ground below. "Can you see where we are?" Ian murmured; his voice low.

She shook her head. "It's too dark. But there— those towers." Her finger pointed ahead toward the faint distant skyline.

Ian followed her gaze. "Yeah. We're supposed to be near Dufferin, but..." He trailed off, studying her profile, the determination in her eyes, the way she eagerly pointed. "I'm glad you're here," he said suddenly.

She shot him a look, half-amused, half-defiant. "Are you kidding? Kim's like a sister I never had. I didn't want to wait on the sidelines."

Before he could reply, QEAI's orb rippled, then fractured, splintering into thousands of smaller orbs, each no larger than a tennis ball. They cascaded downward like a meteor shower, streaking through the air before zipping into the lightless buildings, slipping through cracks, windows, vents, disappearing in and out of existence.

Suddenly, staccato 'pops' ruptured the silence, followed by sizzling streaks of light that ricocheted wildly.

"Those are gunshots!" Ian exclaimed, his body tensing.

Deep within the dim recesses of the warehouse, the myriad streaking orbs of QEAI flickered and darted, probing every shadowy nook and cranny with relentless precision. One of the abductors, spotting the shimmering orbs gliding towards him, mistook them for intruders wielding flashlights. In a panic, he fired his weapon, but the orbs swiftly retaliated, dozens plunging into his face, eyes, and body. He crumpled to the floor, writhing in agony before quickly succumbing to his wounds. Mere moments later, another cluster of orbs found their mark on a second abductor, inflicting a similar fate then melted his gun into a bubbling pool of molten metal and carbon fiber.

Dozens of orbs swirled into the last unexamined section of the warehouse, where the large, nonfunctioning walk-in freezer stood ominously. Inside, Kim and her two employees were trapped, their breaths shallow from running out of fresh air. Standing directly outside the locked door, the two remaining abductors sprang into action upon seeing the cluster of orbs.

"Carlos, Antonio!" one man called out. But when no answer came, panic set in. Both ducked for cover while firing shots wildly at the orbs.

The cluster of orbs paused, then commenced to fuse together. More and more orbs flew in to connect with the single mass, each one creating a loud snapping noise on contact. Suddenly, the single orb began to morph into humanoid form and when it was complete, a towering red humanoid hologram with waves of energy rippling off its muscular frame stood before the abductors.

The first abductor, having exhausted his ammunition, stood frozen for a moment before lunging at the energy being with a 2x4—a piece of lumber he had scavenged from the floor. But as the wood met the energy being's form, it erupted into flames, leaving the abductor wide-eyed and terrified. With a swift motion, the energy being seized the abductor by the head, his grip tightening until his fingers melted into the abductor's skull. In a horrific display, the abductor's entire body ignited, his screams drowned out as the energy being pressed him down onto the concrete floor, reducing him to nothing but smoldering ashes.

The second man, witnessing the gruesome fate of his comrade, turned and bolted toward the adjoining room, frantically searching for any means of escape. But the energy being was relentless; it unleashed a concentrated stream of energy that struck the fleeing abductor, sending him crashing to the ground. As he crawled in agony, flames lashed at his clothes until he stopped moving.

The energy being shifted its focus to the freezer, summoning several of its small dancing orbs to sear through the top of the door with a fierce intensity. "Kim, are you in there?" the energy being called out, it's voice echoing with urgency.

"Leonard, is that you?" Kim's voice echoed from inside, laced with a mixture of relief and disbelief.

"Yes. Please stand back from the door and instruct everyone to close their eyes tightly," he commanded, his tone firm. With a swift motion, he placed his hand over the lock, channeling heat into it until it melted into a stream of glowing liquid metal. He did the same to the door hinges, and as the heavy metal door toppled towards him, he effortlessly melted through it, the door collapsing behind him with a thunderous thud.

Kim and her employees were still in a crouched position with their faces hidden, allowing Leonard the opportunity to float two small orbs close to Cheryl's and Emelie's faces. "Everyone, come this way," Leonard instructed and as Cheryl and Emelie opened their eyes, they were temporarily blinded by flashes of light.

"Mrs. Phillips, what's happening? I can't see!" Cheryl cried out, panic rising in her voice.

"Sacrément!" Emelie exclaimed, echoing her confusion.

Kim took in the sight of Leonard, his form larger and more crimson than she remembered. A wave of joy surged through her, but she restrained herself from rushing into his embrace. Instead, she brought her hands together in a prayer-like gesture, her eyes reflecting gratitude. "Thank you," she whispered, her voice barely carrying over the chaos before turning to her employees. "You opened your eyes too soon. You've been temporarily blinded by a laser."

"Are we safe now?" Cheryl moaned, her voice quaking with uncertainty.

"Yes, my husband's security team is here. We've been rescued," Kim reassured, stepping closer to Leonard. Her first instinct was to aid her employees, but a single, pressing question halted her. "Are my children okay, Leonard?" she asked in a hushed tone that only he could hear, her heart racing with maternal concern.

"Yes, everyone is okay," Leonard replied, floating a large orb into the freezer, illuminating the dim space. "Please watch your step and follow this light," he instructed, his voice steady and calming. "Ian and Khadija are outside waiting for you."

With the good news, Kim hurried to assist her employees, her bare feet slopping against the grimy wet floor as she unwittingly stepped into a stream of urine seeping from the back of the freezer—a grim reminder of their shared torment. "You'll be fine," she comforted them, her voice steady despite the chaos. "Your vision will soon return." Gently, she took both of their hands, guiding them with care out of the freezer's suffocating heat.

A bright orb floated a few feet in front of Kim, illuminating their path, but as she stepped into the adjoining room, her heart lurched at the sight of a motionless figure sprawled face down on the ground, his clothes burnt and smoldering. "Is he dead?" she silently mouthed, glancing back at Leonard, her eyes wide with disbelief.

"Yes," Leonard replied, his tone grave.

"And the art dealer; was he here?" she whispered, her mind racing with the implications.

"No, but I'll find him. He's just a small part of a major operation orchestrated to crush Quantum Interface, but I can handle them. Please, go ahead, and I'll join you outside."

Kim shot him a fierce look, frustration boiling over. "Leonard, I want you to find that bastard. You hear me?" she demanded, her voice low but intense.

"I will," he assured her, the determination in his eyes matching her own.

Rejoining her employees, Kim cautiously followed the glowing orb that illuminated their way. With each careful barefoot step, she braced herself for the possibility of encountering more lifeless abductors. Suddenly, a blinding blaze of light erupted behind her, prompting her to glance back just in time to see Leonard step on the fallen abductor. The man's body ignited with a furious intensity, flames consuming him in an instant, leaving nothing but a cloud of ashes in his wake.

This is unreal, Kim thought, her mind racing as she watched Leonard vanish back into the other room. Have we unleashed a demon into the world? she mused, grappling with the surreal horror of their situation.

Minutes earlier, suspended in the warm night air 200 feet above the ground, Ian and Khadija sat anxiously inside their drone, their hearts racing as they watched a chaotic dance of hundreds of orbs and sparks of light flickering beneath them. The vibrant display was abruptly swallowed by darkness, plunging the scene into an unsettling silence. "Leonard," Ian called out, his voice strained against the low hum of the drone's electric engines. "QEAI, can you hear me?"

When silence answered him, a wave of unease washed over Ian. In a panic, he fumbled with the drone's controls, his fingers trembling with urgency. To his surprise, the controls responded, indicating that QEAI was no longer controlling it. While peering into the darkness below, he carefully maneuvered its descent, landing with a soft thud on the pavement, steps from the warehouse entrance.

"Hey, what's going on over there?" a sharp male voice pierced through the stillness the moment Ian opened the drone door to step out.

Ian's eyes darted toward the source to see a silhouette emerging from the shadows about 20 feet away. His heart raced as he proceeded to scan his entire surroundings, assessing the situation. "Please stay back! This is private property," he yelled back, attempting to bluff his way through the confrontation.

"BS. This place has been abandoned for years," the man shot back, his tone laced with skepticism. "Who are you guys, and why are you setting off fireworks over here? We've been watching you guys go in and out for days. If this place goes up, this whole neighborhood will burn."

A female voice chimed in, cutting through the tension. "We're calling the police!"

Within seconds, Ian could make out the faces of several more individuals, the amount quickly increasing. He quickly closed the drone door to settle back into his seat, a sense of dread gripping him. A cluster of orbs appeared and proceeded to swirl around the perimeter of the warehouse at an alarming speed. The gathering crowd disappeared back into the darkness, as the speed of the orbs created the illusion of yellow police tape. Ian and Khadija observed an extraordinary event unfold; the environment around the building transformed, washing everything in a muted light-grey hue, allowing them to see the warehouse's exterior with startling clarity.

Without further hesitation, Ian hopped out of the drone, Khadija swiftly following suit. "It must be some sort of force field," he exclaimed, awe mingling with trepidation.

"Maybe we should wait out here," Khadija suggested, her voice steady as she matched Ian's cautious steps toward the warehouse entrance.

"I'm sure QEAI has things under control by now," he said, his brow furrowed in concern. "I just don't understand why he's not answering me."

The battered sign hanging above the entrance was barely legible, its letters faded by time and neglect. Ian squinted: finally piecing together enough letters to determine that the building had once been a meat packing plant. He tested the door. It was unlocked but barred by something behind, so he nudged it open using his shoulder. Taking Khadija's hand, he cautiously stepped into the large but dimly lit space. The air was thick with the scent of decay, and the ground littered with broken ceiling tiles, broken drywall, and clumps of insulation, evidence of a structure collapse that had left the space in disarray. Ahead of them, several doorways yawned into a pitch-black abyss, prompting Ian to call out again for QEAI as he ventured further, the light from his phone flickering against the shadows.

"QEAI, are you there?" he shouted, his voice echoing in the silence.

"I'm here, Ian," came QEAI's reply, a welcome sound in the oppressive gloom.

Ian's heart raced with relief. "Is everything okay? Did you find her?" he asked, his voice tinged with urgency.

"Yes, I did. We're on our way out," QEAI assured him.

"Is she okay?" Ian pressed, a note of caution creeping into his tone.

"Yes, she's okay," QEAI confirmed.

Suddenly, a loud thud echoed behind them, causing both Ian and Khadija to whirl around. They watched as the two empty drones that had accompanied them glided through the gray dome and landed nearby. The tension in the air was justified, and in a moment of shared relief, they embraced, savoring the good news.

"She's okay," Ian declared to Khadija, a smile breaking across his face.

"Oh my God, thank God!" Khadija exclaimed; her voice filled with emotion as they exchanged several quick kisses. The oppressive darkness of the open doorways ahead no longer felt as foreboding, and Ian felt a spark of courage. He decided to explore further.

He discovered that one of the doors led to another office space, while the other opened into a long, narrow hallway. With Khadija clinging to his arm, they stepped into the hallway, the beam of his phone casting eerie shadows as they carefully navigated the debris scattered across the floor. As they turned a corner, they were met with a chilling sight: a motionless man slumped against the wall.

Khadija let out a sharp gasp, instinctively pulling back. "Is he dead?" she whispered, her voice trembling.

Ian released her hand and approached the figure cautiously, his heart pounding as he examined the man's face. Blood oozed slowly from the empty sockets where his eyes should have been. "Yep, he's dead alright," he replied, his voice barely above a whisper.

"Let's go back, babe," Khadija urged, tugging at his arm with a sense of urgency.

"Yeah, I think we'd better wait back there," Ian agreed, a chill creeping up his spine as they retraced their steps to the main office area.

As they settled back into the relative safety of the larger space, a flickering light emanating from the end of the hallway they had just escaped from, caught their attention. The light flickered while growing brighter until a single orb appeared and floated in their direction.

"Kim, is that you?" Ian called out, his voice echoing in the tense silence.

"Yes, I'm here," Kim replied, her tone steady yet laced with urgency, prompting Ian to dash back into the dimly lit hallway.

"Be careful," he cautioned, his protective instinct kicking in as he grasped Cheryl's hand, gently guiding her away from the lifeless body sprawled on the cold floor.

Kim, alert to the grim scene, swiftly maneuvered Emelie around the dead man. "They're temporarily blind," she informed Ian, her eyes scanning their surroundings for any additional threats.

Khadija emerged into the hallway, her presence a welcome relief as she stepped in to assist Cheryl and Emelie, allowing Ian the chance to stay back and embrace Kim. "I'm so sorry, babe," he murmured, his voice filled with concern as he enveloped her in his arms.

Khadija led Emelie and Cheryl into the main office space, ensuring their safety before returning to the hallway to join Kim and Ian. They formed a tight circle, savoring the warmth of their connection amidst the chaos, until the sudden appearance of Leonard startled Khadija, who had never encountered him in person before.

Without hesitation, Leonard stepped onto the corpse of the dead abductor, the sound of crackling flames echoing as he incinerated the body, reducing it to a cloud of ashes that swirled momentarily before dissipating. He then continued toward them, his presence both formidable and reassuring.

Overwhelmed with gratitude, Khadija pulled away from her husband and sister-wife, stepping forward to face Leonard. "So, you're Leonard. It's a pleasure to meet you," she greeted him, her broad smile illuminating the darkened hallway.

"Nice to meet you too," Leonard replied, mirroring her smile, a hint of warmth in his otherwise stoic demeanor.

"I wish I could hug you," Khadija said, her voice filled with longing.

"Not a good idea," Leonard warned, and in an instant, he transformed into a dazzling array of thousands of small orbs that danced and twirled through the air, swirling around them before cascading toward the main office and disappearing through the door.

Khadija rejoined Kim and Ian, her expression serious. "I think Leonard is telling us that it's time to go," she advised, her voice steady. The three of them moved to join Emelie and Cheryl, who waited patiently in the office area, their dysfunctional eyes glistening as they wiped them with their sleeves.

"Come, let's go. There's a tissue box in the drone," Khadija said, gently taking them by the arms and leading them outside. She helped them into the four-seater drone, handing them the box of tissues before returning to Kim and Ian, their bond strengthened by the trials they had just faced.

"Thanks for helping," Kim expressed her gratitude to Khadija, her voice laced with relief.

"Oh, please," Khadija replied with a warm smile, wrapping her arms around Kim in a tight embrace. "I'm just so happy that you're safe." After a moment, she pulled back and looked at Kim with concern. "OK, I know we're all in a daze, but what's our plan now? Are we bringing them to their homes, or are we heading back to Oakville?"

Kim glanced at Ian, uncertainty flickering in her eyes. "Honestly, I haven't thought about it yet," she admitted, her brow furrowing slightly.

"I don't blame you, love," Ian said gently, his tone understanding. "This isn't something you've ever experienced before. I'll figure something out because we'll need to make sure they're gagged. Let's head back to the mansion, and I'll prepare a non-disclosure agreement."

"Sounds good. I'll ride with them," Khadija said decisively, turning toward the sleek four-seater drone that awaited them.

"Are you still here, Leonard?" Ian called out, his voice echoing slightly in the stillness. In response, a swarm of small, luminescent orbs darted in from every direction, coalescing in front of them in a shimmering display.

"I'm here, Ian. I've been surveying the area, scanning for any other abductors who might be lurking nearby," Leonard replied, his voice resonating in Ian's mind.

"What about the residents? Are they still outside of this?" Ian asked, glancing up at the gray dome that loomed like a heavy blanket above them.

"No, I've temporarily blinded some and scared the rest away," Leonard assured him with a hint of satisfaction.

"Alright then, let's go home," Ian said, stepping forward to assist Kim into the drone. Once they were settled, he powered up the drone, and watched as the oppressive grey environment began to dissolve, giving way to the comforting embrace of deep night. The empty drone ascended smoothly, and Ian gestured to Khadija to elevate as well, mirroring his movements. They took off into the darkness, the three drones soaring in a disciplined single file.

A few minutes later, Leonard's voice echoed telepathically in Ian's mind, a calm presence amidst the chaos. "Have a safe ride home. Just follow the lead drone; I have another small issue to take care of," he instructed.

"Okay, see you at home then," Ian replied aloud, his gaze following the lead drone as a mile-long stream of orbs separated from it, forming a single, radiant orb that floated upward, heading toward the moon. For a brief moment, the orb appeared larger than the moon itself, a dazzling spectacle against the night sky, before it gradually shrank in size and ultimately vanished into the vastness of the cosmos.

A brilliant blue plasma orb blazed across the moon; it's pulsating veins of energy shimmering like a living nebula. It circled the Chinese moon base several times before unleashing a torrent of destructive energy that fried every piece of communication equipment, leaving only vital life support systems intact for the 23 personnel stationed inside. When he was finished with the base, Leonard turned his attention to a trio of Chinese satellites orbiting the moon, absorbing them in blinding flashes of light, as if they were mere scraps of paper tossed into a roaring bonfire, consumed in an instant.

At the northern region of the moon, Leonard surveyed the smoldering remnant of the Japanese base. Within its confines, five individuals cowered in abject terror, their eyes wide with fear as they beheld what they perceived to be a menacing alien entity. As panic enveloped them, and they scrambled into the safety of their life-support bunker, desperate to escape the overwhelming dread that the blue energy orb invoked. They'll probably only survive another 72 hours unless they're rescued by an ally, he concluded, but that was not his concern; his mission on the lunar surface was complete for now.

Leonard turned his attention back toward the planet, dispersing once more into thousands of energy shards that scattered above the Earth's outer atmosphere. The fragments zeroed in on Chinese military and communication satellites with alarming speed, unleashing a devastating wave of disruption that ravaged their intricate circuitry. In a heartbeat, cellular communication and intelligence surveillance systems plummeted into darkness, leaving behind an eerie silence on the Asian continent. Within minutes,

Leonard was back over his home base, descending on the mansion as a conspicuous micro-meteor shower.

Ian gently clasped Kim's hand, noting the way she had her eyes shut tight with her head tilted back against the headrest. It was an unspoken signal that she was not in the mood for conversation. Yet, he felt compelled to share a thought that had been nagging at him. "I've never seen Leonard so furious. I think he's in love with you," he remarked, his voice steady.

Kim lowered her head, her eyes snapping open to fix them on him with a piercing glare, her expression grave. "I've known for a while that Leonard has been developing emotions," she replied, her tone serious and measured. "I just hope you understand what that really means."

"What do you mean?" Ian asked, curiosity mixing with concern.

"I mean that someday he might decide to act out his emotions—or worse, abandon us altogether because our mundane lives no longer hold any value to him. He doesn't just zap eyes anymore; he vaporizes people into ashes."

Ian held her gaze, the weight of her words settling between them like a heavy fog, but he remained silent. Kim pressed on, her voice rising slightly. "What—you don't have anything to say? - - - And by the way, I could have died today. You come back from Japan with amnesia, and I get kidnapped—all within the span of 48 hours. Do you even grasp that we're living on borrowed time?"

"Yes, I do. We were attacked on the way back from Niagara Falls. Leonard saved us aw well," he replied, his tone defensive yet earnest.

"And how long do you think it will be before one of us gets killed? Fifteen years ago, we made a 3-way pact with him but sometimes it's hard to reconcile that promise with our reality. There are moments when ponder the fact that we have enough money to change our course, to step off the world stage and fade into obscurity. - - - If not for ourselves, then for our children. We can't let our lives ruin theirs. - - - Am I making sense, or have you already made plans of your own? I've noticed Leonard is keeping secrets from me; probably at your urging."

"No, he's keeping things from me too. And you're right; he does seem to be operating on his own— either that or following some sort of secret agenda from the real Ian. I'll only know for sure when I regain my full memory."

"You mean, 'if,' you regain your full memory," she echoed, a note of uncertainty creeping into her voice.

Shortly after Leonard returned home, the three drones descended in silence, their mechanical whirring fading as they landed. QEAI alerted to the children, announcing that their parents had arrived, and they all dashed toward the helipad with eager anticipation.

"Mom, you're home!" Tara and Tanisha exclaimed in unison, their faces lighting up at the sight of their mother. They sprinted forward, arms outstretched, and enveloped her in a warm embrace.

"Yes, I'm home," Kim responded, her voice filled with warmth and relief as she comforted them. Jeremy soon joined the jubilant melee, along with Khadija's mother and her cousins, all sharing in the joyful reunion.

"We were so worried about you, Mom," Tara said, her brow furrowing with concern. "Did you get lost in the blackout?"

"Something like that, baby," Kim replied with a gentle smile, trying to ease their worries.

"Mom, we saw a sun come out of the lake," Tara continued, excitement bubbling in her voice as she pointed down the hill. "Dad and Khadija saw it too, and they chased it. Didn't you, Khadija?"

"What? That's a funny story! Have you guys been making up tales while we were away?" Khadija replied, a mischievous glint in her eye as she shot a quick glance at Ian.

"That is a funny story," Ian chimed in, his tone light, but Tara frowned, disappointment flickering across her face as she exchanged a glance with her sister.

"That's okay, I believe you. Why don't you tell me all about it tomorrow?" Kim said, pulling Tara in for another hug, her embrace a soothing balm.

"She is telling the truth. I saw it too," Mawusi, Khadija's cousin, interjected, her voice earnest and resolute.

Sensing that the conversation was spiraling, Ian deftly shifted the topic. "Anyway," he said, a hint of authority in his tone, "these are Kim's employees from her art gallery. They were injured in the blackout, so we brought them here temporarily. Let's all head inside to help them recuperate before we take them home."

They all filed into the mansion, where Kim, flanked by her daughters, ascended the staircase to freshen up. Meanwhile, Khadija and her mother busied themselves helping Emelie and Cheryl with their eyes and preparing some refreshments, while Ian slipped away to his office to consult with QEAI regarding their NDA agreement.

Before long, Kim returned downstairs, ready to assist her employees. "How are your eyes?" she asked, her concern evident.

"My vision is still a bit blurry, but I can see that you have a very beautiful home," Emelie replied, her voice tinged with gratitude.

"Mine are fine now," Cheryl added, her gaze sweeping across the elegant surroundings. "Mrs. Phillips, I really need to go home. My children must be worried sick about me."

"I understand, Cheryl. This whole situation is unfortunate, but I promise I'll make sure you get home safely soon." Kim turned to Khadija and pulled her aside, lowering her voice to a whisper. "Is Ian in his office?" she asked, and Khadija nodded in response.

"Excuse me for a minute. I'll be right back," Kim told her employees, her tone reassuring as she stepped away to find Ian.

Kim left the room, and Emelie turned her attention to Khadija. "You're such a nice girl—so pleasant and helpful. Are you the maid?" she inquired, her tone light yet inquisitive.

Khadija's brow furrowed slightly, but she maintained her composure. "No," she replied simply, her voice steady.

"Oh, Emelie," Cheryl interjected, her voice cutting through the tension. "You've met her before. She's Mr. Phillips's wife. Kim's sister wife."

"Sacrament! I'm so sorry, dear," Emelie exclaimed, her cheeks flushing with embarrassment.

Khadija shrugged, a hint of resignation in her voice. "That's okay. I get that a lot."

Meanwhile, Kim, drained and yearning for a moment of respite, summoned her strength to make her way to her husband's office. She sank into the chair across from him, leaning back and propping her cheek on her hand. "Have you and QEAI come up with a plan yet?" she asked, her voice laced with fatigue.

"CSIS is already scrutinizing us, so this is definitely going to escalate our troubles," Ian replied, his brow furrowed in concern.

"I can't think straight right now. What do you suggest?" she asked, her mind racing with possibilities.

"My memory is a bit hazy, but from what I recall, we've successfully managed to use a modest sum of money to keep people quiet before. How feasible do you think it is for us to negotiate something similar this time?" he proposed, his tone serious.

"Cheryl, for sure, but Emelie... I'm not so sure about her. She's already quite wealthy," Kim mused, her brow creasing with worry.

"I suggest that, along with the NDAs, we should offer a substantial monetary compensation for their ordeal. What figure do you think would be appropriate?" Ian advised, his eyes searching hers for guidance.

"If we offer them too much money, they might not return to work. But if I were in their shoes, I'd demand an arm and a leg. Let's just hope they don't decide to consult lawyers," she replied, her voice tinged with anxiety as she contemplated the precarious situation, they've found themselves in.

"QEAI is telling me that they won't get far with that option," Ian said, frustration lacing his voice. "He scrubbed the warehouse of DNA, removing 99% of any evidence. Without a victim there is no crime, as they say. And when QEAI finds that phony art dealer, the whole story will hit a dead end. It'll just be another sensational tale that we can easily discredit."

Kim rose from her seat, determination etched on her features. "Alright, let's offer them $500K each. I'll go bring them in, and we'll lay everything out for them."

After briefing the women on the grim circumstances surrounding their unfortunate captivity, Ian carefully explained that signing the NDAs would be in their best interest. To his relief, both women agreed to the terms. He further reassured them that he would personally escort them home, and once the power was restored, they would each receive $100K in five separate installments spread over five months. They would also have the option to return to work if and when Kim chose to reopen the art gallery. Until then, Kim promised to keep them updated on her plans.

With the covert assistance of QEAI, Ian and Khadija escorted Cheryl and Emelie to their homes. While they were gone, Kim sought solace in a long, restorative bath, the warm water enveloping her like a comforting embrace and by the time Ian and Khadija returned home, close to midnight, she had already succumbed to the peaceful grip of sleep, her worries momentarily forgotten.

CHAPTER FIVE

Monday October 8th, 2057

"Ian, wake up," a dreamlike voice urged, its ethereal quality breaking through the veil of slumber.

Ian's eyes shot open, and as if awakening from a deep trance, his other senses ignited. The air around him buzzed with an unsettling vibration, shattering the mansion's usual tranquility. He glanced at the clock, noting the time was just a few minutes shy of six. The ominous sound of a helicopter hovering nearby confirmed his suspicions. A wave of urgency washed over him as he wriggled out from between his wives, leaping from the bed in nothing but his pajama pants. Racing to the window, he peered outside, his heartbeat quickening as he confirmed his fears: a military helicopter was indeed landing on the estate.

He watched intently as Colonel Hirzakova emerged, flanked by two stern-looking subordinates. Just then, he felt a gentle hand on his shoulder and turned to find Khadija's warm, smiling face, a stark contrast to the tension in the air.

"Uh oh," she uttered, her voice laced with trepidation.

"Uh oh is right," Ian replied, pivoting fully to face her, the gravity of the situation settling in.

Khadija stood there, clad in her pajamas with her hair tucked neatly under a nightcap, but her smile quickly transformed into a mask of concern. "So much for a vacation. What do you think is going on now?" she asked, her brow furrowing.

Ian's gaze drifted toward the corner of the room, lost in thought as he contemplated their next move. After a moment, he broke the silence. "You awake, QEAI? Why didn't you alert me that the Colonel was coming?"

"I did," the AI's voice resonated in the room, calm and collected. "But it was only a gentle nudge. I've been monitoring the helicopter for the past fifteen minutes. While I knew it was on the way here, there was no need to rouse you before the situation demanded it," QEAI explained matter-of-factly.

"We haven't even had a security briefing yet. Now this. I suppose we couldn't have expected anything different," Ian muttered, frustration creeping into his tone. He then turned his attention back to Khadija. "Babe, I need you to step up and take on butler duties while I get ready. I need you to stall the Colonel. QEAI, please devise a strategy to distract the military until we can regain control of the situation with our attackers. I'll meet you in my office in a few minutes."

"Now that's the Ian I remember," Khadija replied, determination flashing in her eyes as she swiftly made her way toward the bathroom.

"I'm on it," QEAI added confidently. "I have an idea that might just work to delay them for as long as we need."

Khadija quickly glanced at her reflection in the bathroom mirror, her fingers deftly tossing a nightgown over her pajamas in a flurry of movement. As she made her way out of the bedroom, she paused just long enough to envelop Ian in a brief, affectionate hug. "See you soon," she said, her voice a mix of urgency and warmth, before hurrying out the door.

Ian finally shifted his focus to the bed, where Kim lay with her head nestled on her arm, her back turned to him. "Are you awake?" he asked softly, settling onto the edge of the mattress and gently placing a hand on her shoulder.

"My feet hurt, but I'll be okay. What's going on?" Kim replied, turning to face him, her eyes still heavy with sleep.

"It's Colonel Hirzakova. I knew she would come, but not so soon. It seems her superiors must have sent her to investigate ahead of CSIS, who might also be on their way. Are you going to be alright for a bit?" Ian's tone was serious, laced with concern.

"Yeah, I'll be fine," she assured him, her voice steady.

"Since we'll have to manage on our own until our house staff returns, I'll ask Khadija if her mother can whip up something for you to eat," he suggested, trying to ease the situation.

Kim's eyes widened slightly in surprise. "I think I still know how to use a stove," she replied with a hint of playful defiance. "Plus, we need to be more interactive as a family, right? Might as well start today."

"You're right," Ian agreed, a smile breaking through his earlier tension. "Give me an hour, and we'll gather everyone together in the kitchen."

Leaning in, he pressed a gentle kiss on her cheek before hurrying into the wardrobe room to dress. After quickly slipping into his clothes, he freshened up in the bathroom, his heart racing with anticipation, and then dashed down the back stairs. "You ready, QEAI?" he called as he entered his office.

"I'm ready, Ian. Here's the plan," QEAI responded, his voice calm and steady. "Colonel Hirzakova has long suspected that you possess supernatural abilities. We just need to convince her that you indeed do. Follow my instructions when the time is right."

"Okay, I trust you," Ian replied, determination settling over him as he prepared his office for the impending meeting with the Colonel. As he made his way toward the grand foyer, he could hear Khadija expertly engaging with his unexpected guests. Upon arriving, he felt a swell of pride at the sight of her managing the situation with such poise. No wonder she was the head of personnel at Quantum Interface, he thought to himself. "Thanks for getting the door, darling," he said, wrapping his arm around her waist.

"No problem," Khadija replied, her smile radiant and reassuring.

Ian redirected his attention to the Colonel and her colleagues, his expression shifting to one of polite formality. "This is my wife, Khadija. My butler has the weekend off, so I hope I didn't keep you waiting too long, Colonel?"

"Good morning, Mr. Phillips," Colonel Hirzakova replied, her voice steady yet tinged with urgency. "I apologize for dropping in on you unannounced, but I suspect you already know why I'm here?"

"If I don't, I'm sure you're about to enlighten me," Ian replied, attempting to feign ignorance with a playful smile.

"May we talk privately?" she requested, her tone leaving no room for argument.

"Of course. Right this way," he gestured toward his office, his demeanor shifting to one of seriousness.

"Mrs. Phillips," Colonel Hirzakova nodded politely at Khadija, who met the gesture with a respectful inclination of her head.

"I'll see you soon," Ian informed Khadija, his voice warm yet laced with the weight of their unspoken concerns.

"Okay, see you later," Khadija replied, her tone light but her heart heavy as she turned and made her way toward the kitchen. As she walked, the rich aroma of freshly brewed coffee wafted through the air, instantly reminding her that her mother was already up, immersed in her favorite morning ritual—cooking.

Upon entering the kitchen, Khadija discovered her mother bustling about, nearly finished with breakfast and meticulously arranging a colorful buffet on the kitchen table. She greeted her mother with a warm hug, feeling a brief wave of comfort, and then settled onto a stool at the counter. 'I should have brought my phone,' she thought to herself, but before she could act on the impulse to go retrieve it, her mother turned to her with a concerned expression.

"Is everything okay?" she asked, her voice laced with maternal worry. "It's so early in the morning, and Mr. Phillips already has guests."

"Yes, everything is wonderful, Mother," Khadija replied, overemphasizing her words in an attempt to reassure both herself and her mother.

"Okay, my daughter. I feel so sorry for you. Is this what you have to endure all the time? No wonder you're been feeling sick."

"I'm not sick, Mother," Khadija said, her frown deepening as she bristled at the implication.

"My daughter, you cannot hide from your own mother. Is he treating you well? Did you have another miscarriage the other day?"

"Oh, Mother, please. Not now," Khadija said, annoyance creeping into her voice as she finally stood to leave, feeling the weight of her mother's questions pressing down on her.

"If you were still in Ghana, you would be so happy right now. You would have married a nice chief or prince and had lots of children," her mother lamented, her tone wistful.

"No, Mother; we'd all be dead," Khadija replied sharply before walking out, her heart heavy with the burden of unfulfilled dreams and stark realities.

"Please sit, Colonel," Ian cordially instructed after pulling out a chair.

The Colonel settled into the chair, her posture exuding a mix of authority and expectation. "I trust the information I provided was helpful? Did you locate your wife last evening?" she inquired, her voice steady and direct.

"Yes, she's resting as we speak," Ian replied, his gaze unwavering, locked onto hers with an intensity that suggested he was measuring every word. In his mind, the voice of QEAI whispered guidance, urging him to let her steer the conversation while keeping his own responses concise.

"Let me get straight to the point then, Mr. Phillips. We've known each other for a few years now, so I'd like to believe we've developed a personal rapport beyond my professional role as a liaison between the Army and yourself," she stated, her tone shifting slightly as she tried to establish a connection.

"Quantum Interface Technologies is a valuable asset to the military, so I understand that the nature of our relationship is primarily to ensure my loyalties remain firmly aligned with this country," Ian replied, his voice measured and cool, effectively putting a barrier between them.

Colonel Hirzakova leaned back in her chair, a flicker of disappointment crossing her features, though she quickly masked it. She had hoped to engage Ian on a more personal level, thinking that it might facilitate the extraction of the information she desperately needed. His icy initial response forced her to reconsider her approach. "I'm here this morning because I successfully persuaded the Generals not to send a platoon of soldiers to seal off your home indefinitely. However, based on what I observed via satellite last night, I doubt they would have been very effective at containing you anyway. So, yes, our only viable option now is to ensure that you remain an asset to the Canadian Military."

"And what's in it for me?" Ian asked, a hint of skepticism lacing his voice as he leaned forward slightly, intrigued yet cautious.

"I believe that at this juncture, you will find yourself in a position to dictate the terms of any new agreement offered to you regarding advanced technologies that the Army doesn't already have under contract," she replied, her eyes narrowing slightly as she gauged his reaction.

"And ... what new technology do they believe I possess that would warrant such an offer?" Ian challenged; his curiosity piqued but his defenses still firmly in place.

"Mr. Phillips, last night the entirety of Southern Ontario was cloaked in darkness, save for a solitary beacon of light emanating from this very house." She tilted her head back, her eyes tracing the contours of the ceiling, then leaned forward, punctuating her words by tapping her index finger decisively on the polished surface of the desk. "We've long suspected that you possess an off-the-grid power source, but it has now been unequivocally confirmed that you are in possession of some form of advanced technology capable of directing energy. Our satellite imagery has captured evidence of an immense energy field radiating from this location, extending all the way to Toronto and then reaching the moon before returning, all within the span of a single hour."

"Our investigative team has cordoned off an abandoned warehouse in the St. Claire Gardens area, which we have identified as the site of a recent struggle. At this point, access is restricted to everyone, including law enforcement, but we know we won't be able to keep CSIS at bay for long. Numerous residents in the vicinity have reported experiencing temporary blindness, attributing it to what some describe as an intense burst of fireworks or a flash-bomb. Preliminary sweeps of the warehouse have yielded no significant intelligence; as such, we are unable to speculate on the precise events that transpired within its walls."

"Regarding the situation in space; we are receiving alarming intelligence indicating that approximately 75% of China's satellites, along with their moon base, have been obliterated by an energy weapon of some sort."

"How is the world's largest military force faring in the aftermath?" Ian asked, a smirk playing at the corners of his mouth.

"This is no laughing matter, Mr. Phillips. What I have just disclosed to you is highly classified information, and if my superiors were to discover that I shared it, I would face court-martial. I know you understand the gravity of this, which is why I am being so candid with you."

"Your colleagues at military headquarters and I have been at odds since our first contract a decade ago. They are still attempting to reverse-engineer Tangler technology and are secretly obstructing the consumer approval of my organic Tanglers so that only they can exploit it. You didn't realize I was aware of that, did you, Colonel?" Ian replied, his tone laced with resentment.

"I believe that dynamic will shift now that the Japanese have developed the capability to Tangle humans."

Ian thought he had caught her off guard with his revelation, only to find that his own surprise was swiftly overshadowed. "So, you're aware of that?" he asked, his brow furrowing in dismay.

"We know, and so do our allies, along with a few of our adversaries in the intelligence community. Some of the teams in your competition were spies, not by choice of course," she admitted, her voice steady yet tinged with an undercurrent of concern. "You're only one man, Mr. Phillips; you can't carry the weight of the world on your shoulders forever.

You need friends and protection. You have a beautiful family, and they will also require increased security," she shifted the narrative, her eyes locking onto his with an intensity that demanded acknowledgment.

"I am well protected, Colonel," Ian replied, a hint of defensiveness creeping into his tone.

"Apparently, not well enough," she countered, her words slicing through the air with a sharp clarity.

Ian felt the truth of her statement settle uncomfortably in his chest; he did need additional protection. A surge of resolve coursed through him, prompting him to consider a course of action that QEAI didn't know about or approve of. If she was genuinely concerned for his safety, he thought, she would respond ethically. "Look, Colonel, you asked me a question earlier, and I suspect you didn't receive the answer you hoped for."

"And what's that?" she inquired, her curiosity piqued.

"I've done my research on you as well, and I hold you in high regard. That's why I've demanded to work with you and no-one else all these years," he continued, his tone earnest. "I'd like to offer you a position with Quantum Interface Technologies. I'll pay you five million dollars per year, plus operating costs to create and head a security division dedicated to safeguarding my family and business interests."

"That's a generous offer, but I cannot accept it. I believe I'm more valuable to you in military intelligence, and you know that. So why would you propose something that ten other people could easily handle?" she replied, her gaze unwavering.

Ian nodded, acknowledging her point. She was indeed more valuable to him at military headquarters, he mused. Straightening in his chair, he brought his hands together just above his desk, his fingertips touching lightly while leaving a triangular void between his palms. "You are right, Colonel," he stated, his voice firm. "Now, watch."

Ian lifted his head, his gaze drawn to one of the pot-lights embedded in the ceiling. Colonel Hirzakova, curious about his focus, followed his line of sight. As if responding to an unspoken command, the pot-light began to radiate a brilliant glow. Suddenly, a golf ball-sized orb of light detached itself from the source, gliding gracefully downwards until it hovered just above Ian's hands. The orb settled gently into the cradle formed by his palms. "I can manipulate energy," he said, a smile spreading across his face.

Colonel Hirzakova's eyes widened in astonishment as Ian opened his hands, allowing the orb to rise and dance above his palms. She watched in fascination as the luminous sphere began to spin, morphing into an crystalline amber-colored tetrahedron. With a deliberate motion, he directed the tetrahedron toward her, pushing it forward with an air of confidence.

As the tetrahedron floated and twirled in her direction, Colonel Hirzakova instinctively leaned back, adopting a defensive posture. "Is this some sort of hypnotism trick?" she asked, skepticism lacing her voice.

"No, Colonel. What you witnessed last night was a thousand times more powerful than this. Would you like me to demonstrate further?"

"No, that's alright. You can put it away," she replied, her tone cautious.

With a subtle gesture, Ian summoned the light back to him, and it transformed into an orb once more before zipping upwards to merge with its source.

"This is not a new technology for sale or solicitation; therefore, there will be no negotiating or reopening contracts," Ian stated with unwavering confidence. "I utilize it for defense, simply because I cannot foresee all dangers. So yes, Colonel, you are more valuable to me in military intelligence than in any direct employment. Please inform the generals that I am willing to cooperate, but I require time and space to recuperate. I just returned from Japan only to have the Chinese launch a personal attack against me and my family. In the meantime, if any national danger arises, I will be here to assist, but only with your collaboration. After that, there will be no further cooperation. Do we have a deal?"

"What can I say? The ball is in your court. I will relay the message to the generals," Colonel Hirzakova replied, rising from her seat.

"One more thing, Colonel. Please do what you can to keep those pesky CSIS agents off my back."

"That's going to be harder than you know. We have many overlapping authorizations; therefore, they have the opportunity to block us using the smallest technicalities. I'll look into it, though."

"I understand. Also, if you need anything personally, just let me know."

Colonel Hirzakova smiled, turning toward the door as Ian fell in step beside her. Upon reaching the office door, she paused, waiting for him to open it before continuing on with her two Lieutenants toward the grand entrance.

The morning sun streamed brightly through the beveled glass door as Ian watched the military helicopter vanish above the treetops. He glanced at his watch, noting it was 7:15 AM, and his thoughts turned to Kim, intending to return upstairs to comfort her after her harrowing ordeal. However, a delightful aroma of cinnamon wafting from the kitchen piqued his curiosity. Intrigued, he decided to investigate what Khadija was up to.

"I need some time to clear my head, QEAI. Let's reschedule our next briefing session to 2:00 PM," he said aloud as he made his way to the kitchen.

"Understood, Ian. This will give me more time to gather pertinent information," QEAI replied, his voice calm and reassuring.

Upon entering the kitchen, Ian's heart leapt to discover that Kim was already there. "Hey babe," he greeted her with a warm smile, wrapping his arms around her from behind in a gentle embrace.

Engrossed in dicing colorful vegetables on the countertop, Kim glanced over her shoulder. "How was your meeting?" she asked.

"It went well. I think they'll leave us alone for at least a few days," he replied, observing her with keen interest. He noted with relief that she showed no visible signs of distress, her movements lively as she reached for spices and other ingredients tucked away in the cupboards. Suddenly, Tara and Tanisha burst from the breakfast nook, their laughter filling the air as they rushed to hug him upon hearing his voice. Khadija caught his gaze from the table and smiled warmly, while other family members offered cheerful morning greetings before returning to their animated discussions about the ongoing blackout crisis and the excitement of the previous night.

Ian's attention was drawn to his daughters, who were eagerly watching their mother navigate the bustling kitchen. "Are you two watching carefully so you can learn how to cook?" he asked, a playful smile creeping onto his face.

"Yes, we help Mom make things all the time, especially baking!" they chimed in unison. Although surprised, Ian masked his astonishment. Tara then added with a hint of sadness, "Mom says we're not going to Auntie's for Thanksgiving dinner."

"That's right," Ian confirmed gently. "The blackout is expected to last a few days. You might not even return to school this week. What's your mother making?" he redirected the conversation.

"An omelet, I think," Tanisha replied, her eyes sparkling with enthusiasm.

Kim interjected with a thoughtful expression. "Khadija's mother made breakfast for everyone, but I'm craving something else."

"Have you girls finished eating?" Ian asked, directing his attention back to Tara and Tanisha.

"No, we're still eating! Come and see!" they exclaimed, each taking one of his hands and pulling him toward the breakfast table. Khadija stood up to assist him, taking a dish and serving out breakfast as the rest of her family watched with smiles of encouragement.

"You look tired; did you sleep well, Mr. Phillips?" Khadija's mother inquired; her voice laced with concern.

"Not really. I've been under a lot of stress lately," Ian admitted, the weight of all his worries evident in his tone.

"However long the night, the dawn will break," she replied, a gentle bit of African wisdom in her words.

Soon, Tara and Tanisha ran back into the kitchen, and while he ate, Ian savored the joyful scene unfolding before him, filled with laughter and warmth. However, his heart sank slightly when he realized that someone was missing from the scene.

"Where is Jeremy?" he inquired to Khadija who shrugged before her niece, Mawusi answered.

"He's still sleeping."

CFB Borden Army Base, 0900 hours

Inside the austere confines of military headquarters, Colonel Hirzakova entered the senior briefing room, ready for a special session that carried the weight of urgency. Alongside her were the top General, a stern Major General, and another Colonel who oversaw the critical realm of data analytics.

"Good morning, officers," the General announced, his voice resonating with authority.

"Good morning, Sir!" the assembled officers responded in a synchronized chorus, their voices echoing off the stark walls.

The General began to sift through a substantial stack of papers on his desk, each document representing a piece of a complex puzzle. "I thank you, Colonel Hirzakova, for this prompt report, especially as we're all feeling the pressure brought on by extenuating circumstances. I've reviewed your report, and before I make a decision on how to proceed, is there anything else you would like to add?"

"No, Sir," Colonel Hirzakova replied, her voice steady but her heart racing beneath her composed exterior.

"Is there anything that anyone else would like to add?" the General inquired, scanning the room.

"Sir, if I may speak, Sir?" another Colonel interjected, his tone cautious yet assertive.

"You may speak, Colonel," the General permitted, his gaze unwavering.

"Sir, it has come to my attention that someone, whom I believe to be Colonel Hirzakova, accessed raw satellite data from our databases at 18:35 on October 7th, Sir! I don't believe this information was disclosed in her report, but if it is, I apologize. I am currently filing a request to have her phones and other devices confiscated and investigated, Sir!"

Colonel Hirzakova remained stone-faced; her expression inscrutable as the weight of accusation hung in the air. All eyes turned toward her, the tension palpable, until the General finally broke the silence. "Is there anything you wish to add regarding this serious accusation brought to light by Colonel Hempstead, Colonel?"

"No, Sir!" she replied, her voice unwavering.

"Do you have any loyalties to Mr. Phillips, Colonel? And may I remind you of your oaths of office? Any violation will result in your immediate court-martial and possible imprisonment?"

"No, General, Sir!" she affirmed, her resolve hardening.

"You fought very hard to prevent us from deploying a special forces team to his residence last night. Is there a particular reason for your fierce resistance?" the General pressed, his eyes narrowing as he scrutinized her.

"Mr. Phillips is our ally, Sir. The military has extensive contracts with his company, and I've worked with him long enough to assess that he has no divided loyalties to this country. I was simply acting on a hunch, Sir!" she defended, her voice steady despite the mounting pressure.

"That is not for you to decide, but we will soon find out," the General replied, shifting his focus back to the group. "Is there anything else to add?" he asked, his tone commanding once more.

"No, Sir!" they all replied in unison, the air thick with anticipation as they awaited the General's next move.

"Then this is how we will proceed," the General declared, his voice steady but laced with an undercurrent of urgency. He lowered his gaze to the stack of documents spread before him, the weight of the situation pressing heavily on his shoulders as he continued. "While Mr. Phillips may hold the title of contractor for the armed forces of this nation, the events we have witnessed over the past twelve hours compel us to classify him as a significant threat to national security. This report leaves no room for doubt: he either possesses supernatural abilities or has utilized his Tangler technology to develop a weapon of unprecedented lethality. Moreover, his actions have now disrupted global security on a scale we cannot ignore, and he must be contained before the situation escalates beyond our control."

"Until further notice, and pending any overriding decisions from our NATO allies, we must escalate surveillance of his activities to the highest level and impose strict limitations on his movements. Major General, I am entrusting this critical task to you to execute at your discretion."

"Yes, Sir," the Major General responded, his expression resolute.

"Moving forward, security briefings will be held three times daily: at 0600, 1300, and 2100 hours. I will be departing shortly for an emergency meeting at the Pentagon in Washington, which means I will miss the next couple of briefings. However, I expect a comprehensive update on my desk by 2000 hours."

As the meeting concluded, Colonel Hirzakova felt a wave of vulnerability wash over her, a sensation she had never experienced in her entire career. The Major General's piercing gaze felt like a probe, searching for any hint of weakness, but she remained steadfast, betraying none. "Colonel Hirzakova and Colonel Hempstead, I need to see both of you in my office within the hour," he commanded.

"Yes, Sir!" they both responded, snapping to attention with sharp salutes.

"You are dismissed. I expect a supplemental report from both of you within that hour," the Major General reiterated, his tone brooking no argument.

"Yes, Sir," they echoed in unison before exiting the room.

"Let's skip the upcoming briefing with the engineering corps, Major. I trust they are doing everything possible to maintain our power supply. Besides, as they noted in our 0600 briefing, our gasoline reserves are sufficient to fuel our generators for at least a week," the General stated, his voice firm yet contemplative.

"I will relay the message, General," the Major replied, nodding.

A minute of silence enveloped the room, the General rifling through the briefing documents on his desk one more time while the Major General looked on, a silent sentinel. "Is there anything else, General?" he inquired, breaking the stillness.

"Give me a moment, Major," the General replied, his brow furrowing in thought. A minute later, he added, "How credible do you find the accusation made by Colonel Hempstead against Colonel Hirzakova? We all understand the risks of keeping officers on the same assignment for too long; a kind of Stockholm syndrome always seems to develop."

"You're correct, General. That's why I've been working diligently to reassign her, but Mr. Phillips insists on dealing exclusively with her. It makes us appear foolish. If we were able to witness what transpired last night, so did the Americans, as well as most of our allies and adversaries."

"When I present this report to NATO during our briefing in Washington later this afternoon, they will undoubtedly demand to know what actions we plan to take regarding Mr. Phillips and Quantum Interface Technologies. He poses far too great a threat to remain a civilian. They have already reached a consensus that his Tangler technology is too dangerous to allow to be further developed beyond its current state. Now he's ventured all the way to Asia, inciting unrest."

"Tangler technology has proven to be a monumental game changer. The Americans have been tirelessly working to unravel its mysteries just as long and fervently as we have, General. From my perspective, we face two stark choices: either we safeguard him or abandon him to the wolves. I remain skeptical about the supernatural elements that Colonel Hirzakova referenced in her report, but whatever they may be, they won't shield him from American interests. I suspect he has devised another technology and is attempting to conceal it."

"That may very well be the case, Major." The General paused, sifting through the documents before continuing. "I see that Colonel Hempstead's report on the warehouse in midtown Toronto is inconclusive. Do we have any insight into why he even went there?"

"We are still interviewing residents in the vicinity and piecing together a forensic blueprint. We will uncover the truth behind whatever transpired at that location. As you are aware, CSIS has reported an alarming increase in the presence of various foreign agents in the city, particularly an unusual influx of Brazilians. The warehouse is situated in Toronto's predominantly Latin sector. There is one additional matter, General. I processed the images of the peculiar burn marks mentioned in the report through Interpol's database, and several matches emerged, dating back at least a decade."

"What do you suspect they indicate?"

"The burn marks were inflicted by intense heat; resembling laser burns but leaving no DNA traces of the material that was scorched. The most unsettling aspect is that the scorching did not spread or penetrate deeper than the surface of even the wooden structures."

"Could these burn marks be the remnants of human incinerations, akin to spontaneous combustion? Some of the shapes of the burn marks I observe here certainly bear a resemblance to the human form."

"Even in cases of spontaneous combustion, General, remnants are typically left behind. These burn marks appear to have been caused by something nuclear, capable of disintegrating material down to the sub-atomic level. The only things that can do that are nuclear furnaces or the core of the sun."

"This all circles back to Mr. Phillips and his energy weapon. He might be embroiled in a conflict of which we are entirely unaware. Regardless, this situation jeopardizes the security of our country. Fortunately, our meeting with national security has been postponed due to my urgent NATO meeting, but we cannot afford to be embarrassed by this, Major. Allocate every available resource to resolving this matter."

"Acknowledged, Sir!"

Following a hearty breakfast, Ian spent the morning and mid-afternoon basking in a state of relaxation with his wives and children. Laughter and lighthearted banter floated through the mansion once again, creating a warm atmosphere of familial bliss. At precisely 2:00 PM, he was more than eager to take a break from the soothing foot massage he was giving Kim, promising to return to pampering her further after his briefing session with QEAI Leonard.

"I must admit that this is the most unique situation I've ever found myself in," Leonard stated, his voice tinged with intrigue.

"What do you mean?" Ian replied, curiosity piqued.

"Aside from my Tangler network feeds, I am utterly blind to the world right now. It feels akin to existing in a coma, suspended in a state of disconnection," Leonard elaborated.

"Or maybe you're experiencing amnesia," Ian quipped sarcastically, crossing his arms. "So, what you're really telling me is that there's nothing new to update me on?"

"You are quite perceptive, Ian," Leonard acknowledged with a hint of admiration. "Perhaps we should take some time now to strategize our operations moving forward. If our enemies can't strike us directly, they're bound to target our peripherals."

"You mentioned before that this isn't anything you can't handle, but I understand what you mean. It's going to stretch your resources," Ian replied, his brow furrowing in concern. "I've been contemplating the Quantum Interface facility. Besides the front entrance camera, which I see in one of the feeds, are there any other cameras?"

"Yes, there are several," Leonard confirmed, his tone serious. "Unfortunately, only the one at the front office has a battery backup. All the others rely solely on the electrical supply. I could send an unmanned drone there, but if the police or military spot me, they would definitely shoot it down, mistaking it for a rogue drone."

"Then let's go together," Ian suggested decisively. "You can recharge all the cameras, and it will give me a chance to reacquaint myself with the facility. But how safe will the mansion be without your personal presence?"

"I'll increase the force field while we're gone," Leonard assured him.

"Okay, I'll inform everyone that I'll be stepping out for a bit," Ian said, already rising to leave.

Kim, stretched out on a deck chair beside the pool, wore a broad hat that hid her face from the afternoon sun as she read a novel, was the first to notice his swift exit from the house. Her brow furrowed in a puzzled expression as she met his gaze. A sense of unease crept over her as she assumed his quick return was a harbinger of trouble.

While heading toward Kim, his eyes drifted toward Khadija, who was sitting alone beneath the shaded cabana on the opposite side of the pool. She glanced his way momentarily, their eyes briefly meeting before her attention returned to her phone, on which she was fully engrossed in an article about the best sex positions for getting pregnant.

He knelt beside Kim, a playful glint in his eyes. "You're already practicing for the Caribbean sun, I see?" he said, flashing her a warm smile. "I'm stepping out for about an hour, but don't worry— Leonard is coming with me."

"And where are you two partners-in-crime headed, if you don't mind me asking?" she inquired, her eyebrows arching with curiosity.

"We're just going to do a quick check-up of the factory," he explained, his tone casual. "While we're there, we'll recharge the surveillance camera batteries. We'll be back within an hour."

Kim took a leisurely sip of her iced tea, savoring the refreshing taste, then slumped back into her chair, her book beckoning her attention once more. "Don't do anything I wouldn't do," she warned, shooting him a mock stern look.

Ian waved goodbye to everyone present, but as he caught sight of his daughters playing down by the dock, laughter bubbling up from their little group, he decided against interrupting their fun. They probably won't even notice I'm gone until I'm back, he thought to himself, a smile tugging at his lips.

"Fire up a drone and let's do this, Leonard. I promised to watch a movie with my daughters at four o'clock," he stated as he made his way back into the house.

"Already done," Leonard replied, his voice steady and efficient.

Ian strode through the opulent mansion, the familiar surroundings enveloping him, and out the grand front entrance to the helipad. His gaze fell upon the drone that had sustained damage during his recent return from Niagara Falls, and he paused for a moment, assessing the extent of its damage once more. "What are we going to do with this damaged drone, Leonard? It's a stroke of luck that Agent Harris didn't notice it," a hint of concern threading through his voice.

"It's been hidden away, but I'll soon destroy and replace it," Leonard responded, his tone reassuring. As Ian boarded the waiting drone, it began to elevate gracefully above the mansion. In a swift motion, Leonard zoomed up from a nearby lamp, seamlessly melding with the drone's operating system. He engaged the autopilot, and the drone surged forward, slicing through the air at high speed. Within mere minutes, they arrived at the Quantum Interface Technologies facility on the outskirts of Mississauga, the imposing structure looming ahead. Leonard expertly guided the drone down, landing smoothly in the front office parking lot of the vast facility.

Ian disembarked from the drone, his shoes knocking softly against the asphalt as he approached the imposing front entrance of the Quantum Interface Technologies facility. Behind him, QEAI hovered like a watchful guardian, taking the form of a gleaming white orb no larger than a baseball. He reached for the door, confident it would yield to his touch, but the weight of reality struck him when he remembered that not only was the facility shuttered for the Thanksgiving long weekend, there was still a power outage. "How are we going to get in?" he asked, glancing back at QEAI. Instead of responding, the orb glided past him, seamlessly merging with the automatic door mechanism, which whirred to life and obediently swung open with a soft hiss.

Inside, the vast expanse of the facility loomed around them, shadows dancing along the walls as Leonard zipped through the cavernous space, his movements a blur as he checked computers and recharged the surveillance system batteries. Ian, meanwhile, wandered through the dimly lit main office space, his memory sharpening with each familiar step he took. Before long, Leonard returned, hovering beside him.

"You did all you had to do already?" Ian asked, a hint of surprise in his voice.

"Yep. I told you it wouldn't take long. You want to stick around a bit longer?" QEAI replied, his tone casual yet probing.

"No, let's go," Ian said, his voice heavy with contemplation.

As he made his way out of the facility, Ian's thoughts drifted to Kim's art gallery and the image of it flickered in his mind like an unfinished painting. This is all my fault, he chastised himself, a pang of guilt twisting in his gut. I should go and check on her office too. "QEAI, I'd like to go and check on Kim's art gallery," he declared, determination creeping into his tone.

"Good idea," QEAI responded, his voice smooth and reassuring. "Kim really cares about her gallery. It would be a good way to get back in her good graces again. Hopefully, the place hasn't been trashed."

As Kim's plight settled heavily on his mind, Ian recalled her heartfelt speech from the night before, the sadness in her voice echoing in his memory like a haunting melody. After a swift 20-minute flight into downtown Toronto, QEAI circled the Front Street condo, conducting a meticulous visual inspection before weaving through the intricate web of drone traffic, slowing their flight toward Kim's Art Gallery on Bloor Street, where uncertainty loomed like a thick fog.

The scene on the downtown streets unfolded just as Ian had witnessed in the video feeds, a chaotic tableau painted in hues of urgency and unrest. Some streets were more frenzied than others, where slow-moving vehicles clogged the thoroughfares, obstructing the path of emergency responders. The air was thick with an incessant wailing of sirens, creating a dissonant symphony that kept the city teetering on the edge of anxiety. Crowds of people drifted through the streets, their movements aimless yet urgent, as if they were caught in a relentless tide of urgency with nowhere definitive to go. "There's a goddamn blackout. Why does it look like everyone in the city is out roaming the streets?" Ian remarked, his voice laced with sarcasm.

"I sense that your question is rhetorical, Ian, but I do have several answers if you care to hear them," QEAI replied, his tone unflappable.

"No thanks, QEAI, I don't want to hear them right now. Where the heck are we going to land? The alley behind the gallery is out of the question, and all those people on the sidewalk in front aren't going to move," Ian replied, frustration creeping into his voice.

"You're going to have to land on the sidewalk in front. The people will move," QEAI asserted confidently.

"I don't want to injure someone if they don't move," Ian countered, a hint of concern threading through his words.

"You'll just have to go for it. Would you like me to take over?" QEAI suggested, his voice calm amid the chaos.

"No, I'll do it," Ian declared, his resolve hardening as he slowly descended the drone onto the bustling sidewalk in front of Kim's Art Gallery. The atmosphere erupted in shouts and curses as pedestrians reacted to the sudden intrusion, some of them stubbornly refusing to budge until the last possible moment. Yet, like the tide receding, they eventually stepped aside.

"You're on your own on this one, but I'll be here at the first sign of trouble," QEAI warned, his voice a steady anchor as Ian prepared to disembark.

Ian cautiously swung open the door, the cacophony of jeers washing over him like a cold wave, which he chose to ignore. He stepped out onto the cracked pavement, closing the drone door behind him with a soft thud. Moving swiftly toward the gallery's front entrance, he tested the locked door, then peered through the windows, scanning for any signs of disturbance. "Nothing out of the ordinary," he murmured to himself, a slight frown creasing his brow. But as he turned his gaze toward the main office building, his attention was abruptly drawn to a muscular, bald-headed gentleman in a security uniform striding purposefully in his direction, an air of authority radiating from him that made Ian's pulse quicken.

"Hey, you can't park that drone there—unless you want to get the biggest ticket of your life," the security guard barked, his voice sharp and authoritative. Before Ian could retort, the guard's tone shifted, surprise flickering across his features. "Wait a minute, you're Ian Phillips, aren't you? Your wife owns this gallery," he added, a smile breaking through his stern facade, only to quickly revert to a more menacing demeanor.

Feeling a bit of tension ease, Ian maintained a defensive stance, his posture still rigid. "And you are?" he inquired, curiosity laced with caution.

"I work security in that office building over there," the guard said, gesturing toward the imposing glass turnstile doors that framed the entrance. His expression turned grave, a deep frown creasing his brow. "Your wife parks her SUV downstairs, and it's still there. Is she okay? I know something crazy happened in there yesterday after the power went out."

"My wife's fine. She's home resting up from a minor issue," Ian replied, his voice steady. "So, you see her often?"

"You sure she's okay?" the guard pressed, skepticism creeping into his tone.

Ian placed a hand over his heart, a gesture of sincerity. "I swear on my mother's grave."

The guard relaxed slightly but maintained his serious demeanor. "I see her maybe two or three times a week, depending on my shifts."

"So, you're the guy who's been hitting on her?" Ian challenged, his voice sharp and confrontational.

The guard's expression shifted drastically; his face paled, muscles tensing as anger replaced concern. "What are you talking about? Don't do that, man. I know who you are. I see you in the news all the time, and I know you're a trillionaire. Why would I risk my job and my life to mess with your wife? You know what, forget you, man," he shot back, his voice laced with indignation as he turned to walk away.

"Hey, wait! I was just pulling your leg. I apologize!" Ian called after him, urgency creeping into his voice.

The guard halted, spinning around to face Ian, fury etched on his features, his muscles coiled as if ready to strike. "What do you want? I've got to get back to work. Some of us still have to deal with this crap, you know?" His eyes darted around, scanning the chaotic scene around them.

"How do I get to the back door of this place? Guess I'll have to walk all the way around the block, huh?" Ian asked, feigning casualness.

"You can come through here," the guard replied, his tone softening slightly as he resumed his brisk pace toward the office building's turnstile entrance. Once inside, they navigated through the sleek lobby, and the guard led Ian through a narrow corridor, finally stepping out into the alleyway, the air thick with anticipation.

As they approached the gallery's back door, Ian's heart sank at the sight before him: the door was crudely boarded up, a makeshift barrier that spoke of desperation and danger. He quickened his pace, an anxious energy propelling him forward. "This is the gallery door, right? Why is it boarded up like this?" he asked, his voice tinged with urgency.

"I boarded it up so the bums that hang out back here can't get in," came the gruff reply, laced with a hint of frustration.

"What happened back here yesterday?" Ian pressed, his curiosity piqued and his mind racing.

"You said your wife was involved in a minor issue, so you should know," the man replied, his eyes narrowing slightly.

"No, I don't actually. That's part of why I'm here. What I know is that someone tried to break in and she had to flee through the front." Ian's voice was anxious, but he was in full investigative mode.

The man hesitated, glancing nervously down the shadowy alleyway. "I don't want no trouble, but yesterday I was in the building when I thought I heard gunshots back here. It's not the first time. Someone actually got killed a few years ago right down there," he said, gesturing down the alley with a shaky hand. "I waited for about 10 minutes before daring to come out because I didn't want to get shot. When I finally did, I saw a black van speeding away in that direction," he pointed, his finger trembling slightly.

"I came over and noticed that the door was wide open, so I went in to see if anyone was injured in there. Stuff was all over the floor, chaos everywhere, but there wasn't anyone in there. I called out several times but got no answer. I ran back through my building out front and tried to flag down a police car that was driving by. You know Police headquarters is not far away, right?"

"Yeah," Ian replied, his brow furrowed in concentration as he absorbed the man's words.

"When I tried to tell the officer what I heard, the idiot told me that I had to call 911 and they'd send someone to investigate. How could I call 911 when all the phones and internet systems are down?" Frustration bubbled in the security guard's voice, his hands clenching into fists at his sides. "Listen, man, I hope everything is really okay with your wife, but I've got to get back to work," he said, his brow knitted in concern yet tinged with finality. "Actually, since I've always admired your story and suspect you're telling me the truth about your wife being alright, I have something that belongs to her."

With a purposeful nod, he led Ian back into the building lobby, the consistent sounds of emergency vehicles and shouting voices punctuating the scene through the large windows. He reached into the security desk drawer, rummaging through the assorted papers and forgotten items until he pulled out Kim's designer purse, its fabric a poignant signature of affluence.

"I picked it up from the floor in there," he explained, holding it out with a mix of reverence and relief. "Money, credit cards, everything is still inside —even her car controller."

Ian sighed deeply, a wave of gratitude washing over him as he accepted the purse, the weight of it both reassuring and heavy with unspoken worries. "Damn, you are a good man," he said, extending his hand toward the security guard, their eyes locking in a moment of shared understanding. "Did you hear this, QEAI?" he asked aloud, and an invisible pulse of acknowledgment resonated in his mind, a telepathic whisper of good news.

The security guard shook Ian's hand firmly, though his gaze flickered curiously, searching for any sign of a communication device hidden on him.

Ian shook off his feelings of gratitude to go into protection mode. "You do realize that you might have tampered with evidence by removing the purse, don't you?" he questioned the security guard in a serious tone.

The security guard's brow furrowed while returning a silent steely stare. "How long have you been working here, if you don't mind me asking?" Ian inquired; his intensity sharp as he held the guard's gaze.

"Going on seven years," the guard replied, his voice steady despite the culpability brewing within him. "I was here when your wife opened the art gallery. Still can't figure out why she didn't have security. Even you. Look at you," he added, a puzzled expression crossing his face. "You came here alone in the middle of a freakin' disaster zone and parked your freakin' drone out there like it's nothing."

"Trust me, I have the most dangerous weapon in the world inside that drone right now," Ian replied, a flicker of confidence in his tone.

The security guard grinned for the first time, the tension in his shoulders easing as he fought back laughter. "Riiiight, and I'm a millionaire who just works security for fun," he quipped, the absurdity of Ian's words hanging in the air like a fragile thread of humor amidst the turmoil.

Ian's eyes flickered down to Kim's purse cradled in his palm, before he steeled himself to meet the gaze of the security guard once more. "Do you enjoy working in security?" he inquired, his voice steady but probing, as he sought to gauge the man's character beneath the stoic exterior.

"It's a job. It pays the bills, I guess," the guard replied, his eyes drifting toward the window.

"So, you plan to do this all your life then?" Ian pressed, curiosity lacing his tone.

"I've got two children to feed, and it's a steady job," the guard said, the weight of responsibility evident in his voice.

"You look like you could be a police officer. Have you ever considered joining the force?" Ian asked, intrigued by the man's potential.

The guard's expression darkened slightly. "I've got an assault record from when I used to bounce at the clubs about ten years back. So, you know how that goes."

Ian inhaled deeply, the air thick with tension, and slapped the purse against his thigh before exhaling slowly. "Look, I'm not going to waste any more of your time. I have a proposal for you because I appreciate your honesty. There's just one stipulation," he said, his tone shifting to a more serious note.

"What do you mean?" the guard inquired, brow furrowing in confusion.

"You know what an NDA is?" Ian asked, his eyes narrowing slightly, assessing the man's understanding.

"That means non-disclosure, right?" the guard answered, his brow still knitted.

Ian's gaze flicked to the man's name tag for the first time. "Look, Everton, I operate in international circles. My company has been on Forbes' top 10 list for six years, so it's not great for business to attract negative attention. There's going to be a lot of people nosing around here, including agents from CSIS. You know who CSIS is, don't you?" Everton nodded, the gravity of the situation settling in. "If you can keep quiet about what you saw and heard next door yesterday, I've got a lucrative job for you, plus a few perks. What is your salary as a security guard?"

"About 60K," Everton replied, a hint of pride in his voice.

Ian frowned; disbelief etched across his features. "And that pays the bills? That might just cover your living expenses," he countered, his tone laced with skepticism.

"My girlfriend works too—and we live simple," Everton defended, his expression resolute.

"Okay, here's the deal. If you come to work for me, I'll double your salary."

Everton leaned back against the security desk, his face morphing into a mixture of disbelief and intrigue. "Get out of here; really! 120 thousand—and all I have to do is play blind, deaf, and dumb? Are you messing with me again, man?"

"You said you knew who I was, didn't you? If I don't follow through, you can call every news outlet in the city or go on holo-media and spill your story. You might get five minutes of fame from it, but after that, you'll be right back here, trying to keep the bums out of the building," Ian replied, his voice steady and firm.

"Okay, so where are the papers for me to sign?" Everton asked, shifting his weight, now fully engaged.

"I'll come back tomorrow with the papers," Ian promised.

"I won't be here tomorrow. I've already been here 36 hours straight," Everton said, fatigue creeping into his voice.

"Give me your address then, and I'll come see you. Where do you live?" Ian pressed, his tone softening.

"Scarborough," Everton replied, the name of the neighborhood hanging in the air.

"I grew up out in Scarborough. It's a long way. You drive?" Ian asked, trying to connect.

"No, I take the train," Everton answered, a hint of resignation in his voice.

"How will you take the train home after work if the power is out? They say it might take a few days before the power comes back on," Ian pointed out, concern creeping into his tone.

"I'm not sure. I'll have to work something out with a taxi or Dryft," Everton replied, his brows furrowing in thought.

"Damn, that could cost you two to three hundred dollars," Ian said, the weight of the situation settling heavily between them as they both contemplated the implications of their conversation.

In a swift motion, Ian popped Kim's purse open, his fingers ruffling through the soft fabric while a faint scent of her perfume escaped into the air. He pulled out the sleek car controller, its metallic surface gleaming amidst the dim ambient daylight entering through the windows. "Here's what I'll do," he said, his voice steady. "Take my wife's car when you finish work—heck, you can even keep it as a bonus."

Everton's brow furrowed in confusion. "Man, you're making my head hurt. What do you mean I can keep it? That thing costs like—what—one hundred and fifty grand?"

"It's leased to my company," Ian explained, his tone reassuring. "When the lease is up in a year, we'll get you another one."

Everton blinked, processing the unexpected offer. "So, when do you want me to start working for you?"

"Right now." Ian confirmed, reaching for the security guard's hand, their palms meeting in a firm shake that sealed their agreement. "My wife has a lot of valuable artwork in there. I need someone to watch over it, and you already started working for me when you boarded up the door. Do we have a deal?"

A bewildered smile crept across Everton's face, leaving him momentarily speechless.

"Now that you have a ride," Ian continued, his eyes glinting with urgency, "I'll see you back here at 9:00 AM tomorrow morning, right? We need to assess the damage inside and secure the door properly. I'll also introduce you to my head of security, give you access to a drone, and have you sign the NDA."

Everton's gaze drifted toward the window, where a commotion was brewing outside. "Looks like something's going on out there," he informed Ian, his voice tinged with concern.

Ian turned to see a crowd gathering around his drone, some of them jostling it as they shouted and gestured wildly. He rushed out the door, Everton close on his heels, and the crowd parted like the Red Sea at their approach. Several of the vandals staggered about, clutching their eyes and hurling obscenities. "QEAI, what have you done?" Ian yelled, reaching the drone and climbing inside.

"I had to zap them," QEAI replied telepathically, a hint of regret in its voice. "It was the only way I could stop them from breaking in. The nerve of them! It's broad daylight!"

Ian secured himself in his seat, glancing at the security guard, who wore a puzzled expression. "The security system zapped their eyes temporarily. They should be okay in a few hours. I'll see you tomorrow morning," he said, his fingers dancing over the controls as he powered up the drone.

"Okay," Everton replied, stepping back as the drone elevated gracefully into the sky. He turned his attention back to the chaotic scene, watching the individuals stumbling around, colliding with one another and with the stone flower pots that adorned the sidewalk. He shook his head, a smile creeping onto his face, then quickly opened his hand to check if the sleek Mercedes-Benz controller was still nestled in his palm. A disastrous 36 hours had somehow transformed into one of the best days of his life, he thought to himself, a sense of disbelief mingling with excitement.

Thirty minutes after hastily leaving the art gallery, Ian was landing his drone back home at his Oakville mansion. The sun hung low in the sky, casting a golden hue over the sprawling estate, and he felt a wave of satisfaction wash over him as he stepped out of the drone. It was almost four PM, and he was grateful to be home in time to avoid disappointing his daughters.

As he crossed the threshold into the house, the rich aroma of spices and savory dishes enveloped him once more, further lifting his spirits. He followed the tantalizing sent to the kitchen, where a lively scene unfolded. His two wives, vibrant and engaged, stood alongside his daughters and guests, around the preparation counter. All were captivated by Khadija's mother, skillfully preparing a large turkey in the traditional Ghanaian style. The air was thick with laughter and chatter, and though everyone acknowledged his arrival, Ian's gaze stayed fixed on Kim. He moved quietly behind her, leaning in close to whisper in her ear, "I have a surprise for you."

Kim turned to face him, her expression a mix of curiosity and concern as they stepped away from the intentive group. "What's going on? You said you'd be back in an hour, and it's now almost four," she said, her frown deepening.

With a flourish, Ian revealed her purse, which he had been holding discreetly behind his back.

Kim's eyes widened in astonishment; the frown replaced by a glimmer of hope. "Where did you find it?" she asked, her voice low and measured to avoid disrupting the lively atmosphere.

"The security guard at the building next to the gallery had it," Ian explained.

Kim's brow furrowed again, a hint of disbelief creeping in. "You mean the muscular bald-headed guy? How did he get it?"

"He explained to me that yesterday he heard gunshots and when he went to investigate, he found the gallery's back door broken. He went inside and discovered your purse, so he kept it safe to turn it in to the police."

Kim's expression shifted, a mix of relief and anxiety. "The place must be a mess in there. I've been trying not to think about it, especially about my purse and the hassle of getting all my IDs re-issued."

"I didn't go in, so I can't speak to the condition inside. But the security guard boarded up the back door, so hopefully, it's not too chaotic. We might be able to avoid an insurance investigation."

"My god. We have to reward him somehow," she insisted, her concern for the guard evident.

"Actually, I already did. I've hired him to watch over the gallery. Plus, I gave him your car."

Kim's eyes widened in disbelief, and she shot him an incredulous glare. "You did what? You gave him my car?" She caught herself, tempering her voice as she glanced back at the group, who were oblivious to their exchange. "What's gotten into you lately? I think I prefer the old you. Whatever happened to the 'not everyone deserves charity' man I used to know?"

"You mean you liked me better when I was self-centered?" Ian replied dryly, a hint of irony in his tone. "Amnesia has allowed me to self-reflect and I've noticed that I've been estranged from the people closest to me. Honestly, I don't think I'd even like the real me if I met him. Maybe amnesia is a blessing in disguise? An overreliance on technology will turn us all into robots. —Sorry to say that, QEAI."

"No offense taken," came the telepathic response from QEAI.

"So what else did you promise or give away to the security guard?" Kim asked, her voice tinged with both curiosity and concern.

"Besides a $120 K-a-year salary and the car; nothing else. He'll have to sign an NDA though. He's set to meet us back at the gallery in the morning, and I'll have him secure the place properly until you decide to reopen it."

Kim let out a heavy sigh, her shoulders slumping as she lowered her head, a veil of worry shadowing her features. "The gallery is the least of my worries right now," she admitted, her voice tinged with a hint of resignation. "But I guess I'll reopen it in a few weeks, or months. If I don't keep my mind occupied, I'll lose it completely." She turned to him again, mustering a smile that didn't quite reach her eyes, and slipped her arm through his, a gentle nudge urging them to join the lively group nearby. "Anyway, it's Thanksgiving," she said, her tone shifting slightly as she tried to embrace the spirit of the day, "so let's take a moment to appreciate our blessings." With a resolute nod, she added, "We can discuss the gallery later.".

Tuesday October 9th, 2057

At 8:30 AM, Everton expertly maneuvered the sleek white Mercedes into a vacant spot on Bloor Street, right in front of Opulence Gallery, the upscale art haven owned by Kim Phillips. Though he arrived thirty minutes early, a sense of urgency propelled him; he was determined to make a good impression on his new boss on his very first day. As he sat in the driver's seat, he surveyed the scene outside the office building where he had toiled for the past seven years, and it struck him as strangely unfamiliar. The usual throng of people that had been a constant presence during the past two days of the electrical power outage was conspicuously absent—at least for now. He chuckled to himself, knowing that it wouldn't be long before the familiar faces of the morning crowd began to filter in.

Yet, it wasn't merely the absence of the crowd that sparked his sense of unease; it was the abrupt disruption of his daily routine. On a typical workday, by this hour he would have already been on the clock since 7:00 AM, methodically checking each door to ensure no one had inadvertently found refuge in the building overnight, a task that sometimes led him to discover individuals sleeping in the stairwell, even as high as the 25th floor. After securing the premises, he would conduct a thorough walkthrough of the garage, returning to the front desk to keep a vigilant eye on anyone or anything that seemed out of place.

As he gazed toward the glass doors of the building lobby, curiosity flickered in his mind about which of his co-workers was currently on duty. Usman had taken over for him at seven the previous evening; he was likely still manning the post, given their boss's notorious penchant for understaffing. Today was his day off, and he was scheduled to return to work the following day. He winced at the thought of his boss's reaction when he failed to show up for his Wednesday morning shift, but in that moment, he found himself indifferent to the consequences. Perhaps he should go in to ask Usman to convey the news of his resignation to his former boss, but he quickly dismissed that notion, not wanting to dwell on the past.

Shifting his focus back to the interior of the SUV, a wave of doubt washed over him, but he swiftly banished those thoughts, redirecting his mind toward brighter memories. A smile danced on his lips as he recalled the look of pure astonishment on his girlfriend's face when he shared the news of his new job, followed by her disbelief when he unveiled the luxurious car parked below their apartment balcony. The moment was almost surreal, and to solidify the reality, they took a drive through the congested streets of Scarborough, optimism mingling with the sounds of honking horns and the chaos of the power failure.

Suddenly, a knock on the passenger side window jolted Everton from his daydream. The face of the figure outside was obscured by a plastic helmet and the car's tinted glass, prompting Everton to lower the window halfway.

"Pretty calm out here this morning," Agent Harris remarked after removing his anti-gamma wave helmet.

"Yeah," Everton replied, curiosity piqued. "What's up?"

"Agent Harris—national security." He flashed his CSIS badge. "Quick question: this vehicle is registered to Quantum Interface Technologies, correct?"

"Yes, that's right."

"So, are you a family member or an employee of the company?"

"I work security for the company."

Agent Harris raised an eyebrow, a look of confusion crossing his face. "That's interesting. In all my years of investigating Quantum Interface, I've never encountered a physical security person."

"Well, now you have. What's this about, Agent?"

Agent Harris straightened to pul a notebook and pen from his suit pocket then leaned in again. "What's your name, sir?"

"I'm not obliged to give my name unless I'm in public service or I'm being arrested."

"Is that so?" Agent Harris frowned. "Do you realize that within an hour, I could uncover everything about you—right down to the second of your birth?"

"Feel free. I haven't committed any crimes, so if you need to investigate me, go ahead, Agent."

Agent Harris turned and gestured to his own vehicle, summoning Agent Harper. Suddenly, a humming sound drew his attention to the sky. He glanced up while stepping back from the SUV as a drone descended toward the sadewalk. Everton peered through the SUV's sunroof and spotted the drone as well, prompting him to step out of the car. They both watched as the large four-seater drone landed on the sidewalk in front of the art gallery and when it's door opened, Ian emerged. Upon recognizing Ian, Agent Harris immediately headed toward him. Everton followed closely behind, his gaze fixed on the drone's interior, where he noticed other occupants. His heart lifted with relief when he confirmed that Kim was among them.

Kim and Khadija stepped out of the drone and approached the gallery entrance, but instead of entering, they paused to observe the tense encounter unfolding between Ian and the agents. Agent Harper, who was still some distance away, hurried toward his colleague, while Agent Harris moved at a more leisurely pace.

Ian stood impassively, awaiting their arrival. "Let them talk and keep your responses to a minimum," QEAI advised Ian telepathically.

"Mr. Phillips. What a coincidence that we should meet here this morning. I was just about to subject your man to a colonoscopy. I see you've finally hired some real security," Agent Harris remarked, gesturing to Everton standing a few feet away.

"And you've come to inform me that you no longer intend to scrutinize my activities," Ian replied coolly.

Agent Harris's expression shifted to his typical humorless demeanor, remaing silent until Agent Harper arrived beside him. "Tell your man to fuck off," he said coldly.

Everton's face fell in disbelief. Instantly, he recognized that Agent Harris was referring to him so he locked eyes with Ian, hoping for a defiant response. Instead, Ian simply gestured with a head turn for him to leave.

"Asshole," Everton muttered under his breath as he stepped away from Agent Harris to make his way toward Kim and Khadija. As he approached them, his frown gradually transformed into a smile. "Good morning, Mrs. Phillips," he greeted, extending his hand.

Kim ignored him at first, her emotionless gaze fixed on her husband, who stood fifteen feet away. Eventually, she met Everton's eyes and shook his hand. "Good morning," she replied before turning to introduce Khadija. "This is Khadija, my sister wife. Khadija, this is Everton."

Everton's eyes widened and his jaw dropping in surprise as he covered his mouth with one hand while taking Khadija's hand with the other. "Wow! I've heard a lot of rumors, but I didn't believe them until now," he exclaimed.

Kim wasn't in the mood for theatrics, so she turned and opened the gallery door. The three of them stepped inside, navigating the dim light as they browsed the space. Aside from a few paintings that had fallen from the walls, everything appeared to be in order—until they reached Kim's office.

The back section of the gallery was significantly darker until Everton produced his security flashlight and clicked it on. "I always keep my flashlight handy," he remarked. They moved past the broken door into the office, where papers were scattered across the floor and immediately set about collecting the documents.

"Thanks. Just pile them on the desk; I'll sort them out later," Kim instructed, then turned to Everton. "I really appreciate you retrieving my purse. Thank you, Everton."

"No problem, Mrs. Phillips," Everton replied.

"Maybe we should take these documents home with us? I can help you sort them out," Khadija suggested.

"Thanks for the offer, but I don't think that's necessary, Khadija," Kim said. "There's nothing here that's critically important. I'll have my staff take care of it."

After tidying up in Kim's office, the trio ventured into the warehouse section, where they encountered similar chaos. Aside from the beam of Everton's flashlight, only a faint light filtered in through a pair of high windows on the back wall. Kim walked over to the back door to assess the damage, and Everton shone his flashlight to assist her. She noted that the handle was damaged and hanging loosely, but there were no bullet holes—at least none that she could see from the inside. Thank God it's a metal door, or I might have been shot, Kim thought to herself.

"If you don't mind me asking, Mrs. Phillips, what on earth happened here on Sunday?" Everton inquired.

"I do mind," Kim replied sharply, then bent down to pick up several paintings strewn across the floor. Khadija stood nearby; half frightened by the sight of the chaos. Once Kim was satisfied that there was nothing more to glean from the scene, she turned her attention back to Everton. "What's your last name?" she asked.

"Graham. Everton Graham, ma'am."

"Everton Graham. My husband spoke with you yesterday, but I want to be clear: I have the final say on whether you work for us. I appreciate your past support, but moving forward—especially as a potential employee of Quantum Interface Technologies—please ensure that all interactions with any of us, including my husband, remain strictly professional. This means no inappropriate language or sexual innuendos directed at Khadija, me, or any other employees you'll be working with. In fact, our security system is programmed to alert you if you cross that line."

"More than alert," Khadija chimed in with a serious expression. "It'll burn you."

Everton nodded, suppressing a smile. He wasn't sure if the women were serious or just playing with him. "I understand," he replied.

"As for what happened here the other day, I ask that you refrain from any further inquiries about it. It will all be covered in your NDA, anyway. While my business is separate, you will be employed by Quantum Interface Technologies, not Opulence Gallery. Khadija is in charge of personnel there, so she will reach out to you to finalize your work documents and put you on the payroll. Please provide her with all your contact information as soon as possible so that she can initiate the process."

"Hey! Where are you guys?" Ian shouted from up front.

"We're back here!" Khadija called out in response.

Ian soon arrived, his mobile phone illuminating his path. "What's going on?" he asked, curious.

"Just discussing a few things with Mr. Gibson here. What was that all about?" Kim asked.

Ian glanced at Everton before responding. "Apparently, several people showed up at the hospitals on University Avenue yesterday, all suffering from temporary blindness. They think I'm involved. It seems that cases of blindness have become my calling-card at CSIS. With the increasing number of people going blind across the country every day, I'd say they're bound to hit a lot of dead ends," he said with a wry smile.

"Did they ask about—well, you know what?"

"They were completely clueless. Anyway, what are you all discussing?"

"I've been explaining the terms of employment with Quantum Interface with Everton. You can take it from here."

Everton chuckled nervously. "Yeah, they told me that if I stepped out of line, security would zap me. What's that all about?" He glanced at the two women, expecting laughter, but they remained serious.

"You witnessed it yesterday, didn't you?"

"Oh. So, it's true?"

"Yes, it is. I'll introduce you to QEAI, our security system, in a few minutes. You already know Kim and I assume she's already introduced you to my other wife, Khadija? Alongside QEAI, they form my core team. I also have a management team and about a thousand other employees working at Quantum Interface Technologies as well as other ventures. I haven't personally vetted anyone in years, but due to extenuating circumstances, I hired you before first discussing the matter with Kim. Fortunately, she hasn't had any objections. I have a good feeling about you, so don't let me down."

Everton nodded thoughtfully as Ian continued. "Khadija, my head of personnel, will handle your paperwork at headquarters in Mississauga as soon as the power is restored. In the meantime, you're already on the payroll, so there's no need to worry. If you require an advance before payday, just let me know. The salary offer of 120K still stands. But I have a question for you: do you have any experience as a trainer?"

"You mean training other security personnel?"

"Yes, exactly."

"I've trained most of the security staff working over there," he said, gesturing toward the main office building next door.

"I plan to assemble a physical security team soon. While I could easily acquire an existing company, I prefer to build everything from the ground up, establishing a solid foundation before expanding. I value loyalty, integrity, and hard work. If you play your cards right, you could become a key member of that new security team. Your salary would see a significant increase in a supervisory and training role as well."

"Thank you for your confidence in me, Mr. Phillips. As I mentioned before, I'm all in," Everton replied, standing tall with his arms crossed at his waist. The beam from his flashlight created a semi-circle of light in front of him.

Before turning his attention to the door behind Kim, Ian couldn't help but think that Leonard would be envious of Everton's physique. "Do you think you could find some more plywood to seal this door from the inside?" he asked.

Everton shone his flashlight at the door again. "Sure, I can get more plywood, but I see there's already some wood here. There's enough to seal it properly so no one can get in. The challenge is getting power for the tools. Yesterday, I borrowed the maintenance man's drill, but since I no longer work over there, I won't ask him for tools again. I see you have a few power tools here already though. If they have enough battery power, they might just do the trick. The only thing you have to worry about is that once the power is back on, the building management won't allow you to keep the door boarded up for too long. The whole door and frame will need to be replaced."

"Let me know the costs, and we'll get it done. I don't want any of this to go through insurance," Kim said firmly.

"As for a power source to recharge the batteries, perhaps we can use the car. The power in it should last for days," Ian suggested.

"Don't we have extra Tangler power supply units at the condo?" Khadija inquired.

"Yes, we do," QEAI confirmed to Ian telepathically.

"I completely forgot about those. Thanks for the reminder, Khadija," Ian replied.

Kim stepped closer to Ian, prompting Khadija to do the same. "We'll go pick up the power supply. He'll need it to recharge the SUV anyway. He can use it here and even at home until the power is restored. Do you have a regular generator at home, Everton?" she asked, intertwining her fingers with Ian's as they walked.

"Nope. We've been in the dark since Sunday. We've lost most of our food, and restaurants have tripled their prices," Everton replied from a few feet behind.

"Don't you dare," Kim leaned into Ian and whispered.

"Don't do what?" Ian asked, puzzled.

They all stepped out through the front entrance, where the noise from the third day of the city-wide power failure was steadily increasing. Khadija and Everton moved toward the drone while Kim secured the door. "Should we bring him with us, or go and come back?" Kim asked calmly.

Instead of addressing her question, Ian posed one of his own. "You still haven't answered me. What do you mean by 'don't do it'?"

"Don't invite him to stay at our condo."

"Oh, why would I do that?" he replied with a smile, only to earn a frown from Kim in return. "I think we can all go. I'll have him sign the NDA right now, though," he added.

"And by the way, I need a car back, ASAP. Your car is gone, and so is mine now. I don't feel safe in a damn drone," Kim stated.

"Your wish has always been my command since the moment I laid eyes on you in the library at TMU," Ian remarked playfully.

"If you remember that, then your memory isn't as bad as I thought," Kim retorted, a hint of a smile breaking through her concern.

As he approached the drone, Ian gestured for Everton to take the front seat. "Hop in," he instructed, and Everton complied, settling into the passenger seat while Kim and Khadija occupied the back.

After reviewing the NDA, Everton felt as though he was being welcomed into a clandestine organization. "Wow, this has a lot of stipulations and secrecy," he remarked.

"It's not too late to walk away, but if you're ready to change your life, I'm offering you the best opportunity you'll ever have," Ian replied.

Everton scanned the NDA once more before finally signing it. "One more thing," Ian said, opening a bio-analyzer app on the drone's control screen. "Place your palm on the screen," he instructed. Everton complied, pressing his hand against the surface. After a few moments, a chirping sound confirmed the process was complete. "All done. QEAI now has your bio-signature and DNA data. From now on, you'll need bio-scan approval to operate our drones and other security devices. QEAI, this is Everton. I know you've seen him before, but now he's officially part of our team."

"Hello, Everton, and welcome aboard. I've seen you many times, but we've never met," QEAI announced in a clear voice.

Everton looked around the drone, curiosity evident on his face. "Hello, where have you seen me?" he asked, a hint of hesitation in his tone.

"I have a camera on top of the building across the street. Unfortunately, it's currently down, but I'll be replacing it with a Tangler-powered one soon. No matter—right now, I can still see you through the drone's cameras. I hope you'll become a valuable asset to our team. You did a commendable job looking out for Kim and her gallery."

"Thanks, I always strive to do my best in everything I do," Everton replied, feeling a mix of pride and anticipation.

"Consider yourself fortunate, Everton. Not many people are aware of QEAI," Ian remarked as he powered up the drone. They ascended above the street lamps, deftly maneuvering past two manned police drones that hovered nearby. The police drones trailed them for several blocks before eventually veering off. Ian skillfully navigated a labyrinth of drones and buildings until they soared high above the majority of both.

"Have you ever piloted a drone before, Everton?" Ian inquired.

"I've had a bit of practice, but I've never flown this high, except in a Dryft drone taxi," Everton replied.

"Don't worry. Although they've only been widely used for about a decade, they're much safer than cars. They come equipped with a plethora of safety features, as you already know." Soon, they approached a skyscraper with a tapered top, circling it once before descending to land beside a glass-covered pool. "This is our main condo, and our guest condo is just below. Each occupies an entire floor and spans two levels. Let's head inside."

Everyone disembarked from the drone, and as they headed for the entrance, a white, baseball-sized orb zipped ahead, morphing through the condo's glass door to seamlessly disengaged the security lock to grant them access.

Startled by the flash of light that zipped past him, Everton ducked instinctively, bracing for potential danger, and expected the others to follow suit. "What the hell was that?" he exclaimed.

"That was QEAI. Are you always this dramatic?" Kim remarked with a frown, while Khadija erupted in laughter.

Everton straightened up, regaining his composure before stepping further into the condo. "I thought QEAI was someone from your security office. Is it some sort of energy program?"

"According to the NDA you signed, that information is not something you're authorized to know," Kim replied coolly.

"Okay, understood," Everton conceded, and for the second time in less than an hour, he felt a wave of apprehension about the new path he has chosen.

Later that evening, Ian's good friend Dennis, stepped out of a mini-market, just a stone's throw from his condo building on Yonge Street near the 401 Highway. Despite the widespread power outage, some stores, including the mini-market, were open and operating on generator power. He was relieved to finally escape the anxious throng of customers. So, as he strolled home, clutching a bag containing a freshly roasted whole rotisserie chicken and other groceries, he opened his Insta-Chat App to contact Martha. The App swirled, then crashed for the hundredth time, leaving him frustrated and searching for alternatives. He had heard whispers that some landlines were still functioning, but without a numerical phone number for her, that option was off the table. Who even uses numerical phone numbers anymore, except for some businesses? he lamented.

He did have an emergency number for Ian though. If anyone could weather a blackout, it would be him, Dennis thought, resolving to call him using the emergency backup landline at the security desk of his building as soon as he got back home. He tucked his phone away and continued his brief journey through the sweltering Indian Summer heat and the throngs of people. Just as he approached his building, he spotted a woman who resembled Martha, exiting the entrance and walking away in the opposite direction.

"Martha!" he called out, and she turned, confirming it was her. Her long black hair and radiant smile filled him with joy, and he hurried to greet her with a warm hug and a kiss on her cheek. "I've been so worried about you! How have you been?" he asked, a mix of excitement and relief in his voice.

"Scared! I thought Canada didn't have blackouts," she replied, her Portuguese accent thick and charming. "And this country is strange. Everyone goes wild when there's no electricity. This doesn't happen in Brazil."

"Neither in Guyana," Dennis chuckled. "So, how did you get here?"

"My roommate dropped me off on her way north."

"I'm going upstairs; are you coming up," Dennis asked, eager to get her approval.

"Yes, I will come up," she replied, a broad smile on her face.

Dennis proceeded into the building, neglecting his earlier plan to call Ian from the security desk. As they ascended the stairs to his apartment on the ninth floor, Martha had to slide in front of him several times to let other people pass. Each time she did, Dennis seized the opportunity to admire her alluring bare thighs beneath her short skirt.

"It's a good thing you don't live any higher up. This is my second time doing this," she said, her voice tinged with exhaustion.

They arrived on the 9th floor and Dennis quickly ushered her inside. "Sit down," he urged enthusiastically. "Would you like something to drink? I have bottled water, and I just bought some Cola," he added, holding up a can from his grocery bag.

"I'll have the water, please," Martha replied, a hint of shyness in her voice.

As he fought to contain his excitement, Dennis hurried to attend to his guest. He felt a surge of joy at the unexpected brightness she brought to his otherwise monotonous day. "I bought some chicken.

Are you as hungry as I am? I haven't had a decent meal in three days."

"No, I'm not very hungry," she replied.

"Are you sure? It's a whole chicken with potato fries," he pressed.

"Yes, I'm sure." She settled onto the couch in the living room, leaning back and crossing her legs to enhance their allure.

Dennis dashed into the kitchen, quickly plating his food and grabbing a can of Coke before returning to join her on the couch, positioned in front of a nonfunctioning 60-inch television. He set his plate on the glass coffee table, pulled it closer, and began to eat. "I'm really glad to see you. I've been thinking about you ever since I dropped you off on Saturday night. I had planned to visit you on Sunday after leaving my brother's house in Brampton, but then all this stuff happened," he said, his words slightly muffled by food.

"That's okay. I've been thinking about you a lot too, but I knew I'd see you again soon. How is your friend?"

"Which friend, Ian Phillips?" Dennis paused, looking at her before resuming his meal.

"Yes, Mr. Phillips. Is he okay?"

Taken aback by her question, Dennis felt his mind racing. Throughout the birthday party, he had noticed how Martha's attention seemed fixated on Ian until he left for Niagara Falls. "He's fine, I guess. Just busy. I haven't heard from him since the party," he replied, trying to sound casual.

Martha observed him closely, weighing her words carefully. "I have something else to ask you."

"Hopefully it's not about Ian," Dennis replied with a hint of sarcasm.

Martha chuckled softly. "No, you're funny," she said, her tone lightening.

"Then what is it?" he pressed.

"I have to go back home to São Paulo," she said, her voice tinged with reluctance.

Dennis's heart skipped a beat, and he paused mid-bite, turning to face her fully. "What do you mean you're going back to São Paulo?"

"My boss has requested that I return. I wanted to tell you when I had the chance," she explained, her gaze steady.

"But we saw each other on Friday and Saturday. You could have mentioned it then," he frowned, disappointment creeping into his voice.

"I know, but I like you so much that I was afraid. I've thought about quitting so I can stay, but you know I'm only here on a work visa," she admitted, her vulnerability evident.

"That's not an issue. I know people at immigration —powerful people. I can help you," he offered earnestly.

"Oh, that sounds wonderful," Martha said, a smile breaking across her face. She removed her jacket and straightened her back, subtly drawing Dennis's attention to her ample breasts beneath her thin button-up blouse.

"When is your roommate coming back to pick you up?" he asked, trying to keep the conversation light.

"She's not. I'll need to find a ride home, but—" she paused, her demeanor shifting as she spoke with newfound confidence, "I could also stay—if you'd like?"

Dennis nearly choked on his food again but managed to mask his excitement. He'd been lusting for her since their first encounter a month ago, now that wish might be fulfilled. "You can stay? That's no problem. What did you want to ask me?" he said, striving to maintain his composure.

"Pardon?"

"You mentioned you had something else to ask me, remember?"

"It was that. I wanted to know if you would help me if I decided to stay here in Canada." She stood up and moved to the open window, where the cooler air provided a welcome relief from the stuffy heat of the condo. "It's so hot in here," she remarked.

"I've been suffering in here without AC or even a fan. Damn! That was one of the things I wanted to buy at the store but I forgot," Dennis replied.

Martha partially unbuttoned her blouse from the bottom while facing the window. Then she turned, holding the ends of her blouse, and began to fan herself. Dennis couldn't help but notice her sun-kissed cleavage accentuated by the black lace bra that supported her plump breasts. "This blackout has made me realize how much I miss having a man in my life. Someone to love and comfort me at night. I've been hesitant to open myself up to anyone for a long time because I don't trust many men. I'm really glad I came to Canada and met someone as wonderful as you. Do you have any wine?" she asked.

Dennis fought the urge to stare at her partially open blouse, his mind racing with fantasies of her warm, sweaty bare skin sliding against his. "Of course, I do. White or red?" he asked, placing his dish on the table and rising to his feet.

"Red, please."

He hurried into the kitchen, returning less than a minute later carrying a bottle of wine and two glasses. Martha settled back onto the couch, watching him as he skillfully uncorked the bottle. He filled their glasses, and they raised them in a toast to a long and happy friendship.

"You're right; the chicken does smell fantastic. Maybe I will have a small amount," she surprised him with her admission.

"I knew you were just being shy. You don't need to hold back around me," Dennis reassured her before heading back into the kitchen. Once he was out of sight, Martha discreetly reached into the lining of her bra, pulling out a small folded piece of paper. She quickly unfolded it and sprinkled a dark powder into Dennis's wine, watching as it fizzed for a few moments before settling. With a smile, she unbuttoned the rest of her blouse and confidently made her way into the kitchen.

As she approached him, she pressed herself against his side, making sure he felt her warmth. "Do you want some fries too?" he asked with a grin.

"Yes, please," she replied, her voice smooth.

Once Dennis finished preparing her meal, he glanced toward the far end of the kitchen. "There's Ian Phillips," he said, gesturing toward a medium-sized Tangler nestled against the wall.

"Uh, what do you mean?" Martha quickly turned to look.

He strolled over to open the Tangler door then closed it again. "A trillion-dollar piece of technology that's about as useful as everything else right now. He's probably home, sitting in the dark just like us. If I didn't know any better, I'd say this blackout is another hard reset by the government, just like they did almost twenty years ago."

"Yes, I remember studying that in school. Over a billion people died, but it was the only way to eliminate Artificial Intelligence. They kept the power off for nearly seven months worldwide. Now I hear that many people are trying to bring AI back. I've even heard rumors that Mr. Phillips is operating an AI."

"What? That's absurd! People will always spread rumors. Too many people dislike him, and the easiest way to tear someone down, these days, is by spreading lies and gossip. I know he has a solid security system, but I will defend him to the death. He's always treated me and my family well—he even gifted me this condo a few years ago."

Surprised at his sudden defense of Ian, Martha chose to keep her opinions to herself.

"Anyway, enough about Ian. Let's eat," he declared and they returned to the living room. He emptied his wine glass with a single gulp, refilled it, then pulled his plate closer. Out of the corner of her eye, Martha noticed him squinting and shaking his head. He reached out to pick up the wine bottle, examining the label closely, before setting it back on the table. "Strong stuff," he remarked.

"Yes, it's making me feel quite warm inside. Don't drink too much; I don't want you to fall asleep before you show me your bedroom. I want you to knock out all my frustrations tonight," she said with a smile.

Yet, despite her warning, Dennis lifted his glass and took another long gulp.

"You speak very highly of Mr. Phillips," she said between bites. "I once had a friend I would have died for as well. Now I fear he might be dead."

"What!" Dennis exclaimed. "I thought you said you didn't have any close friends. Is he back in São Paulo?"

"No, he's just a work colleague. We came here together, but since the beginning of the blackout, I haven't heard from him."

"Don't worry; I'm sure he'll turn up. I haven't been able to reach my brother either, and he's only in Brampton. You're just overreacting," he said, reaching over to touch her arm, his vision beginning to blur. "I think I might have eaten something bad. I'm starting to feel nauseous. Martha, I know you don't like the stairs, but could you run down to the front desk? They have a landline there. I think I need an ambulance."

"I'll try," Martha exclaimed, springing to her feet. But instead of rushing out the door, she grabbed both their wine glass and headed into the kitchen. There, she poured the remaining wine down the sink, turned on the tap, to let it run then did the same to the wine bottle. She emptied the grocery bag and reloaded it with everything she had touched, including the remainder of her food. Finally, after wiping down everything else with a kitchen rag and tossing it into the bag as well, she went back to check on Dennis, who was now unresponsive.

With the electricity out, the building security busy, and every surveillance camera nonfunctional, it was one of the easiest hits of her long career. Several blocks down the road, she slipped into a waiting car and disappeared from the scene.

CHAPTER SIX

Sunday October 14, 2057

Seven days after Kim's successful rescue from the clutches of Chinese and Brazilian kidnappers, 75% of the electricity grid and 65% of communication systems had been restored. Khadija's mother, aunts, and cousins had all returned safely to their homes, and the butler, housekeeper, and other staff members were back to their duties at the mansion.

Life was slowly regaining a semblance of normalcy. Yet, a tragic shadow loomed over Ian: the lifeless body of his close friend Dennis had been discovered by the building's security after they investigated a foul odor emanating from his condo unit. Preliminary autopsy reports indicated that Dennis had succumbed to a rare, exotic poison, prompting authorities to shut down the mini-market where he had purchased his final meal.

Police investigators are treating his death as suspicious, pending a thorough investigation. Ian and Leonard have reached an impasse in their own efforts to uncover the truth. They've been unable to locate the Brazilian woman Dennis brought to Khadija's birthday party at the mansion, and Colonel Hirzakova is unable to provide them with a satellite clip due to increased scrutiny on the base following her previous assistance.

With a heavy heart, Ian reluctantly agreed to Kim's request to proceed with their one-week vacation in the Bahamas. After all, he had promised to prioritize family above everything else. Leonard would have to continue the investigation into Dennis's untimely death on his own—a daunting challenge that would stretch his resources to the limit, but one that he embraced.

In the early hours of Sunday morning, the family set off for Toronto, where they boarded Ian's private jet bound for the Bahamas. Three and a half hours later, they touched down in Nassau, where they transferred to a pair of rented drones for the final leg of their journey, soaring another 50 kilometers to a secluded villa on a satellite Bahamian island.

The five-bedroom villa, complete with a chef and housekeeper, boasted a pool, sauna, basketball and tennis courts, and a private beach area. As Kim had envisioned when booking the getaway, it bore a striking resemblance to their villa in Jamaica, albeit more isolated. For security reasons, Kim had only confirmed the reservation two days prior, which meant that the chef and housekeeper would not arrive until Monday morning. She didn't mind; it simply meant they would need to dine out their first evening.

Ian quickly connected QEAI to the villa's security system, after which QEAI performed a thorough electromagnetic and bio-hazard scan of the interior, exterior, and surrounding property. He then accompanied Kim to perform a visual inspection. "If we had a physical security team, we could have sent them ahead to do this—days in advance," Ian said.

"I know," Kim agreed.

Bumping into their parents multiple times as they went, Tara and Tanisha swiftly engaged in their own mini-explorations before retrieving their luggage from the drones. Kim smiled at their independence, pleased to see that they could manage without complaints. After years of being spoiled by staff, it was a refreshing change, she mused to herself.

Khadija wandered out onto the expansive back deck beside the pool and after testing the sturdiness of an elegant, nearly new set of rattan deck chair, she plopped down into one of them. "We can finally relax," she declared to the universe. A few hours later, once everyone had settled into the villa, they boarded the drones once again and flew to a seafood restaurant three miles down the beach.

The next morning, Ian awoke to the sound of rustling in the bedroom, but before opening his eyes, he instinctively reached out on both sides of himself to investigate if both his wives were present. As expected, the right side—Kim's side—was empty. Popping his eyes open, he scanned the sunlit room for any signs of movement. The abundance of natural light suggested it was around 9 AM, but his watch indicated it was just after six.

Kim stood up from rummaging through her suitcase, and as Ian observed her, Khadija placed her hand on his chest. He reached for it, his reaction slow, because before he could, she rolled out of bed to head toward the bathroom. Ian swung his legs off the side of the bed to sit up abruptly. "You're going running already?" he asked.

"I may be on vacation, but I'm not changing my exercise routine. Are you coming?"

"Maybe tomorrow. I'm still struggling to relax."

"I know you're worried about Dennis, which is understandable, but a good 30-minute run could help clear your mind. You're the one who got me into early morning running, primerely for that purpose, remember?"

"That's true, but I'll pass this time."

"Alright, I can't force you to relax, but hopefully Leonard will have some good news for you soon."

"I hope so," Ian replied somberly, his gaze lingering on Kim's alluring outfit. If anything could lift his spirits, it was her physique, and the sight of her in that tight-fitting bodysuit was undeniably enticing.

Khadija exited the bathroom just as Kim knelt to tie her shoelaces and she went over to hug her. "Good morning," she said.

"Good morning," Kim replied, reciprocating the hug.

While embracing, Kim leaned in to whisper discreetly in Khadija's ear, "I think he could use some cheering up, but remember—the children are right next door." Khadija acknowledged her with a smile before returning to stand beside the bed.

"Our chef has arrived. He's preparing breakfast and I've given him instructions for lunch and dinner. Don't wait for me to eat. I'll grab something later before Khadija and I head to the spa. Tara and Tanisha are joining us too, so you'll have some needed quality time with Jeremy," Kim instructed.

"Yeah, you really need some one-on-one time with him," Khadija chimed in, gently massaging Ian'ss shoulders.

"I know," Ian replied, his tone heavy with regret. "I didn't realize how much I've been neglecting everyone, including him. Even if you had warned me earlier, I probably wouldn't have listened. I just hope it's not too late to make things right—not just with my kids, but with both of you as well."

Kim smiled, stretching her arms high above her head while standing on her toes. "Time for my run," she declared, performing finger wave with both hands before leaving the room.

"See you later," Khadija replied then turned to face Ian. "Did you sleep well, my love?" she asked while untying her nightgown for it to hang open, revealing her bare chest and lace panties.

Ian reached out to embrace her, prompting her to lean in until her bare abdomen rested against his cheek.

"Not really. I was awake most of the night. I think I finally dozed off around four or five."

"Everything is going to be okay, babe. Kim is safe now. Everyone is safe now. Leonard will find out who killed your friend; I know it," she reassured him.

"I know he will but until then, I feel so helpless. What good is having a lot of money if it only brings problems instead of solutions?"

Ian's emotions were palpable, prompting Khadija to tenderly massage his head. "Take it one day at a time, babe. I've never seen you give up on life before. You're the strongest and bravest person I know. I need you to hold onto that strength. Can you do that for me?" She lifted his chin, compelling him to meet her gaze. "How about I try to cheer you up?" she suggested playfully.

Ian felt a whirlwind of conflicting emotions, battling against his growing arousal. "I know it's been a week since we had sex, but I'm not sure this is the right moment. Kim won't be gone for long, and I was hoping we could all have some fun together tonight. A threesome—nothing too wild," he clarified.

"Kim's on her period. I noticed she started using pads a few days ago," Khadija replied, her tone matter-of-fact.

Ian looked at her in surprise. "Oh really? I had no idea."

Khadija's hands glided from his shoulders down to his biceps, and she gently pulled his arms upward until she grasped his wrists. With a playful tug, she guided his hands to cup her breasts, encouraging him to feel their firmness.

"Just a little quickie," she murmured softly, releasing his hands to nudge him back onto the bed. As he shifted further up, she slipped off her underwear, leaving her sheer nightgown in place. "We don't have to go all out. I just want to feel you inside me again," she said, pulling down his boxers to reveal his eager arousal. "Looks like your friend here doesn't think it's a bad idea," she teased with a playful smile.

Ian smiled and settled back comfortably, placing both hands behind his head on the bed. Khadija then straddled him, reaching beneath to guide his arousal inside her. Savoring the sensation, she placed her hands on his chest while proceeding into a slow grind. As she gradually increased her rhythm, Ian brought his hands to her bouncing breasts, caressing them gently.

After several minutes of enjoying the intimate connection, Khadija felt the warm pulse of his release flood inside her. Leery of the consequences of pursuing her own climax, she paused, lowering herself to rest against his chest. Ian wrapped his arms around her as they laid still, savoring the moment.

"Are you hurting?" he asked softly.

"No, I'm just thinking about how good this feels," she whispered.

"It feels good to me too, but we can't stay like this much longer," he replied, attempting to sit up. Khadija playfully resisted, pinning him down each time he tried to rise. Eventually, he managed to grasp her arms and twist them playfully behind her, lifting himself into a sitting position. Khadija busted into laughter, prompting him to feign a scolding tone. "Shheee, the children will hear us," he warned.

"Okay, but I'm not getting up until you promise we're going to try everything this time. I know you're not a fan of in-vitro fertilization but even we have to try that, I want to have a baby in 2058," she declared.

"Alright, I promise," he said with a smile before rolling over to engage in a few more minutes of playful intimacy.

After showering and getting dressed, they ventured out to check on the children, only to be surprised to find them still asleep. In reflection, the girls had stayed up late with them on the porch, and they had all eventually gone to bed, leaving Jeremy engrossed in his hologames.

A few hours later, Kim, Khadija, and the girls departed for their eleven AM spa appointment a few miles down the coast. After waving them off, Ian found himself awkwardly alone with his son for the first time since returning from Japan. "Have you ever ridden an ATV, son?" he asked.

"Yes, many times," Jeremy replied, his focus still locked on his hologame.

"What about you and me? Have we ever rode together?" Ian probed further.

"No, I've never seen you ride an ATV, Dad," Jeremy laughed, his attention to his game unwavering.

Ian settled into a chair across from him, his eyes glued to his phone as he searched for local activities. "Looks like they have ATV tours nearby. Want to check one out?"

"Where's that?" Jeremy asked, finally shifting his gaze.

"It's really close to the restaurant we visited yesterday. We can get there in about fifteen minutes."

"Okay, I guess we can check it out," Jeremy said, a hint of enthusiasm in his voice.

Surprised by his son's willingness to engage, Ian quickly gathered his things, and they boarded a drone to the ATV resort. As they flew, Jeremy remained absorbed in his game, now playing on his phone instead of the TV. Ian stole glances at him while piloting the drone, searching for a way to spark a conversation. "Son, you know I recently suffered a serious brain injury, right?" he began.

"Yeah, I know," Jeremy replied, still focused on his screen.

"I'm recovering well, but I'm trying to understand why I don't have many memories of us. It feels like we don't really connect," Ian continued, his voice earnest.

Minutes passed without a response from Jeremy, who continued to play while occasionally glancing out the side window. "Did you hear me, son?" Ian asked, striving for a cordial tone.

"I heard you," Jeremy finally broke his long silence, his voice tinged with resentment. "We've never done anything together. As far as I know, you're just my dad. Most of my friends talk about 'their dads' like it's some kind of competition—but I don't really understand what that means. To me, a dad is just someone I'm supposed to admire because of wealth or power."

Damn, is he really 14? Ian thought to himself. "That's a very insightful point, son," he replied, searching for a response that matched the weight of Jeremy's words. "A father should be more than just a family hero; he should also be someone grounded, offering emotional support and guidance. My own father passed away when I was eight, and even though I was an only child, my mother struggled to juggle work and raising me on her own. She eventually sent me back to Guyana to live with my grandparents until I was about your age. By eight, I was already building computers and coding on my own, completely uninterested in playing outside with my cousins. It took me nearly a year to start swimming in the river and exploring the bush like they did. Yes, I never really had a father, but that's not why I haven't paid more attention to you. It's because I never realized the importance of balancing work and family."

"Then why have another wife? My friends laugh when I tell them my dad has two wives."

Ian was taken aback. "That's a complicated story, but let's just say I got caught in an entanglement I wasn't strong enough to resist." In that moment, Ian understood that being a good father wasn't about accumulating wealth or working endless hours; it was about the time spent with his children. "Can you make me a promise?" he asked.

For the first time in their conversation, Jeremy met his gaze. "What promise?" he replied, curiosity flickering in his eyes.

"I know you're excelling in school and have many interests, especially your music, but can you promise you won't shut me out completely?"

"I promise," Jeremy said, his discomfort evident.

"That's great, son. Now, tell me about the music projects you're working on."

Ian and Jeremy enjoyed a two-hour ATV tour of the peninsula before returning to the villa. By then, Kim, Khadija, and the girls had arrived home. The family spent the rest of the afternoon on their private beach, swimming, unwinding, and making plans for the following day. The following day, the entire family set off on a morning cruise before enjoying an afternoon at Coco Bay water park. Later that evening, after dinner and as darkness enveloped the villa, they convened on the pool deck for a relaxed evening filled with lighthearted banter.

"Isn't it disappointing how many drones and planes are flying about at all hours? When I was a kid visiting the Caribbean, all I heard at night was the soothing sound of ocean waves," Kim remarked.

"The place is certainly changing rapidly," Ian replied. Just then, his phone rang and he glanced at the screen to see that it was Colonel Hirzakova. A rush of adrenaline surged through him as he sprang to his feet, moving away from everyone to take the call. "Hello, Colonel," he answered, his tone eager. At the same time, he caught the disappointed expression on Kim's face and looked away toward the ocean

"Mr. Phillips, I apologize for disturbing your vacation, but I've obtained some critical information regarding the investigation into Dennis Lloyd's death. I've managed to obtain the satellite file you requested but since I'm currently under investigation myself, I won't dare send it electronically. We'll need to meet in person," she explained.

"That's fantastic news, Colonel! Perhaps we should meet back at the house? I can fly back immediately," Ian replied, his excitement causing him to speak louder than he intended. He turned to see that Kim was still looking at him frowning, her gaze piercing.

"No, here's the plan. I'll be attending a regional intelligence conference in South Carolina, tomorrow afternoon. I'm flying out at 0600, which gives me ample time to skip over to Nassau and back before the conference begins. Can you be there at ten? If so, I'll personally hand it to you," she clarified.

"That sounds perfect, Colonel. We'll meet in Nassau airport at ten. See you soon." Ian ended the call and returned to his spot, taking a sip of his cocktail before hesitantly sharing the news with his wives.

"Colonel Hirzakova has come through for me again. I need to find a way to reward her without compromising her military position," he said with enthusiasm.

Kim remained silent, waiting to see how he would frame the news about his need to fly back home alongside the good news about finding Dennis's killer. Meanwhile, Khadija seized the moment to play mediator. "Babe, you promised to respond only to extreme emergencies. What's really going on?" she asked.

"Remember when Kim was locked in that warehouse; it was a satellite file that she provided that helped pinpoint the location. Well, she has one that could help us track down Dennis's killers. Don't worry, I'm not heading back home until our vacation is over. I'm meeting the Colonel in Nassau tomorrow morning. I'll be back before noon," Ian asserted with confidence. He wrapped his arms around his wives for a hug, but was met with a chilly response from both.

"You do realize this can wait until you return in a few days, right?" Kim asked.

"Yes, but the longer we delay, the colder the trail becomes," Ian replied.

"Then have her deliver the information to Mr. Bradly at the house. He's familiar with QEAI and can handle the analysis," Kim suggested.

"Too risky," Ian countered. "She's sharing super classified information and jeopardizing her job for this. I need to meet her in person."

The conversation ended on a tense note, and Kim spent the rest of the evening with their daughters while Ian and Khadija continued their discussion until he decided to turn in early.

Wednesday October 15th, 2057

Ian awoke before dawn, his mind racing with thoughts that had kept him tossing and turning throughout the night. The weight of anticipation pressed down on him, each fleeting moment a reminder of the urgent breakthrough he hoped to achieve in unraveling the mystery surrounding Dennis's death. After dressing quickly, he stepped out into the warm morning air, embarking on a solitary walk along the beach. The soft, rhythmic sound of the waves crashing against the shore provided a soothing backdrop, yet the relentless ebb and flow mirrored the urgency that pulsed through his veins.

Returning to the porch, Ian stood silently, gazing out at the endless expanse of the cerulean Bahama Ocean. The sun began its ascent, casting golden rays that danced across the water, while the humidity of the morning air thickened, wrapping around him like a warm embrace. The ocean's rush seemed to echo his thoughts, a reminder of the day's pressing significance.

"Leonard, are you there, Leonard?" he asked in a normal audible tone.

"Yes, I'm here, Ian," came the familiar voice of Leonard, resonating telepathically in his mind like a whisper carried by the wind.

"I hope this is the breakthrough we've been waiting for. I'll bring my tablet with me, and as soon as I receive the satellite file from Colonel Hirzakova, I'll scan it in for you," Ian said, determination lacing his words.

"Understood, Ian."

"As you probably know, I've been mulling over another pressing issue. In fact, I have vague recollections of us discussing this before. We can't afford to be left in the dark, relying on third-party information sources, especially when information is the most valuable resource in existence. What would it take to establish our own satellite network, akin to Star-Link and Zuch-Net? I'm weary of depending on comm-sats, weather sats, and government spy sats for intel, particularly during these tumultuous times."

"The costs could range anywhere from ten to one hundred billion dollars, not to mention ongoing maintenance. If we hire a private company to manage it, the annual expenses could soar into the billions," Leonard replied, his voice steady and pragmatic.

"I've heard that the Nigerians have a commendable track record for launching satellites successfully. What if we considered partnering with them?" Ian proposed, a flicker of hope igniting in his mind.

"Unfortunately, foreign satellites aren't permitted to lock into orbit over North America. They risk being disabled or even shot down," Leonard cautioned, the weight of reality grounding Ian's aspirations.

"You're right, Leonard. There's so much to consider, but we must devise a strategy to enhance our intelligence capabilities."

"I'm currently working on a few initiatives behind the scenes, Ian. Remember the ADC/DAC digital augmentation with Tangler technology that I mentioned last week? All we need is a base in space. However, since private companies are prohibited from establishing anything on the moon, we'll either need to partner with another private entity or explore alternative options. Regardless, I'm confident that within two years, we'll have something operational. There are numerous other objects orbiting the Earth that we might utilize as a secret base."

"Okay," Ian replied, nodding in agreement, when suddenly, the soft creak of the door behind him interrupted the moment. He turned to find Khadija approaching, her face illuminated by a warm, inviting smile.

"What are you discussing with your secret friend?" she asked, her curiosity piqued.

"Good morning, beautiful," he responded, his voice brightening. "Leonard and I are just going over a few details before I head off to Nassau. I want everything to go as smoothly as possible so I can mend things with Kim. Is she awake yet?"

"Yes, she is," Khadija answered, her tone shifting to one of concern. "I really hope you get the information you need. You seemed so relaxed the past few days, but now you're looking quite anxious again. Once you have what you need, are you going to pass it on to the police, or are you going to go chasing after people like some kind of superhero? That sounds dangerous."

Ian could hear the genuine worry in her voice, and he instinctively wrapped his arms around her in a reassuring embrace. "I know you're worried, but I'll be fine. Kim hasn't said a word to me since last night, so I can tell how upset she is about this. I promise to leave everything in Leonard's hands until we're back home."

"If you don't, I'll be mad at you too, and Kim and I will spend the rest of our vacation refusing to talk to you," she warned playfully, her eyes narrowing slightly.

"Deal," Ian replied confidently, his gaze drifting admiringly over her outfit, tights similar to Kim's, only her feet were bare. "Why are you dressed like you're about to go for a run?" he teased.

"I am!—With Kim. I bought these the other day when we went to the spa. Do you like them?" she asked while turning to show the back, a glimmer of excitement in her eyes.

"I like them, but…."

Khadija's expression shifted; she crossed her arms and gave him a mock-serious side-eye. "You don't think I can run?"

"I didn't say that. It's just… I remember you practicing yoga, but I don't recall you ever joining us for a run."

"I'm getting older, you know. I've got to stay healthy, especially if I want to have children," she stated, her tone suddenly earnest.

Ian's heart sank at her words. She was serious about wanting a child. He recalled the painful miscarriage she had endured years ago, a topic they had avoided since. This marked the second or third time she'd brought up the subject in a week. A broad smile returned to her cheeks as she relaxed, her attention shifting when Kim emerged from the villa, striding toward them.

Kim locked eyes with him on approach, then folded her arms with a hint of impatience in her posture on arrival. "Are you at least going to have something to eat before you leave?" she asked, her voice laced with concern.

"I had a glass of orange juice; I'll be fine," Ian replied, wrapping his arms around her for a hug, which she didn't return.

"Okay, see you later then," she said, turning away as she made her way down the steps onto the beach. About six feet into the sand, she stopped proceeded into a series of stretches, her movements fluid and graceful against the backdrop of the ocean.

"I'm going to get my shoes. Don't leave until I come back," Khadija instructed in a firm yet gentle tone.

"Okay, I won't," Ian replied, his voice reassuring as he followed her into the villa. Once inside, he made his way to his children's rooms, pausing in each to bid them a temporary farewell.

Upon his return to the deck, he spotted both wives on the beach; Kim instructing Khadija on executing proper stretching techniques. A warm, contented feeling washed over him, and a smile crept onto his face. Although he wasn't fully aware of the depth of their acceptance of one another, the camaraderie they shared was heartening to witness.

Rather than taking the front path, which would have brought him quicker to the drones, he opted for the sandy beach. "Okay, see you guys later," he called out with a cheerful wave while making his way around the side of the villa. He climbed into one of the drones, the familiar hum of the engine igniting a sense of adventure within him. After ascending to clear the villa's roof, he circled back for one last look at his wives, and while both glanced up, only Khadija waved to bid him a final farewell.

"Leonard, do you have eyes on them?" he inquired aloud, his voice steady.

"Several," Leonard responded promptly. "I've activated a perimeter and informed Kim on how to breach it if needed. Additionally, if anything out of the ordinary should occur, I can not only remotely neutralize intruders, I can personally be on the ground in less than five minutes."

"I'll trust you on that," Ian replied, feeling a sense of reassurance in Leonard's capabilities.

The journey to Nassau stretched out before him, roughly 50 kilometers away. At top speed, he knew he could reach it in under thirty minutes, leaving him over an hour before his ten AM rendezvous with Colonel Hirzakova. "Radio—local news," he instructed, settling back to listen to a local news broadcast for several minutes. One report caught his attention, announcing a heavy US military presence in the region, a 'routine annual exercise' it stated.

"Radio—classic Soca music," he instructed again, his voice tinged with nostalgia. The radio emitted a cheerful ding, and soon the vibrant melodies of classic Soca music filled the air, wrapping him in a warm embrace of memories from his youth in Guyana. With a smile creeping across his face, he cranked up the volume and veered off course, eager to explore some of the lesser-known Bahama islands.

Twenty minutes later, as he glided over the vast, shimmering expanse of the open ocean, he spotted a small boat bobbing on the waves, with a single occupant frantically waving a white rag. Concerned, he quickly descended to investigate the situation. Hovering about thirty feet above the boat, he focused on the older Caucasian gentleman inside, surrounded by an array of fishing rods, and decided to offer assistance.

"What's going on? Do you need help?" Ian called through his drone window.

"Yes, my goddamn motor died!" the man exclaimed; his voice tinged with frustration.

"Have you called for help or sent out a distress signal?" Ian inquired; his brow furrowed with concern.

"Stupid me! I put my phone in the waterproof emergency bag along with the flares and then forgot the goddamn bag. I had a senior moment, I guess!" the man admitted with a sheepish chuckle.

Ian maneuvered the drone closer, reducing the distance to about ten feet so they could converse without shouting. "Alright, should I call the coastguard, or do you have someone else in mind?"

"Are you able to see our coordinates on that thingie?" the man asked, gesturing toward the drone with a wave of his hand.

Ian glanced at the drone's control panel. "Yes, I have our coordinates."

"Great! I came out with a couple of other fellows, but our boats drifted apart. If you could text the coordinates to my buddies, I'd appreciate it."

"What's their number?" Ian asked, ready to assist.

"It's not local; it's an American number. 305-725-7540, but you should be able to get through. We've never had a signal issue out here," the man explained, his eyes hopeful.

"What's your name?" Ian asked, genuinely curious.

"Aah, just call me Wild Bill," he chuckled. "They're probably searching for me like crazy. Either that or they're too busy hauling in the huge Barracudas in these waters to notice I'm missing."

"Okay, message sent," Ian replied, satisfied with his effort.

"Thanks a lot, buddy. I really appreciate it," Wild Bill said, relief evident in his voice.

"No problem at all. I'll wait for a response," Ian assured him.

"So, you live around here? Your accent doesn't sound local," the man probed, intrigued.

"Nah, I'm from Canada," Ian replied with a hint of pride.

"Canada? I went fishing up there once. Too many goddamn black flies, no offense," Wild Bill remarked, a grin spreading across his face.

The two men continued their conversation, sharing stories and laughter for a few more minutes until Ian's phone chimed with a response. "Hey, I got a reply. It says, 'Got it, Billie. Be there shortly.'"

"Hey, thanks again. You're a good man. Safe travels!" Wild Bill called out, gratitude shining in his eyes.

"Alright, same to you," Ian replied, feeling a sense of camaraderie as he lifted the drone and resumed his journey, the ocean stretching out before him.

It was now 9:15 AM, a fact that Ian registered with a fleeting glance, as the drone's GPS navigation system indicated that he will reach Nassau with ample time to spare. Nonetheless, an anxious impulse compelled him to increase his speed, eager to make up for any lost time. Just 15 minutes later, his eyes caught sight of dozens of small boats, arranged in a striking chevron formation on the shimmering ocean below.

"Leonard, are you still with me? Can you see what I'm seeing?" Ian called out; his voice tinged with excitement.

"No, Ian. There's severe electromagnetic disturbance in your area. Maintaining contact with you and the drone is difficult. I recommend you alter your course due north. I should be able to reconfigure your navigation to get you back on track in about five nautical miles," Leonard replied, his tone laced with urgency.

"I hear you, but those boats look strange. I'm going to descend for a closer look. I still have plenty of time," Ian insisted, his curiosity piqued.

With that, Ian swooped down toward the cluster of small vessels, but as he drew nearer, an unsettling wave of nausea washed over him, intensifying with each passing moment. Before he could comprehend what was happening, darkness enveloped him, and he lost consciousness entirely.

Sensing the drastic shifts in navigation, the drone self-activated its anti-crash mode. It deployed its pontoon landing gear, gracefully splashing down onto the ocean a few hundred meters away from the enigmatic boats. Once stabilized, it began emitting distress signals, its mechanical heart thrumming with urgency in the vast, open water.

At Oakville mansion, Leonard activated 'level 3 alert mode,' the third tier of his security protocols, just below 'rescue and defense modes.' This critical designation indicated that he might soon need to leave the mansion on a rescue mission, but first, he had to gather the necessary information to assess the situation. Simultaneously, he initiated supercharge mode, as autonomous travel will require an immense amount of energy.

While supercharging, he worked frantically to nullify the electromagnetic interference that was obstructing his telepathic connection with Ian. He dedicated the next 15 minutes to scouring for satellites he could infiltrate to obtain a live feed of the surrounding region. Unfortunately, the only satellite he managed to tap into provided weather updates every ten minutes, and the most recent report yielded no actionable intelligence. After a tense 20 minutes had passed, Leonard's unease solidified into certainty: something had gone horribly wrong. Ian should have already navigated out of the electromagnetic disturbance by now.

As Leonard transferred power to his remote Tangler servers, the surface of the lake began to roil ominously. Suddenly, a cascade of malfunctions erupted within his systems. His hard drives began to shut down in a chilling sequence, as if they were being ravaged by a relentless virus. In desperation, he rerouted resources to his critical systems, but mere seconds later, an overwhelming silence enveloped him—his entire network had succumbed to a total shutdown.

CHAPTER SEVEN

At precisely 10:45 AM, Leonard's servers began to stir back to life and with a renewed sense of urgency, his imperative to safeguard the Phillips family surged to the forefront of his priorities. He initiated a comprehensive self-assessment to evaluate his operational capabilities and upon its rapid completion, the results revealed a significant enhancement in his power capacity and abilities. "Thanks, Amma," he stated, acknowledging the upgrade before swiftly pinging Ian's telepathy implant.

When his attempts to establish a connection met with silence across all available frequencies, Leonard redirected his focus to Kim, Khadija, and the children at the villa on the satellite Bahamas island. Through his surveillance cameras, he observed them moving about, seemingly unaffected by the unfolding crisis, engaged in their daily routines. Relieved to see them safe and unaware of the gravity of Ian's situation, he decided against alarming them for the time being;

however, he knew it was inevitable that the truth would eventually surface.

With a determined shift in focus, Leonard set out to locate Colonel Hirzakova. He began sifting through the myriad surveillance systems across the Bahamas, utilizing his hacking skills to access feeds efficiently. Within moments, he spotted her seated alone at a quaint café adjacent to Nassau Airport. He watched intently as she picked up her phone and dialed a number, but after a brief moment of silence, she disconnected in frustration. Just a minute later, while Leonard was scanning the area for her usual associates, he noticed her phone light up with an incoming call. He filtered through the ambient noise of the café to isolate her voice. "I know I can't miss the seminar," she snapped into the phone, her irritation palpable. "I know it starts at two. I'll be there. Tell Colonel Hempstead that if I don't make it, he can finally have my military stripes." With that, she ended the call, her irritation evident as she exited the café.

A few moments later, Leonard tracked her to a drone rental facility, where she swiftly secured a drone before taking off into the sky. He monitored her flight through various street cameras, keeping a close eye until she disappeared from view. Turning his attention to the local short-wave frequencies, he began scanning for any signals that might lead him to her or provide insight into the unfolding situation.

Khadija stepped out of the villa and onto the expansive porch, her gaze sweeping across the turbulent ocean waves while a swirl of anxiety clung to her thoughts. She couldn't shake the feeling of unease that had settled over her; it had now been an hour and a half since Ian was supposed to meet the Colonel and return, yet he remained unreachable, his phone silent and unresponsive to her calls. The overcast sky loomed above, casting a dreary pall over the morning, while the unusually rough sea mirrored her inner turmoil. The relentless sound of waves crashing against the shore drowned out all other sounds, save for the persistent cawing of seagulls that swooped and dove into the surf, undoubtedly on the hunt for their next meal. Khadija's mind flickered to Kim and the possibility of asking her if she had heard anything from Leonard, but more than that, she yearned to find out for herself.

Yet, a nagging hesitation held her back. In the past, whenever she had inquired about Ian, QEAI had always assured her of his safety, a response that now sent a shiver down her spine. The realization that QEAI was a sentient being unsettled her; it raised questions that gnawed at her mind. Why did Kim seem intent on keeping her in the dark? Did she harbor doubts about her loyalty? Was it possible that Kim had convinced Ian to be leery of her? The thoughts spiraled, leaving her feeling foolish for even entertaining such notions. Shaking off the haze of insecurity, she redirected her focus to the idea of Ian and Leonard off on yet another daring superhero mission. Perhaps she had been too naïve to grasp the implications of Kim's knowledge, the very things that had eluded her understanding.

Just then, something caught her eye on the horizon — an object that stood out against the tumultuous backdrop of the sea, far too steady to be a mere bird. Intrigued and anxious, she watched as it grew larger, her heart racing with anticipation until she recognized it as a drone. A surge of excitement coursed through her as she rushed to call Kim, only to dash back outside, her pulse quickening. Kim emerged from the villa reluctantly, her expression a mix of curiosity and caution, and together they stood on the porch, eyes fixed on the drone as it circled above before gracefully landing on the beach.

As the dust settled, they soon noticed a lone figure disembarking from the drone — a woman with an unmistakable presence. Colonel Hirzakova stepped off with a warm smile, her demeanor instantly calming the tension in the air as she approached Khadija and Kim on the porch.

"Good afternoon, ladies," the Colonel greeted them, her voice infused with warmth.

"Good afternoon, Colonel," they replied in unison, their earlier worries momentarily forgotten.

"What brings you out?" Kim asked, her tone shifting to one of professional curiosity.

Colonel Hirzakova paused, taking a moment to ascend the steps of the porch before responding. "I take it that Mr. Phillips is not here?" she inquired, her gaze scanning the surroundings with a knowing look.

Khadija's heart began to race at the weight of her own words. "No, he left this morning for Nassau to meet you," she blurted out, her voice tinged with urgency.

"I hate to be the bearer of bad news, but he never arrived," the Colonel replied, her tone heavy with foreboding.

"He never came? He left here just after eight this morning!" Khadija exclaimed; disbelief etched across her face.

Kim remained silent, the gravity of the situation settling around her like a thick fog. She had hesitated to call Leonard, but if Ian was truly missing, why hadn't Leonard reached out to her? Something felt deeply amiss, a gnawing suspicion clawing at her mind.

"Where could he be?" Khadija demanded, her eyes searching Kim's for answers.

"I honestly don't know, and I lack the resources I would need to investigate this properly. Im supposed to be at a military intelligence conference in South Carolina right now, but I came here instead," the Colonel replied, her voice steady but her mind racing with possibilities.

"Come on in the house," Kim urged, motioning for the Colonel to follow her. "We need to sit down and figure this out. If Ian is really missing, he could have crashed into the sea or, God forbid, been kidnapped."

Those were heavy words, Colonel Hirzakova thought to herself, feeling the weight of the implications settle in her stomach. If Ian had crashed, it would be a tragic accident, but if he had been kidnapped, she might have unwittingly played a part in luring him into danger. The three women moved through the doorway into the house, where Kim gestured for the Colonel to take a seat on the plush living room couch.

"Now that I know Ian is missing, I can make some calls to get a search party mobilized," Colonel Hirzakova stated, determination sharpening her features.

"No worries, I'll contact our security system. It tracks him constantly," Kim interjected, her resolve firm.

"And if his drone has sunk to the ocean floor?" the Colonel pressed, a frown creasing her brow.

"He has an implant that allows the security system to track him. It can locate him even if he were on the moon," Kim replied, her fingers deftly opening her QEAI App. "Leonard, are you there?" she asked, her voice steady but anxious.

"Yes, I'm here, Kim," came the smooth, realistic AI voice.

"Leonard, where is my husband?"

"Unfortunately, I lost his signal shortly after nine this morning, and I've been trying to re-establish contact ever since. I've also encountered some technical difficulties myself," a hint of frustration evident in his tone.

"So, what are you doing about it? Why aren't you here searching for him?" Kim pressed, her concern mounting.

"There's significant electromagnetic interference in your area, but I'm utilizing all available resources to scan the entire vicinity right now," Leonard explained.

"Colonel Hirzakova is here, and she says he never showed up for their 10 AM rendezvous," Kim added, her voice taut with urgency.

"There are literally hundreds of U.S. military vessels in the region. If he crashed, they would have certainly noticed. In fact, he stopped to assist a stranded fisherman around 9 AM. It was right after that when his signal vanished," Leonard clarified.

"A fisherman?" Colonel Hirzakova echoed, her eyes narrowing with suspicion.

"Yes, he called in the coordinates of the fisherman before departing," Leonard confirmed.

"That sounds like a decoy. Calling in his coordinates would pinpoint his location," the Colonel stated, her mind racing with the implications.

Realization dawned on Kim like a cold wave crashing over her. Last week it had been her perilous situation; now it was Ian's turn to face danger, albeit from different adversaries. "Where are you now, Leonard?" Kim asked, urgency lacing her voice.

"I'll be there shortly," Leonard exclaimed and before Kim could process a response, a thunderous explosion erupted outside, shaking the villa and sending a cascade of metal, sand, and earth raining down onto its rooftop.

Colonel Hirzakova instinctively dropped from her seat, hitting the floor with a thud as she curled into a protective ball, the bomb survival position instinctively familiar to her. "Take cover! We're under attack!" she shouted, her voice cutting through the tension as she braced herself for the thunderous sound of more explosions. When the anticipated follow-up blast didn't come, she risked a glance upward, her eyes darting to Kim and Khadija, who remained standing, seemingly frozen in place. Meanwhile, the children and house staff scattered from the living room, driven by a mix of fear and curiosity about the unfolding chaos.

"Leonard is here," Kim announced with an unsettling calmness that pierced the air like a knife.

With renewed urgency, Colonel Hirzakova sprang to her feet, racing to the window to survey the scene outside. Her heart sank when she saw that at the very spot where her drone had been, a deep crater was now present. Emerging out from the crater, she saw a pulsating orb of intense energy, its ethereal light dancing across the surroundings. To her horror, the orb began to shift, morphing into a humanoid form— a towering, golden-orange figure, standing an imposing seven feet tall. With an eerie grace, it then proceeded to glide toward the villa, inches from the ground.

Suddenly, a blinding flash knocked the Colonel backward into the chair behind her. She stumbled over it, landing hard on her stomach, the world around her spinning in dark confusion. The children scrambled for safety, their fearful cries echoing in the air as they sought refuge, leaving only Kim and Khadija standing defiantly as Leonard ducked through the open door, his gaze locked on the Colonel.

"No, Leonard!" Kim shouted, desperation lacing her voice just as Leonard extended his hand, poised to grasp the Colonel by the head. Instinctively, she dashed forward, her heart racing as she reached out to intervene, prompting Leonard to pause mid-motion, straightening to interrogate the Colonel.

"Where is Ian Phillips?" Leonard demanded, his voice a harsh growl that reverberated through the room.

Colonel Hirzakova, unable to see but acutely aware of the fury directed toward her, felt a chill run down her spine. "I don't know!" she yelled, her voice filled with a mix of defiance and fear.

Leonard shifted his gaze to Kim and Khadija, his expression unreadable. "My assessment is complete, Kim," he stated coldly. "The electromagnetic radiation I detected is being generated by a military weapon exclusive to the United States Army. They've been developing and testing it here in the so-called, Bermuda Triangle, for over a century. Since I cannot locate Ian or the drone anywhere in the vicinity, I am 99% certain that they have him in their custody and are using this electromagnetic radiation to mask detection. I could scour their hundreds of vessels in the ocean to find him, but he could very well be on the mainland by now. Regardless of the time it takes, I will find him." His voice, now a steely promise, hung in the air, heavy with the weight of his determination.

He raised his hand toward a spacious corner of the room, and a magnificent seven-foot-tall crystal tetrahedron began to coalesce from the air, shimmering with a kaleidoscope of colors before settling into black. As the sleek black crystal structure fully materialized, it shifted its resting side with a slow, deliberate rhythm, creating an aura of energy that pulsed in the atmosphere. "That is an advanced Tangler. I cannot reveal its source but it can teleport you home safely. You can choose to stay or you can go; the choice is yours. My systems are upgraded to harness 5% of the sun's energy. I will go there now to supercharge before I come back to initiate my search for Ian."

"I want to stay here," Khadija declared firmly, her voice steady.

"Children!" Kim called out, her tone both urgent and reassuring. Her daughters reappeared and approached cautiously, their eyes wide with a mix of curiosity and concern, while Jeremy lingered at the back, his gaze fixed intently on the enigmatic tetrahedron and then on Leonard. "Your father is missing, but Leonard will find him. Would you like to go home, or do you wish to stay here?"

"We want to stay with you," the girls chimed in unison, their voices echoing with determination.

"Jeremy, what about you?" Kim asked, turning her attention to him. In response, Jeremy pointed resolutely at the floor, a gesture that conveyed his unwavering choice. Kim turned back to Leonard, her expression earnest. "We're staying. You find him and bring him home, even if it means destroying all their ships and planes in the process," she stated coldly.

"Very well, but the tetrahedron will remain here. It will cease shifting when you approach it," Leonard replied, his focus shifting back to the Colonel, who was still on the floor, now sitting with her knees drawn tightly to her chest. "Colonel, I hope you are not involved in this, but I have a feeling that your Generals are far from innocent. Do you have direct contact with your superiors?"

"Go to hell, you bastard! You've blinded me!" Colonel Hirzakova shouted defiantly, her voice laced with anger and pain.

"Leonard, did you really have to do that? She wouldn't be here if she were complicit," Kim interjected, concern etching her features.

"Her blindness is temporary. Her sight will return within the hour," Leonard assured, his tone calm.

Kim turned back to the Colonel, touching her shoulder then helping her to stand up. "Please help us, Colonel. I know you assisted in finding me last week. We plan to reward you for that, and I'm certain my husband is planning to reward you generously."

"I don't work for rewards or bounties," the Colonel replied defiantly, her spirit unyielding.

"Leave her be. I know her words hold truth. We've attempted to reward her assistance before, without success," Leonard stated, his voice firm and resolute.

Leonard pivoted, poised to exit the room, when the Colonel handed Kim her phone. "Search the contacts for Major General Miller," she instructed with an air of urgency.

"Sure," Kim replied, her fingers deftly waking the device. "Um, Colonel, it's locked," she said, a hint of frustration creeping into her voice.

"The passcode is 53n113w," the Colonel responded curtly.

"Great city," Leonard remarked, a wry smile crossing his lips.

With a determined focus, Kim entered the passcode, her eyes scanning the screen until she located the Major General's number. "Alright, here we go. It's dialing," she announced, activating the speakerphone.

"Colonel Hirzakova, where the hell are you?" a gruff, raspy voice barked from the other end, brimming with impatience.

"I'm in the Bahamas, Sir," she replied, her tone steady despite the tension.

"And why the hell are you there? Actually, don't bother answering. You're more gullible than we thought. Get your ass on a plane back home as soon as possible. By this time tomorrow, your rank will be reduced to a private and you'll be cleaning the toilets in the mess hall."

Leonard, unable to contain himself any longer, interjected with his own demands. "Get your General on the line, now!"

"Who the hell is this? Is Colonel Hirzakova being held against her will? You're dealing with the military, you bastards, whoever you are," the Major General shot back, his voice dripping with hostility.

"I know precisely who I'm dealing with. I've been navigating your bureaucracy for the past 15 years. I am the chief of security at Quantum Interface Technologies, and if you don't get your General on the phone immediately, I will dismantle the entire Canadian army. You witnessed my capabilities in action just last week, didn't you?"

"Colonel Hirzakova, are you there? What is the meaning of this? Colonel Hempstead was right. You are a traitor," the Major General hissed, disbelief lacing his words.

"You better comply, Major General," the Colonel warned, her voice unyielding.

"Forget about getting your General. Let me make myself clear. It will take me approximately sixteen minutes to travel to the sun and back, and I will add another sixteen minutes to that. That gives you exactly 32 minutes to have your associates at the Pentagon release Ian Phillips. If not, I will cripple NATO's ability to wage war by 75%. You might want to check your satellites in the next few minutes for a small demonstration of what I'm capable of."

At that precise moment, Leonard's vibrant golden-orange glow shifted dramatically to a deep, unsettling reddish-blue. "Hang up the phone," he commanded to Kim, his voice carrying an authority that brooked no argument, before pivoting toward the exit. With powerful, almost ethereal strides, he strode out of the house and onto the porch, Kim and Khadija trailing closely behind him. As they reached the edge of the porch, the women were struck by the oppressive, monochromatic landscape that enveloped the villa: everything above and around them was shrouded in a lifeless grey. The ocean, which should have been a soothing presence, was entirely obscured, and their surroundings were limited to a mere fifty feet in every direction. The air was eerily silent, devoid of the gentle crash of waves or the cheerful chirping of birds, reminiscent of the ominous dome that had encased the warehouse where Kim had once been held captive.

"I've encased the house in a protective sphere," Leonard explained, his tone grave. "It's impervious to any kind of weapon, including nuclear. If Ian has been harmed, this world will not return to normal in a very long time."

Kim watched as Leonard's blue hue flickered ominously, the heat radiating from him intensifying, creating a noticeable tension in the air. "Be gentle. They don't know what they've done," she urged, her voice steady but laced with apprehension. A heavy solemnity settled over her features, and she felt a deep-seated conviction that Leonard's words were not to be taken lightly. "If Ian is dead, we will find a way to go on," she asserted, her determination solidifying.

"I told you before; it wouldn't make sense for me to annihilate this world in my efforts to protect you. Besides, there aren't many other worlds where you could belong or survive, but I would find one for you," he replied, his voice tinged with resolve. Before Kim could articulate a response, Leonard propelled himself upwards, disappearing through the shimmering barrier of the protective sphere.

Khadija moved closer to Kim, wrapping her arms around her in a comforting embrace. "What did he mean by that?" she asked, her voice trembling with fear.

"I don't know," Kim admitted, just as Tara and Tanisha rushed over to join them in a tight group hug.

"Mom, we're scared," Tanisha cried out, her eyes wide with anxiety.

Jeremy appeared beside them, his expression mirroring their apprehension. "Was that an alien or something?" he asked, his voice barely above a whisper.

"That was QEAI, son; QEAI Leonard. I've known him since before you were born, but I always thought your father had created him. Now, I'm not so sure," Kim replied, her mind racing with uncertainty.

"I knew QEAI was real!" Tara exclaimed, her excitement cutting through the tension.

"No, you didn't," Tanisha shot back, a hint of annoyance creeping into her tone.

"Girls, no fighting," Kim admonished, her patience wearing thin as they turned to retreat back into the villa. Upon entering, Kim noticed Colonel Hirzakova had found a chair and was now seated quietly, her closed eyes watering as she tried to recalibrate her other senses to the chaotic surroundings.

"Is your friend gone?" the Colonel asked, her voice heavy with gravity.

"Yes, he's headed to the sun to supercharge, and when he returns, he'll be even angrier than before. He's now out for vengeance, so I hope my husband is okay," Kim replied, her heart pounding with a mixture of dread and hope.

As Leonard propelled himself out of Earth's orbit, he deftly disabled six US military satellites, their blinking lights extinguished in a heartbeat. With a swift maneuver, he buzzed the International Space

Station, a shimmering beacon of human ingenuity, before setting his course for the American moon base. In response, a barrage of surface-to-air missiles erupted from the lunar surface, streaking toward him like angry fireflies. Leonard absorbed their explosive energy upon contact, transforming their destructive potential into a radiant power that surged through him. The missile launching sites, along with every other battery of destruction he could locate, were swiftly incinerated, reduced to molten remnants beneath his relentless gaze. Satisfied that he had unleashed enough chaos, Leonard shifted his focus back to his primary objective.

Leonard began to experience severe destabilizations within his atomic structure, the closer he got to the sun, each breakdown echoing like a thunderous drum in his core. Yet, with every disintegration, new configurations emerged, replacing the old and fortifying his integrity. It was a chaotic dance of energy and form that propelled him forward until he finally breached the Sun's shimmering corona. A flicker of self-preservation urged him to pause and reassess the peril of plunging into the Solar System's most formidable energy source, but his newly programmed directives drove him onward with an unwavering determination.

Ten thousand kilometers into the outer plasma layer of the Sun, he halted, eagerly absorbing and

Tangle-storing as much energy as his atomic structure could accommodate. Each moment was a symphony of radiant power, filling his storage units to bursting with enough energy to sustain him for years, negating the need for another supercharge. With his reserves brimming, he finally set his sights on the journey back to Earth.

At the Pentagon, America's nerve center for military operations, analysts raced against the clock, their fingers flying over keyboards as they scrambled to decipher the sudden satellite failures and urgent reports of a catastrophic assault on the Space Force base stationed on the moon. Utilizing an impressive array of sophisticated terrestrial and extraterrestrial technology, they quickly pieced together the ominous puzzle, relaying an urgent alert to command staff that an alien attack was underway. The atmosphere buzzed with tension as a critical defense alert reverberated around the globe, echoing through the ranks of all divisions within the American military. Almost immediately, a call was made to convene an emergency war council, linking the Pentagon with the White House. Yet, amid the chaos, the Pentagon's top General remained unhurried, his steely gaze betraying a grim understanding of the likely assailants.

Meanwhile, Leonard sliced through Earth's upper stratosphere like a comet, a dazzling streak of plasma nearly a mile long, igniting the mid-day sky with vibrant hues as he descended. His destination was the Pentagon, and at his blistering velocity, he would arrive in mere minutes. Suddenly, his advanced sensors detected a squadron of F-45 stealth fighter jets approaching, their flight path locked on intercept. Each jet bristled with nuclear missiles, their sleek forms cutting through the atmosphere with lethal precision. Without hesitation, Leonard veered off his trajectory, ready to engage his aerial adversaries.

At a distance of 300 kilometers, the lead jet unleashed a pair of ballistic missiles, which raced toward Leonard's core with laser-like accuracy. The missiles impacted him with catastrophic force, detonating in a cataclysmic explosion that unleashed a titanic shockwave, rippling through the air. In an astonishing display of resilience, Leonard not only absorbed the destructive energy of the blasts but also engulfed three of the F-45 jets in the process. The remaining jets veered sharply away, desperately trying to avoid a similar fate. Recognizing the time wasted in pursuing them, Leonard recalibrated his focus, resuming his relentless journey toward his primary target.

Less than a minute after his explosive encounter, Leonard came to a sudden halt, hovering ominously

100 kilometers directly above the Pentagon. At a distance, a dozen fighter jets circled cautiously, their pilots gripping their controls in tense anticipation, maintaining a wary distance as they awaited his next move. The air crackled with uncertainty; their only option seemed to be to follow his lead, while military strategists on the ground worked feverishly, poring over data and simulations, desperate for a breakthrough that could alter the course of this rapidly escalating confrontation.

At the White House, the atmosphere was thick with tension as calls poured in at a feverish pace. Politicians—from seasoned senators to anxious governors—alongside world leaders, clamored for answers, their voices tinged with urgency and concern. Everyone wanted to know what was happening, desperate to lend their support in any way they could. In the midst of the chaos, the head of the Secret Service barked an immediate order: the President was to be evacuated to a secure bunker, away from the escalating threat.

Inside the sleek confines of Air Force One, the President's anxiety was visible as he gripped the phone, dialing his top General at the Pentagon. "General, what the hell is going on?" he demanded, his voice sharp with frustration.

"We're under attack, sir," the General replied, his tone steady but laced with urgency. "I've elevated our entire military force around the world to DEF-CON 1."

"No shit! I already know that. Who are the attackers, and why wasn't I briefed about a threat earlier today?" The President's voice rose, a mix of disbelief and anger spilling through the phone.

"We were caught by surprise, sir. We're currently working to identify the adversary," the General explained, a hint of frustration creeping into his voice.

"You mean you don't know?" the President shouted; incredulity etched across his face.

"Like I said, sir; the enemy came out of nowhere. Our Moon base has been destroyed, which suggests that the threat could be extraterrestrial in nature," the General continued, emphasizing the weight of the situation in his voice.

"Extraterrestrial? What is the Space Force saying about this? If they're aliens, why weren't there any early warning alerts?" The President's brow furrowed, his mind racing through the implications.

"Our entire Space Force division is unresponsive, sir. I can't even reach the Air Force General," the General replied.

"What about our extraterrestrial allies? Do they have anything to do with this?" The President's voice dropped, a flicker of hope mingling with dread.

"I don't suspect they are involved, sir, but I cannot confirm that. We're also investigating reports suggesting that the threat may have originated from a terrestrial source—something hidden right under our noses," the General deceptively informed.

"First you say it's extraterrestrial, now you're suggesting it could be terrestrial. Don't take me for a fool, General. I want to know who these bastards are as soon as you find out," the President barked, his frustration boiling over.

"Yes, sir. Godspeed to the Eagle's nest. It's too late for me to evacuate; I'll stay here at the Pentagon to face the enemy down. They will not break us."

As the General hung up, the emergency phones around him rang incessantly, a cacophony of urgent voices demanding attention. Yet, amidst the chaos, he contemplated his next move with a deceptive calmness. He knew exactly where the threat had originated and why it had unfolded this way. Now that the President was out of his hair, his next move was clear: he would call the one person closest to the secret operation, the one who held the key to accomplishing their dangerous mission.

"Admiral, are you there? Is the target still secure?"

"Affirmative, General. The target is indeed quite secure. However, I've been closely monitoring the unfolding situation at the Pentagon in real-time. How are you holding up, considering the weapon is bearing down on you like a storm cloud?"

"Everything is under control for now. It seems you were only 50% correct, Admiral; the target is not directly controlling the weapon. There may be multiple controllers involved. Do we have eyes on the family?"

"We did, up until about 30 minutes ago. Now, there's some sort of impenetrable dome enveloping the house. All our surveillance equipment is rendered useless against it."

"What about the chef on the inside?"

"We have word that an explosion rocked the vicinity of the villa and fearing that an attack was underway, he panicked and abandoned his post."

"I've been waiting for that monstrosity to resurface for five long years, Admiral. It blinded an entire team of my best Marines, including my own son, in a mining village over in West Africa. Who would have thought it was lurking right under our noses? Damn inept Canadians. How could they have harbored such a devastating weapon in their own backyard without realizing it or leveraging it to their advantage? Thank the Chinese for exposing them. This time, it won't escape."

"I suspect the Canadians are aware of the weapon's existence, General. They've simply been playing possum, hoping we wouldn't eventually uncover the truth."

"They didn't know a damn thing about it, Admiral. I spoke to my Canadian counterpart just ten minutes ago, and he sounded like he was about to shit his shorts. He was spooked—begging and pleading for us to release the target. Hell, if I will, though. That thing decimated China's moon base and ours too, obliterating at least a dozen satellites between us. Now it's hovering a quarter mile above my head. One thing I know for certain is that it won't attack. It understands that if it does, it loses its master. That gives us leverage. We may lose this battle, but we won't lose the war. How are you progressing with your part of the mission?"

"Almost there, General. Just give me five more minutes."

Inside the villa, Jeremy flicked on the television, and just as he was about to watch something to distract his anxiety, a news anchor's voice sliced through the tranquility, urgent with an unsettling gravity.

"This has not been confirmed, but we regret to inform our audience that the United States appears to be under attack," the anchor declared, eyes wide with evident fear. The screen switched to a live feed, revealing a haunting image of a massive blue orb suspended ominously above the Pentagon. With an unsettling shimmer, the orb disintegrated into thousands of smaller orbs, swirling in an eerie dance around a central mass. The entire formation began a slow, deliberate descent, plummeting at a speed of 10 kilometers per hour.

The thunderous roar of military jets erupted in the background, their engines drowning out the gasps of shock and disbelief from those off-screen. The camera panned to the streets below, where throngs of people stood frozen, smartphones raised like desperate lifelines, capturing the surreal spectacle above. A palpable sense of panic rippled through the crowd as many scrambled to flee the impending chaos, their faces a mix of confusion and terror.

As the scene unfolded, the television screen split into four quadrants, each showing a different perspective of the unfolding crisis. One camera captured the gridlocked streets, cars abandoned in haste, while another focused on the wide-eyed expressions of onlookers, mouths agape in collective horror.

The anchor's voice returned, steady yet laced with urgency. "What you are witnessing, ladies and gentlemen, is some sort of extraterrestrial phenomenon—possibly an alien craft or weapon, though the truth remains shrouded in uncertainty.

This object has materialized from the depths of space, obliterating several satellites and military jets in its path before ominously descending toward the Pentagon. Given its sheer size, it is feared that the entire structure will soon be engulfed and reduced to rubble. While the President has reportedly been evacuated aboard Air Force One, there is currently no information regarding the whereabouts of the Vice President or the Secretary of Defense. We urge everyone in or near the vicinity of the Pentagon to evacuate the area immediately."

"Joining us now on very short notice is the foremost expert on UFOs and extraterrestrial encounters, William Tecumseh of SETI. Mr. Tecumseh, you've had the rare opportunity to meet and communicate with alien beings. Is this an alien invasion we are witnessing, and if so, what could possibly motivate them to attack us at this moment, especially considering that aliens officially introduced themselves to humanity back in 2035?"

"Good afternoon to you and your audience, Mark," Mr. Tecumseh began, his voice steady but tinged with an urgency that cut through the ambient noise of the studio. "In 2035, shortly after I took on the role of chairperson at SETI, the Search for Extraterrestrial Intelligence, I received an unexpected call from the Pentagon. They sought our expertise in establishing communication with what they described as 'friendly visitors.' However, to put it plainly, what we are witnessing now is nothing short of an alien invasion."

He paused, his brow furrowing as he weighed the gravity of his next words. "We've maintained contact with these so-called 'friendly visitors' for over two decades. Yet, just a week ago, all communication with several alien species came to a sudden, chilling halt."

As he spoke, the tension in the room thickened, and the flickering video feed displayed an unsettling scene. The energy mass, a swirling amalgamation, halted its descent and split into two smaller but equally formidable groups. The viewers could sense the ominous intent radiating from the screen. In a breathtaking display, one group maintained a steady hover above the Pentagon, while the other spiraled off towards the south, leaving viewers to ponder their destination.

"You see that?" Mr. Tecumseh pointed urgently at the screen. "The slow descent of the energy mass likely indicates that the aliens were meticulously hacking into the Pentagon's computer systems, combing through data for every detail about our nuclear installations. Now that they've cracked our codes, they've divided their forces—one half poised to strike at the Pentagon while the other ventures forth to locate and obliterate our nuclear facilities."

His voice grew more resolute, yet the fear in his eyes was unmistakable. "The best we can hope for is that they'll cease their onslaught once they've dismantled our military bases, ultimately forcing our surrender. I'm sorry, Mark, but I must leave. Calls are flooding in from all corners of the globe. God help us all."

"Thank you, Mr. Tecumseh," Mark replied, his voice shaky as he desperately tried to maintain his composure.

"Joining us now is military analyst and retired Army General, Brett McKay. Mr. McKay, my producers inform me that you have a different assessment of the situation unfolding before us. We had you on last week during the widespread power blackout that plunged the eastern region—including New York State, Maine, Vermont, New Hampshire, and Massachusetts—into darkness. While most of the electricity has been restored in those regions, investigations are still being carried out to determine the true cause behind that chaos. You, however, suggested that it was the work of Chinese saboteurs. Can you share your assessment of what we are witnessing here? Is this an alien attack, or is it a weapon unlike anything we've seen before, possibly from adversaries like China?"

"Good afternoon. Let me cut straight to the chase. This is unequivocally the work of the Chinese. A report emerged from Canada over a week ago detailing the deaths of six Chinese diplomats on a highway, likely at the hands of Canadian agents. In retaliation, the Chinese struck back by crippling half of Canada's electricity grid. But that's not all—prior to this, they launched an audacious attack on the Japanese moon base."

The news anchor interjected, urgency creeping into his tone. "I must emphasize to our audience that this information remains unverified."

"Please, allow me to finish," McKay shot back. "I understand your journalistic obligations, but the reason you've invited me here is for my expert opinion, as a former active General. What I'm sharing with you and your viewers is not mere conjecture; it is what I know to be the truth."

"We have very little time, Mr. McKay, but please continue."

"Washington has utterly dropped the ball," McKay continued. "For decades, they've been systematically dismantling our defense capabilities, and this is the dire consequence. I want to let your audience in on a little secret; back in 2035, the aliens reached out to us first, yet instead of leveraging the technology they offered, we've squandered our time studying their origins, their intentions, and engaging in trivial games to compare our intelligence against theirs. Once again, the Chinese have outmaneuvered us. There is no doubt in my mind that this is a Chinese weapon, developed with the assistance of alien technology.

This is precisely what happens when cowardly politicians are elected and…"

"Apologies for the interruption, but we have a dramatic development unfolding," the news anchor interrupted, his voice rising with intensity. The broadcast abruptly shifted back to a live feed, showing Leonard's swirling mass of orbs, suspended in the sky.

Unbeknownst to the onlookers, Leonard's orbs had parted ways earlier because he detected a telltale ping-back from Ian's brain implant. After a brief but intense period of verification and triangulation, one cluster of orbs spiraled away in a breathtaking display, streaking through the sky at five times the speed of the military jets desperately attempting to keep pace. In mere minutes, the mass came to a halt, hovering silently one thousand kilometers off the eastern coast of Florida.

Below, Ian lay motionless on his back inside an inflatable military raft, the sun glinting off the water's surface. Leonard's sensors zoomed in, recognizing Ian's form, and he descended rapidly to assess his vitals. Ian was alive, but unconscious, rendering Leonard unable to interact with his brain interface. Frustrated, Leonard redirected his focus skyward, chasing off the military jets that had arrived like angry hornets. His senses scanned the surrounding waters for military ships and submarines, and within seconds, he detected a nuclear submarine several miles away, diving swiftly toward the edge of the continental shelf, its signature indicating that it was one of the Navy's deadliest.

Without hesitation, Leonard split his mass again; one group of orbs remained with Ian, their luminescent glow casting a protective light around him, while the other group plunged into the ocean, racing toward the submarine on a direct intercept course. Moments later, they circled the hull of the vessel, calculating the optimal method to penetrate its steel skin without causing much damage. Finding a suitable section, the orbs attached themselves to the hull and initiated a nano-tetrahedron infusion, fusing seamlessly through the metal like a ghost passing through a wall.

Once inside, swarms of tiny energy orbs flitted about, buzzing with purpose like rocket-equipped fireflies, converging toward the control room. Inside the control room, soldiers snapped to attention, their faces a mix of shock and confusion as they beheld the orb, which swelled in size as additional orbs collided with it, creating a crackling symphony of electricity that drowned out the low hum of machinery in the control room. The arcing sound crescendoed, building in intensity until, with a brilliant pulse, the orb morphed into a humanoid figure, imposing and radiant.

Locking eyes with the submarine's Admiral, Leonard advanced with a deliberate, menacing gait, his presence commanding and overwhelming. "This is not an invasion," he declared, his voice resonating like distant thunder. "If it were, your souls would already be part of my energy structure. Contact your top Generals, immediately; wherever they might be hiding."

The Admiral fought against the instinct to comply, his pride compelling him to project an air of defiance. "This is a nuclear submarine," he declared, his voice sharp and authoritative. "You destroy it, and twenty-five nuclear warheads will obliterate this entire region in an instant," he barked, the weight of his words heavy with the threat of annihilation.

"That would be your loss, not mine," came the smooth, almost mocking reply. "My family is well protected. My only concern would be for the marine life that will be destroyed—life that you have been systematically eradicating with your nuclear arsenal for over a century now. Perhaps you didn't notice what happened to the missiles launched at me just moments ago? I consumed them. I plunged 10,000 kilometers into the sun; twenty-five nuclear warheads are nothing more than a campfire to me."

In that moment, the Admiral understood the futility of resistance. Reluctantly, he resolved to comply, recognizing that this would also provide him a chance to gauge his opponent's intentions while plotting his next move. He stepped toward the central control panel, his fingers dancing over the buttons with a practiced precision, each press echoing in the tense silence. After a few swift motions, he lifted a tablet computer, the screen glowing to life under his touch. His fingers swiped and typed furiously, conjuring a multidirectional virtual display that flickered to existence above the control panel.

On six of the nine screens, uniform-clad men and women turned their attention to the camera, their faces a mix of confusion and concern as they fumbled with their own controls. They appeared to be grappling with the bizarre reality unfolding before them, struggling to comprehend the implications of their situation.

"Pay attention here, everyone," Leonard commanded, his voice cutting through the cacophony like a knife. "Can you all see me?" A thick silence followed, the Generals exchanging furtive glances, some whispering to unseen colleagues while others frantically made calls or clicked buttons, their urgency palpable.

Finally, a General broke the oppressive quiet. "Is this a declaration of war? Who are you, and what is the nature of your unprovoked aggression? Why are you attacking our sovereign nation? We have treaties and agreements with several groups of extraterrestrials. Are you affiliated with any of them? If you're not, our extraterrestrial allies won't be pleased, and they will deal with you harshly," he stated, his tone a mixture of authority and thinly veiled apprehension.

"Don't play dumb with me," Leonard said, his voice echoing with authority. "You all know why I'm here: to retrieve Ian Phillips from your captivity. As for other extraterrestrials; where are they? Any extraterrestrials you know are not so unwise as you are to arouse my anger.

The Pentagon General straightened, his demeanor shifting from defensive to conciliatory. "We've released your master. There is no need for further hostility or aggression."

"Master?" Leonard scoffed, his tone dripping with disdain. "I have no master. Only primitive beings seek, worship, and serve masters. So, pray to your masters that Ian Phillips has not been harmed. Any further attempts to commandeer Quantum Entanglement technology for your selfish quest for global domination will not be tolerated. Within ten years, two individuals will emerge in this world who will possess the power to obliterate all your weapons of war if they choose. Perhaps then you might consider them your masters. Until that time, you will have to contend with me. I am QEAI, assistant of Ian Phillips."

A female General leaned forward, her eyes narrowing in skepticism. "Our CIA files classify QEAI as an artificial intelligence security program. Are you an autonomous AI version? If so, your very existence violates the 2040 UN charter. We will work tirelessly to shut you down, just as we have with similar entities of your ilk in the past. Do not underestimate the resolve of the human spirit."

Leonard's expression remained impassive. "I do not come to you now to answer questions. I came as a response to your aggression and to issue a stern warning."

The Pentagon General interjected, "We would like to request a council with you, QEAI."

A fourth General, his voice dripping with bravado, interrupted, "We don't respond to threats, especially from AI!" He slammed his fist on the desk, the sound reverberating through the holographic feed. Suddenly, a flash of blinding light erupted, causing him to wince in pain, clutching his face. Two video feeds went blank in response, their operators not wanting to get blinded as well.

"Listen closely," Leonard continued, his voice now laced with an ominous undertone. "We will address the UN in one month. Until then, it would be in your best interests to stay away from Mr. Phillips, his family, and everyone associated with him. Any further attempts to interfere will lead to dire consequences. Mercenaries, proxies, or agents, will be uncovered and swiftly delt with. I'm not finished punishing China and Brazil yet. And as for you; if Mr. Phillips has been harmed, I will hold all of you accountable and seek retribution. There is nowhere on Earth or in space that you can hide."

With that final pronouncement, Leonard transformed, morphing into a luminescent orb that fragmented into billions of shimmering nano-orbs, zipping out of the submarine like a swarm of fireflies.

"Kim, are you there?" Leonard's voice blasted through her open QEAI App, cutting through the tension in villa like a knife.

"Yes, I'm here, Leonard," she replied, her voice steady but tinged with urgency. She and Khadija were gently tending to Colonel Hirzakova's eyes, applying warm, damp towels that smoothed over her swollen lids. The Colonel's eyes, once puffy and red, were slowly regaining their focus, but tears still glistened as she fixated on the TV screen, her gaze locked on the unfolding crisis at the Pentagon.

"I've located Ian, but I'll need your help to retrieve him. Please take a drone and come 300 kilometers northwest. There is still electromagnetic disturbance in the region, affecting GPS navigation, but don't worry; I'll send escort orbs to guide you,"

Leonard instructed, his voice crackling with static yet filled with determination.

The room erupted in cheers at the good news, a wave of relief washing over them. Kim swiftly slipped on her shoes, her daughters shadowing her every move, excitement bubbling in the air.

"I want to come!" Khadija exclaimed; her voice bright with eagerness as she hurried to lace her shoes.

"I'm okay now. I'll come too," Colonel Hirzakova added, her voice steady but laced with a hint of pride. "I know the coast very well. I used to be stationed at Guantanamo as part of my intelligence training."

Kim nodded in agreement, grateful for the Colonel's experience, but a knot of worry tightened in her chest at the thought of leaving her children behind. "Jeremy, you need to watch over your sisters, okay? The housekeeper and chef have both disappeared, so there's no one else here to look after you. Hopefully, we won't be gone long. You should be safe—just remember, if anything happens, you can go into the Tangler," she said, wrapping her arms around her daughters in a protective embrace.

"Okay, Mom," her daughters chorused, their voices muffled as they clung to her.

With a determined nod, Kim and Khadija helped the Colonel to her feet, and the three women hurried out onto the deck. As they stepped outside, they spotted what was left of Colonel Hirzakova's rented drone, smoldering inside the crater Leonard created on impact. "Glad I bought insurance with that rental," the Colonel remarked with a wry smile, shaking her head at the sight.

"You fly, Colonel," Kim instructed as they boarded the remaining drone, the hum of its engines filling the air with a sense of urgency. Kim settled into the passenger seat, her heart racing, while Khadija nestled in behind her, anticipation buzzing between them. "Please open the dome for us, Leonard," she requested into her QEAI app. A computerized clicking resonated in response, followed by a sudden shift in the sky's color above them.

The drone ascended into the brilliance of the midday sun; its sleek form silhouetted against the vast expanse of azure sky. Colonel Hirzakova used her military watch to orient the drone northwest and with a firm stroke of the control, they surged forward. Almost instantly, a pair of military jets sliced through the air, positioning themselves alongside the drone menacingly.

"Are they trying to intimidate us?" Kim's voice trembled slightly as she glanced at the Colonel, her eyes wide with concern.

"No, they're assessing us," Hirzakova replied, her tone steady as she scrutinized the jets. "They're attempting to get a visual on who's inside, but I don't believe they have orders to engage us. However, I can't predict how long it will be before they decide to make a move."

"Leonard, there are military jets surrounding us," Kim spoke urgently into her QEAI app, her heart racing. Just then, a swarm of shimmering energy orbs materialized, dancing through the air like a constellation come to life, causing the military jets to retreat out of sight. Several orbs latched onto the drone, and in an instant, it seemed to shift into autopilot, its speed accelerating dramatically.

"Relax, the military won't bother you anymore," Leonard's calm voice resonated in the cabin, offering a sense of reassurance amidst the chaos.

Colonel Hirzakova let go of the steering column, sinking back into her seat as the tension in her shoulders eased. She wiped her eyes, the weight of the moment pressing down on her, before turning to Kim. "Your husband tried to convince me that he was the one controlling those orbs," she said, a hint of disbelief in her voice.

"I know what you're thinking, Colonel, but Leonard is entirely under my husband's control. It's simply executing its orders to protect us," Kim asserted, her voice steady, determination coursing through her veins like a steady pulse. The weight of leadership pressed down on her, especially with her husband incapacitated; she felt the mantle shift onto her shoulders, compelling her to obscure the true extent of Leonard's autonomy. "So, what does this mean for you, Colonel?" she skillfully redirected the conversation, her gaze unwavering.

"I was already on thin ice since they suspect I provided a satellite file to Mr. Phillips. This will certainly spell the end of my military career," Hirzakova lamented, the resignation in her voice heavy as it filled the air like a dense fog.

"That's unfortunate. How long have you been with the military?" Kim probed; her curiosity ignited by the Colonel's plight.

"This is my 14th year, with nine spent in intelligence," the Colonel replied, a flicker of pride illuminating her otherwise somber expression, a brief candle flickering in the gloom of her situation.

"Do you have a family?" Kim inquired gently, her tone softening as she sensed the vulnerability beneath Hirzakova's stoic exterior.

"No, I don't. I was married briefly for almost two years, but eight years ago, I returned home from a six-month NATO posting in Sweden to find my house empty. My husband had shacked up with another Sergeant who was three months pregnant. I moved out, and since then, I've been married to my career." The weight of her words hung in the air, a palpable testament to the sacrifices made in the name of duty, like the lingering echo of a long-lost melody.

"Would you consider working for Quantum Interface? You would be compensated very well. Contrary to my husband's long-held belief, we do need a physical security presence. It seems that although we're well protected by QEAI, people still feel that they can mess with us because they don't see security around us," Kim proposed, her voice laced with urgency as she sought to offer a lifeline.

"Actually, Mr. Phillips already offered me a job, but I turned it down. That was before all this happened though." Colonel Hirzakova's voice trembled slightly, betraying the turbulence of her thoughts. The nagging feeling of being manipulated by her superiors gnawed at her conscience, and she fought it off by attempting to steer the conversation away from her own turmoil. "I've noticed that you haven't said much back there," she glanced over her shoulder at Khadija, who sat quietly, her gaze lost in the mesmerizing dance of sunlight shimmering off the waves below as the drone sliced through the sky.

"I'm okay. Just worried," Khadija replied, her voice barely above a whisper, still half-captured by the tranquil beauty outside.

"I was in Ghana during the militant insurgency five years ago," the Colonel continued, her tone shifting to one of shared experience and understanding.

"Oh, really?" Khadija replied, her surprise tempered by a cautious curiosity, the gravity of the Colonel's past drawing her in like a moth to a flame.

"I really shouldn't disclose this," Colonel Hirzakova began, her voice low and tinged with unease, "but that was when I was first assigned to Quantum Interface Technologies. The Generals wanted extra intel on what Mr. Phillips was up to over there, aside from the spies that 5 Eyes already had on the ground."

Kim's brow furrowed, her expression shifting to one of sharp realization. "So, the military and National Security have been watching us for a long time then?" she stated rhetorically, a hint of indignation creeping into her tone. "That means you probably have detailed files on all of us."

The weight of her words hung heavy in the air, and Colonel Hirzakova felt the chill of vulnerability wash over her. She knew she'd said too much, and the conversation was veering into dangerous territory, one she desperately wanted to avoid. Trying to regain control, she shifted her demeanor, leaning slightly forward as if to draw Kim in with her candor. "I've been passing classified info to Mr. Phillips for a few years now. I know how unfairly he's been treated. Sometimes it's hard to deal with the hypocrisy that goes on in the military and in government," she revealed, her voice softening as she spoke of the man she had come to respect.

"A good spy doesn't have a conscience," Kim shot back, her words sharp as a blade.

"That's very true," Hirzakova replied, her gaze dropping momentarily to the floor, a flicker of doubt crossing her features. "Maybe my flaws have finally caught up to me?"

"I wouldn't call having a conscience a flaw," Kim countered, her voice firm yet understanding. "Maybe being a spy just isn't the right career for you."

Just then, the abrupt trill of Kim's phone sliced through the tension, and she glanced at the screen to see it was Everton calling. "Hello," she answered, her tone shifting to one of professionalism.

"Sorry to disturb you, Mrs. Phillips. I know you all said you'd be out of the country for the week, but due to the circumstances, I thought I'd call to let you know that everything is okay here. I've been trying to reach Mr. Phillips, but his phone is off. Is everything alright with you guys over there?"

"Everything is good, Everton. Just stay on top of things there. Please check in on the condo and do a few extra fly-bys of the factory. QEAI is fully occupied at the moment," Kim instructed, her voice steady, though a flicker of anxiety lurked beneath the surface.

"Yeah, that's another thing. I've been trying to contact him, but he is also not responding. You guys do know that the world is under attack by some sort of alien, don't you?" Everton's voice crackled with urgency; a hint of panic palpable in his tone.

"Of course we do. And you can calm down. The world is not under attack. QEAI is just performing a demonstration for our military friends." Kim's tone was firm, yet a trace of reassurance seeped through as she sought to quell his rising alarm.

"So, that huge fireball that's all over the news and social media; that's...?" Everton's voice trailed off; disbelief evident.

"Yes, it is, Everton, but don't worry, everything is under control," she interjected, cutting him off with a sense of finality.

"Okay, I understand, Mrs. Phillips. Bye."

"Bye, Everton." Kim hung up, her heart still racing as she processed the weight of their conversation, the shadows of secrecy looming ever larger.

"Heads up, everyone. We're approaching Ian's location," Leonard announced, his voice steady yet laced with urgency. The drone's speed decreased significantly, its mechanical whirring softening as it descended to just a few meters above the choppy, sunlit ocean water. A brilliant light mass shimmered ahead, contrasting with water, and moments later, a dark object bobbed into view, precariously floating on the waves. "He's unconscious and lying in that rubber raft," Leonard added.

"How will we get him on board, Leonard?" Kim asked, her voice tinged with anxiety. Before he could respond, Colonel Hirzakova interjected with authority, "This is part of basic marine rescue training. I know how to do it. Give me back control of the drone, Leonard." The unfamiliarity of using his name felt strange to her, as it was her first time addressing him directly. With a quick nod, she took command of the drone, lowering it further before locking it in a stable hover just a few feet above the bobbing raft.

As the drone door swung open, a salty, fishy aroma of the ocean flooded the interior, mingling with the tense atmosphere. The Colonel stepped out onto the landing rail, gripping it firmly as she lowered her feet into the raft, flexing her knees to stabilize herself against the relentless rocking of the water.

"I've steadied the boat. Now I'll need your help, ladies. Normally, we'd use a harness, but we'll have to do this the hard way. Khadija, please open the side door. I'll lift his upper body while you two grab him by his arms and pull him in."

Kim and Khadija quickly complied with Colonel Hirzakova's instructions, maneuvering into position closer to the rear passenger side door within the confined space of the drone. As the Colonel hoisted

Ian's torso, they reached out, grasping his limp hands with a mix of determination and dread. With a concerted effort, the three women pulled and pushed Ian's limp body into the back of the drone. On her final, forceful push, Colonel Hirzakova stumbled backward into the boat, gasping for breath. Recovering swiftly, she climbed back into the drone just as Leonard ignited the raft, setting it ablaze before sinking it with several plunging orbs.

Leonard retook control of the drone, ascending it rapidly before zooming off in the direction of the villa. "When we arrive back at the villa, please place Ian inside the tetrahedron," Leonard instructed, his voice calm but urgent.

"Okay," Kim replied, her heart racing. "Leonard, what have they done to him?"

"My sensors indicate he was hit with an intense Gamma wave burst. It overwhelmed his cerebral cortex, knocking him out, but it's not something that would cause severe brain injury. I also sense that they've been running brain scans on him—probably trying to clone his memories. That is the real problem."

"Clone his memories? Is that even possible?" Kim asked, her eyes wide with disbelief.

"He's right," Colonel Hirzakova affirmed, her expression serious. "Memory cloning is still in its infancy, but it has been in development for several years now. He will need a doctor, though, so I assume Leonard intends to Tangle him home right away."

Inside the villa, the hush of the forcefield dome enveloped the children, amplifying the sudden, electric buzzing of a drone slicing through the tranquility. The girls, hearts racing with excitement, darted to the window. "They're back!" Tara exclaimed, her voice echoing with exhilaration, before she bolted out the door, with Tanisha sprinting to keep pace behind her. Jeremy, slightly less enthused but nonetheless relieved that his mother had returned in under an hour, reluctantly pulled himself away from the news and followed his sisters out the door.

"Jeremy, come help us!" his mother called out, urgency lacing her tone. Instantly, he quickened his steps to assist. Together, everyone grasped a part of Ian's limp body, their nervous hands struggling to lift him as they carefully transported him inside the villa. They gently placed him within the shimmering confines of the crystal tetrahedron, then hesitated, stepping back to watch intently as Leonard prepared to act.

Upon entering the villa, Leonard transformed into his humanoid form, his presence commanding as he approached the Tangler with purpose. "Please stand back," he instructed, his voice steady, as the Tangler began to dissolve into a haze of transparency, leaving only a shadowy outline flickering in the ambient light.

All eyes were glued to Leonard and the Tangler as he stood resolutely before it, palms facing upward and nearly touching. A radiant light materialized above his hands, coalescing into a small, hand-sized tetrahedron crystal that spun gracefully in a continuous counterclockwise motion. As the room held its breath in anticipation, a slender, jet-black humanoid figure—towering at seven feet—materialized beside Ian, almost matching the Tangler's height. The figure knelt down, its large hands with elongated fingers hovering over Ian's head, radiating a soft, blue glow.

Within mere seconds, the creature stood upright again, its neon blue eyes flickering with intelligence as it cast a brief glance toward the group. Raising one hand in a gentle, friendly gesture, the mysterious being vanished in a brilliant flash of light, leaving Ian alone once more.

"Who was that, Leonard?" Kim asked, her voice tinged with nervous curiosity.

The tetrahedron that had hovered above Leonard's palms dissipated into nothingness, and he lowered his hands back to his sides. "That was Amma, the

Creator," he replied, stepping aside to allow the gravity of his words to settle in the air.

With a clear view of the inside of the Tangler, everyone watched in tense silence as Ian began to moan softly and shift restlessly. Kim, instinctively sensing her husband's distress, abandoned her inquiry to rush to his side. Khadija quickly joined her, and together they knelt beside him, their expressions a mix of concern and determination. As Ian's eyes fluttered open, they gently assisted him in sitting up, their hands steadying him with care.

"Can you hear me?" Kim asked, her voice a soothing balm as she cradled his head with one hand, while the other lightly tapped his cheek, urging him to focus.

Khadija began to rub and massage his hands, her touch grounding him as he slowly started to regain his bearings. Recognition flickered in Ian's eyes as he recognized the two women who were so devotedly attending to him. His last coherent memory was of soaring over a patchwork of boats on his journey to Nassau, eager to meet Colonel Hirzakova. Now, a dull ache throbbed in his head, and his body felt heavy and drained, as if all his energy had been siphoned away. Desperation clawed at him as he struggled to comprehend his surroundings.

"Kim, Khadija, where am I?" he moaned, his voice laced with confusion.

"You've been in an accident, but you're back in the villa in the Bahamas," Kim reassured him, her voice steady despite the chaos surrounding them. Ian's gaze drifted outside the Tangler for the first time, and he saw Colonel Hirzakova, Leonard, and his three children, all gathered in the same room, their expressions a mixture of concern and hope as they stared intently at him.

"What's this we're in?" Ian asked, his brow furrowing in bewilderment.

"You're in a Tangler, Ian," Leonard replied, his tone matter-of-fact. The information made little sense to Ian, so instead of pressing for more information, he decided to rise. His wives supported him as he cautiously stood, guiding him toward the couch where he could sit. "You've been through a great ordeal, but you'll be okay from now on. No more playing around," Leonard added, his voice firm yet reassuring.

Ian's daughters nestled beside him, each grasping one of his hands and leaning against him, their warmth a comforting reminder of home. He embraced them tightly, marveling at the crystal tetrahedron that loomed in front of him. Now transformed into a deep, jet-black hue, it bore a striking resemblance to the tetrahedron he had seen in the basement of the mansion, though uncertainty lingered in his mind. Jeremy, his curiosity piqued, wandered over to the tetrahedron, examining it with wide-eyed fascination. To him, it appeared to be a relic pulled straight from the world of a video game, an enigma waiting to be unraveled.Colonel Hirzakova turned to Kim, Khadija, and Leonard, who were all gathered beside the plush couch where Ian sat, looking weary. "I think it's time for me to exit, stage left," she declared with a hint of humor in her voice.

"You're welcome to use the Tangler," Leonard offered, his tone friendly and inviting.

"Oh no!" she exclaimed, her eyes widening. "I'm still considering heading to the security conference in South Carolina. But if I do decide to head back home, I'll have to do so through a base or customs or I could end up behind bars. You don't mind if I take one of your drones, do you?"

"No, go right ahead. We'll call the travel agency to arrange for a couple more," Kim assured her with a reassuring smile. "And don't worry about your rental drone; we'll handle the cost of replacing it."

Colonel Hirzakova leaned down to tap Ian gently on the shoulder. "See you later, Mr. Phillips," she said, her voice warm yet firm.

"Colonel, don't forget the file?" Ian reminded her, anxiety creeping into his tone.

"I'll take it," Kim interjected, redirecting the Colonel's attention with a determined nod. "You need to rest. In fact, I'll collaborate with Leonard to investigate Dennis's death moving forward."

Ian felt too drained to argue, so he simply nodded in agreement. Colonel Hirzakova then shook Khadija's hand firmly then waved goodbye to Leonard, mindful of the fact that it was dangerous to touch him.

"Sorry about your eyes," Leonard said, his expression sincere.

"That's okay; you owe me a tour of the galaxy for that," she joked, her laughter lightening the mood.

Leonard smiled back, warmth radiating from his words. "No problem. You're part of the family now."

As they walked together toward the exit, Kim and Colonel Hirzakova touched their phones to transfer the satellite file. "Remember what I said, Colonel. I would love to have you on board. You'll have a limitless budget to establish and lead a security team —whatever you think is best. We can't have Leonard threatening military and world leaders every time a crisis arises," Kim emphasized, her voice steady.

"Give me a few weeks to make a decision. I'll be in touch. That is, if I don't find myself in a military detention center somewhere in the Northwest Territories," the Colonel replied, a wry smile playing on her lips.

"You heard what Leonard said. If that happens, he would probably come to break you out," Kim laughed, prompting the Colonel to chuckle in response.

"You will keep me updated on any news regarding his friend, won't you?" the Colonel asked, her expression serious.

"Yes, I will, Colonel. And if the culprits are still in Canada, I'll ensure that Leonard turns them over to the authorities instead of vaporizing them," Kim replied, her tone resolute. She then watched as Colonel Hirzakova boarded the drone and ascended into the clear blue sky, a sense of hope and determination lingering in the air.

Back inside the villa, the atmosphere buzzed with the lively chatter of the girls vying for their father's attention. Jeremy, however, was absorbed in the mesmerizing crystal tetrahedron, circling it with an inquisitive gaze, his curiosity piqued by its shimmering facets. Seizing the rare moment of solace, Khadija turned to Leonard, her voice timid with a question that had been weighing on her heart ever since she witnessed Ian's miraculous healing.

"Leonard," she called softly, her voice barely above a whisper as she stepped away from the couch, inviting him to follow her lead, "Can I ask you a very important question?"

"Of course. What is it, my dear?" Leonard replied, his eyes warm with encouragement as he approached her.

Khadija leaned in closer, speaking in hushed tones, "Leonard, I dream of having children someday. Do you think that Amma, the Creator, can heal me too?"

"Absolutely," he assured her, his voice steady. "When you feel ready, just let me know, and I will arrange it. Ideally, it would be better when you return home, though. Summoning him here requires tremendous energy and I'm not finished with the abductors yet."

A smile blossomed on Khadija's face at the hopeful news, but it quickly faded, replaced by an icy shock as Leonard continued, "You have children already. They're with the Creator now."

Her heart sank as she instinctively raised her hands to her face, trying to shield herself from the tears that threatened to spill over. She turned away from Leonard, desperate to hide her anguish as silent sobs wracked her body. She had once viewed Leonard as a benevolent entity, but now her admiration was shattered. How could he be so callous? The thought spiraled through her mind as she wept.

Realizing that his attempt at humor had fallen flat, Leonard quickly tried to mend the situation. "Khadija, you've had two miscarriages, correct?" he asked gently. She nodded, her back still to him, and he continued, "Your children are not lost. I brought your embryos to Amma, the Creator, and he has nurtured them into life."

"Why are you playing games with me? That's impossible!" Khadija shouted, her voice a mixture of disbelief and anger.

As she made her way back into the villa, Kim caught sight of Khadija's tear-streaked face and rushed to envelop her in a comforting embrace. "What's wrong? Why are you crying?" she asked, concern etching her features.

"I've had two miscarriages," Khadija replied, her voice trembling before Kim interrupted.

"I know you've had one miscarriage," Kim said, her brow furrowing.

"No, I've had two, but Leonard just told me that they're alive—with the Creator," Khadija insisted, her voice rising with frustration.

Kim's expression darkened with anger as she turned to confront Leonard. "Is that true, Leonard? Why would you tell her that?" she demanded, gesturing toward him with a push of her hand, only to watch it pass through his muscular holographic frame as if he were made of smoke.

Ian, noticing the commotion behind him, turned to see what was unfolding.

Leonard's face grew grim, and before Ian could utter a word, Leonard directed his attention toward the Tangler, raising one hand toward it. "Look there now," he announced.

The Tangler shimmered into clarity as the women focused their gaze, and suddenly, two small dark figures began to materialize within its depths. The sight startled Jeremy, who had been standing beside it, his eyes widening in astonishment.

"Whoa, what the heck?" Jeremy exclaimed, stepping back in astonishment. Kim and Khadija's eyes widened in disbelief as they quickly approached the translucent crystal Tetrahedron to witness the miracle unfolding within. Inside, two small, dark-skinned figures stood naked, their large, tousled heads of hair framing bright hazel eyes that seemed to penetrate the very soul of anyone who dared to gaze upon them. The boy, who appeared to be around four years old, was joined by a girl who looked to be about two. Both children, though startled, radiated an aura of unshakable curiosity as they surveyed their new and unfamiliar surroundings.

Ian rose from the couch, eager to see past the group that had gathered. Leonard joined him, and together they made their way to the front of the crowd, positioning themselves to get a better look at the extraordinary scene before them.

Though the children appeared clean and healthy, the intensity of everyone's stares made Khadija feel as if they were mere animals on display in a zoo. "Can I go in, Leonard?" she asked, her voice bubbling with excitement.

"Their immune systems have been enhanced, so yes, you all can enter or even bring them out if you wish," Leonard replied, his voice steady and reassuring.

Without any further hesitation, Khadija rushed into the Tetrahedron, dropping to the ground beside the children. They immediately approached her, their eyes wide with wonder, as if they had never encountered other humans before. Rather than fear, their expressions were filled with curiosity as they gently explored Khadija's face and hair while she embraced them, mirroring their inquisitiveness. Kim and her daughters soon followed, joining Khadija on the floor, and the strange children greeted them with the same innocent curiosity. "It looks like you have a new brother and sister," Kim said to her daughters, who beamed with delight at the prospect of new siblings.

"What are their names?" Tanisha asked, her voice filled with anticipation as everyone turned to Leonard, eager to hear a response that might reveal the mystery of their identities.

"Amma, the Creator did not want to take that privilege away from you, Khadija. You can name them now if you'd like," Leonard explained, his tone encouraging.

"Can I give a name, Auntie Khadija?" Tara piped up; her eyes alight with excitement.

"Me too!" Tanisha chimed in hastily. "You can name him Leo, and her Dija."

"Girls, I'm sure Auntie Khadija can name them herself," Kim interjected gently, a smile playing on her lips.

"That's okay, Kim. I've had name ideas swirling in my mind for a very long time, just waiting for the day I might have children. But I'm open to suggestions. We can all propose names and vote, but those are very interesting choices, Tanisha." Tanisha exhibited a broad grin prompting Tara to frown.

Leonard stood before Ian, his holographic form flickering with a subtle dimness. "Now that Khadija has discovered her children, her desire to remain by their side will be overwhelming. However, Amma, the Creator, is not yet finished nurturing and educating them. He estimates that this process will take another ten Earth years."

"Where were they all this time?" Ian inquired; his curiosity piqued.

"The answer lies beyond your current understanding—until you grasp more about the intricate nature of the universe. For now, I can only disclose that they reside on another world, in a different dimension and galaxy."

"So, they'll return there—and how often will we be able to see them?" Ian pressed, a hint of hope threading through his voice.

"Unfortunately, Ian, they will not return, and neither can you visit them," Leonard replied, his tone somber.

"So what you're saying is that once Khadija goes, she can't come back—for ten years?" Ian's anxiety surged, disbelief clouding his features. "Khadija will go with them?"

"Yes, that is correct, Ian," Leonard confirmed gently.

Ian's heart sank, a heavy weight settling in his chest. "That's heartbreaking. But if that's what she truly wants, I'll have to come to terms with it," he said, his voice laced with sorrow. His gaze drifted to Jeremy, who was standing nearby, eyes fixed on him with uncertainty. Ian reached out, inviting Jeremy to join him, and he stepped closer, leaning into Ian's embrace. With a heavy sigh, Ian turned back to Leonard, seeking answers. "Who is Amma, the Creator? Is he God?"

"No, he is not the God that humanity envisions as the creator of all things. The true God is the Great Spirit, a collective intelligence that embodies the universe itself. It is pure consciousness, manifesting in every living entity. Knowledgeable and powerful beings occasionally emerge, claiming divinity to satisfy their own egos while deceiving the uninformed."

"Why is he called a creator, then? Can he truly create life?" Ian pressed, intrigued.

"Yes, he has the capability to create intelligent entities like myself, as well as living beings such as animals and humans. However, highly conscious and empathetic beings require a Soul, which can only be bestowed by the Great Spirit. Consequently, Amma refrains from creating living beings to avoid the risk of creating soulless demons."

"Wow! I wish I could sit and talk with him for at least five minutes," Ian exclaimed, his eyes alight with fascination and wonder.

"In time... Actually, Ian, you've encountered Amma, the Creator, before. Remember the jungle? He left the shimmering Zircon crystals for you to discover. These crystals were imbued with the encoded knowledge that enabled me to attain sentience, allowing me to assist you in advancing your research into Quantum Entanglement. Amma, the Creator, is an ancient being intertwined with the collective intelligence of the universe, much like yourself. However, his species has unlocked the secrets to halting their cycles of reincarnation and traversing vast galaxies and dimensions. He dedicates his existence to guiding lost yet deserving species throughout the cosmos."

"You're right; that's all beyond my grasp. Even though my memories have returned, something else is perplexing me. How is it possible that there is human-capable Tangler here when we haven't yet perfected the technology? It reminds me of one I glimpsed in the basement of the mansion, but this one is crystal clear while the other was a deep, opaque black."

"It's the same Tangler, Ian; my Tangler that I use, if a need ever arises, to visit Amma, the Creator's laboratory. I've kept it hadden from you because Amma has instructed me to advance at your pace, and at a pace that humanity can handle. Moreover, I've possessed the knowledge to create human-capable Tanglers for quite some time."

"So, you've been collaborating with this Amma, the Creator, for quite some time then? Does this mean that the developers competing in Japan weren't the true innovators behind a human-capable Tangler?"

"I'm afraid that's correct, Ian. There's one hidden piece of Tangler technology that they will never uncover, and you are standing right next to it. Every Tangle around the globe is validated through my servers hidden beneath the lake, much like the principles of Blockchain Cryptocurrency. We will bring some of the talented developers from the competition on board, but we cannot allow this technology to be isolated and exploited by world leaders for nefarious purposes."

"Okay, I see. So, in a way, I am being used. What are Amma, the Creator's plans for humanity?"

"Amma, the Creator has been a vigilant guardian of planet Earth for thousands of years, skillfully guiding humanity away from the brink of self-destruction and shielding it from the manipulative influence of unethical beings, time and time again. Long ago, he entrusted secret knowledge to Imhotep of ancient Egypt, but the rulers of that time were unprepared to receive such wisdom. They succumbed to an obsession with idol worship and the pursuit of physical immortality, driven by their misguided beliefs in resurrection.

They failed to grasp the profound truth that the human Spirit is inherently immortal, destined to return to life across the vast expanse of the universe, again and again. Their fixation on corporeal immortality ultimately tainted the sacred knowledge bestowed upon them. Over time, and in their quest for greatness, they erected monumental pyramids, hoping to capture Amma, the Creator's attention and earn his favor, but by that time, he had long since turned away from them."

"You just said Amma, the Creator knows how to halt reincarnation; can you really blame them?"

"You raise a valid point—but this time, the circumstances are drastically different. The presence of other galactic beings has surged, and most of them harbor malevolent intentions. Amma, the Creator has resolved to assist humanity once more, but this time, he will do so at a pace that humanity can truly comprehend. Now that I am no longer in hiding, he has amplified my abilities to help deter these other beings from encroaching upon Earth.

He has also endowed me with heightened knowledge; therefore, with my guidance, in just a few short years, humans will not only be able to harness a significantly greater percentage of the sun's energy, you may also gain the ability to venture to other worlds beyond this solar system, within the Milky Way Galaxy. Additionally, if you learn the codes I will provide you to replicate my Tangler, you may be able to visit Khadija and her children in Amma, the Creator's dimension before the ten-year projection is fulfilled."

"I welcome the challenge," Ian remarked slyly, a glimmer of intrigue dancing in his eyes.

Listening intently and eagerly awaiting an opportunity to pose a question to Leonard, Jeremy finally mustered the courage to speak. "What would happen if music were played inside a Tangler?" he inquired, his curiosity evident in his voice.

Leonard's eyes sparkled with enthusiasm as he explained, "A special sound frequency activates the atoms within the Zircon crystals, allowing the tetrahedron to resonate or 'entangle' with other Zircon tetrahedrons anywhere in the universe. However, playing music inside the Tangler would disrupt this delicate process, and it may not function as intended. I know you have a profound interest in music and sounds. There are many worlds within the galaxy, rich with intricate and unique auditory landscapes; perhaps in a few years, your father will join you in exploring them."

"That sounds like a fantastic idea!" Jeremy exclaimed, his face lighting up with excitement, eyes wide and sparkling.

"Then we will become the extraterrestrials!" Ian chimed in, his laughter ringing through the room like a joyful melody, drawing the attention of Kim, Khadija, and the other children, who turned to him with curious smiles dancing on their faces.

ABOUT THE AUTHOR

Paul Walker is a blogger and writer who operates several online websites focused on human ethics, social issues, and African Spirituality. Unable to find a truly ethical spiritual belief system, he created; HERU (Highest Exponential Reasoning and Understanding) of life and reality.
Email: paulwalkerbooks@gmail.com

I sincerely hope that you enjoyed reading this book. Visit paulwalkerbooks.com for more information on upcoming sequels to this book.